KATHERINE ASHE

Montfort

The Early Years

ISBN: 1-4392-6466-X
ISBN-13: 9781439264669
Library of Congress Control Number: 2009911613

visit: simon-de-montfort.com

Montfort

The Founder of Parliament
The Early Years
1229 to 1243

VOLUME I

BOOK 1: THE COURTIER

BOOK 2: THE EXILE

Acknowledgments

The actual, unquestioned events in the life of Simon de Montfort are so mutually contradictory, and there are such important gaps in the documentary evidence surviving from the thirteenth century that, to explore a plausible sequence of cause and effect, I've taken freedoms beyond those allowed a historian. *Montfort* is offered under the aegis of fiction.

I owe a debt of thanks to Dr. Henry Pachter, who urged me to pursue this adventure; to Dr. Madeleine Cosman, founder of the Institute of Medieval and Renaissance Studies at The City University of New York, who encouraged and guided me; to Mark Peel of The New York Society Library, who let me keep the Society's copy of the *Chronica Majora* for years on end; to Dr. Karen Edis-Barzman, and The Center for Medieval and Renaissance Studies at Binghamton University, for their generosity in granting me access to their research facilities and lecture series; to Emile Capouya, Jonathan Segal and James Clark for their advice; to Lucia Woods Lindley, who funded my travels in France and England; and to my husband, who has been very patient.

Contents

Book I

THE COURTIER

Chapter One

SIMON
1229-1230

HE WAS TALL AND SLENDER, at that time in life when the body in a sudden rush to adult height becomes long limbed and angular. He was dressed in white. His hair was dark, his skin was fair, but his eyes had the stern frown of acute nearsightedness. He stood on the quay at Dover, peering for his baggage among the cargo tossed by the ship's crew to the landing. Mist and sheaves of sleety rain swept across the harbor, blending the gray air into the cold, slate-colored sea. It was February of the year 1229.

A superb white horse with a fine bridle and high-cantelled saddle was hoisted up from the ship's hold. As the animal got its footing on the quay and sailors unfastened the hoist-cinch from its belly, the youth in white claimed it. Leading his horse to the heap of baggage, he pulled out a weighty leather sack. Rummaging further through the heap, he retrieved a pot helmet and a shield as plain and white as his clothes, for he was a new-made knight not yet in liege to any lord.

With his sack lashed behind his saddle, his helmet hooked to the saddlebow and his shield slung over his shoulder, he mounted and was on his way in the foreign, English countryside where his future lay before him. He didn't mind the rain, for he was happy. More than happy, he was towering, as only the young first stepping into life can be.

His family was Norman and noble, balancing between power and genteel poverty and on the down side now. But they could trace their lineage from William the Conqueror. His father, for whom he was named, had been a hero of the Third Crusade in Palestine, and leader of the war against the Albigensian heretics in France. The crusader died at the siege of Toulouse, struck on the head by a stone hurled from a mangonel. In the eleven years since then the family's fortunes had disintegrated.

The hero's widow, in her grief, had spent her love upon this namesake son, her youngest child. She was deeply devout and, though she too died before the lad was eight, she imparted her religion to him. Every thought, word and deed was to be held up to the light of faith and balanced. Nor was this a forced mental exercise for him. It was fed by his deepest feelings. His mother, the Virgin, the Church all blended to a rich amalgam in his heart, an alchemy the heady fumes of which infused his every action with a sense of divine purpose. Though he might doubt the rightness of his acts, might bitterly revile his failings, he never would doubt himself, doubt that his responsibility was of the highest order.

This earnest faith, and his family's service to the Crown of France, led Queen Blanche to choose the crusader's orphan as companion for her son. The boy had grown up at the Court in Paris beside the child-king Louis IX, who was later to be Saint Louis. With Louis he was educated in theology and logic, history, Latin grammar and rhetoric, and the military arts from the techniques of the two-edged sword and jousting at the quintain, to the deployment of armies in the field. In the scholarly subjects he had proved a good student. But in the military arts he had excelled.

The youth trotting through the wintry Kentish countryside was thus a special mix: of scholarship and courtliness, of spiritual devotion, and of military skills as yet untried.

As he ambled along the rain-soaked highway, the sound of hoof-beats coming on at speed broke into the youth's daydreaming. A rider caught up with him and drew rein.

The lad looked narrowly at this imposed companion. He was a burly man, red haired, in his mid-forties and wearing chain mail armor. His surcoat and his shield were black crisscrossed with gold: the arms of Maltraverse, well known on both sides of the Channel. But, over the gold pattern, a red swallow was painted, the mark of a landless son.

Maltraverse smiled genially. "I see I be well met on the road," he said in the provincial dialect of French spoken in England.

The youth was not glad for his company but returned the greeting civilly.

"Poitouvin?" the knight in black asked, hearing the crisp accent. He was at a disadvantage, the youth's white shield told nothing but its newness.

"French," the youth replied, distinguishing himself as from France proper, not one of England's dukedoms on the continent.

"French, Poitouvin, they're all the same to me," Maltraverse shrugged. "You go to Westminster?"

"Yes."

"Come to make your fortune from us, eh? Take service with the king? Henry favors anybody so long as he's not English." His tone had bitter edge beneath his smile.

The Frenchman didn't answer. For a while they rode on in silence through the dreary, rain-drenched countryside. Broad, empty fields spread to the horizon with only a small, dark mass ahead to mark, in the youth's weak eyesight, a hut or modest inn.

Maltraverse put his hand on the white horse's rump. "Fine horse. French too?"

"Yes. My brother raises them."

"Let's have a joust for it." The challenge was in earnest with nothing of sportsmanship in it. The challenger was no more than a well-born highwayman intent upon the easy prey of a novice knight.

The youth squinted toward the hovel ahead, but doubted any help would be found there. "How can we joust? We have no lances."

"I will provide," Maltraverse gave an ironic bow from his saddle.

As they approached the shabby thatch-and-wattle inn, the innkeeper emerged. It was clear at once that he was party to the black knight's highway ventures. Seeing Maltraverse, he nodded then waddled into his stable, emerging with two long poles of ash wood sharpened to lethal points.

The youth had jousted in lesson tourneys beyond number, but he had never faced real combat before. He peered at Maltraverse's horse. Its hipbones jutted, sliding back and forth like shuttles underneath its skin. He knew his horse was heavier by far. In jousting, the weight and speed of the horse and its rider's skill counted for more than a knight's own bodily strength. The highwayman was a powerful brute, but the novice thought that he might beat him.

There was no choice in any case. His own armor and his sword were in the bag behind his saddle. But clearly Maltraverse did not intend to give him time to arm himself. He unhooked his helmet from his saddlebow and laced it on, unslung his shield from his shoulder, slipping his left forearm under its leather strap, and took the pole the innkeeper was handing up to him.

The knight in black turned his horse into the field across the road. The white knight followed. They rode away from each other until some two hundred yards lay between them. Then they turned and faced each other. At this distance the novice could see no more of his adversary than a dark shape melting at the edges into the gray rain. In his practice jousts, he had learned to be quick at the last instant as he closed with his opponent. And at close range his eyesight was excellent. He adjusted his shield, then lowered his lance, couching it along his right arm.

Maltraverse stood with lance lowered, then spurred his horse forward.

The youth touched his spurs to his mount's flanks. The horse leapt forward, stretching its strong legs out to the swift volant. The English horse reluctantly ambled from trot to gallop. Streaking across the ground, the novice met his adversary well into the Englishman's half of the field. His lance struck the black shield hard. The black knight -- horse and rider -- hurtled to the mud.

Maltraverse scrambled from his downed and kicking beast.

The youth reined in his horse and turned back, pointing his lance at the downed man's chest.

"Cursed jade slipped in the mud!" the Englishman grumbled.

Smiling broadly with pride in himself, the young Frenchman raised his lance. "Would you try again?" Maltraverse's horse and armor were his, won fairly. But for him this wasn't business yet, jousting was still fun.

The highwayman stared, incredulous, then accepted the offer with a shrug. He found his dented shield, caught his horse, which had gotten to its feet and wandered a few paces, and he remounted. Both man and horse were caked with mud.

The white knight and the mud knight dashed toward each other. Now the mud knight's lance smeared the white shield. But the novice caught the highwayman so squarely with a blow that he was lifted from his saddle and sent flying -- while his horse went on. This time there could be no question of the horse's slipping.

Maltraverse lay sprawled in the wet earth, inert for several moments.

The youth caught the straying horse, dismounted and did what he could to wipe the dirt from it. He retrieved the battered black and gold shield and fastened it to the saddlebow of the horse he had twice won, then he remounted. Leading his prize by the rein, he rode back to the highwayman.

The mud knight raised himself up on one elbow, pulled off his helm and rubbed his head. "You're as fine a knight as any, lad," he grinned as he handed over his helm.

The young Frenchman smiled broadly at the praise. "My name is Simon de Montfort. I shall be at King Henry's Court. You can ransom your horse and armor there."

Maltraverse nodded.

Leading his booty horse, Simon went back to the road, brimming with this bright omen of his arrival.

Chapter Two

THE MAKING OF AN EARL
1230

BUT GREAT THINGS ARE SELDOM accomplished easily, even with the best of omens.

The doors of Westminster Hall stood open like a towering pair of wings earthbound in cumbersome oak, hinged with iron, strapped with iron and bossed with iron defenses. But they stood open, with neither steward nor guards nor even a porter anywhere nearby.

Simon paused in the courtyard. From the doorway there came sounds of raucous laughter and the yelp of a large dog, and odors of spoilt meat and unwashed men. This was not what he expected. Fearing he might appear a country lout hesitating outside, he stepped forward and squinted into the hall.

At the Court of France Simon knew everyone. He could place a name to any courtier from his posture and motions, though the features of face and dress were only hazy colors to his eyes. Expressions of the face, be they hostile, friendly, rude or kind, were lost on him except in close communication. Hence the world at large supposed him proud, aloof, when he was merely braced for the mysterious, unknowable and possibly dangerous middle and far distance. He lived cautiously, staying afloat in the unseeable seas around him by clinging firmly to a raft built of firm notions of what was right.

What he saw now was not right at all. His twenty feet of fairly clear vision gave him ample evidence. The Court of England at Westminster was as far from the proprieties of the Paris Court of the Regent, Queen-Mother Blanche, as two royal meeting chambers could be.

High in the gables of the hall, hawks perched sullenly, whitening the black rafters with their droppings. The walls, painted to look like brickwork, were peeling; and two rows of square stone pillars filing down the room's length were peeling as well. Portraits of ladies, drawn in brown paint and dressed in a style two generations out of date, peered from the pillars' flaking sides like frightened ghosts trapped in a dissolute gaming-den.

Drunken men, dirt-spattered from the morning's hunt, lounged at trestle tables set among the pillars. They played at cards or dice, or picked at the cold remnants of last night's feast. Gold chains, buckles and fibulas, gifts from their youthful patron, brightened their soiled riding-robes. Coarse jests passed loudly from table to table. The laughter was cruel, if also hearty, for these were the chosen, the king's own friends who could afford to ridicule anyone.

One of these rough courtiers, seated near the door, noticed that he was being scrutinized. He nudged the man sitting next to him, gestured toward the tall youth hovering in the entrance, and grossly mimicked the stranger's stare. In the strong accent of Poitou he remarked to his friend, "Yet another sapling come to find his spot of sun here in the royal woods."

"He'll find we grow thick, and the shade's too deep for newcomers," his friend retorted in the same accent.

Further down the hall another courtier, grease dribbling on his surcoat, waved a piece of meat in the air. A hawk dropped from her perch, veering toward the morsel. But as she neared to strike, three massive tawny hounds bounded from beneath a table, bellowing like thunder and earthquake. The hawk flashed back to her perch in panic, flinging a gobbet of excrement at the youth's white robe as she swooped above his head. The two Poitouvins burst into uproarious laughter.

Simon took a napkin from the table nearest him and dabbed away the streak of filth as best he could. Coolly, he ignored the pair of laughers, and the other courtiers near them who were watching him with sneering smiles.

At the far end of the hall two men stood higher than the rest on what Simon supposed must be the royal dais. Their postures showed they were conversing earnestly, though their faces, for him, were as blank as two thumbs. As still no one had come to announce him he made his way forward, around tables and through a maze of lounging legs and dogs, until he reached the foot of the dais.

One of the men, dressed in a black robe draped with massive golden chains and jeweled pendants, was clearly a high Clerk of the Court. The other, with a circlet crown over his fine brown, chin-length hair, was Henry III, King of England, Lord of Ireland, Duke of Anjou, Maine, Poitou and Gascony.

Henry Plantagenet was twenty-two, tall yet almost delicate in build, with a self-conscious grace. He had a neatly trimmed brown beard, perhaps to make himself look older, beards were not in fashion for young men. But his most striking feature was the sagging of the left side of his face. At first Simon supposed this was an affectation, a pose of ennui. But the drooping eye and cheek moved almost not at all. Palsy marred the young king's face.

Noticing the stranger intently peering at him, Henry broke off his conversation with the clerk, and darted a glance about the hall. "Where's the steward to see to this person? Is everybody free to come and stare at me!" No steward appeared. The king turned toward the youth, "Well?" he snapped, "what do you want?"

Simon bowed low, "It is for the Stewardship that I've come, my lord."

"Impudent, isn't he," Henry raised his one mobile eyebrow and gave a short laugh. Amused by the bold newcomer, he took a sip of wine and said, "The office is taken, though it may not seem so from the housekeeping. Who are you?" But he turned back to the clerk before Simon could answer. "I never should have made FitzNicholas steward. The disorder only grows. Perhaps I should appoint him to your office of the Treasury. His penchant for increase might work for me there."

The Treasurer, Peter de Riveaux, laughed with a courtier's practiced grace.

"My lord, it's not the household stewardship I've come for," Simon explained, fetching from the blousing of his robe two rolled documents with dangling wax seals in royal and papal gold. "I've come to receive the Stewardship of England and the earldom of Leicester. I am Simon de Montfort."

Henry frowned to Riveaux, "It seems he's serious. How tedious." He took another sip of wine as Simon handed the documents up to him. Giving his goblet to Riveaux, the king unrolled the parchments and glanced through them. Claims from hopeful Norman lordlings came to him all too frequently. Thanks to a good memory, he was adept at dealing with them swiftly and decisively.

"Your father forfeited his rights to the earldom of Leicester and Stewardship of England when he chose to pledge his liege to France, rather than England."

"The Pope assured my father of safekeeping for *all* his lands and titles when he went on crusade," Simon insisted. "And your father, King John, observed that surety by placing our English holdings in the care of our cousin Ranulf, Earl of Chester."

"Yes, yes," Henry whined in annoyance, "your brother's been here about this already! But as a vassal of the King of France, he cannot also be in liege to me. Your family's claims are forfeited, regardless of the Pope!"

Offering a third roll of parchment, Simon pressed on, undaunted. "My brother, Count Amaury de Montfort, abandons all his English claims to me, in exchange for my rights in France. And I've come to pledge my liege to you, my lord." He bowed again.

Henry tipped his head back. "This fellow's giving me a headache." He leveled a glare at Simon. "I tell you, you're too late! Leicester has been given outright to the Earl of Chester. Be that an end of it! Good day, Sire Montfort." Turning to Riveaux, he hissed, "Find a bailiff and toss him out."

"My lord!" Simon protested. But Henry didn't deign to look toward him again. The youth bowed icily. "On my way here, I overcame a knight of Maltraverse who would have robbed me. I make over his horse and ransom to you, my lord, in thanks for the kindness I've received this day!"

As he turned on his heel and made his way back through the hall, a blear-eyed courtier he passed remarked, "If Queen Blanche thinks she'll slip her spies in amongst us as easily as that, she's a simpleton."

Simon's face reddened. His pent humiliation burst to rage. Turning on the drunkard, he grasped him by the breast of his robe and dragged him to his feet. But before he could do more, two royal bailiffs seized him by the arms, propelled him out of the Court, and closed the great oak doors behind him.

Back in France after his failure at Westminster, Simon wandered about the old tower hall and the fields of Montfort l'Amaury in grim dejection, trying to think what to do next. He sent word to Queen Blanche of his failure. But, too chagrined, he did not return to the Paris Court.

The prospect of being Earl of Leicester and Steward of England had not been his ambition for long. Had his father survived, and his conquests held, young Simon could have been a lord of the Pyrenees: the Count of Foix perhaps. But his father had not lived.

He could barely recall his father, tall, dark-bearded, in chain mail that sounded like the rustle of a thousand coins. The funeral in Carcassonne was his first clear memory: his father lying motionless upon a beige stone bier, his face broken, tinged purple, his lips drawn back in a strange smile. Simon was five years old. He turned his head and gazed for a long time at the statue to his left: the fair young Virgin wailing, with the beautiful, bearded, blood-streaked Christ stretched out across her lap. Looking to his right, he watched his mother, not so young but just as fair, weeping in bitter grief.

Simon always had supposed his brother Amaury would hold the English titles, and that he himself would stay by Louis and serve in the French Court. For half his life, he and the boy king had practiced combat, studied, eaten their meals together and slept in the same room. But, as they grew toward manhood, their closeness gave Queen Blanche concern. When Amaury was refused the Leicester titles, she decided to send Simon in his place. For Simon, though he loved Louis as his dearest friend, and respected him as his sovereign, the prospect of a life of title and honor all his own surpassed every attachment.

With the presumption of youth, he had assumed that given Amaury's opportunities, he would have done far better. But now his first attempt in the world had failed miserably. He was plunged into depression – though it was some comfort that what he had seen of England's Court did not appeal to him at all.

"They're barbarians!" he shouted at Amaury. "I'd as soon go live in Ireland!"

"We have no earldom in Ireland," Amaury replied coolly, sitting in their father's old oak chair in the gray stone hall of Montfort l'Amaury. "You must try again."

"And subject myself once more to their filthy hands?"

"Write a letter," Amaury smiled.

Simon sent a messenger to England with a letter offering his liege again. Weeks passed with no reply. Then Amaury was summoned to the Court in Paris. He returned with the news that King Henry was planning to invade France to regain his and his lords' lands in Normandy. Amaury, now Marshall of France, was to provide auxiliary warhorses for France's knights, and pack horses for the army's supplies.

In April, answer finally came from King Henry. Reading the letter as the English knight who brought it waited, Simon laughed out loud and bitterly.

"What amuses you?" his brother asked.

"No doubt the King of England imagines he can buy my knowledge of our plans for the war. He offers me four hundred marks! Cheap mercenary service! 'Until such time as I may come into the earldom.' He told me plainly it was given to Ranulf of Chester. Now that I might be useful, he'd dangle it before me like a piece of meat before a dog!"

"What answer would you have me bear to my lord the king?" the messenger asked, bending like a reed in the blast of the youth's fury.

"Your lord deserves no answer!" Simon's anger was rising out of control. He pushed his way past the English knight, went to the stables, saddled his horse, took up a pike and galloped headlong down the cobbles of the village's steep street until he reached the level field below.

At the far end of the field was a quintain for practice jousting: a dummy mounted on a post with paddle arms outstretched. Simon jabbed his heels into his horse's belly. The startled animal leapt forward, then stretched into the reaching rhythm of the careening volant. Streaking across the field, Simon held King Henry's drooping eye and smirking lips in mind. As the quintain's leering Saracen face neared, he struck its paddle arm with a blow that sent it spinning and its wooden pivot screaming. He reined in his horse sharply, turned and galloped at the quintain again, striking its still spinning arms so that it whirled and shrieked at higher pitch. Again and again he battered the quintain. Only when his horse was creamed with sweat and heaving with exhaustion did he turn back up the cobbled road, passing the departing messenger who eyed him with a sidelong look of unconcealed fright.

In June, a summons came for Amaury to attend King Louis, ready for war. King Henry had landed in Brittany and was moving his forces east.

The summons that came for Simon was not to war, but to Queen Blanche's private chamber.

The paneled room, with its ornate chairs and great oak bed hung with damask draperies dotted with gold fleurs-de-lis, was as familiar to Simon as any chamber at Montfort l'Amaury, though it was beyond bounds for most of France's courtiers. Sitting in her chair beside the hearth, where a small fire burned to ward off the spring damp, Queen Blanche extended her hand to Simon without need of words for greeting.

He took the Queen Regent's hand and pressed it to his lips, as he had always done. But this time it was with a strong and unfamiliar sense of shame, for he had shown himself a failure. Queen Blanche's austere beauty and regal bearing filled to the full his idea of royalty, and shaped his notion of the Queen of Heaven. And she had deigned to be a mother to him – all the mother he could well remember. His own mother faded into Blanche's image in the far recesses of his memory.

Her long, solemn face was framed by her white wimple and silk veil of blue, her V-shaped lips were a pale pink. She smiled, "It is a serious misfortune to us that you've not succeeded to the English earldom of your father."

Her words pitched him deeper into shame and confusion. "We're at war… I'm glad not to be forced to raise my hand against France."

"If we had someone in King Henry's Court, in Henry's confidence, this might not have happened. You do understand my meaning?"

A look of fear came into Simon's eyes. He thought he did know what she meant. To fight in wars, to die with honor was what he hoped, even expected of his life. But to be a spy, an agent for a lord other than the one to whom one's liege was pledged, was traitorous and vile. To be caught as a traitor was to be hanged or worse, and to deserve a shameful death.

"We want you to use every means you can to secure the earldom, and become close to Henry. Earl Ranulf of Chester, whom your letter said holds Leicester, is with Henry now. He's known to be a man of honor. Go and speak to him directly of your rights."

The personal debt that Simon owed the Queen Regent was great, but further, she was his sovereign. He could not refuse, however much his conscience might rebel at the commission. He felt like a fool not to have grasped her intentions sooner, to have been so dazzled by the earldom in such innocence. The drunken lout at Westminster had known better than he.

As Amaury joined France's forces ranged against King Henry, Simon set out to join the opposing side. He did not hurry. He had no desire to take part in this battle. The attraction of the earldom had taken on a complication that he had no notion how to solve.

But by the time he reached the place where the armies ought to be, King Henry's brief, ill-organized campaign was ended. Most of the lords with him had gone south to Poitou, or home to England. But Earl Ranulf, Simon learned, was still in Brittany: at his castle of Saint Jacque de Beauveron, near Mont Saint Michel. He sought him out.

The Earl of Chester was a sturdy, gray-faded old man who had outlived all his close family. In the somber hall of Saint Jacques he received his young cousin with curiosity. "I've heard about your visit to King Henry. How you bestowed on him a ransom. And nearly thrashed Drogo de Barentin."

Simon glanced down in embarrassment, his dark eyelashes brushing his cheeks. "He insulted Queen Blanche. The Court of England was not as I expected."

Noting this callow blend of delicacy and honor, Ranulf raised his head like an old hound on the scent of an intriguing quarry. "No. I suppose it wasn't. It's just two years since King Henry cast off his childhood guardians. They ran the Court and country for their own profit, with no concern for England's good. We all rejoiced when Henry rid himself of them. But since then he's surrounded himself with tipplers and flatterers. He could be a good king, if he had wise councilors and better friends." The old earl studied Simon, "I knew your father well. A fine and handsome man. You look much like him."

"Some say so." Simon smiled at what he considered a high compliment.

"Simon de Montfort," Ranulf savored the name. "He was a great leader! In Palestine. Then against the heretics in southern France. We had no commander when we started for the south. And no one wanted to command us after we set fire to the church at Bezier, roasting some six thousand heretics. Blood-lust. We were savage after that. It was your father who dared take control. He curbed the bloodshed. Yet he was a stern warrior for the Church."

Ranulf seemed to drift, to lose himself in memories of times past. Dreams of golden times, when songs of brave and righteous knights were sung in every court. He sang, half to himself, the song of Simon de Montfort, "He was a Mars for war, a Paris for beauty, a Cato for wisdom…" The old man broke off abruptly, asking, "Do you know the prophecy that the English would rise up and overthrow their king, and make your father king?"

"I've heard of it," Simon confessed. "I'm told that father took it as a jest, but said that it was wicked to overthrow a king whom God had given, however evil he might be. He was glad that he never set foot in a land given to such prophecies."

"Well," Ranulf coughed, "England is not as bad as that." He studied his young cousin with increasing interest. "I've held his English earldom in safekeeping."

"King Henry says you hold it outright by his leave."

"By his leave, I hold it in safekeeping. I'd be poor indeed to accept gifts that aren't the giver's to bestow. But I haven't had the time to care for Leicester's holdings as I ought." He narrowed his gaze at Simon. "Your brother, now that he's Marshall of France, can never hold Leicester as well."

"Amaury has granted all his English rights to me, in exchange for my share in Montfort l'Amaury."

"Then there's nothing to oppose your title to the earldom."

"Nothing but King Henry, and yourself my lord."

A down-turned smile bent the old earl's lips. "Henry's thinking if it's mine, as I've no heirs, when I die Leicester will go to the Crown. Never doubt that Henry knows exactly what he's doing."

Servants were setting a trestle table in the hall in preparation for the evening meal. Ranulf took Simon by the arm and led him to the table. "You'll stay with me a while? I'd like to know the son, as I once knew the father. In August I return to England. Stay with me till then."

Simon stayed at Saint Jacques until the earl was ready to leave. Then Ranulf said, "Come to England with me. I'll deal with Henry for your Leicester earldom, if you'll pledge your liege to him."

Simon's second visit to Westminster differed from his first in the extreme. King Henry held Ranulf in high regard. The Earl of Chester was one of the few lords who had defended his father, King John, when the barons rose against him and won Magna Carta. And Ranulf had been among those who had guaranteed Henry's own reign at its start.

When King John died in ceaseless civil war against his lords, his queen, Isabel of Poitou, brought their nine-year-old son Henry to London to be crowned. On the way, the barons, led by William of Pembroke, seized the queen's cortege. Little Henry, gazing up from his pony at the armored men, asked in his solemn, childish voice, "My lords, have you come to kill me?" Softened, William dismounted and knelt, saying, "No, my lord, we've come to take you to your throne." Since that moment, the fragileness of life itself for one who holds the Crown was never very far from Henry's consciousness.

Today there were no lounging drunkards, hunting dogs or hawks in Westminster Hall. The floor was swept and strewn with fragrant rushes. The trestle tables laden with stale food were gone, and the few clerks and bailiffs in attendance observed an air of dignity about the person of the king.

"Welcome, Earl of Chester. We're pleased at your return from France," King Henry smiled unctuously.

Ranulf, not deceived, glanced sourly about the room. He eyed the telltale streaks of bird droppings on the high rafters. "Your hawks have outgrown their mews and now perch in the hall?"

Henry laughed uneasily, fighting the sensation of being reduced to a mere boy again, rebuked by this old man. But he made no reply.

Ranulf came to his point. "I'm aware that you refused to convey the Leicester honors and titles to my cousin Simon de Montfort."

"That's so. They're yours, lord Earl," the king answered.

"By my promise to the Pope, I hold them in surety for Montfort."

"They were forfeited, and I gave them to you outright," Henry insisted, his resistance hardening.

"I never considered the surety to be forfeited!" Ranulf bellowed, turning livid. "By my honor, it would be a blight against my name to withhold the earldom from my cousin of Montfort. If my lord will not agree, then, by my faith, I will adopt my cousin Simon, and make him heir to both Leicester and Chester!"

Henry was shaken by this unexpected move, as was everyone who heard it. Simon most of all.

After some hesitation, the king answered in a pleasant, mollifying tone. "Good Earl, we didn't know you felt so strongly on this issue. In deference to the honor you express, we accede to your interpretation of the surety. But let this be no precedent. We do not intend to bring into question old Norman claims for titles latterly bestowed elsewhere. We agree to this grant, as a special recognition by the Crown of one who's served us long and well. That is, if the knight pledges his liege to us."

"I will my lord!" Simon said promptly.

"Then we will write to the sheriff of Leicester, and wherever else there are rents due the Leicester Honour, and direct the monies to be remitted to Simon de Montfort." Henry smiled to Ranulf, then turned to Simon, adding in a tone less sweet, "Attend us, and we'll accept your liege on Tuesday next when Court will be in Wales."

"You'll invest me with my titles, my lord?" Simon asked.

"In due time," Henry replied coldly. "We were hasty once in granting the stewardship of our household. How much more careful ought we be, before we grant the Stewardship of England? We'll know your merits first."

King Henry's words pleased Ranulf, but not Simon. The titles Earl and Steward were as much his right as were the rents. Yet he had gained so much that day, it seemed unwise to press the matter further. He bowed and said no more.

On Tuesday, at Painscastle, near the Welsh border, with the courtiers, clerks and clergy witnessing, Simon knelt to Henry, his hands clasped before him as in prayer. The king stood with his hands enclosing Simon's as the youth spoke his vow of liege.

King Henry now had claim to Simon's loyalty and service, above all others except God Himself.

Chapter Three

THE HONOUR OF LEICESTER
1230

AFTER HIS LIEGE-GIVING AT PAINSCASTLE, Simon rode east toward Leicester to take possession of his lands. A smile was on his lips and cloudless joy was in his heart. He peered at the manor houses he passed, certain that his own would be far finer, the great mansion of an earl.

To either side of him spread broad fields furrowed in long waves like the sea: fallow green fields where sheep and oxen grazed; spring-fields of oats, peas, beans and barley; and winter-wheat fields where the August mowers moved with a graceful swinging of the scythe. The world was rich and verdant, and his own parcel of this wealth soon would be delivered to his hands.

Some eight days after leaving the royal Court he was nearing his goal. The last two miles of road, he was told, passed northward up a hill. From the hill's summit he would have a fair view of Leicester.

When Simon reached the hill's crest, he saw not a fine manor, but the *town* of Leicester, lying in a marshy river's bend. Not only was it a town, but it seemed very strange.

Squinting, shading his eyes from the bright sun with his hand, he saw a city wall that was no more than an erratic, broken line. Any proper town, even to his poor eyes, showed a fretted skyline of close-packed, peaked roofs. Here, beyond the wall, there were only a few scattered gray masses that could be rooftops. The rest was green, merging with more green that seemed to be a forest on the town's farther side. He knew no proper town could afford precious space within its walls for trees.

Leicester appeared half-abandoned, as if defeated in some war long past that had erased all but a glimmer of its life. Though his father destroyed towns in southern France, Simon was too young to have seen them. But here was a ruined town, and it was his father's legacy. A sense of foreboding came over him.

From the foot of the hill to the broken city wall lay Leicester's manor fields. The road to the town passed between the spring bean-field to the west and the wheat field to the east, then cut diagonally across the spring field.

Chewing his lower lip, Simon rode slowly down the hill and along the road by the fields. There were only a few rows of beans and peas in cultivation. All the rest was weeds. Further east, in the fallow field, just a few cattle grazed.

He made his mind a blank, rather than give room to superstitious thoughts of curses from his father's enemies. Ahead of him was an intact gate. As he came nearer, he could see the rubble of the city wall was boulders of cut stone and Roman tile, held in shattered mortar. He guided his horse westward to where a conical mound loomed high, and the city wall was gone entirely. Atop the mound more broken stones marked the remnants of a tower.

Simon chewed his lip harder. He had given up his share of Montfort l'Amaury for *this*.

A shallow, reedy river, the Soar, flowed by, forming the town's western border. He walked his horse along the riverbank, threading his way between boulders of broken stone half-buried amid frothy, flowering wild carrot stalks so tall they reached his horse's chest.

Circling behind the cone shaped mound, he found an oblong building: a hall. Its roof had burned; only massive, charred trusses remained. But the walls were sturdy, made of well-cut stone. Simon's despair lifted for a moment. Then he thought what it must cost to fix the roof, thought of the fields and their slim hope of profit and his heart sank again. Bleakly he waded through the lacy wildflowers.

He rode at a pensive walk past the corner of the hall, and found that the yard widened to a tidy lawn kept trim by a pair of sheep. A freshly renovated church stood at the end of a well-trod path that led into the town. He was not much surprised. Most manors had their own chapels. When a church was abandoned, Franciscans often took it over, restoring it to use for their preaching.

Simon took note of the worn path and the costly stone carvings adorning the church's newer parts. It seemed the friar who had settled here was a man highly regarded.

His curiosity piqued, he dismounted and went inside. Leicester's oppressive air of desolation lifted at once as he passed through the church door.

Glazed windows filled the nave with bright light in diagonal streams of red, yellow and blue. The altar, in the apse, was fenced by a tall roodscreen with slender columns painted blue and gold. Fine wood paneling closed off one aisle, forming a private chamber. Though Simon saw no one, the church was vibrant with life. The multicolored air itself seemed singing.

Simon knelt to pray, but the reality of Leicester and the ruin of his hopes swept over him. He struggled to keep from crumpling and weeping like a child. Covering his face with his hands, he tried to force his mind toward prayer. Not the disarray of King Henry's Court, not Earl Ranulf's idle remark that he had failed to care for Leicester, nothing had prepared him for this catastrophe.

As he knelt, crushed beneath a sense of loss and helplessness, the door to the private chamber swung open. The sound of sandaled feet scuffed briskly toward him. Wiping his eyes, Simon straightened, very much embarrassed. He ought to have gone first to the sheriff to announce his arrival properly. Plainly dressed, dusty from the road and with no servants in attendance, he must appear far short of an earl's dignity. To say nothing of groveling in tears like an infant.

The monk, in the coarse brown woolen cassock of a Franciscan, approached with both his hands held out in greeting. "Do come this way, my lord Montfort. The archdeacon's expecting you."

Simon was dumbfounded. How did this man know who he was? And what was so high a personage as an archdeacon doing in this wreckage of a town? Not trusting to his voice, wiping his eyes with his hand again, he nodded to the monk and followed him silently through the chamber door.

The room he entered was small, sunny and filled with books: large leather-bound volumes, little books bound with wooden covers, and packets of parchment tied with string. Loose sheets of parchment: blank, written upon, and palimpsested, were strewn everywhere.

At a table by a lancet window sat a wiry, sharp-jawed monk with pale, creased skin. Wisps of gray hair fringed the smooth dome of his tonsure. He seemed as fragile as the ancient tome he read. Shutting the book with a clap, he turned as Simon was shown in. "Lord Montfort!" he smiled as easily as if they had been friends for years, and the robustness of his voice gave any frailty in him the lie. "No doubt you're wondering why I'm not at Lincoln, where I ought to be, but occupy your chapel?"

"I... yes," Simon stammered.

"In my youth I served in Leicester, and I come here still as my retreat. But now that you're in residence, I'll leave. You have the chapel's advowsen, so you may choose whatever priest you will."

"Father, I know no one in England. Nor, from the look of the fields, can they support a priest. Or me," Simon said bleakly. "Please. Remain here if you wish."

The archdeacon's gray eyes studied the youth, then his papery features bent to an even warmer smile. "The manor is in poor condition. I've written on the subject of land management, and some regard has been paid to my scribblings. I'd be glad to offer any help I can."

"Good father, help from you would be most welcome." Simon brushed away the moisture that still dampened his cheek. "Can you tell me... what happened here? Why is the town in such decay?"

The priest folded his thin hands together on his lap and the long sleeves of his robe draped over them. "The last, shall I say *active*, Earl of Leicester – for your father had claim to that title but was never here – was Robert Whitehands, who raised an army for Queen Eleanor of Aquitaine against her husband, King Henry the Second. Henry ordered the town destroyed, the population sent away. When King Richard came to the throne, forty years ago, he restored Earl Robert to his titles and his lands. The hall was restored, though it was struck by lightning and burnt recently. The town itself recovers only slowly. Since Robert died, there's been no lord to take an interest here. Leicester once was a great city. In Roman times. There are remnants. A few arches still standing. Now and then an ancient bowl is dug up in a field. This is Leicester's age of sorrows."

"And I must share them," Simon tried to smile.

The archdeacon said gently, "Perhaps together we may bring life here again."

It was evening when Simon finally left the chapel. In the late-lingering twilight, he led his horse into the center of the town. Walking north along the main street, he passed broken house-walls, the inner chambers open to the sky, their floors rank with weeds. Here and there a foul-smelling cabbage patch was neatly hoed where a townsman used the walled space for a garden.

Soon the main street was crossed with straight roads east and west, a grid as ancient as the first Roman soldiers' camp. Here stood some blocks of half-timbered two-story houses with steeply pitched slate roofs. A few had shop windows, battened shut with wooden covers at this hour of the night. How much of their trade was taxed for Leicester's earl? Simon understood the care of manor lands, but nothing of the unique fiscal duties that an English town might owe its lord. He felt very far from home, and far from all he knew.

Above the doorway of an inn a sign showed a bishop, one hand raised in blessing and the other offering a bag of coins. Seeing this as a hopeful portent, Simon called out loudly in the quiet street and soon a boy came running from the door to take his horse.

The Inn of Saint Nicholas had just one private room. Simon took it, flung himself down on the bed's straw mattress and escaped into sound sleep.

In the morning, he awoke bewildered but with the weight of despair growing lighter in his young heart. He thought of the archdeacon and gave a prayer of thanks for the blessing that had brought him this first friend. After a breakfast of bacon, bread sops and milk at the inn's single, smooth-worn table, he set out to find his way back to his friend.

The archdeacon was a complex blessing. His name was Robert Grosseteste. In all of England there was no man of keener mind and deeper spiritual perception. Though he was of common English birth, the breadth of his learning – or his insistence upon the rightness of his own ideas – had earned him his French surname Grosseteste: the Swelled Head. But no one made jest of his knowledge. He was not only Archdeacon of Lincoln Cathedral, he was Provincial of the Orders of Franciscans in England and Provost of the Oxford Colleges. His works on agriculture were the standard for manor management. But his fame was greater for his essays on Greek philosophy, mathematics and medicine; his researches into the natural sciences; and his translations of the Old Testament directly from the Hebrew. His writings on theology influenced Rome. And he was known to have the gift of prophecy.

In the weeks that followed, Simon met with Grosseteste every day. He listened closely to the scholar's views on everything from Leicester's possible revival to England's politics: current and past.

One morning, soon after Simon arrived, the sheriff brought the records of the rents and fees due Leicester's lord. Earl Robert Whitehands' son, Robert FitzParnel, had died without an heir. The inheritance had passed to Whitehands' sisters, Simon's grandmother and his grand-aunt Margaret. Whitehands had held seventy-eight fiefs, scattered over England. Of these, Aunt Margaret, who was Countess of Winchester, received twelve. All the titles, and the remaining sixty-six fiefs, had passed to Simon's grandmother, and now to him.

But before Simon could smile with satisfaction, the sheriff pointed out that sixty of those fiefs belonged to Leicester's sixty knights, whose services the king claimed in time of war. The knights owed their earl no rent, though one had to deliver a red rose annually. How this floral rent had come to be, the sheriff couldn't say. But just six fiefs, the manor fields and forest of Leicester, and the earnings of a defunct mill remained to support the earl. Even the town owed nearly nothing. Lord Whitehands graciously had forgiven its fees.

Grosseteste bent his mind to find a way for Leicester's fields to yield a profit. The manor lands had been tilled by Leicester's villeins, growing wheat and oats, peas, beans and barley from time immemorial. But, with so few villeins left to work the land, the archdeacon proposed a radical plan of fencing the fields to raise livestock.

Simon grasped at the idea eagerly. "I could buy some of my brother's brood mares, and raise and train destriers!" Amaury was rebuilding his fortune by supplying King Louis's stables with fine warhorses, and everywhere Simon went, his horse drew admiration.

Grosseteste thought the proposal was good. Simon relied upon his friend entirely. The archdeacon made no mention of what Leicester's villeins' rights in the matter might be.

The new holder of Leicester returned to France. But, once in France again, there were issues more pressing than horses on his mind. He stopped at Montfort l'Amaury just long enough to obtain his brother's promise of four brood mares and a stud for 500 marks, to be paid after a grace period. Then he went on to Paris.

It was months since he had been to the Court of France. In the vast, double-gabled hall of the palace on the Isle de la Cite, the steward, elegant in his livery of blue with golden fleurs-de-lis, announced, "The Lord of Leicester, Simon de Montfort."

Simon moved forward among the somberly robed courtiers who spoke in discreet murmurs. They smiled and nodded to him as he passed. Most had known him since he was a child. His success pleased them, both for their fondness of him and their hopes for France's strategies. Simon acknowledged their smiles with polite nods, and walked to the blue-canopied royal dais.

Seeing Simon coming through the crowd, King Louis grinned happily to his mother, who sat on a twin throne by his side. "Simon's returned at last."

Queen Blanche frowned slightly as Simon bowed. "We're pleased to see you. We've not had any word from you for months."

"I beg my lady's forgiveness." Simon knelt and kissed the hand that she extended. The kiss earnestly begged forgiveness, though he doubted she would grant it. His failure to write was no small thing and was, above all else, what he had come to Paris to resolve. He straightened and bowed to Louis.

"I've missed you badly." Louis's smile in his broad face betrayed the pain of boyish friendship deeply hurt. "Could you not write at least?"

"At Henry's Court I was accused of spying," Simon said carefully, keeping his eyes averted from the queen's. "I dared not write. And I had no servants, no means of sending word to you from Leicester."

Queen Blanche dismissed his excuses with a wave of her hand. "You know, no friend of France needs suffer lack of servants to bring letters."

"My lady?" Simon said evasively.

"We never meant to send you out into the world without support. You know that."

"My lady, I cannot accept your help... without making return." He brought the words out painfully, but he had come to his decision and was firm.

The queen pursed her mouth in a way her courtiers knew to fear. "We'll speak of this another time."

Louis looked from Simon to his mother uneasily.

But Blanche went on, more lightly. "There's another here who's been grieved by your silence. Johanna!" she called.

Out of the milling crowd of courtiers, a young woman of dreamy, dark-haired beauty drifted toward the dais. Though she was well into her twenties, her cheeks tinted with a blush and she kept her gaze modestly low.

"You've not greeted Johanna," the queen nodded to Simon.

Simon colored nearly as deeply as Johanna. This meeting he dreaded almost more than facing the queen mother. He took her hand and kissed it with a formal touch of his lips.

"I'm certain you have much to tell each other, being parted for so long," Queen Blanche waved them toward the door that opened from the hall out to the royal garden. "I give you both leave to go. Attend us at supper."

Saying nothing, Simon and Johanna, the Princess of Flanders, wandered from the Court out to the garden. Like Simon, Johanna had long lived at France's Court, an honored semi-hostage. Her father, Baldwin IX of Flanders and Emperor of Constantinople, had died in 1205, shortly before she was born. At age seven she had been wedded to Ferdinand, the Prince of Portugal, whom she loathed. Captured by France at the battle of Bouvine, the prince for years was a prisoner in a tower of the palace on the Isle de la Cite, while his child-bride played with Louis and Simon. Before Ferdinand's release, Queen Blanche had seen to it that Johanna's marriage was annulled.

Damask roses, heavy in their lush September bloom, drooped in the parterres, giving the warm air an intoxicating fragrance, a sensuality all the more disturbing to the still-virgin young woman and her shy seventeen-year-old betrothed. Strolling to the walkway on the parapet along the garden's edge, they sat on a stone bench. Simon gazed fixedly down at the creamy brown surface of the Seine heaving below in curling white ripples.

The princess gently took his hand and pressed it. When she could bear his silence no longer, she ventured, "Tell me of Leicester. Do you like it?"

"It's a ruined town, half deserted," Simon said bleakly.

"Oh, surely you make a jest! The holdings of an earl? I think there is no higher rank in England, save that of prince and king."

"It's the truth. Leicester was sacked decades ago and never has recovered. I'm living in a squalid inn. There's a hall, but it has no roof, and I've no means to repair it."

Johanna wasn't daunted. "Then Queen Blanche will help us. She's offered..."

"I know what she offers," Simon answered curtly.

"I can't believe a word of this!" The girl withdrew her hand from his, trying another tactic. "It's simply that you don't care for me. Else you would have written."

He took up her hand again, kissing it gently, "Have I ever lied to you?"

For years they had known each other, for years he had known that she loved him. He was far from hard of heart. Though he had not yet felt the yearnings of desire for anyone, and looked upon such feelings as a child looks on a mystery, her pain touched him. Worse, he knew he was about to cause her much more pain.

"I could *not* write. I'm sorry." He paused, then forced himself to bring out the next chapter of the hard text that he had come to Paris to recite. "Johanna, I can offer you nothing."

"You're an earl! Steward of England!"

He shook his head. "I don't have the titles yet, only the rents and they're nearly nothing."

"But you can't be poor!" she protested. "You serve France! Queen Blanche favors our marriage for that very reason."

"No!" Simon shouted. "I do not belong to France, or to Queen Blanche any longer! I've given my oath to the King of England, and I cannot serve two masters."

Johanna looked away from him, thoroughly accustomed to his outbursts. "Don't be foolish, Simon," she said coolly. "You'd best control yourself before we go to supper."

"Control myself? If Queen Blanche forces me, I must tell her so!"

"Then, Simon," Johanna turned on him, as icy as he was hot, "I hope I'll not be there to hear a traitor speak!" She got up and left the parapet, sternly holding back her tears as she stalked through the garden to the palace.

Simon remained sitting on the bench, alone and staring at the Seine.

Supper went quietly despite Johanna's fears. But afterward, Blanche summoned Simon to her private chamber. A clerk of the Court was there, writing from the queen's dictation. Blanche broke off as Simon entered the room.

"I'm giving you a draft upon my personal treasury," she smiled, her long white teeth showing between her V-shaped lips. She gestured toward the clerk, "Philip will go with you tomorrow to see you have new clothes made, appropriate to your new rank. When you leave for England, he'll go with you. I'm giving him an open draft upon my funds held by the Templars. They have a banking house at York. I'm sure that can't be far from Leicester. Whenever you need money, feel free to have him call on them. You see how well I trust him. And trust you. Needless to say, Philip can be relied upon to bring your letters to us."

Motioning for Philip to leave, she changed her tone. "How do you find Johanna? Has she not grown even lovelier than when you saw her last?"

Simon stood stiffly facing the queen, but didn't speak until the clerk had left and closed the door behind him. Then he brought out his words slowly, tortuously, as if each syllable cut him. "My lady, I cannot accept your generosity."

Blanche's smile bent to a frown. "This is not a question of my generosity, but of your duty."

"My duty is to my liege lord. And he is now King Henry."

The Queen Mother's face lost even the delicate tint it had, and two red spots, fine traceries of veins, appeared on her cheeks. "Philip will go with you," she said in a tone that brooked no countering. "You will keep us informed."

For Simon, Blanche was the most wise, most kind, most perfect of women. His feelings were too urgent for the love of a son, too childish for the passion of a lover. And he was stepping far outside the bounds of service to the Court of France, the only world he knew. He stood rigid, his heart pounding, his head a blank of confusion but for one single thought. His face reddened, twisted like a punished child's, but he would not relent. "No!" the words burst from him, "I must serve King Henry now!"

"You refuse me?"

He couldn't answer. Trembling, unsure his legs would hold him, he turned and ran out of the room.

"Yes!" Blanche cried after him, "Run from my sight! Ingrate! Traitor! Thou hadst best flee France!"

His heart pounding as if it would break through his chest, Simon dashed down the familiar, darkened corridor, the corridor full of memories that always had ended with the good face of the Queen Mother of France.

Suddenly, out of the shadows at a turning, someone caught him and held him fast. He struggled to break free, but the voice of his captor stopped him.

"I know what she asks," the voice said, "and I know your honor. That you must say no."

Simon's determination shattered, leaving him trembling in Louis's arms.

The young king held him close. "You've not been treacherous with us. I'll always count you as my dearest friend."

Simon couldn't speak.

"I wish you well in England," Louis whispered. "But if all does not go well, come back. You'll always have a place by me."

Simon started to bow, but clutched Louis's hand and kissed it instead.

Louis held him tightly for another moment, then released him. "Go! I regret your leaving far too much. Go, while I can part with you."

"Pray for me," Simon whispered. Turning, he ran on down the corridor. He ran out through the courtyard to the stable, ordered his horse saddled, and rode to Montfort l'Amaury without looking back.

Chapter Four

The Tyrant
1230-1231

IN THE GRAY STONE HALL of Montfort l'Amaury, Simon dined with his brother. He told him nothing of what had passed at Court. He only said, "I must return to England at once. Can you have the horses ready?"

Amaury assumed that Simon's quick return must be on urgent business for Queen Blanche. He hurried his stablemen to comply. Before evening, Simon, with one of Amaury's servants and a hostler, led away a fine stud and four mares.

Torn between elation at his freedom, and isolation from all that had formed his family and the world he knew, Simon tried to concentrate his thinking on the future, and avoid thoughts of the past. He sorely missed companionship: the sharing of a laughing observation with Johanna, who had been more of an older sister to him than a future bride; the discussing of ideas with Louis; the steady, guiding presence of Queen Blanche. Every thought of the queen stabbed him with pain. His conscience was crushed by her accusations. As soon as he reached Leicester, he made confession to Grosseteste.

"Yet it was she, you say, who determined you would come to England and seek the titles," Grosseteste pondered. "You've given an oath before God. It would be at peril of your soul if you betrayed King Henry. You've done as you must. Queen Blanche acts for her country's best interests. But each of us must act for our soul's health first."

Seeing Simon's loneliness, Grosseteste commended a young man, Thomas deMesnil, to serve as his steward. Round-faced, curly haired, rosy-cheeked and merry, deMesnil was of the knightly class, could read and write in Latin and French, and keep fiscal accounts. Though Simon had no money to pay a salary yet, the archdeacon advised Thomas's father that his son would do well to be close to this rising star in the firmament of earldoms.

Simon had almost no money left at all. Not even enough for his shabby room at the Inn of Saint Nicholas. The innkeeper suggested, "Take a loan from the Jews," and directed him to their neighborhood on the far side of Saint Nicholas's Church, under the crumbling arches of the ancient Roman baths.

Wooden sheds leaned up against the weathered stone, creating housing that was cramped, humble and flimsy. Jews could not own land. But, as no one claimed the arches, the Jews were free to settle there. Simon approached the first makeshift hovel. Boards, propped up like an awning, shaded a broad counter and shop window. Behind the counter an old man sat, rocking gently back and forth with a book open in his hands. His eyes were shut. Simon thought he was asleep. But as he turned away, the man opened his eyes and called out, "What can I do for the young lord?"

"You know me?"

"Doesn't everyone in Leicester, lord Montfort?"

Simon had never sought a loan before. He was deeply embarrassed, but he stated his need plainly. "I'm short of funds. I was told that you lend money."

"Of course. I'm a goldsmith, but few in Leicester buy gold cups or brooches. So I lend. What do you need?"

"Twenty pounds. To keep my horses stabled, and to travel to my fiefs to collect the rents. I won't need the loan for long, only a week or two." It was nearly the end of September, and Simon's outlying manors' rents were due at Michaelmas, September 29th.

"I'm glad to be of service to my lord," the old man smiled. He arose and went into the depth of his small chamber, returning in a moment, carrying a wood-bound ledger like a tray laden with a balance scale, an inkpot and a quill.

"Twenty pounds in silver pence," the moneylender intoned, his trembling, rheumatic hand carefully inscribing the entry on a ledger page, "...lent to the lord Simon de Montfort, on this twenty-fifth day of September, in the year of Christian reckoning 1230, at customary compound weekly interest."

A younger man, who had been sitting at the back of the shop nodding and reading with his back toward the window, got up and hauled a heavy leather bag from underneath his chair and hefted it onto the counter. The old man dipped his shaking hand into the bag, drew out and weighed twenty pounds of pennies.

At the beginning of October, Simon and deMesnil went on a tour of the six fiefs of the Leicester Honour. Every property they visited was sunk in deep neglect. They gathered just enough to pass the winter at the inn. Simon had to ask the Jew for an extension of his loan.

Spring brought relief from an unexpected quarter. Ranulf, chagrined that he had let the Leicester fiefs decline, invited Simon to visit him, and pressed on him a loan of a thousand marks. Returning to Leicester in triumph, Simon had a new roof constructed for the hall, set his six fiefs in order, repaired his mill, and paid his villeins to fence Leicester's fields. The fence encroached upon the Countess Margaret's demesne, rousing her steward's protests. But otherwise, all seemed to be going very well at last.

Simon returned to the Jew to repay his debt. Putting a bag of twenty pounds of pennies on the counter, he asked, "What fee do I owe you?"

"Fee? We do not charge a fee. We charge ten percent on loans for a fortnight. But you kept my money thirty weeks. At interest compounded, that is eighty-four pounds in silver that you owe me."

Simon's mouth opened, but at first no words came out. His education with the King of France did not include finance – that was the concern of France's clerks. At age eighteen he was completely innocent of compound interest. When he found his voice again he blurted out, "I will not pay it! Take your twenty, and I'll pay you ten more for your troubles. That is plenty!"

"At ten percent I ask far less than the Hospitallers. Ask anyone! You know what 'compound' means?" the old man cried.

"I don't know, and I don't care! It's usury!"

"Oh, such a word. You think to hurt me with that word? Pay me what you owe me!"

"I will not!" Simon turned away, tossing a few pennies in the street. "Take that for your 'compound'! You'll get no more!"

"Do you imagine we don't know how to collect our debts?" the old man cried.

The next day, as Simon oversaw the repairing of his hall's roof, the sheriff came to press the Jew's complaint. Simon staunchly refused to pay. His builder too was in debt to the Jews, and goaded his young employer on.

Simon sought out Grosseteste in his chapel.

"I know Isaac and his family well. We read Hebrew together," the priest smiled. "I'm sorry that you fell into his debt. Understand, the Jews are barred from most crafts, as the guilds are Christian. I've founded a house in London for their conversion, not only for their souls, but to curb the sin of usury, the bleeding of the debtor for one's own profit. Would there were such a remedy for Christian usurers.

"Let the Jews go to your house in London then!" Simon was in high temper. Leaving the church, he passed the hall, striding toward the Jewish neighborhood. His builder and the workmen followed him. As they went through the town, the workmen shouted to the shopkeepers and passers-by, "We're going to the Jews!" Soon Simon was at the head of a mob.

Reaching the Roman arches, the Leicester folk worked themselves to a frenzy, tearing the flimsy wooden hoardings from the ancient stone. The Jews: men, women and children, clutching their belongings, grabbing leather bags, ledgers and books, rushed screaming from the crashing sheds. In moments the old arches were vacated, and heaps of broken wood, tumbled bedding and furniture lay in the street. The townspeople scrambled through the wreckage, looking for silver and gold.

Simon, excited to a blinding state of rage, pursued the Jews. His builder, the workmen and many more went with him.

The Jews, with two or three men together hefting the heavy leather bags, fled by the city's western gate and crossed the bridge over the River Soar. They did not stop until they reached a nearby manor where the steward knew them well and opened his doors. It was the Countess Margaret's manse.

Simon followed. He beat on the door and demanded that the Jews be sent out. The steward refused.

The men of Leicester made camp in the manor yard and meadow.

Night came. Simon's temper cooled and he began to look about. Living as he had within the sheltered, polite confines of the Paris Court, he had little experience of common folk. He saw the agitated, angry faces of the mob, and he began to feel disturbed about the people who had followed him.

Bonfires were burning. A gibbet had been raised. Simon had not known how readily the common, law-abiding man could become dangerous. A spirit seemed unleashed, an exhilaration eddied through the crowd, a blood-lust quite unlike the thrill he knew in practice combat. This was not one man testing his strength against another, but many men as one, knowing their strength and yearning for mayhem. He had meant nothing of this sort, but only to send the Jews to Grosseteste's London house.

The manor's steward, protected by armed porters, was coming toward him. "Lord Montfort, you are trespassing again! First you erect fences, impinging upon my lady's land, and now the whole of Leicester's camping at her door!"

"I beg my aunt's pardon for these offences. No offense has ever been by my intent." Simon hoped graciousness would appease the steward, but the man seemed to have taken a personal dislike to him. Nor had the countess ever responded to his overtures. He realized that somehow he must disburse the mob and send them back to Leicester.

He shouted for attention, then ordered. "Put your fires out! Take your gibbet-beams apart, and go back to your homes!"

Someone yelled from the darkness, "Not till we're rid of the Jews!"

"I promise you! As your lord! They will not return to Leicester!" The Leicestermen seemed unimpressed. "Tomorrow! I will put it in writing with the sheriff!" Simon pledged.

Reluctantly the men put their fires out. As the flames died, the seething spirit of the night seemed to fade with them. A grumbling crowd crossed back over the bridge, dragging their gibbet.

Simon had been a leader for the first time in his life, and it was shameful. The Jews left Countess Margaret's manse, scattering all over England with their story of the tyrant Simon de Montfort, who had driven them out of their homes.

The word "tyrant" would cling to Simon's name forever after. He had made a bad beginning.

Chapter five

KING HENRY'S COURT
1231-1235

MAY CAME. SIMON PAID HIS villeins not to plow and sow, but to complete the fencing of the fields. The villeins were intrigued at first. He lent them money to buy sheep and rented to them two of the fenced fields. Soon the hilltop view of Leicester offered a bizarre landscape in a world of open, three-field cultivation. Grosseteste's radical experiment was a reality.

But the villeins, unaccustomed to a single yearly income at sheep-shearing time, by summer were complaining that their lord had forced a perilous change. The word "tyrant" was heard again.

By October of 1231, a modest income trickled in for Simon from his mill and fiefs, and the foals born in the spring gave promise of good profits. Simon took on a squire. Peter was a journeyman barber who not only shaved chins but, like most barbers, was a surgeon. And he could cook. For Simon, Thomas deMesnil and Peter, life in Leicester's hall with rudimentary furnishings was comfortable. Simon's fortunes seemed to be improving.

Then in the spring of 1232, after the hard work of sheep shearing, his villeins lodged official complaint. Their ancestors had plowed the fields since times before the Normans came, before even the Romans. However sparse their harvest was, they meant to plow again and have the fences down. They took their complaint all the way up to the Crown.

Simon was summoned to Court at Windsor. Before King Henry, he argued the merits of Grosseteste's plan for raising livestock where labor to till fields was scarce. He stressed the benefit to England when her knights could buy fine warhorses. Henry grasped at once his own best interest. He ordered that the fences would remain.

Their rebellion scotched, the villeins took more earnestly to shepherding. In two more years, with the increase of their flocks they were prospering. Even a small industry of weaving was begun. An alderman built a fulling mill.

Simon saw no gain from this success beyond the customary rents from his fiefs. His income remained dependent upon those rents, the earnings of his repaired grain mill and profits from the sale of young horses. Nonetheless, by living frugally, he managed to return eight hundred of Ranulf's loan of a thousand marks.

Then he heard that the old earl had died. Feeling heavily the loss of his kind cousin, he had Mass said for Ranulf, and waited settlement of the estate to learn to whom he should remit the last two hundred marks.

Now he could turn his attention to his titles, Earl and Steward. For Simon, life at Henry's raucous Court was as enticing as a sojourn in the halls of Hell. But the titles rested with the king's whim. No force of argument, no feat of arms could win the titles for him, only King Henry's good will.

Simon presented himself at Court.

King Henry greeted the young tyrant of Leicester with a bemused, "How are your villeins, Sire Montfort? Still complaining that you fence their fields?"

Simon smiled, he could make good report. "No, my lord," he said brightly. "Their profits, through my efforts with them, doubled this year past. They are pleased as wives who, laboring for one, have gotten twins."

"Well said for a comely, knavish lad!" the drunken Roger Bigod, Earl of Norfolk, winked. "How many twins is it you've begotten on your villeins, through your efforts with 'em this year past?"

"My lord?" Simon blushed crimson in confusion. But his embarrassment was ignored in the general laughter.

As the din abated, the knight Giles Argentine called out, "Who here's gotten the most children from a single birth?"

"I have twin sons!" one knight proudly declared.

With twinkling eyes Richard de Montfichet offered, "I knew a knight in Palestine who claimed five at a single birth out of a Berber camel-driver's daughter."

"To that knight!" Henry toasted.

"To that camel-driver's daughter!" Bigod waved his goblet high.

Sipping his wine, King Henry became pensive. "I know of no child I can rightly claim. I've been thinking lately that it's time I married."

A murmur of approval rustled through the room.

Henry went on, "I've commissioned the Bishop of Ely to find me a bride. But, truthfully, I fear the outcome of his tastes," he twisted his lips sourly. "Friends, whom do you think I should marry?"

The question turned the Court at once into high gamesomeness.

"The richest!" Bigod shouted.

"No, no, it were mean for the king to wed for money," the knight Richard of Hurle countered.

"Well, the fairest then!" Bigod offered in his soused geniality.

Henry caught up his words, "The fairest, yes. But who *is* the fairest?"

"Johanna of Flanders is as fair as any man could wish," Simon put in.

Henry turned to him. "You sought her hand yourself, did you not?"

Simon feared how much Henry might know of his attachments to the Court of France. But he summoned his best courtliness and bowed, "I did. And would your steward offer you any but the finest wines that he himself has tasted?"

"Well said! I like you, Simon," the king laughed. "Why did she turn you down?"

Simon answered cautiously, "It was her guardian's bookkeeper who turned me down , on seeing my accounts."

Henry waved his goblet toward his friends. "If her guardian's bookkeeper is keeper of her chastity, she'll bear no interest from me!" Unlike the regal French, Henry knew finance and could make jest of it. "What other winsome lady shall I marry?"

Drogo de Barentin shouted, "What of the Lady Nova whom Cardinale calls a blonde goddess?"

"And godlike in her purity as well," Henry retorted. "No, she won't do."

The Royal Clerk John Mansel simpered, "My lord, it's clear the loveliest of ladies is your own sister Isabel. The proof's the Holy Roman Emperor's eagerness to have her as his bride."

"If so, Frederic drives a hard bargain," Henry laughed dryly. "He gets a dowry with her that would sweeten the worst hag's looks. Friends! How shall I outshine the emperor in marrying?"

"Why not the fairest with no dowry at all?" Richard of Hurle made a flourish with his feathered cap. "Show the emperor that England's king is rich enough to spurn such haggling!"

"I like that," Henry mused, sipping his wine. "Hurle, I commission you to visit every Court that's in financial ruin. Find me the loveliest dowerless bride in the world."

"You can't be serious! This is no joking matter!" Henry's sturdy, red haired younger brother Richard, Earl of Cornwall, broke in.

"Of course I'm serious," Henry beamed. "What better way to find a wife: loving, faithful, full of eternal gratitude and beautiful as well?" He stretched out his hand holding his goblet, "I shall seem to her like the prince in the tale, come to save her from her life of sweeping ashes."

"Henry, you're losing thirty-thousand marks with Isabel!" Richard's florid face grew redder. He was nineteen and the image of his uncle Richard the Lion Hearted. Life for him at his brother's court was unending frustration, which he relieved often and loudly with his sensible outbursts. Many thought that he would be the better king.

"Recoup at least some part of our losses through your marriage," Richard urged, "or we shall be ruined, ourselves!"

"Send my brother to that bookkeeper of Flanders," Henry waved Richard away. "Montfort, take him to Johanna. There's a pair!"

"What he says has merit, my lord," Simon said quietly.

"Sire Montfort, I was just beginning to like you," Henry frowned. "Don't be grave. Tell us more of your twins of Leicestershire. It was the challenge of your twins that started all of this."

"My lord, no challenge will you find in me. As your liegeman, all I have is yours."

"This generous spirit I like well," Henry laughed, placing his hand on Simon's shoulder. "But your twins you keep. They're something each man must get for himself."

Simon began regular attendance at the royal Court as a petitioner for his titles. He followed the Court on its annual travels around the countryside: from Westminster to Windsor, to Winchester to Woodstock, then back to Westminster again. His persistent presence was noted. One day he was summoned to the king's private chamber.

Henry was lounging upon an old, curtained bed. It was the only piece of furniture in the room. The bedposts bore gouges from decades of traveling, and the browned curtains of needlework were threadbare in their folds. The king plumped a sagging feather pillow underneath his arm, then began the interview with, "They tell me, Sire Montfort, that you were reared with King Louis."

Simon's heart clutched. Had he been accused again of spying? He answered carefully. "That's true. I spent some years at France's Court as a page. And as companion to the king. But I've no ties to France now." He added quickly, "I assure you that my fealty is to you, my lord."

Henry waved his hand as if he brushed Simon's distress away like an annoying cobweb. "I'm not accusing you of anything. I merely want to know about the Court of France."

"My lord?" Simon asked, trying to look ignorant.

"I'm not asking for state secrets! I want to know about the manners of the Court. How the king is served at table. The furnishings of the rooms. In conscience, you can manage to tell me that sort of thing I would suppose."

"My lord," Simon breathed with relief, "I will be happy to tell you all I can."

Henry poked up his crushed pillow. "Begin with Louis' chambers. Are the walls painted? Is there glass in the windows?"

Simon could not imagine these were Henry's chief concerns of France, but he blessed his luck for such an easy way to gain a closeness to the king. He described in detail the furnishings and manners of the Court of France, from the colored window glass to Louis's bed curtains, and even the formal posture of the royal equerry as he held the king's stirrup when Louis mounted his horse.

Henry was entranced. He had come to the throne when England was in civil war and the Court in disarray. The court ministers of his childhood had pilfered freely from the Chancery and Wardrobe purses, leaving a paltry minimum for the child-king's maintenance. Decay and shabbiness were all he knew. But there was in Henry a spark, an essence of an artist. Simon's tales of royal splendor fanned the spark to flame. Time and again he summoned Simon to his chamber to tell him more of France. The buildings, the jewels, the food, the furniture, the customs and celebrations: every aspect held him fascinated.

One morning Henry, almost giddy with his new idea, informed Simon, "I'm going to redecorate my palace at Westminster. It's not been painted since grandmother's time." In understatement more profound than he knew, he added, "The hall, I think, may be unseemly to our dignity," and he asked, "Can you draw?"

"Only poorly," Simon admitted.

Henry was delighted. He loved to draw. It was the one thing he knew he did well. But if Simon could draw, it would be improper for the king himself to do it. "Good!" he said decisively, "I'll draw. You advise me."

After that, Simon and King Henry met daily as if in conference of the deepest secrecy. The young Frenchman's closeness to the king became the chief meat of Court gossip. Some were certain Henry planned a new campaign to retake Normandy and was extracting the young Frenchman's knowledge of King Louis' military strength. Others leered at Henry's fascination with the comely foreigner. But no one guessed the truth: that on huge sheets of parchment Henry was recreating the Battle of Antioch in ten colors.

Then the painters, carpenters and drapers came and the renovation of Westminster Hall began in earnest. King Henry was interested in nothing but his furnishings and plans; and Simon, his advisor, was supreme. For every tint of paint, every fold of drape, Henry asked Simon's opinion. Even at supper the king ignored his courtiers to question Simon on the precise hue of red that would be proper for a door. Or might the ceiling be enriched with gold?

When table manners rose to his attention, Henry had a clerk write down what Simon told him of the customs at the Court of France. The clerk then read the list of do's and don'ts aloud to the assembled Court. Henceforth every person dining in the Royal Presence must be mannerly after the French mode. He must use napkin and washbasin, not lick his fingers or, worse still, use his robe. His voice must be moderate and his language fitting to the royal dignity. Drink must be only in moderation. So the list began, and continued for pages. The result was a far quieter and better-ordered Court.

Among Henry's courtiers, resentment against Simon grew, festered and became deep and aggravated. From "the tyrant of Leicester," his unpopularity advanced to "the king's cursed foreign friend."

But the faded, peeling imitation brickwork of the hall was vanishing, replaced by knights, horses, ships, siege-towers and embattled Antioch, topped by a broad border of crimson with the golden lions of Plantagenet *en passant guardant.*

Henry studied his achievement and was pleased.

When the king resumed his normal business, hearing pleas and granting charters, Simon remained firmly by his side.

Jealousy among the courtiers gave rise to a whispering campaign: the Frenchman was a spy for Queen Blanche. The king's cousin, William Longspee, the Earl of Salisbury, cautioned, "Recall if you will, Henry, that blood is thick."

"What do you mean by that, Lord William?" Simon demanded.

"I mean that your brother is Marshall of France, a country with which we are not at peace!"

"I won't hear these accusations," Henry declared firmly. "Sire Montfort has paid his liege to me. Be that an end of it."

But that did not make an end of it. Silenced, the jealousies and suspicions merely crept deeper.

Simon's time at Court extended into months: months filled with feasting, hunting, and a little business of state. A year, and then another passed. Henry sought Simon's opinion on nearly everything, and heaped him with favors. All but the one favor he sought: the granting of his titles. Whenever he uttered the words "earl" or "steward," the king frowned so sternly that Simon ceased to ask for fear of angering him. Henry knew very well that, once the titles were granted, Simon would not linger willingly at Court.

For Simon, life at Henry's Court brought loneliness so deep that he dared not let it touch even the outskirts of his thoughts. The hostility of the courtiers was palpable, as if a wall enclosed him. He was utterly isolated but for his attendance upon Henry, and that was not companionship, it was strained work.

Loathing the ribald license of the English courtiers, he sometimes yearned to quit his efforts for the titles and retreat to the shelter of monastic life. But Father Grosseteste replied to his unhappy letters by urging patience, and assuring him that his place was at the Court where he would do great things some day. For solace, the archdeacon sent him books: Eusebius's gory catalogue of martyrs, and his own grim tract on the desert hermit, Saint Mary the Egyptian. Life clearly could be worse, but Simon was not comforted.

Once, when the Court traveled south, Simon took brief leave to visit his grandaunt Loretta at her convent near Hackington.

Loretta was the widow of Robert FitzParnel, the last of the Beaumont Earls of Leicester. She had grown up at the Court of Henry II: before King Richard of the Lion's Heart had let the Court fall to neglect as he pursued his foreign wars; before the chaos of the civil wars of King John's time; before the depredations imposed upon the child-king Henry by his Poitouvin guardians. Loretta was regarded as one of the last living authorities on how the Court had functioned in its prime.

No one at Court seemed to know quite what the duties of the Steward of England were. "Why should I trouble myself for this honor," Simon asked his aunt, "if it's nothing more than holding the king's washbasin?"

"Whoever told you that is either ignorant or lying!" the old lady retorted. "It isn't that at all. The Steward has the keeping of the door. He controls who may– and who may *not* – be heard by the king."

Loretta nodded her head as the vast power her words implied reached Simon's comprehension. "It can be the most important position in the realm," she said quietly. "After the king himself, of course. Why do you suppose Ranulf made Henry promise the earldom and the stewardship to you? For justice's sake? Certainly not! Justice was on Amaury's side, for all that might have been worth! No, Ranulf thought you'd be a good influence on Henry. We talked of it, Ranulf and I."

Simon digested this stunning information for some moments, then said, "Henry's lords would never tolerate such power in my hands. They call me a 'foreigner,' as if *they* were English, and not as Norman as I when you but look to their ancestors. Did I tell you that I'm learning to speak English?"

"Whatever for!" Loretta recoiled as if even a passing knowledge of the language of the peasantry might taint a noble person.

"I can speak directly to my villeins now, which is more than most of the lords who call me foreign can claim."

"And your friendship with the king?"

"Henry relies on me more every day. He's been giving me presents. But it fuels the lords' resentment to a heat I fear."

"What sort of presents?"

"Escheats mostly. When a property is forfeited through crime or lack of heirs and passes to the Crown, Henry's been granting it to me. Five fiefs so far, though none of them is very large. I couldn't afford to travel with the Court otherwise."

"You're dressing well enough," Loretta smiled. She was enjoying the fine sight her nephew made in his short white riding-robe embroidered with a dotting of the fork-tailed red lion rampant of Montfort.

Simon, at twenty-two, was tall and muscular like his warrior father, and his features were maturing to a beauty rare in a man. He had the deep-set eyelash-shadowed eyes of his father, his father's straight nose and delicately curved lips, and the strong, fine hands of a swordsman.

He was aware of his comeliness, even dimly aware that his success with Henry was in some part due to his physical attractiveness. But he was not vain, the difference being that he did not value himself for his appearance, any more than he valued his increasing skill at what passed for wit at Henry's Court. But he knew that these things helped him. He glanced down at his plum-colored stockings and his elegant, embroidered robe, and laughed, "This English Court unteaches my French lessons of humility."

"Humility, Simon, is a lesson that you've yet to learn." Loretta narrowed her eyes wisely, "I doubt you ever will."

Chapter Six

A ROYAL WEDDING
1235-1236

"FREDERIC'S REMINDING ME HOW MUCH he wants my sister Isabel," Henry remarked to Simon as they stood in the grassy, walled courtyard of London Tower, inspecting the latest present from the Holy Roman Emperor. It was a camel.

"Oh, take the beast away," Henry told the stableman, "and see its picture's painted before it dies like the last one." He turned from the shaggy animal and walked back to the hall, with Simon following.

"Frederic's determined I shall keep a bestiary as he does, but he doesn't take my climate into account. I suppose I must send Isabel off soon. I've made a list of the people who will go with her. Let Frederic support them for a change. I'd like you to look over the list with me."

Simon nodded. "Will the dowry go with her?"

"Only part. I don't have the funds to spare. Do you suppose it's true that Frederic keeps a harem?"

"I've heard it said. I find it hard to believe."

"I don't. You should see the letters Isabel receives. You'd think some love-struck Saracen had written them. A propos of love, Richard of Hurle is back. He's found my future bride. You don't look joyful, Simon. Why the long face?"

"You know I'm of your brother Richard's opinion. The Crown can ill afford such jests."

"When you hear whom he's found, you'll pull a longer face. What do you say to Eleanor of Provence?"

Simon was stunned. He had never seen Eleanor to know whether she was a beauty or a hag, but it was his father's war against the Albigensian heretics that had destroyed Provence and brought her family's ruin. She was the last woman on earth whose Court he would willingly attend.

"Ha! That did surprise you," Henry laughed. "She sent my brother a poem she'd written, full of fancied chivalry, and so impassioned I told Hurle to have a look at her."

"She hardly sounds the modest bride you had in mind."

"Be that as it may, Hurle says she's definitely the prettiest."

"My lord, whatever good is to be had from Provence, King Louis has in marrying the eldest daughter. He secures his southern border. You can gain nothing by a marriage to the younger one. Count Raymond cannot even pay the dowry he owes France."

"Precisely," Henry smiled.

"My lord, this is foolhardy!"

"I intend to marry her."

"She's a heretic!" Simon burst out.

"That she may sympathize with them, I don't doubt. Am I in more danger of being tainted by my wife's views than Louis is?" Henry teased.

Simon winced but countered, "My lord, Louis gains peace on his southern border. What motive can you have?"

"I lust for her."

"A woman you've never seen?"

"I lust for her in imagination. From Hurle's description. Simon, I'm in love! I'm on a cloud! Do you know she keeps a Court of Love? My grandmother Eleanor held a Court of Love. That was a great woman! Unfortunately I never knew her."

"You're in love with your grandmother, whom you never knew, so you marry a woman with the same name and the same bad precepts?"

"I've sent the Bishop of Ely and Robert of Hereford back with Hurle to negotiate the marriage, with a letter from me in Frederic's passionate style. I expect she'll be here by Easter. Then we'll see what you say of my bride."

"Please excuse me from the Court," Simon said curtly.

"Oh no, my would-be earl, my would-be Steward of England! If you try to stay away I'll have you summoned. I'll have you bear the office of steward for my wedding and the coronation of my queen."

"You will invest me with my titles?"

"I didn't say that. Let me see how well you play the part. Is that not fair?"

"Most fair, my lord," Simon bowed frigidly.

"Don't sulk... though the expression does become you. Remember that, Simon. Sulk for the ladies, it's your winning look."

"Would that I could win my lord to reason."

"Reason? I suppose, like you, I should court a rich woman twice my age for the sake of her fortune?"

"If you mean Mahaut of Boulogne, any stories of my ever courting her are gross exaggerations. She knew me slightly at the Court of France, but she's old enough to be my mother."

"There, you see. You need the money but you won't take an old hag to bed for all her fortune. You've no business lecturing me. You're no different, and I'm glad to hear it."

With due pomp the Princess Isabel was sent on her way to wed the Holy Roman Emperor. And messages came from Provence of the rapid close of Henry's suit for Eleanor. Her father had never dreamed of so fine an offer for his second daughter's hand. He didn't quibble. Far from waiting for the better weather of spring, Eleanor, with a great entourage, was sent to England at once.

"I want a surpassing celebration!" Henry bubbled with excitement. "Bring the citizens of London out to meet my bride. With banners and music! Yes! And a feast upon the road! You must arrange it for me, Simon. Make it outshine anything ever seen in France. Let my subjects show their love for me on my most happy day!"

Simon bowed coolly and said in obvious avoidance of the nuptial occasion, "I shall be glad to serve as steward to the honor that your subjects bear their king."

Henry scowled at his chilly reply. "It really hurts you that I'm marrying a Provencal?"

"Yes, my lord."

Life at Henry's Court was a gamut of jealousy, insinuation and overt insult that Simon steeled himself to bear. But the Court of a heretical Provencal queen struck at his last refuge: his faith.

In one final attempt to win his titles, he threw himself into the preparations for the celebration. He visited the masters of the London guilds, gaining promises from the fishmongers, butchers and bakers of foods for the feast – prepared, delivered and served gratis. From the vintners' guild he obtained wine.

"Perhaps the king would like our pageant wagon of 'The Miracle of Cana'?" the Master of the Vintners suggested. "It's a great fountain of wines which we display on the feast day of our patron saint."

Simon readily agreed, and this gave him a new idea. He visited the masters of all the guilds, then all the parishes of London, and found that many had such wagons for their saints' festivals. The wagons bore elaborately built and decorated settings where the parish and guild players portrayed their saints' miracles. The holy pageants suited Simon's humor perfectly: they would make a fitting welcome for a heretic.

As Henry devoted his attention to his and his attendants' clothes, and gave orders to his courtiers to do the same, Simon was amassing an event like nothing ever seen before. At no cost to the Crown.

The site of the celebration was to be a stretch of road between London and Rochester, the route the wedding party would follow on their way to the royal city. The challenge of organizing a stupendous festival in the open air, on empty country fields, in the midst of winter was immense. In addition to the wedding party, provision must be made for the Londoners: guild members, parish players and their families, teamsters with their wagons of supplies, and unguessable numbers of spectators.

With his oppressive attendance at the Court relieved by the demands of his work, Simon felt like a prisoner liberated. He roamed the city, cheerfully expanding the event to encompass all the population reachable by parish or by guild. He found use for his studies in deploying and supplying armies at war, as he organized shelter and commissaries for the bystanders and the great feast and pageant for the wedding celebrants themselves. The project engaged him totally. If he had a moment to reflect, it was not spent upon the lady being greeted, but on the titles, Earl and Steward, shimmering at the end of the campaign.

Eleanor arrived at Dover on January the thirteenth, 1236, the day before she was expected at the earliest. Henry and his Court were on their way to meet her at Dover, but found her outriders already at Canterbury. A great assembly came with the bride: her father's kinsmen from Provence, her mother's kinsmen from Savoy, and numerous waiting ladies, knights, troubadours, clerks, servants and pages. Eleanor had gathered her attendants all the way from Provence to the French port of Wissant, where she had embarked. Roger Bigod remarked it was remiss of her not to have brought along her ship's captain, sailors and any mermaids she encountered in the Channel.

Henry III and Eleanor of Provence were wed in Canterbury Cathedral. Archbishop Edmund Rich performed the marriage rite. Then the combined royal entourage went on to Rochester, where Henry and Eleanor spent their first night.

Snow, sleet and frigid wind swept the road from London to Rochester all through the night. In the blast of the gale, by the whipping lights of torch-flames, oxen dragged wagons laden with folded tents, trestle tables, barrels of serving vessels, kettles, costumes, firewood and foods for the feast. Hogsheads of wine loomed through the snow-swirled air, rocking on their carts toward the vintners' designated spot along the royal wedding party's way. Gaily painted pageant wagons lumbered, their wonders cupboarded behind their folded panel doors. Men, women and children, the guild and parish players, trudged beside the wagons, bundled and huddled against the freezing night.

Simon, with the help of his squire Peter and steward deMesnil, directed each arriving caravan to its appointed place at the roadside, and allotted each arriving group its area in the fields for tents and supplies.

Through the bitter night the Londoners came in hundreds, then thousands. Not only the performers and the cooks and servers of the feast arrived, but everyone from nuns and priests to jugglers, pickpockets and cutthroats came. All wanted to see the royal bride and the winter festival. London emptied to populate the road.

As the long, cold night went on, a new city grew in the fields. Masses of people clustered by bonfires that blazed in orange streams into the dark, sleety wind. To keep spirits high among the circles of frost-chapped faces in the firelights, troubadours sang songs of ancient loves, of beauties whose love-glances never died: Helen and Isolde, Guinevere and Blanchefleur.

Morning opened with a sky of infinite bright blue above a world encased in ice. The road, swept clean by the night's wind, was like a band of polished silver. Trees glinted in the sunlight: their branches, sheathed in crystal, scattered rainbows from each prismed twig. The stubble in the fields was white as winter fur.

The encampment of Londoners, a long dark smudge on the white landscape, swarmed like a hive. The sleepless cooks and players made their last preparations. Scents of wood-smoke and of dainty dishes wafted in the icy air. Seamstresses sewed last-minute repairs. Guildsmen unpacked and counted silver serving vessels while apprentices tied swags of evergreens to litters that would bear the feast.

Simon was everywhere, like a general seeing to the readiness of his troops before battle. He checked the cook sheds, the teams of bearers and the pageant wagons' readiness. As he went his rounds, suddenly the noisy clatter of the camp was broken by the blaring of brass horns. Above the curve where the road crested a distant hill, bright pennants were fluttering.

The cooks began to ladle their hot victuals into silver chargers.

Players hurried to their places on the pageant wagons. Saint Laurence climbed upon his grill of painted flames. Saint Lucy, in a flutter of nerves, searched her pockets for her eyeballs. Saint Sebastian adjusted the arrows piercing his breast. Saint George's dragon was stoked until its three nodding heads belched flames as well as smoke. And Hellsmouth roared with flames so hot the miserable parishioners who played the Damned could shed their cloaks and stand in their thin under-shifts. Theirs was a pageant usually performed in summertime.

The Royal Progress came on with banners of red, blue, yellow, white and black with splashing fringe of gold. Heralds and flag bearers in the red and gold livery of Plantagenet blew horns, beat drums and held aloft a forest of flags that snapped in the brisk wind. The lords of England followed in fur cloaks and pheasant-feathered hats, their horses caparisoned in satins with heraldic embroideries and fringes to their hocks.

The Londoners swarmed toward the parade. Jugglers tossed fruit to the riders and danced over ropes of sausages. Guild masters, in their finest fur-lined robes and jewels, bore holly-swagged litters heavy with silver vessels heaped with rich, rare foods: pimpernel and lark pastries, sugared flawns, black puddings, squabs in wine, pies filled with salmon and with luce, and boars bursting with plums and apricots.

Cherub-faced apprentices served as cupbearers with brimming beakers of hippocras and mead. The Master of the Vintners hurried with a litter of cups and ewers from the guild's "Fountain of Cana," where the wine had frozen in arches and cascades like the buttresses and pinnacles of a fanciful cathedral made of crimson ice.

At the side of the road the pageant wagons displayed their saints. The child Saint Philomel climbed to the top of a living pyramid of angel acrobats costumed in white robes and goose-feather wings. Saint Michael, in gold armor, brandished a silver sword and held aloft a torpid snake. Saint Margaret, her face blackened and bloody, her skirts painted with flames, stood in a huge cauldron, her shivering arms uplifted joyously. Saint Lucy thrust out her hands, each holding an eye. Saint Magnus knelt before a sturdy, leather-aproned butcher who hacked at the saint's neck with a gigantic wooden axe. Saint George, in silver helm and suit of mail, battled his fire-spewing dragon as its flames melted the frozen earth to mud beneath his feet.

Children of Saint George's parish, dressed as monster pups, darted through the march to offer chalices of soringue of eels to King Henry, for eels were known to be his favorite dish.

Among the marchers, after the heralds, the flag bearers and lords, came curtained, horse-borne palanquins with swaying golden tassels. Ladies peeped from the curtains to take the dainty foods offered by the masters of the guilds. Whenever a lady could be glimpsed, cries rose from the onlookers, "Is that she?" The Londoners vied to catch the first sight of their queen-to-be, the beauty who had won King Henry's heart.

The royal bailiffs, dressed in scarlet livery with golden lions *en passant guardant*, came next.

And then there was no question: King Henry and Eleanor of Provence rode side by side. In furs and cloth-of-gold, the King of England sat upon a splendid chestnut destrier manteled in broad stripes of red and gold. His bride, in cloth-of-silver lined with ermine as white as the fields, rode beside him on a milk-white palfrey draped in midnight blue.

Eleanor held her head high, already a queen. She was sixteen, and everyone agreed her beauty beggared Hurle's description. She had the luminous petal-pink complexion of her mother, Beatrice of Savoy. Her eyes were large and lustrous blue. Her forehead, like a fawn's, was wide and round. She wore no veil; her hair, a treasure of bright golden curls, fell freely upon the shoulders of her cloak. But more than Nature's gifts, a studied grace flowed in her every gesture. She was sensuous. In the arts of desire the lady was well schooled. She filled to the full the ideal of a people whose doctrine of love the Church declared perverse, lubricious and heretical. Henry was dazzled, madly in love.

Simon, with his sheaf of lists and maps of the festival grounds, found himself at the roadside as the royal couple passed. The bride, laughing at a jest of Henry's, turned aside an instant. Her glance met Simon's narrowed gaze. Then she moved on.

Simon looked after her. He could not draw his gaze away, though soon he could see no more than a glint of golden hair beyond the intervening riders.

"My lord," deMesnil, at Simon's elbow, tried to draw his master's attention. "She is a rare beauty," he nodded solemnly. "I pray she'll prove a proper queen."

Simon said nothing. He had no words for the sudden emptiness he felt, the sensation that his heart had gone where his eyes could not, and left a gaping vacancy in his breast. He coughed, and realized he hadn't been breathing. Pulling his gaze to deMesnil was like turning away from sunlight to resume a life in dismal shade.

Seeing his master's expression, deMesnil looked away, down at his feet, stymied with embarrassment.

At London Bridge, the Gate of Eden, borrowed from Saint Paul Cathedral's "Play of Adam," spanned the road between the bridge's double row of shops. The shivering, leaf-clad Adam and Eve bestowed their blessings. The Royal Progress marched beneath the painted alabaster arch, as passing from the Fallen World back into Paradise.

The flags of the lords, as they arrived at London Tower, were arrayed on the battlements. Long ropes of holly swagged the walls. Doves were loosed, flying in a shimmering white cloud over the castle's crenellated keep.

The next day in London Tower's hall Queen Eleanor was crowned. Another feast was held and Simon served as Steward, bearing the king's washbasin.

Henry was never happier. The grandeur of the Progress had transformed his kingdom to a world of pleasure, with him its easy, radiant monarch. "Love is a surpassing, joyous thing, is it not, Simon?" he murmured, toying with his bride's slender fingers.

Simon, in the short red and gold tabard of the royal livery, stood behind them. "Judging by your visage it must be, my lord, though of my own experience, I cannot say." Since he first had seen Eleanor she had been a magnet to his eyes, though his mind deplored her manner and looked upon her beauty as her evil agent. Restraint, like an iron vice upon his feelings, gave his voice hard edge.

The young queen, stung, turned toward him. She let her glance pass slowly up to his face, as unabashed as a caress. "Who is this steward of yours who confesses that he's never been in love?"

"My name is Simon de Montfort." He pursed his lips, knowing his words would offend a Provencal.

The queen recoiled as if she had been struck. It was the name of the man most hated by her people, the man who had laid waste to southern France.

But her languid gaze struck Simon with a force at least as strong. His heart seemed to abandon his breast entirely to hover, quivering, in her golden hair. His body waged war with his will, declaring itself independent and in liege to her. Blushing hotly, he frowned and held the basin lower, covering his short tabard's hem.

Henry, seeing his bride's distress and Simon's fierce glare, whispered in Eleanor's ear, "It was Sire Montfort who arranged our Wedding Progress. So far as kings have friends, he is my friend." Taking up his goblet, he arose and announced to the whole assembly, "At this merry nuptial, with Heaven as our witness, let Provence and Montfort be reconciled!"

In the glaring light of the entire room's attention, the young queen smiled obediently. She drank from the goblet Henry held to her lips, then said, "My lord, I'll try to learn the name in this new form, and not think on what's past."

Chapter Seven

THE COURT OF LOVE
1236

THE COURT WAS CHANGED COMPLETELY by the coming of the queen. Drunken carousals ceased. Many of the courtiers who had arrived with Eleanor remained; among them were the queen's uncles, Peter and Boniface of Savoy. Peter was in his forties: witty, discreet, filled with taste in all the arts and politically astute. Boniface was burly, simple, jovial and not yet twenty. Henry loved them both, and made Peter officially a royal counselor with a lavish income and the title Earl of Richmond. Instantly the Savoyard achieved what Simon could not do in six years. His elegant robes and dainty beard, his lean and fluttering gestures, became a constant presence by the throne.

From a hale-fellow bluffness, the Court swung to its opposite: a feminine gentility redolent of the French south. In years past, the few ladies of the royal family had lived away from Court. Now they were summoned as companions for the queen. It wasn't long before Queen Eleanor announced she would commence a Court of Love. Henry, eager to please, declared Westminster Hall hers for certain hours on fixed days of the week.

Simon begged to be excused from Henry's Court. He pled his long absence from Leicester and the neglect of his estates. But truly, despite the king's toast, he was definitely not reconciled to the new queen. While she might forgive him, since he was not his father, he could not forgive her for what she was herself. And he was beset by dreams of her, dreams from which he woke burning with shame.

He fled to Grosseteste, finding the archdeacon in his study at Lincoln.

"It's true. The Church isn't pleased with this Court of Love," the old priest mused placidly, sitting in the sunlight at his table with his writing spread before him. "But Henry's own faith is not at issue. This is a passing whim. He wants to gratify his bride. We must be cautious lest, if we oppose the queen, he may be moved to defend her. Unopposed," Grosseteste toyed with his writing stylus, "he'll soon lose interest in this Court of Love when its newness is dulled. The Church means to ignore it."

"But how am *I* to ignore it, Father!" Simon protested. "I'm a stranger to myself. I jest with the king, I play to his moods in hope someday he'll grant my titles – the foolishness I hear issuing from my mouth puts me to shame. And now this queen! I beg you, let me join your Franciscans!"

Grosseteste regarded Simon with the calm of a man whose life has known no fleshly temptations. "The Church doesn't lack friars, but a man of faith close to the king She can ill afford to lose."

"Aren't there plenty of bishops, priors, archbishops? It's their business to deal with the king as men of faith!"

"You know as well as I how few of them these days are men of faith. They hold their benefices thanks to their high kindred or their money, and they advise the king with their eyes fixed firmly on their own gain."

"Am I any better? I merely have less success!"

Grosseteste studied Simon; he seemed unable to put his thoughts in words. At last he said, "I have a certain gift of insight. But of this I cannot speak. Not now. Believe me when I say to you, your place is at the Court."

"You will oppose my entering the Order?"

"Yes."

"On what grounds!"

"I'll find grounds if need be."

"Then you are not my friend!"

"Perhaps," the archdeacon said quietly, "but we are in this life for more important things. If you no longer hold me as your friend, know that my love and prayers go with you nonetheless."

Furious, Simon turned and left. Then at the door he paused and turned again; the emptiness he faced in losing this one friend was too bleak. He surrendered. "Father, if I must live at Court I'll need your counsel. But I beg you, tell me how I can go on in faith?"

"The answer is in the living," Grosseteste replied. "That is life's test, isn't it?"

Simon confined his deepest reasons for alarm not to Grosseteste, but to the anonymity of Coventry Cathedral's confessional on his way back to Leicester. To the shadowy figure behind the booth's grill, he spoke of his besetting dreams of "his lord's wife," a thing the priest undoubtedly had heard from many other men. He came away with advice to pray and to be strong against temptation. From a monk he bought a hair shirt and wore it beneath his courtly robes of scarlet and white. The shirt's roughness made him irritable and did not stop his dreams.

Not long after he reached Leicester, Simon received a summons from King Henry. All the lords of England were called to attend the Royal Court at Westminster. Anxious, uncertain and deeply unwilling, Simon returned to the king.

Standing before the hurly-burly havoc of the mural of embattled Antioch, the lords of England, dressed in their finest robes of satin and fur, talked earnestly. Archbishops, bishops and abbots milled at the fore, beside the dais steps. Their crimson copes and tall mitres were stiff with thread of gold; their croziers like a fence of gilded shepherds' crooks. The hall buzzed with speculation as to what the king was going to announce. Among the optimists there was the ever-present hope the king was planning to invade Normandy to retake their lost lands. But the pessimists outnumbered, observing that King Henry's French, and now Provencal friends would never countenance the project.

Whispers and frowns met Simon as he entered. The Earl of Hereford, Humphrey de Bohun, muttered loudly enough for him to hear, "There's Queen Blanche's man. So long as Henry befriends him, our Norman lands are lost."

Simon, vexed in the extreme at being there at all, blushed livid with rage and moved to strike Bohun. But someone caught his arm.

"Ho, Montfort! Such a hothead still?"

Simon spun around to see who gripped him so powerfully, and greeted him so familiarly. "Walter Cantaloup!" He stared at the huge, jocund fellow dressed in priestly robes. "What brings you here?"

"I've come for Worcester. Our bishop isn't well and sent me instead." Walter was of that monumental Norman build, the ideal image of a knight. But he was a fine scholar and an ardent Franciscan. They had met when Simon and Louis, escaping from the palace on the Isle de la Cite, sat on the floors of musty tenements in the Latin Quarter hearing lectures by the scholars of the university. Queen Blanche, discovering her son's truancies, had brought his clandestine studies to an end, but Louis' scholar friends were invited to the Court.

Simon embraced Walter, forgetting Bohun's insult in the joy of meeting an old friend. "I'm so glad to see you. You must be heaven-sent!"

His smile showed such relief that Cantaloup felt abashed. "Sent here just to keep you out of brawls?" was all the young priest could reply. They moved to the side of the hall to talk until the king's meeting began.

Eventually King Henry entered from the door beside the dais and took his place upon his carved-oak chair. He was dressed in full state with jeweled crown and fur-trimmed crimson robes. Peter de Riveaux, the Minister of the Treasury, followed him and went to the fore of the dais. A bailiff pounded his staff for attention. The room quieted. The meeting began. Walter hurried to his place at the hall's front, among the bishops. Simon remained where he was in the hall's side aisle; he was only an untitled onlooker.

Riveaux stood straight and stiff before the assembly. He took a deep breath as if about to plunge into an icy pool, then in his high-pitched Poitouvin accent he announced, "Good fathers of the Church and lords of England! King Henry hereby announces that, whatever he may have done before, he now and henceforth will, without hesitation, submit himself to the advice of all of you, his faithful, natural subjects."

The lords and clerics looked from one to another, eyebrows raised approvingly. Simon was amazed at this change from Henry's usual unconcern for his subjects' views.

Riveaux went on. "But those who, in the management of the king's affairs, till now have been in charge of the accounting of his treasury, have rendered incorrect count of the funds held by them. Owing to this the king is destitute of funds, without which any king is desolate."

The listeners' smiles dissolved. A sullen murmuring crept through the room.

Riveaux shrilled above it. "He humbly therefore demands assistance, on the understanding that the sums raised shall be expended for the necessary uses of the kingdom."

Having made this announcement, the Treasurer bowed and retreated to stand behind the king's chair.

The hall was utterly silent. In the silence came a single, loud voice, "The mountain labored and brought forth a mouse."

The whole assembly broke to mocking laughter.

King Henry gripped the arms of his chair, his expression gray as ash.

Now the lords' responses came swiftly. "Why should we give money to the king? What does he do for us?" Gilbert Marshall, the Earl of Pembroke, challenged. "Does he defend our borders?"

"No!" several voice cried in unison.

"Does our feeblest enemy fear Henry?" Pembroke pressed. Laughter rippled through the hall. Pembroke played upon it. "Are we so much weaker than England's foes that we let ourselves be robbed? We know he'll only give our money to his leeching foreign friends! Are we such slaves?"

"No!" the shouts came heartily.

Henry sat tense and grim.

Finally the lords quieted to hear their king's response.

With the composure of true majesty, the stamp and chief aim of kingly nurturing – the object of which is to hold the Crown at any price – Henry spoke mildly. "We must beg our subjects' forgiveness for having served so ill as to deserve this harsh rebuke. We would remind you that our recent expenses have been unique, in the dower of our sister Isabel, now empress, and in our own marriage."

"The king should live within his means like every other man!" the Lord of Cadnor, Richard de Grey called out.

"I promise to do nothing in the future without your advice, if you will help me now," Henry insisted.

"You say that, yet you're petitioning the Pope for revocation of the Magna Carta!" Richard de Montfichet threw back.

"That's not true!" Henry protested. "We grant it was suggested. But we did not agree. On contrary, we promise you, we will observe the Charter."

Simon stood leaning against a pillar, studying the queen's relatives who stood near him. Isabel's dowry he knew was paid only in part. And the wedding celebration, though lavish, had been no great burden to the Crown. But the Provencals and the queen's uncles of Savoy were dressed in far more costly robes and jewels than they had worn at the wedding feast. Simon guessed how Henry's funds had been spent.

When at last King Henry could bring the meeting to an end, the lords and clergy withdrew, but the king did not permit them to leave London. After several more days of bickering, they agreed to raise the funds he asked. Only then were they allowed to return to their homes.

Simon was commanded to remain at Court. Henry appointed him to assist in collecting and recording the new tax as it was received at the Exchequer.

One afternoon when his tax-collecting duties were slack, Simon went to the hall in search of Henry, but found instead the queen's Court of Love in session. Richard, the king's brother, sat talking with a lady. Otherwise there were few in Simon's range of vision whom he recognized. Most of those attending were the queen's people and ladies only recently come to Court. He turned to leave.

But the queen, seeing him, called out, "Simon de Montfort! Welcome to our court. Come forward."

He had no choice but to obey. He came to the fore, by the first row of benches.

"Today we are discussing Tristan," the queen said sweetly, in the manner of one talking to a child, or to a fool. She gestured toward an elderly waiting woman sitting by her. "Lady Alice contends that the sword Tristan placed between himself and Queen Isolde, as they slept in the grove, was the True Cross. What is your opinion?"

"That's blasphemy!" The rude words broke from Simon's lips.

A tight smile curved the queen's bow mouth. "You speak strongly, Sire. But you are quite wrong. Would you have love fulfilled?"

"Yes. When it is sanctioned and lawful." Simon gazed upward in exasperation, casting his glance anywhere but at the queen.

"But desire is far purer than possession," she insisted.

"Tristan had possessed the queen. They were adulterers, madam." As he spoke his eyes met Queen Eleanor's and his gaze locked in hers. In that instant the desire he had been struggling to suppress spoke all too clearly through his eyes. Confused, mortified, he blushed deep red and looked away.

The queen's lips opened slightly in surprise. The view into his heart had been all too clear. Lady Alice gave a knowing smile. Queen Eleanor spoke in soft, measured tones, "Then why, Sire Montfort, did Tristan place his sword between himself and Isolde, when at last they might have surfeited their love?"

Burning with embarrassment, he could only manage to reply sullenly, "That I cannot know. Yet I am certain it was not the Cross."

Ladies Alice simpered, "He's the cub of his father. But without the claws."

A surge of anger rose in him. His fists clenched till his nails dug in his palms, but he was too confounded to make answer.

Thoroughly enjoying the suffering of the son of their old enemy, Lady Alice put the question to him once again. "Sire Montfort, do you truly believe – that which is possessed is preferable to that which is desired yet denied?"

Simon turned on her, his anger sweeping his mind clear. "Yes, madam. If what *you* believe were so, then devils who live in torment, yearning for lost Grace, would be in better stead than angels who reside in Heaven's bliss!"

A young woman seated on a bench near him remarked, "Well said!"

He glanced down at her. Like many there, he had seen her at the wedding feast but had no notion whom she was.

"Indeed," the queen laughed lightly. "You speak like an angel, Sire Montfort. We, here, are only mortals. We hold *wanting* as the better passion, for it keeps our eyes upon our earthly lack, setting our gaze heavenward."

"I think, madam," Simon retorted hotly, "your gaze is then not heavenward, but lover-ward," and his eyes met hers again.

The Provencal ladies burst into mocking laughter. Simon clenched his jaw and glared at the embattled towers of Antioch on the room's wall. Now even his words betrayed him.

Queen Eleanor was blushing and her answer was flustered. "You speak too boldly, Sire. You've much to learn of courtesy." The ardor she could see in him ignited a glow in her: in part a triumph, in part the lure of the most forbidden. She felt a shudder of her inmost body, a sensation that, for all her studies of the theories of love, she had not known before.

Simon turned to leave, but the queen said quickly, "Sir, you've not yet been dismissed. Please sit. And learn from our debate."

At that moment the one consuming passion Simon felt was to be gone from the hall. But against such a command he was powerless. The young woman who had spoken in his favor smiled up at him, and made room by her on the bench. Simon sat, his face flushed, his heart wrung with annoyance and shame.

"You've not been to the Court of Love before?" the lady beside him asked.

"No."

She whispered, "You did well, for one who gave all the wrong answers." And she laughed a warm and gentle laugh.

The friendly lady was slightly younger than Simon. Her large features could be called ill favored, framed by a plain white wimple and gray veil. Her robe was of coarse russet cloth such as was worn by the poor, but the style and cut were fashionable.

"I said what I believe is true," Simon replied, trying to calm his ringing nerves.

The lady smiled, "Bad consciences are easily offended."

Simon glanced at her, alarmed that she too seemed to see into his heart. But the direction of her look made it clear she was referring to the queen. "You don't hold their views?" he asked.

"Certainly not."

He felt soothed by this woman's presence, put at ease by her amiable smile. But his harried thoughts still came out of his mouth unguarded. "So there's at least one person here with whom I can speak without offending."

The lady laughed lightly.

An old woman sitting behind them poked Simon's arm, "Pay court to her and you'll soon know the truth, 'Desire's better than the having!'" and she chuckled as at a great jest.

Perplexed, Simon looked to the somberly clothed lady by him for an explanation.

She glanced down. "I've taken holy vows."

"Oh," he nodded. He tried to turn his attention to the debate on the dais, but his eyes kept moving back to her. At last he whispered, "May I ask why?" Then, "Please! You needn't answer that. I fear I'm offending you, too."

"It's no offense. I was married when I was quite young, to a much older man, and when he died I took the vows."

"Oh, that don't tell him!" the old beldame behind them poked Simon again. "The old Earl of Pembroke, William Marshall. She was only nine when she was married. Widowed at fifteen. Now what sort of marriage is that, I ask you."

"Mary, you're too indiscreet," the lady in russet chided her waiting woman.

Simon was not shocked. Such matches were common among the nobility, where marriage was the means to secure fortunes and political alliances rather than the consecration of a bond of love between a man and woman. The lady sitting by him must be the Countess Eleanor of Pembroke, King Henry's youngest sister. Henry had spoken of her fondly. Simon looked on her with growing curiosity.

The queen noticed. With a laugh spurred by a prick of jealousy she called out, "Eleanor, you seem already to have tamed our Simon de Montfort. See how he keeps his gaze heavenward."

Simon looked abruptly to the queen.

Her pearly teeth showed in her smile, "Sire Montfort, I think you'll teach our precepts back to us before you've left our court."

Chapter Eight

COUNTESS ELEANOR
1236-1237

LIFE AT COURT WAS NOT the misery Simon had expected. Attendance at the Court of Love was an attraction. He sat at the rear of the hall, apart from the other courtiers, talking with the Countess Eleanor. At first they talked of the Court of Love. Eventually he asked her about herself.

"My lord William Marshall was over seventy, and I was just turned nine," Eleanor said brightly of her wedding. "I was terrified. My father had been killed – if not by my new husband's own hand, then by his agency. My mother had left for Poitou with my sister, who was to be married to Count Hugh of La Marche. As it happened, mother married Count Hugh herself and remained in Poitou. My brother was upon the throne, but in the thrall of the very lords who had undone our father. Except for my good governess, Cicley de Sanford, I was utterly alone, and much afraid at being sent as wife to a strange old man."

"Children ought not to be used so," Simon said darkly. He himself had been sent to strangers when he was a child, but her case seemed far worse.

"Truly, it turned out not badly after all, " the countess smiled, well-pleased with the warmth of his comment. "Of course, Lady Sanford would not have tolerated my mistreatment. And in Sir William I found a truly kind, gentle and considerate man. He doted upon me like a grandfather, and I was happier than I have been at any other time. Of course, I was too young for what are called marital rights. And before I came of age, Sir William died. I grieved for him. Who could be as sweet to me as he had been? Lady Sanford pictured to me the certainty of my being married again without regard to my wishes. She advised that my only recourse was to take holy vows. So I did. And there is the whole of my life."

The countess smiled with a charm that made her story seem a happy one. She did not add that her husband's sons had been jealous of her while the old man lived, and took their revenge when he died, refusing to return her dowry. Without the dowry, which was hers by right, she was penniless but for her brother's absentminded care. He had given her a small castle, an extraneous bit of the royal holdings, where she found that being poor was no great burden. But here among the splendid Court, her poverty led to fury every time she glimpsed the Pembroke clan. And her cheap russet robes shamed her. Like Simon, though for very different reasons, she too attended Court against her will.

Simon had not given thought before to the hapless condition of princesses, bartered in political negotiations, with no more control over their destinies than had a heifer in the marketplace. The only princess he had known was Johanna, and her betrothal to him had been at her own insistence.

"I think the choice you made was a good one," he said thoughtfully. "I would take holy orders, but my spiritual counselor insists my place is here."

"My brother commanded that I come to Court for the queen's sake, though it's little to my liking. So we both are here despite ourselves," the countess's brown eyes twinkled. "We must make the best of it."

And they did. In the days that followed, Simon came to every meeting of the Court of Love, and found the countess waiting for him. They occupied a bench that suited them well, at the rear of the hall. It not only afforded a degree of privacy, but at that distance, should his gaze turn toward the queen, she was no more to his eyes than a mere dab of pink and gold. And the irritating chatter at the dais faded in the close attention he paid to the Countess Eleanor.

In the countess, Simon found a friend, the first in all his life with whom he truly could speak freely. She was well read and had an analytic turn of mind. Their topics ranged from the Court, to theology and even to philosophy. Time and again she echoed his deepest feelings. And she had insights of her own that enriched his understanding. They talked for hours, locked in conversation long after the Court was dismissed.

Over the weeks, as these intense meetings went on, the Countess Eleanor's appearance, for him, underwent a change. Her nose no longer was too large. All other noses were too small. Her wide lips gave perfect form to the flow of her thoughts. Her grave, almond-shaped eyes were comforting. The queen dwindled from his dreams, though never fully vanished.

Simon felt at ease, truest to himself, when he was with the countess. Through her, he seemed in step with his own soul. He found himself counting the days, and then the hours, till the Court of Love was next convened. The countess, sitting by his side, was all the happiness he asked. Her absence was a dull and constant pain that left him restless, conscious of his loneliness. The more he was with her, the more her gentle, vibrant voice impressed itself upon his heart; the more her brown eyes soothed and were the only antidote against his isolation. He was in love.

This was not the physical obsession he felt for the queen, but a yearning all too like the passion that the Court of Love described: the severed soul's desire for its lost half. Months passed. Simon stayed at Court, though Henry twitted him, "Aren't your Leicester holdings being neglected?"

Simon and the countess were a fixture of the Court of Love – remarked and, with the tact of *courtesy,* left to themselves.

While the Court was at Westminster, whenever King Henry had no need of him Simon contrived to be with Eleanor.

She had a merlin. Though hawks no longer roosted in the hall, falconry was at the height of fashion. The countess's merlin, flown too young, was not well trained and would fly off to perch in a tree, instead of returning to her mistress's gloved hand. Simon made himself useful, casting lures to retrieve the bird and training her to return properly. Thus he managed to spend whole afternoons alone out on the fields of Hyde with Eleanor.

Seeing him so interested in hawks, she gave him the merlin. It was the first gift that passed between them. But it made a barrier, for she no longer had a reason to walk out alone with him.

Stricken, Simon let the hawk go free.

"You lost the merlin?" Eleanor asked, when they next met in the Court of Love. "But you had her trained so well to come to you."

In misery, Simon shook his head, "Not so, my lady. She loved heaven more than she loved me."

His words' double meaning pierced the countess's heart. She said nothing, but, her fingers trembling, she drew from around her waist the nun's knotted rope belt she wore, and placed it in his hand. It was the perfect token of the bond of *courtesy's* impossible, obstructed love, and of her love for him.

The next day Simon left the Court. He went to Leicestershire and threw himself into a tour of his outlying fiefs. The slightest thing amiss, the grudging gesture of a villein, would make him fly into a rage. It would have been far better for his tenants if he had a war to fight.

For he was fully tasting now the anguish that the Court of Love extolled: the lack that made one long for death: the lack of Eleanor: Eleanor of the holy vows: of the faith he held as firmly as she. Eleanor the unthinkable. Yet he could not stop thinking. Dreams of the queen had filled him with shame, but now desire for the countess burned in him both night and day. Yearnings for her stalked him through his waking hours; and his sleep was a single, endless dream of passion and torment in Hell.

Outspoken critics of the Court of Love, he and the countess were exemplars of its code: her giving, his accepting of her token was the symbol of *courtesy's* perfect, unconsummated love. But for them, the matter was no courtly gesture. It was truth itself. For there could be nothing but love unfulfilled. Love everlastingly yearned for, and denied. Simon saw the Court of Love did not exaggerate: it described passion rightly. Yet the Courtiers of Love could sate their passion. Nothing but their preference for yearning held them back. Not so for him. His lady was a nun.

Attending Court became an agony that made his previous annoyances paltry in comparison. He and the countess dared not speak. At supper in the royal hall, if her eyes chanced to meet his he felt as if his life poured from his veins. Yet if he skulked at home in Leicester, his idle time filled up with thoughts of her.

He volunteered for military service in the Welsh marches. Taking his squire Peter with him, Simon joined the English camp in Snowdonia, and fought battle after battle against the Welsh Prince Llewellyn.

Fighting with a rage and an abandon that seemed to welcome death, he became well known among the Welsh. His white shield with the red, fork-tailed lion rampant of Montfort struck terror among Llewellyn's followers.

Battle, with its all-consuming, desperate focus of attention, was relief for Simon. He dreaded only the long hours of inaction. Then he would sit reading in his tent, as Peter made their supper or sharpened his sword. Caesar's Gallic wars and the battles of Arthur were his constant study as he strove to keep his mind from Eleanor. With his commander, Henry d'Urberville, he discussed the tactics of the Welsh campaign. He gained d'Urberville's respect so far that he was made prime counselor for the war's strategy.

At Court, reports of Simon's combats glorified him with a hero's fame. The epithets of "tyrant" and "the king's foreign friend" were said no more.

King Henry chided his cousin William Longspee for grudging the favors he had lavished on his friend. "It is far better liege Sire Montfort pays the Crown than do our English-born subjects."

Queen Eleanor pouted daintily, "My lord, you do mistake him. It's not the Crown to which Sire Montfort pays this liege. His liege is paid to Love."

The queen spoke truly. In the dank, dreary mountain camp, far from the Court, far from any reminder of the lady – except the knotted belt he could not bring himself to cast away – Simon's thoughts still clung to his obsession. The very disdain that he always had felt for such flaws of character, such weakness of mind in others, left him without defense, without the means to master his own feelings.

At night, in full awareness of his foolishness, he would gaze at the moon and take a doleful comfort in the thought that it was shining upon her as well. By day, everything he saw became transformed with the thought of her. The leafless autumn trees, the broken rock and steep inclines of the Welsh mountains strained to become the tender, grassy field where she stood watching as he hailed her hawk out of the sky. The cot in his tent became too easily the bench where they so often sat. D'Urberville's intelligent eye disturbingly converted to her understanding gaze. Even the gross, shambling walk of a squire, by contrast reminded him of her grace.

If the world had seemed brighter, in sharper focus when she had been near, now a gray and suffocating mist engulfed all things in an eternity of moments that passed one by one in a slow march that staggered Time. In Simon's breast there was a constant, palpable pain, as if a cord truly stretched from his breast to the heart that he had given to her keeping. The sensation was all too like the pull upon the fallen soul that the Court of Love described.

A morbid fascination grew in him for the doctrines of the Court of Love. When a troubadour came to the camp, he questioned him as an authority on love's cures.

"There are just two cures," the troubadour said conclusively. "Marriage and death."

"Marriage?" Simon asked, perplexed.

"Whenever love's compelled, it will soon die."

Simon found this precept as absurd as Tristan's sword being the Cross. And the Court of Love was very wrong in claiming that desire set one's gaze toward Heaven. The simple faith he had enjoyed in virgin calm was now destroyed. He thought only of Eleanor. His consciousness of sin wracked him. Did he not constantly defile her holy vows in mind? Was that not as wrong as doing so in fact? Clearly this love was not heaven-bent, but was Hell itself.

He felt damned. He had never felt so far from God. So smashed into a million piercing splints of shame. Never again would he feel the superiority, the confidence in a purity that placed him on a higher plane than other men. His misery did not bring humility, but a self-abasement as extreme as his pride had been. Never again would he judge other men as lesser beings than himself. *He* was the vilest sinner, worthy of the lowest depths of Hell.

Absence had not brought relief, but an entangling skein of yearnings, shame and agony. Yet when, in late October, King Henry summoned Simon back to Court to make report on the Welsh war, he went with more unwillingness than ever he had felt before, mixed with a deep sense of foreboding.

Entering the hall of London Tower, where the Court was lodging, Simon found his brother Amaury was there on embassy from France. To his great relief, neither the queen nor the Countess Eleanor were present. After he had given his report, King Henry ordered him to remain in London for some days of consultation. Simon left the royal presence arm in arm with Amaury, to share his brother's room at an inn.

"Louis has heard splendid accounts of your triumphs in the west," Amaury told him cheerily. "But you're looking thin and pale. Have you been injured? Are you sick?"

"I'm well enough," Simon replied evasively.

"No. You should see a doctor."

"A doctor cannot help me."

"How can you know?" Amaury pressed. "Some rheumy humour has infected you perhaps..."

Simon cut him off. "My ills aren't of the body."

"What else can it be? Ah... surely it can't be that you're pining for a lady," Amaury smirked.

Simon turned away from him, nettled.

Amaury crowed, "My brother is in love at last! But seriously, hasten the wedding. This going about pale and suffering isn't healthy."

"There can be no wedding," Simon snapped.

"No wedding? But of course there can. Your prospects are as good as any lord in England, if you'd but achieve them. As for lineage, we're descended from William the Conqueror – almost as nearly as the king himself. How dare anybody look down on Montfort?"

Simon cringed at his brother's pompous claims. "It's none of that."

"Well, what then? What else can it be?" Amaury demanded.

Hard pressed, Simon muttered, "She's King Henry's sister..."

Amaury was overjoyed. "Here I'd thought my little brother was a dunce! Seven years in England and the titles not yet won. This certainly will do it! Well done!" He cuffed Simon's shoulder, "Does she return your love?"

Simon drew the knotted belt from his robe's sleeve and showed it to his brother, "Amaury, she's a nun."

But the Marshall of France was an optimist, and not the least discouraged.

In the Tower of London, Countess Eleanor sat in her chamber, tearing a small note into pieces and burning the pieces in a candle-flame. She let the wax seal melt until its image of the fork-tailed lion rampant of Montfort dissolved into a little pool of red among the letter's ashes.

Lady Mary watched her mistress worriedly.

The countess moved as if remote from herself, remote from everything, her thoughts too crowded and confused to take on form. In early childhood she had learned to shelter in oblivion whenever life's demands were too complex. She could act as was required, yet suspend thought. Nonetheless, her heart pounded as she put her hooded cloak over her head and shoulders, and went out her chamber door. She did as the note asked.

Though it was early in November, the weather was still warm. She kept her hood up to avoid being recognized as she passed the Lanthorn Tower. Here, where the castle and the city rampart met, the wall was being torn down and rebuilt. She picked her way across the rubble and walked on beside the Thames.

A barge with a tent pavilion was moored to wooden pilings a few yards past the broken wall. A boy sat on a piling and played upon a pipe. He looked up when the hooded lady stopped in front of him. As she must be the one he had been paid to wait for, he took her hand and helped her onto the gently swaying deck.

The barge's tent was of red satin trimmed with heavy golden fringe, the sort of pleasure-chamber that a wealthy courtesan might own. Within, wide benches on each side were cushioned with deep satin pillows in blue, red and mauve, and more pillows were heaped upon the floor. Daylight, tinted red as it passed through the fabric walls, gave the atmosphere a lurid glow, which was perfumed with a heady scent of civet and attar of rose.

Eleanor sat stiffly on the bench, isolated from the place, from her own thoughts, from everything. The lubricious impropriety of the barge was but a pinprick of embarrassment compared to the distress that would consume her if she let herself think any thought of what the next hour might hold. Not docile by nature, she was rather determined and strong willed. But, as a child who could be sent to wed her father's killer, she early learned to combat stress with mental abdication. She sat staring at the curtains opposite. They swung apart slightly, then closed with the rocking of the barge. At each parting, a sliver of the distant shore of Lambeth showed in brilliant white daylight. She imagined herself on that far shore.

There were footsteps on the deck. Eleanor glanced up as if startled from a dream.

The curtains at the bow of the barge parted. Simon appeared. He looked pale, haggard and tense, then shocked. He had supposed the summons he received was some cruel ruse, a practical jest spawned by a courtier's ill will. He had not meant to come. But, being idle, the chance of finding a culprit upon whom he could vent his rage lured him. He had fully expected to find no barge at all at the quay, but a gaggle of laughing barons. When the barge was actually there, he assumed his mockers lurked inside. He had thrust the curtain back, ready to throttle the laughter out of someone's throat.

But *she*, and no one else, was there. And the sensuous atmosphere was overwhelming. Could she actually have summoned him here? Deathly pale, he stumbled to the bench opposite her.

Hands icy, they both sat staring away from each other.

Eleanor said nothing.

Scraps of thought flickered across Simon's mind, gone too soon to frame in words. Then one thought rose from the welter: the troubadour's advice – and the words he had rehearsed a thousand times since then, but never believed that he would say.

His heart was pounding, he could barely breathe. Haltingly he began, "I've been wanting to speak with you. I didn't know I'd have a chance... to see you... so privately." He stopped. He felt faint and sick.

Eleanor was watching him.

He stared fixedly at the barge's red silk wall. His heart clutching, he blurted, "Would you marry me?" The words sprang from his mouth like an animal at bay springs for its life. He turned and looked at her, his eyes wide with the hopelessness of what he asked.

Their eyes met, full of despair at the hurt they worked upon each other.

"I cannot... you know," Eleanor whispered. She knew *courtesy* too well not to understand what Simon's response might be. She knew her words could cost his life, as he knew his words asked the price of her immortal soul.

They both knew she spoke wisely, as they both could only wish, when she said no. Yet, the hopeless words spoken, they could not look away. And both their wills were cancelled in that gaze.

Vision ended with the touching of their lips. Then his arms were around her, and they were lying amid the heaped silk cushions of the barge. They kissed, embraced, and her russet skirts were gathered up into their hands. Tears streamed from their eyes, tears of frustration, fear, and the immense joy of their love.

Chapter Nine

FLIGHT
1237

THE NEXT DAY SIMON BEGGED leave of King Henry to return to Wales at once. He intended never to come back. He was sick with rage at himself. If he had been in a misery of yearning and shame before, his misery now was multiplied by guilt.

As squire Peter packed his master's linens, robes and chain mail into leather sacks, Amaury questioned Simon.

"Did you have a chance to speak with the lady?"

Simon could not read his brother. He assumed that people were as direct of purpose as himself. His brother was a puzzle he had long since ceased to try to solve. There was a blind spot in Simon: he would never understand duplicity. Avoiding his brother's gaze, he stiffly nodded.

"So now you're going away?"

"Amaury, I can't stay here! I must not!" He broke to crying uncontrollably.

Amaury studied his wretched brother, and understood completely. "You're a dunce, Simon! It's no good doing anything for you. You're sure to undo it!"

Simon left for Wales, but not by a direct route. As they rode toward the southwest, his squire was puzzled, worried, "Master, I don't recall this road to Wales," Peter ventured cautiously.

"We go to Cornwall," Simon replied in a tone that brooked no further comment.

Simon had heard of a tournament in Cornwall; he was going there. He mentioned this detour to no one. Country tournaments at that time were such mayhem that they were banned by the Crown. Nevertheless, the meets were held clandestinely. News of them passed by word-of-mouth, and victims of *courtesy*, like Simon, found them especially appealing.

At a tourney, if a man survived he could win the booty of several knights in a single afternoon. If he died, he achieved *courtesy's* true aim: surcease of pain. The meets were so near kin to suicide that anyone who took part in them risked excommunication. For young men of light mind, this hardly mattered. For Simon, damnation seemed already earned. His soul was in such agony that the torments waiting him in Hell seemed but a welcome variation from what he suffered now.

He took a plain white shield and surcoat. To bear the rampant red lion of Montfort, the arms of a known royal favorite, to an illegal country joust would be an outright insult to King Henry. In the turmoil of Simon's mind, such delicacy of good manners could still hold sway.

The event was held in a shallow, basin-shaped valley beneath a hill that bore a rustic castle on its hunch. The ancient tower was of rough, tar-blackened wood, typical of the old strongholds of Cornish earls. But it stood alone and bleak. It was the field that drew the throngs of visitors. Bright tents covered the valley's gentle slopes in a dazzling array of reds, blues, whites and yellows, with stripes, chevrons and powdered blazonings. The breeze crackled with pennants above a seething swarm of men on foot and horseback, and horses being led, harnessed and draped in vivid mantlings.

At the center of this whorl of activity, like the sinkhole of a whirlpool, was the jousting ground: a broad, flat oval of green lawn bordered by a sturdy wattle fence. At each end of the oval there were entry gates. Midway along each side of the fence stood a tall, awninged pavilion: one for the judges, the other for the lady spectators.

Simon left his squire to set up his tent as he went to register with the judges.

"Your name?" the judge muttered over his wax tablet without looking up.

"I've come in white so that I'll not be known," Simon said curtly.

The judge marked his tablet with an X. "You'll be of the red team." He handed Simon a red linen tabard. "You'll be paid five marks. If your team wins, you'll have your share in the booty. A boundary is disputed..."

Simon cut him off. "I care not for the cause, or for the booty."

The judge looked up. "When the horn sounds, join your team at the west gate." He was a minor local lord and he pitied the unhappy youth, glad that he himself had reached the fair pastures of middle age unscathed by such foolishness.

Simon had arrived late. There was just time for him to reach his tent, arm and mount. As Peter, in grim disapproving silence, laced his master's padded pourpoint shirt and helped him pull his chain mail hauberk over his head, the horn sounded, summoning the combatants to the gates. Simon quickly took his helm and red tabard, and mounted his horse.

In this first and principal event, twenty horsemen on each side would come against each other at one time. For sheer disorder, this was the deadliest of combats. To be unhorsed meant certain death from trampling on the crowded field. And with booty as their chief reward, the members of the winning team might turn upon each other to reduce the sharers in the spoils. Unlike the jousting games that Simon knew in France, or real battle, where ransom was won by sparing one's opponent's life – deadlier than war itself, these English country jousts attracted none but fools and suicides.

The helmeted knights passed through the gates, reining in their mounts to a restrained walk. The horses rolled their eyes and swiveled their ears nervously at the excited noises of the crowd. Each knight wore over his hauberk the red or blue tabard of his team. As they passed through the gates, pages handed each combatant a long, sharp-pointed ash wood lance tipped with ribbons in the team's red or blue. The knights formed two lines, the red team at one end of the field, the blue at the other. Onlookers along the fence and in the ladies' pavilion pointed out and cheered their local favorites, anonymous in their steel helms but known by the blazons on their shields.

The knights took their places in the lines. Their lances, held upright, formed a tall rank of spars, their red and blue ribbons fluttering as prettily as if at a joyful festival. The combatants were a varied lot. Simon squinted through his helm at the far line of riders. The distant, blurred forms of horse and man that he could see ranged from massive to thin and slight. He selected the most massive for his target.

The two lines of combatants faced each other with a distance of two hundred yards between them. Some of the horses pawed the ground and shifted their weight anxiously, their mantles flouncing at their heels. At the horn's blast, like vast wheels the heavy lances rotated to couch at horizontal. The riders started toward each other, moving from walk to trot to gallop, and the full volant. The on-coming ranks of riders frayed and broke as horses lagged behind or sped ahead.

Simon's powerful horse stretched out to the volant, his feet thrusting the earth away until it streamed in a green rush beneath him. Simon crossed the midpoint of the field, dashing toward the strongest, foremost knight of the opposing team. Well-schooled in combat, ingrained lessons swept all other thoughts out of his mind. He forgot his pain, forgot even his lady, as he peered at the man careening toward him. His mind was free. Closing in, he saw his opponent's flaws and adjusted for his strike.

As the forty horsemen dashed toward each other, bristling with lances, Simon and his opposite clashed first. The point struck Simon's shield and slid off in the air, as Simon's point hit shield and skidded inward, driving through the blue tabard and chain hauberk beneath.

The man, impaled on Simon's lance, rose in his saddle, then pitched to the ground. Simon had to drop his lance or be unhorsed himself. The riders on both sides were closing, lance-points coming on at speed. Simon spurred his horse's flanks and dashed for the wattle fence. He turned at the safety of the fence in time to see the riderless horse he just had won, caught in the clash, knocked down and trampled in the mayhem.

In a moment the combatants still upon their mounts spread out. The joust was done. The slaughter in the field lay stark and red. Five of the horses and twelve of the forty men now lay upon on the grass, crushed and mangled in a bloody swath. One man, his body broken, reached out begging for the *coup de grace.*

Simon, moved to pity by the man's raised, trembling hand, rode over to him, dismounted, and with his sword did quickly what the man begged.

Since fighting in Wales, Simon had known what it was to kill a man, the unique resistance of armor, flesh and bone against his sword, the perverse instant when his hand, his blade and another man's life were one. But he had never killed before except in defense of his life. This stroke, given in cold blood, was very different. It had an odd effect: it brought him to himself. His pain came flooding back.

Taking off the red tabard of his team, he used it to wipe the man's blood from his sword. Then he dropped the gory rag, sheathed his sword, mounted and rode to the judges' pavilion.

As attendants cleared the field of its still-living and lifeless debris, Simon spoke with the judges, then rode to a gate where a page handed him a new lance. The crowd murmured with fresh interest as the unknown knight in white drew a nun's rope belt from his sleeve and tied it to his lance point. Simon made a circuit of the field at a trot, the rope belt dancing against his lance's shaft. A herald called his challenge to all comers for single combat.

"He means to die here," a burly Cornishman chuckled. "That's a fine horse – well worth doin' him the service." With a broad grin to his loutish friends, he put on his pot-helmet and spurred his horse to the end of the field, opposite where Simon now was waiting.

Simon removed the rope-belt from his lance and tied it around his upper arm. The horn sounded. The two combatants lowered their lances and their horses started toward each other, pounding across the flattened, blood-wet grass. Simon watched his opponent coming near. He let his own lance droop and canted his shield low, exposing his left side. The Cornishman, intent on the white shield, aimed his lance point low as well, forgetting his own shield entirely. Such blatant idiocy was too much for Simon. Though he might want to die, he would not die at the hands of a fool. He swung his lance up at the last instant, striking the man hard in the chest. The Cornishman fell to the ground, gasping and spouting blood.

Simon took the reins of the horse he had won and rode to the gate where Peter, pale and anxious, stood watching. As he handed the booty horse's reins to him, his squire begged, "Please, master, isn't this enough?"

Without answering, Simon turned, took a new lance from a page, and went to wait for his next challenger.

A knight in red with a white blazon on his shield was moving to the position opposite. At the horn's blast, Simon and the far knight couched their lances, and spurred their horses toward each other. As he approached at speed, Simon could see the red knight had a true and calculating eye. He came on with more skill than any other on that field so far. Simon could not insult this man by defending himself poorly; he adjusted his shield and aimed his lance point well.

The two riders met at full volant. Their lance points screamed against their shields and deflected outward, harmlessly into the air.

As Simon reached the far side, reining in his horse, he turned abruptly, peering back at his opponent. Surely his mind was deceiving him. He squinted, trying to wring vision from his eyes. But the blazon on the shield, now at the far end of the field, was merely red with a white tinge. A page was handing him a new lance. His opponent had re-armed and was waiting.

Simon took the new lance. At the signal he started back across the field, squinting at the nearing blazon as he galloped. The white shape finally cleared. Like a demonic cancellation of his own red lion arms that he had put aside, the arms that came at him were the exact reverse. Upon a blood red ground, instead of white, there stood, the same in every way but white as death instead of red, the rampant, fork-tailed lion of Montfort.

The ghost-pale lion vanished in a sudden, blinding blow.

Simon opened his eyes to an expanse of sky. The red knight emerged, towering against the blue.

Simon realized he was lying on the ground. A lance point hovered just above his chest. The red knight was no unearthly vision of portent. He was very real. And he was demanding his victim's name to claim his ransom.

Simon raised himself on an elbow and removed his helm, which the red knight permitted. "I came in white so that my name would not be known. I'll tell you, but only on your word that you'll tell no one else."

"On my honor, I'll keep your secret safe," the red knight replied graciously.

"My name is Simon de Montfort."

The red knight, who should have raised his lance at being answered, instead thrust Simon flat against the ground. "I've given you my word!" he said menacingly. "Mock me and I'll kill you where you lie!"

"I tell the truth!" Simon bellowed from the ground, confounded at this sudden and uncivil turn matters were taking.

The red knight seemed puzzled for a moment. Then he asked, "If your name truly is Montfort, where is your family seat?"

"At Montfort l'Amaury, in Normandy," Simon threw back.

The knight raised his lance, then turned and galloped away.

Simon sat up and watched as the knight rode to the judges' pavilion. In a few moments a page came leading Simon's horse. "Sire," the boy said, "the victor wishes you to accept the return of your mount. He asks to speak with you."

"Tell him I won't accept my horse. He's won it fairly, and I've no wish to be in his debt. But I will speak with him."

The page, with the destrier still in lead, hurried back to the red knight at the pavilion, as squire Peter helped his master to his feet. With Simon clutching his bruised ribs, the two made slow and limping way to the pavilion.

The red knight stood waiting with his helmet off. He was in his early twenties with caramel-blond hair and tense, alert brown eyes. On foot he was powerful, barrel-chested, but below average in height. There was a timidity in his stance that had not been apparent on horseback. Almost shyly he bowed, "My lord Montfort of Montfort l'Amaury, I am Peter de Montfort of Gloucestershire."

Simon stared at him a moment, then burst into a laugh that made him clutch his hurting ribs. At once the reversed arms made sense: the lion of Montfort differenced for a cadet branch of the family.

"We must be cousins!" Simon laughed.

"My lord, I pray I haven't hurt you," Peter de Montfort looked alarmed as Simon winced with pain.

"You did well. Where did you learn such jousting?"

"I taught myself," the Gloucestershire knight said modestly.

Simon studied this Parsifal-like prodigy and, chastened, changed the subject. "We must come to terms about my horse and ransom."

"My lord, I beg you don't speak of it. I cannot take your horse, nor anything from you." Peter de Montfort was under the impression that Simon was the Count Montfort of Montfort l'Amaury, head of the far-flung Montfort clan.

"You leave me deeply in your debt," Simon protested. "What can I do for you?"

"It is enough, my lord, that you're not seriously hurt."

"What will you do now?" Simon pressed. "Where do you go from here?"

Peter shrugged. "Nowhere in particular until the joust at Dunstable."

"Then come with me to Wales. It may seem far from Court, but a battle well-fought in Snowdonia can earn you more in honor than all the country jousts in England ever will."

Peter's face brightened. "I'd like that. Yes, I'll come."

Chapter Ten

ODIHAM
1237

SIMON WAS TOO BRUISED TO travel quickly. It was the second week of December when he, his squire Peter and his cousin Peter reached the English army encamped in Snowdonia.

A priest came to the new arrivals' tent. "Make confession, my sons," he urged. "No wise man goes to battle unconfessed."

Cousin Peter went at once. When he returned, he gave Simon so grave a look as to suggest he thought his unshrived, new-found relative might be a pagan.

Shamed, Simon limped to the priest's wooden shed that served as the army's chapel. The certainty that he was damned, and justly so, had kept him from confession. On his knees before the gentle father, the thin membrane of his self-control tore open, and all the tortures of his soul came tumbling forth. He told not only of the joust, but of his months of lustful obsession, fulfilled in his carnal knowledge of a nun. Crumpling, he wept at the priest's feet.

The kindly priest's capacity for mercy was not overwhelmed, not even by such an extraordinary confession. Knowing that a soldier's life may be too short for lengthy penances, he comforted Simon with words of Christ's forgiveness even for crimes worse than his, and gave him a penitence of fasting, prayer, and a self-inflicted lashing to chastise his body for its having seized dominion of his soul.

Tears drenching his face, Simon kissed the good priest's hands and no longer felt so utterly lost. Tucking into his robe's sleeve the little whip the priest gave him, he returned to his tent, stopping on the way at the carpenter's shed for a handful of nails.

At his tent, Simon found his cousin Peter had gone off for the day with the army. To ensure his privacy, he sent his squire Peter on a quest for healing herbs, a task he knew would keep him away for at least a couple of hours.

Alone, he knotted the whip's end and set a nail into the knot. A feeling of elation came over him. Hopeless, helpless, a victim of a passion that had shackled him for months, he felt he was at last truly in possession of a cure. No fatuous suggestions of a troubadour, but pain itself would curb desire, train it like an unruly beast until it knew its master. He could ignore pain when need be in battle, but he took no perverse pleasure in it. Yet freedom from the suffocating shame and guilt, and the constant yearnings of desire, was a prize immeasurable compared to the penance. He would make his passions subject to his will once more.

Simon stripped naked, and lashed his back and chest, striking with the full force of his rage urged on by his body's betrayal of him. With each stroke the whip's nail tore flesh away. Simon lashed the harder. Pain was victory over the enemy that had stolen his mind, his heart, his very soul from him.

Peter the squire returned to find his master lying on the tent's bare ground, unconscious, naked, soaked with blood, with long, deep gauges racked through his torn skin.

Peter fought back an impulse to cry out. Pressing his lips tightly together to keep silent and hold in his grief, he dragged his master's body onto his camp cot. And he set about the business of washing away the blood. Grinding the fresh, healing herbs with fat to make an unguent, he salved Simon's flayed back and chest, as his master no doubt had intended in sending him to find the herbs today. Peter loved his master tenderly, with the love that a generous servant has for a good man he serves. He gently packed the deepest cuts with boiled lint, then bound Simon's body with clean bandages.

If the penance was severe, so had been the sins. But, as the priest reminded Simon, no sin was too great for the Lord's forgiveness. His body healing, Simon felt the burden of his guilt passing as well. He even felt at one with his faith, though never again would he be proud and certain of his virtue.

D'Urberville never questioned Simon's injuries: a man's dealings with his own soul were a private matter requiring respect. The commander simply listed Simon with the army's injured. To Simon's cousin Peter, who was stricken with dismay, the faithful squire explained what little he felt he could say discreetly of his master's recent somber and distracted moods. Cousin Peter nodded gravely. He knew that if Simon had not had some weight upon his soul, he would not have been at the joust.

While Simon lay in his tent, his wounds healing, his cousin was battling the Welsh with such distinction he acquired the ekename Iron-Arm, and high praise from their commander Henry d'Urberville. Evenings, Peter would sit by Simon, regaling him with merry accounts of the day's rout, however dull or horrid the action really had been. Their friendship became close, with the mutual trust of men who have a warm feeling for each other, without explanations needing to be spoken.

One day in the latter half of December, when the army was out in search of the Welsh and no one was left in the camp but squires, the priest and the wounded, an old woman arrived, mounted on a mule and attended by a single, foot-sore servant. She found her way to Simon's red and white striped tent.

Simon woke from a sound sleep to find Lady Mary standing by his cot, regarding him sternly. He thought at first he must be dreaming, but when she sat upon his cot her weight convinced him that she was no dream.

"Did Eleanor send you?" he asked, sitting up and drawing his blanket around his bandaged chest.

"She did not. I come of my own," Mary replied.

"It's a hard trip..." He had no idea of what to say to her.

She studied him, her little eyes screwed up in her plump face. "Are you wounded?"

"I'm recovering..." He glanced away, embarrassed under the crone's steady gaze.

"Good. You must leave here at once," she commanded.

"Leave?"

"My mistress is with child."

Simon looked at her as if not comprehending. Then, as her words sank to his understanding, he cried, "Oh, my God. What have I done!" His lashings had not dimmed his love, nor had they averted its result. He covered his face with his hands.

The old woman shook him by the shoulder. "You must marry her!"

"How can I! Her vows...!"

"Indeed, 'Her vows!' What of her vows now!" Mary grasped his wrists and pulled his hands down from his face. "She must marry you! When this child's born, it could succeed to the throne! There are those who might use it, use her, so long as Henry has no heir. Do you understand me? She must marry!"

Simon met Mary's implacable glare. He did understand. Henry had enemies, and an unguarded royal bastard might well serve their purposes. "Is it known at Court?"

"Not yet. She's gone to her manor at Odiham. Go to her there at once!"

Simon needed no more urging. He pulled a woolen robe over his bandages. Then, flinging a cloak over his shoulders, he took a leather sack that held some coins and clothes, saddled his horse and rode out of the camp, leaving Lady Mary to follow later with his squire.

By traveling fast despite his pain, Simon reached Odiham on Christmas Eve.

The manor of Odiham possessed a massive castle tower, a crown-like octagon of beige stone seated on a grassy knoll. A channel made an island of the knoll on three sides. A natural stream closed the fourth side, crossed by a drawbridge mounted on a gatehouse by the water's edge. With the bridge raised, as it was now, the place was as secure as any fugitive could wish. Henry had allotted the royal holding to his sister for a home when her husband died, and her step-nephew, the unpleasant Gilbert of Pembroke, turned her out without her dowry or a roof over her head.

An old man leaned from an upper window of the gatehouse. He was fishing; a long line dangled from his window to the stream. Simon hailed him, gave his name and asked to have the bridge lowered.

The old man leaned his pole against the sill and disappeared, then reappeared, hobbling up the slope to the castle.

Simon let his horse graze on the frosty grass. His thoughts, turning over and over in his mind during his journey, had taken form and were bursting to be said.

Finally the shambling old man returned. He called out across the stream, "My lady will see you." Then he limped into his gatehouse. In a few moments, which seemed an eternity to Simon, the drawbridge swung down.

Burning with impatience, Simon galloped across the bridge and up the slope.

Countess Eleanor was sitting in the wide, circular hall of the tower. Fire blazed in a huge hearth. A few sprigs of holly were propped in a jug in half-hearted salute to the Christmas season. Cold sunlight, beaming from a high window, washed Eleanor's white veil with a stream of light against the dark brown of her robe. Two maids sat sewing beside her. As Simon came in the two women arose to leave, but their mistress gestured for them to stay and they sat down again, looking ill at ease.

Simon bowed, but the words he had rehearsed so many times came haltingly under the cold stare of three pairs of eyes. "Lady Mary... told me..."

Eleanor interrupted him. Her voice was flat. "I did *not* wish you to come here. Mary went to you against my expressed command. Mine was the fault. Mine are the consequences."

"Not so, my lady," Simon said softly. "As you cannot deny my share in the fault, you must grant me leave to do my best in the mending."

"My vows..."

"Your vows are gone! They *were* gone! *That* you know as well as I. At least accept the sacrament that mends chastity's loss!" He knelt to her, "I cannot argue my merits as a husband. I've neither titles nor wealth befitting the daughter of a king. But I plead our marriage for our souls. And for yours and the child's safety! Eleanor, you must marry me."

The countess's stern gaze softened. She still loved him, and her heart was reached by the glimmer of hope that his words evoked.

It was an absurd hope, but it glistened like a mirage over the emptiness to which she had withdrawn when every thought of the future was too frightening to think through to its conclusion. She said low, "If only my vows could be annulled…"

Seeing she still loved him, Simon pressed, "We'll go to Canterbury. We'll beg the archbishop to lift your vows. Surely, under the circumstances, he will do it! We will leave at once!"

Chapter Eleven

A SECRET MARRIAGE
1238

AT CANTERBURY, ELEANOR AND SIMON learned that the archbishop was in London. They went on. But at London they thought it best to go first to the king. They told Henry everything, and begged his mercy and his help.

Henry looked kindly on his sister and his friend. "The two people I love best, after my wife. Can I be angry that you love each other? Let's celebrate the wedding, and be happy in what Heaven's brought."

"But my vows..." Eleanor urged.

"The archbishop will take care of it. He'll have to," Henry waved away her fears.

Despite Eleanor's uncertainty, her brother made arrangements for the wedding. The next day, which was Twelfth Night, January sixth, 1238, in the chapel of the king's private chambers, Eleanor and Simon were secretly wed. The royal chaplain of Saint Stephen's Church, Westminster, officiated, and the king and queen were the only witnesses. There was no pomp, no ringing of bells. The bride wore the somber robe of a nun and the vows were spoken in hushed tones. Both bride and groom were ill at ease with the proceedings. But the king willed it.

When the sacrament was done, the queen smiled teasingly to Simon. "Admit now, Sire Montfort, is not *courtesy* far stronger than the strongest vows?"

Abashed, Simon confessed, "My lady, you've won every point."

"Ah, no," she tossed her golden curls, "I've still a point to win!"

Henry promised the bride and groom that he would deal with Archbishop Rich. Assuring them that all was as good as done, he sent them back to Odiham to enjoy their new-wed state in privacy.

At Odiham, Eleanor and Simon spent days in languid bliss. Days of pleasure amid the heaped fur coverlets of the chatelaine of Odiham's great oak bed. Snow fell silently beyond the shuttered windows. Fire glowed in braziers set about the floor, but the second-story solar remained chilly. Simon and Eleanor nestled in their bed with suppers of spiced meats and wine.

Her long brown hair falling around her shoulders, framing her solemn face, Eleanor traced the scabs of Simon's scourging with the tip of her finger. "You love me so much as this?"

"Yes," Simon said softly, gazing in the darkness of her almond eyes. "No. I love you more. You see how swiftly my repentance is forgotten." He embraced her, kissing her lips, then covering her face with kisses.

Another time she pondered, "This child of ours, what name shall we give it?"

"Henry, if it's a boy," Simon said decisively. "But if it is a girl... my mother's name was Alice..."

Eleanor smiled, well pleased. "You'd name our first-born son after my brother. I thought perhaps you'd want him to have your father's name."

"We'll get to that. And Amaury, Guy, Richard, William, John..."

"Stop!" Eleanor burst out laughing and struck him with a pillow.

"I'm forgetting our daughters," Simon went on undaunted. "Eleanor of course, then Isabel, Amicia, Margaret..."

"Stop. Stop!" Eleanor thumped him soundly with the pillow. "I'll be having children till I'm sixty!"

"No! We'll have them all at once. I've heard tell of a knight who claimed he had five children at one birth from a Berber camel driver's daughter. He's inspired me."

"You lie!"

"Yes, I lie!" He turned upon her playfully.

"No, no! You tell untruths!" She fended him off with her hands and her cold bare feet. "No woman ever had five children at one time. It wasn't the camel driver's daughter, but the camel driver's bitch!"

Days passed. Lady Mary and the squire Peter arrived, joining Eleanor's servants in the mood of gaiety. Odiham was bright despite the chill, blue fog that rose up from the stream, and the soft snow cradling the castle's knoll in whiteness.

But those happy days were few. Henry blundered. He did not approach Archbishop Rich first privately, but had the marriage of his sister to Simon de Montfort announced to the assembled Court. If he thought the tactic would compel Rich to rescind the countess's vows, he was quite wrong. Rich was furious. He flatly refused to grant the annulment.

A royal messenger carried the news to Odiham, bringing the lovers' carefree time to a quick end. Simon and Eleanor returned to Court, as the struggle between the king and the archbishop grew to an impasse.

A meeting of the barony was called in the crisis. But the lords of England had their own objections to the marriage.

The Earl of Norfolk, Roger Bigod, was the first to complain. Standing on a bench so all could see him, he called out, "We weren't asked when the king gave his sister Isabel to the emperor, with a monstrous, fat dowry! Then he came begging us for money! He promised to take our advice, if we gave him what he wanted. Has he done it? No!"

"The king does as he pleases for his foreign friends!" Gilbert of Pembroke cried. His own interest was deeply involved, as the dowry he withheld from his step-aunt Eleanor now could be construed as owed to her husband.

The room was in an uproar. Simon, standing by the king's chair with the Treasurer Peter de Riveaux, watched the protest, stunned. That the lords of England hated him was a truth he lived with every day, but he had not expected such rebellion.

In the midst of the shouting, Richard, the king's brother, came to the foot of the dais and bellowed at Henry, "If our sister was to marry again, it should have been to someone who brought benefit to the Crown! What army do we gain by this marriage? What peace do we assure? What land is brought under England's influence? None! There is no gain! As in everything you do, brother, England is the loser!"

Riveaux tried to quiet him. But, once started, Richard would not stop. "Thirty-thousand marks you've given to the Emperor with Isabel! And what gain have we there? Frederic returns her ladies, and asks us for a hundred knights to fight his own subjects in Italy! Do you send back the hundred ladies as a fitting answer? No! You summon the knights! Frederic will rebuild the Roman Empire, as he's sworn. And he'll conquer England by driving us to bankruptcy! Brother, then you'll see. You'll be no more than Lord of Ireland! Your own marriage..."

Henry finally cut him off. "I think, brother, you've wandered from your point."

"I am *on* the point of your ever seeking England's loss!" Richard's fury was unstoppable. "As for our sister's marriage to this foreigner you dote upon, there's hardly a knight in the world who wouldn't have been preferable! A man with no titles. A mere fourth son, with nothing to his name but what you've given him!"

Fury gripped Simon. Too angry to speak, he came down the dais steps and grabbed Richard, hurling him onto the floor. The burly prince fought back. But Simon was upon him, beating him bloody in the face until four bailiffs pulled him off. As the bailiffs pinned Simon's arms behind him and dragged him back up the dais steps, he shouted at the prince, "That's a lie! A damnable lie!"

"Be quiet! Don't make matters worse!" Henry snapped sharply at Simon, though the sight of his contentious brother's blood-smeared face gave him a twinge of pleasure.

Getting to his feet with the help of the earls Bigod and Humphrey de Bohun, Richard wiped his face. "You keep a vicious dog," he snarled at his brother.

"No more vicious than your tongue," Henry retorted.

Coolly the king addressed the Court, "It's an ill day when the king's brother-in-law calls the king's brother a liar, and the king's brother has given him such ample provocation." Turning back to Richard, who was tenderly touching his cut face, he asked curtly, "But what of your own marriage, Richard? Have you not married according to your choice? And without the lords' consent? What right have you to rail against our sister, when she's only done the same?"

Henry hit his mark. Richard was reduced to grumbling, "It's not the same. My wife's the daughter of an earl."

"Indeed. You make a valid point," King Henry smiled. "Our sister ought not to marry a man with no titles. A mere fourth son, as you so feelingly put it. It is too long that we've withheld the titles for which Sire Montfort has so patiently petitioned us."

Several lords started to object, but Henry raised his hand to quiet them. "Let us not concern ourselves with issues of lapsed Norman claims. On the merits of his services to us in Wales, Sire Montfort has shown himself full worthy of our sister's hand, and has earned the titles that we grant. We hereby declare we shall invest the lord Simon de Montfort with the titles Earl of Leicester and Steward of England."

Turning back, Henry saw Simon's amazed gaze, and he burst to laughter. The king was in a highly amiable mood, no doubt fed by the amusing sight of Richard's bloody face. With a wave of his hand he added, "As our sister and new brother need a fitting home, we grant them as a wedding present our royal castle of Kenilworth."

Simon, overcome, knelt and kissed Henry's hand. No date was set for the formal investiture, but the king's word was given before the assembled Court and lords of England. At once Simon had gained all that he ever hoped. And more.

Chapter Twelve

ROME
1238

BUT THE MOST PRESSING PROBLEM was not yet resolved: the lifting of Eleanor's holy vows. Without that, the marriage was invalid.

Archbishop Rich was obstinate. To him, a vow before God was a vow eternal and unchangeable. Despite the marriage, despite the appeasement of the barons, and of Richard – to whom Simon gave a horse and publicly apologized – despite even the announcement of the countess's pregnancy, Edmund Rich refused the annulment. Private meetings with the archbishop brought only bitter arguments. By March, Henry admitted failure. Edmund Rich would not relent.

The king called Simon to his chamber. "The papal legate is relieving the vows of knights who've pledged themselves to the crusade, but changed their minds." He looked meaningly at Simon. "They need only pay a price."

Simon frowned. The notion Henry seemed to be suggesting was so unthinkable that he could only suppose he didn't understand him.

Henry explained in a tone that would have made his meaning clear even to an imbecile. "The legate says the Pope is not in need of more crusaders now, whereas the Church *is* needing funds. You have to grant these Italians, there's reason in their arguments. Just possibly the Church might find that it could spare a nun? For some more useful recompense in gold?"

Simon was appalled. The purchasing of holy things was the abominated sin of simony. He turned away, not knowing what to say to so outrageous a suggestion from his king.

Henry shouted at him, "Don't turn away from me! This may be our only hope! It's not as though you'd got some country wench with child. This nun's bastard about to be born is nothing short of a catastrophe!"

King Henry was Simon's master. To oppose his will, or worse, to shame him with the reproach that his demand deserved, would counter the submission that had been pressed into Simon's mind throughout his years with Louis. He controlled himself, and said with all the tactful evasion he could muster, "I don't have that sort of wealth in any case."

"I'm sure you could find it! Are there not moneylenders to grant credit to the king's own brother-in-law?"

Recalling his disastrous venture with the Jews of Leicester, Simon blanched. "I cannot do this. And even if I had the wealth of Croesus, to offer money in exchange for a nun's vow..."

"Don't be a scrupling fool! Are you more virtuous than the Pope himself?" Henry grasped Simon's shoulders. "If Rich is bent upon humiliating me, we must go above him. This bastard is your doing, Simon. You must set this right!"

"By Heaven, Henry! Don't you think I would do anything I could to secure my marriage to Eleanor?"

"Then find the money, and go to Rome! I'll pay your travel costs."

To offer money for a nun... For Simon, all that he had gained, or hoped to have, hinged upon his doing as his king commanded. In counterweight was his deepest, most emphatic sense of what was right. His counselor, Grosseteste, had refused him escape into the haven of monastic life, insisting that his place was at the Court. And now there seemed no choice. He submitted to his king.

Simon had felt sunk in guilt before. But now he felt lost in confusion, as though he had stepped off the foundations of what he believed, and swam in a flood in which all values lost their meaning. Perhaps his soul was Heaven's price for what he had cost Eleanor? The thought that he had escaped with no more than an act of penance now appeared absurd. He felt damned. All things in his life seemed to witness he was beyond holy grace. Perhaps this was divine justice.

There were no money-lending Jews in Leicester any longer, but the Knights Hospitallers had opened a house to serve the prospering town. Simon applied to the Hospitallers.

"What assurance can you give that you'll be able to repay so large a sum as what you ask?" the Master of the Hospitallers asked politely.

"The demesnes and fees of the Leicester Honour bring me four-hundred and fifty marks a year. This years' sale of livestock will yield another two hundred. The escheats granted to me by the king bring two hundred more."

The Master looked grievously unimpressed.

"And I am King Henry's brother-in-law," Simon added, invoking Henry's argument, though he doubted it would weigh. But mention of the king's name had magical effect. The Hospitaller gladly granted him the loan.

With the draft upon the Hospitallers' banking house in Rome in hand, Simon parted from Eleanor. They were standing in the sun-filled courtyard of London Tower. The queen's and the countess's veils and skirts ruffled in a surge of March wind, and the queen shaded her eyes against the brilliant daylight.

"I'll wait for you at Kenilworth," the countess said, as she kissed Simon farewell. "I shall be there, praying. God be with you! "

"May He be with us both," Simon said low, though he had no doubt the Lord would not be with him. He knew the action he was taking was damnable, but there was no recourse now.

When Simon and the countess finished their leave-taking, Henry added, on a practical note, "We won't announce the birth until November. We've troubles enough without a child coming too soon." August was the true term of the countess's pregnancy.

As squire Peter held his master's stirrup, and Simon mounted his horse, Eleanor put her hand upon her husband's arm. "You will be back on time?" Her tone begged to have him nearby when their child was born, but also that the length of time her fate would be unknown, would itself at least have a known end.

He pressed her hand. "I will be back by August. I give you my promise."

It was early May when Simon reached Rome. He had lived in cities all his life, walking freely through the stews of the Rive Gauche or London's fairest districts and worst shambles. But Rome came as a shock.

At times during his journey, when he could separate his travel from his task, he had been happy for this chance to see the greatest of all cities. What had he expected of the seat of western Christendom? A City of God? A shining goal of pilgrimage? A new Jerusalem? There were the expected multitudes of nuns, monks, priests and bewildered pilgrims. But these were a thin swirl, like oil over the dark and turbid waters of the native populace. Pickpockets were everywhere, nimbly at work among the pressing crowds. Loiterers leaned against the sun-blazed buildings, studying the passing throng with narrow eyes, their manner advertising that for a modest fee they'd gladly plunge a blade in someone's throat.

Simon supposed his heart would rise in joy at seeing the Lord's chosen seat. Instead he found himself uneasy, wary, drawing inward as from an unclean thing.

Apart from its people, the ancient city itself amazed him. On every street were marble statues, mounted upon every public building and down every lane. Statues of the saints were dear to him. The ancient, solemn prophets at Chartres spoke to his soul. But here the statuary was like none he had ever seen before. Pagan deities, emperors and senators, fleshy as living men, displaying naked to the glaring sunlight what no man bared to anyone except his wife.

Simon had read Caesar. He knew well the Rome of antiquity, the mighty force that wrested empire out of a world of tribes. What he was ill prepared for was the living presence of that pagan world. Rome was an immense bloom of great age: nibbled by time and rot, but with its masculine member erect, and its sardonic, sensuous perfume all-pervading. The walled compound of the papal enclave was but a scab, an adhesion, alien in its healthfulness on this corrupt, flaunting body.

Simon passed the papal gates without entering. His plea before the Pope was to be heard the next day. His immediate task was to bring letters from King Henry to the emperor, and to the empress their sister from both Henry and Eleanor.

Frederic II, the Holy Roman Emperor, was at odds with Pope Gregory. He had seized papal lands, justifying his attack by cheerfully declaring that he only relieved His Holiness from the cares of worldly wealth. The Pope responded to his wit with excommunication. Frederic's insouciant reply was to put his crown upon his head and ask his courtiers if he seemed any different. In an age steeped in the spiritual legacy of Saint Francis, with a modesty and fear of God that reached even to kings, Frederic was an anomaly: a man untouched by faith.

His mother, Queen Blanche of Hainault, at the age of forty – and just after her husband's death – had claimed at last to be pregnant with an heir. Her claim was so implausible that she insisted upon giving birth in a public square with all the populace to witness. Blanche died giving birth, but with her dying hands she gave the orphaned new-born Frederic into the care of her Muslim physician.

Brought up by Muslim scholars to fill the role of a Christian king, the child grew to manhood with no faith at all, but a fine-tuned sense of expediency. That sense, in time, won him an empire. Without conscience, Frederic wielded absolute, unconstrained power. He was called, though not in praise, the *Stupor Mundi*: Wonder of the World.

The emperor was in Rome to negotiate with Pope Gregory. At the moment, his military attentions were focused on his rebel subjects in Milan. During his Roman sojourn he occupied an ancient, hilltop villa, and it was there Simon delivered the letters from King Henry and Eleanor.

To the street, the villa offered a long, windowless buff wall with patches of scaling crimson paint and a single, pedimented door.

Simon showed his letters and their royal seals to the chain mailed guards who clustered by the entrance. A password was given through a peephole, and the heavy door creaked open.

Within, the vestibule was dim, lit by elegant, ancient hanging oil lamps of bronze. It took Simon's sun-struck eyes some moments to adjust to the darkness, as the porter led him through a series of connecting rooms. The first object to emerge from the shadows was a statue, human in size but of a monstrous being, half man and half goat. The creature leered with a knowing, intimate gaze; its stare seemed to pierce all pretenses of virtue, to claim a kinship with shared depths of foulness beneath. The thing was no more than immobile stone, but its salute chilled Simon with a cringe of revulsion.

The porter, a proud, devoted servant, smiled, "The emperor's a great lover of art."

Underfoot in the first chamber there were intricate mosaics: tiny stones of white, beige and brown pieced to form pictures of maidens bearing flowers and fruit. The richness of such work, made to be walked upon, struck Simon: a floor of such extraordinary fineness, trod upon by wealthy men and their minions for a thousand years.

The walls of the next chamber were a dull black. But, as his eyes grew used to the soft lamp-glow, Simon saw here too were images. He squinted and moved closer to a delicately drawn mural that appeared to be a pattern of knots. Closer inspection brought the heat of a deep blush to his face. He moved away. The knots were composed of men, women and even beasts massed in an orgy of unspeakable couplings.

The porter grinned.

Now sunlight filtered from an inner court, and soon they walked beside the court itself, along a columned corridor open on one side to a garden. Peacocks strutted through parterres of roses and sweet herbs, trailing their gold-eyed tails through the scented greenery. The perfume of the air was intoxicating, penetrating. In each corner of the garden stood an orange tree, dotted with starry blooms and vivid orbs of fruit. Small white monkeys clambered through the foliage, ransacking the fruit. Chattering and shrieking, they hurled their orange missiles at the strolling, sedate birds.

In a room beyond the far end of the garden, the Emperor Frederic held his Court. Here the distracting murals were discreetly curtained behind rich damask draperies woven in a pattern of pomegranates worked in thread-of-gold: the image of abundance in the East. Abundance too was the theme of the floor; its chips of colored-marble formed naked, merry Bacchae. But most of the mosaic was concealed beneath the elegantly slippered feet of the emperor's petitioners. Porphyry columns rose to a gilded, deeply-coffered ceiling that cast back the hanging lamps' lights with a golden glow. The room was like a treasure cabinet, open only to the eyes of those few whose lives had brought them to admittance to this opulent sanctum.

The emperor was seated on a gilded, gem-encrusted throne; his very person was poised like a jewel within this setting that beggared the word *extravagance*. Intricate gold chains, hung with precious stones, glittered upon his robes of purple silk and ermine. A ruby, like an all-seeing eye, protruded from the froth of gems that was his crown. As base iron is drawn to a magnet, riches clustered about Frederic, gathering to a stupefying single point of awe.

But the man within the setting did not dazzle. Frederic was small, impish, with a fringe of graying reddish hair. His pale, wizened face hung over a frail chest. His boney arms ended in hands with fingertips that swelled in soft pads like a frog's.

Courtiers from every Christian kingdom mingled in the chamber with swarthy men dressed in the gaudy, rich robes of the East. All the world seemed drawn to pay court to this imp who gathered so much to his little self.

On the dais, beside the emperor's throne, stood a man Simon recognized. He was Michael Scott, an astrologer, a panderer, a mountebank or worse, a black magician whom King Henry had refused to hear. He seemed on equal footing with the emperor's black-robed secretary.

When the steward of the Court announced him, Simon drew the letters from his robe, placing them in the secretary's outstretched hand. The letters for the empress were noted and tucked up the secretary's full, black sleeve without comment. He then read King Henry's letter in a murmur into the emperor's ear.

A look of surprise crossed Frederic's bemused face. He chuckled to himself, "This Simon brings Rome a new simony. Soon the Pope will see his priests buying their way out of their benefices, just as they've bought their way into them. It serves us well to help him."

He looked down at Simon at the foot of the dais, and said aloud for all the Court to hear, "Lord Montfort, our brother of England asks our aid in your petition to the Pope. We're pleased to be of service. As you're wedded to our empress's sister, we look upon you as our own brother. You'll be our guest here while you are in Rome." He beamed an impish smile. The beautiful and young could always interest him, for he was a voyeur.

Simon suppressed an urge to make excuse and rush back to his lodging. He had entertained no expectations that Henry's letter would rouse help. But now that help was readily granted, he felt as if some crawling creature of the night had settled on his skin. Reason told him this was arch stupidity. The most powerful man in Christendom, after the Pope, was offering him aid and hospitality. With a deep bow, he accepted Frederic's offer.

The light from the courtyard garden had grown blue with evening, and the piercing screams of the white monkeys were long hushed, when the emperor's Court was finally dismissed. Apparently at Frederic's order, Scott appeared at Simon's side to guide him to where he would spend the night.

"When will I see the empress?" Simon asked, as they passed through a dim maze of corridors. "Her brother and sister look for word from her."

"The empress is sequestered," Scott replied. "She sees no one but her own household. Our emperor follows the practices of the East." He gave a simpering laugh. "I suppose you've heard rumors?"

"There are tales..."

"Of a harem... I assure you, they're not tales. Frederic is licentious, yes. But who amongst us can cast the first stone? And he is so much more. Brilliant! Scientific! He conducts experiments of the most wondrous kinds."

"Such as?" Simon asked coolly.

"For a time, he isolated infants from the moment of their birth, to learn what language they would speak, left to themselves. They had fine nurses, but no words were spoken that they ever heard."

"What language did they speak?"

"They all died. We have no notion why!"

The astrologer prattled on, ignoring Simon's look of shock.

"He's made Arabic numerals the counting method in his lands. It's so very practical! And poets, and musicians, he supports them all."

"How did you come to be so close to him?" Simon asked. The mountebank whom Henry had rejected seemed perfectly in keeping with his horrid master.

Scott's sweaty, flaccid face beamed with pride. "When I first proffered my services, the emperor was good enough to set me a task. He asked the precise – precise, mind you – distance from his throne-room's floor to the sun. I calculated the figure and presented it to him. Then, for several months, he kept me by him in his travels. When we returned to the same room I had measured, he asked me to do my figures once again. To my utter amazement, the distance from that floor to the sun had decreased by three inches! The emperor embraced me, took me into his household, and admitted he had raised the floor by three inches to test me."

"You bribed someone who told you."

"Of course. The distance to the sun is none of my concern. But my horoscopes are accurate. He relies on them for every move he makes. He's asked me to cast your chart. At what date and time, and where, were you born, Sire Montfort?"

"I don't believe in horoscopes," Simon said flatly, appalled to see how superstitious gullibility walked hand in hand with power and corruption.

"You'd best comply. In this small thing, and *all* the emperor asks. He's taken a lively interest in you. My lord Montfort, you stand upon the threshold of great favor and advantage."

"I ask only his commendation to the Pope."

"Why do you pretend to such severity? If you were half as pure as you would have me think, I doubt Fate would have brought you here. "

Arriving at their destination, Scott placed his hand on Simon's shoulder like an intimate advisor. "You know the dream of Herakles? When he reached manhood, the hero dreamed two women came to him. One, beautiful in gauzy robes that displayed all her charms. She was Pleasure and she promised everything he wished, wrung from others' labors with no effort of his own. The other, muffled up, modest, gaunt and stern of face, was Dame Virtue. Need I say more? Accept what Fate allots, my friend. You've come to Dame Pleasure's door."

The next morning Simon was brought to join the emperor at his breakfast in a garden on the villa's roof. All Rome was spread before them: its ancient, crumbling monuments to empire scattered upon the hills and clustering down to the Tiber's bank. The air bore a fetid smell, overpowering the scent of myriad roseheads nodding on the roof. The light was glaring and the heat singeing. Green leaves withered in its assault.

The emperor was seated on an ancient chair of such dainty workmanship that he appeared to float upon its slender crescent legs. A high table bore woven-gold baskets of fruit: oranges and strawberries, and fruits too early for the season: plums, cherries and peaches brought from Sicily and Africa. Cakes scented with orange water, and almond- cream pastries were heaped upon a salver of gold.

The emperor, stuffing his mouth with strawberries, the red juice oozing from the corners of his thin lips, gestured for Simon to sit by him. A servant brought a cushioned stool. "What do you know of Henry d'Urberville?" Frederic asked without greeting or preface.

"I served under him in the Welsh war. He's a fine commander," Simon answered, relieved to speak of familiar things. His state of confusion had become vertiginous. In the sensual reek of the emperor's villa, he felt that all his unacknowledged, vilest impulses had turned outward, joining sins far past his most shameful imaginings to make a world that mocked and welcomed him upon the brink of Hell. He knew now from experience that the emperor did indeed keep a harem. To speak of the war in Wales was to reach back to sanity.

"D'Urberville holds a most high opinion of you." The emperor picked a strawberry husk from between his teeth. "He's leading my campaign against the Milanese with the hundred English knights that Henry has been good enough to give me. You will join them."

"My lord, I beg pardon. I've made promises to return to England by August."

"Six weeks. Surely my assistance with the Pope is worth that?" Frederic's small eyes smiled, but with a coldness that would not allow a difference of opinion.

Simon bent under the emperor's gaze. "I shall be glad, my lord, to serve you in Milan."

"Good. Do try some of the almond creams."

Later that morning Simon presented himself at the Vatican. Passing through the tall doors, he found he was trembling, with perspiration breaking coldly on his brow. Sin, corruption, the taint of the emperor's bower, must be writ upon him clearly to the eyes of these clean monks and priests who moved about him everywhere. Yet no one seemed to notice him. He showed his papers, and was ushered to the papal Court to wait his turn.

The room was spare white stone, lit with a wash of sunlight from tall, slender windows. Lordly men and women, and many of very modest mien, stood in the chamber. But most of those present were clerics: abbots, priests, nuns and monks, their black and gray and brown robes a dull background to the scarlet of the cardinals of the Curia.

Distracted as he was, Simon had barely taken note of his surroundings when his name was called, his case was to be heard. He made his way to the front, where the papal throne of pale marble was set upon a dais of wide marble steps.

Pope Gregory IX, aged and slender, seemed as fragile as a feather resting on the crimson cushion of the towering stone chair. He was dressed in white from the cap that covered his tonsure to the tips of the shoes that showed beneath his robe. A crucifix hung on a chain about his neck; all else of him was plain and white except the papal ring.

Simon saw all this, and in the next moment saw Archbishop Rich standing in the fore near the dais steps. The archbishop had arrived in Rome before him.

A clerk was reading Simon's petition aloud to the Pope and Curia. When the reading was barely begun, Rich stepped forward and interrupted.

"Your Holiness, I myself repeatedly, against great pressure, have forbidden the lifting of this nun's vows!" His words rang crisp and clear against the soaring walls. His plump face was a mask of strained emotion. "It is in breach of all respect due to the Church in England that this man comes before you. He deserves excommunication for this impudence alone!"

Simon stood defenseless under Rich's assault. Sin had brought him to abandon his conscience, and hopeless resignation had brought him to Rome. Now the judgment he had earned would come.

Yet he heard his own voice speak, as if some part of him still struggled with his fate. He sank to his knees before the papal throne. "Your Holiness, have I not the same right as any Christian to seek Our Lord's most high recourse on earth?" It was as if his spirit, flown free of his guilt's constraint, were crying out. "Your Holiness, I pray you to believe that it is not in disrespect of the Church that I come here! Lost though I may be, I hold the Church as dear as does any man."

"Respect for the Church were better served if you both refrained from interrupting," Pope Gregory said gently.

The contenders were silenced for the moment, and the reading of Simon's petition continued. When it was done, the Pope turned to Archbishop Rich, "Tell us now your objections to the granting of this request."

"Your Holiness," Rich began, quaking with anger, "it is quite clear. A vow before God cannot be eradicated! The fifth chapter of Ecclesiastes speaks specifically to this." He reached for a Bible that his clerk handed to him, the passage marked with a slip of vellum. Opening the book, he read, "When thou vowest a vow unto God..."

Pope Gregory stopped him. "I assure you, Archbishop, we know the passage. Please go on with whatever else you have to say."

"Your Holiness, I will speak directly," Rich shut the book with a resounding clap. "This nun has fallen into shame. But, because she's prideful and the sister of a king, with her fellow sinner's wealth she hopes to wipe away her guilt. She is but adding simony to the mass of her wickedness! I beg you, have her confined to a convent of strict rule where her weak soul may find support. As for this man!" Rich bent his glare at Simon kneeling near him, "This man, who would doubly cuckold Christ Himself! First by seducing His avowed bride, then by offering payment for her like a common whore! Excommunication would be but a mild punishment!"

Dead silence followed his tirade. The assembled Curia and the crowd of petitioners were mute, shocked by his words. Simon hung as one suspended by a thread in a vast void. Hollow, empty as a shell, he stared but his eyes saw nothing, and no sound came to his lips.

Pope Gregory's slight frame hunched in the papal chair for several moments that seemed an eternity for all but him. He pressed his dry, pale forehead with his fingertips, then clasped his hands against his breast in prayer. At last he straightened.

"Archbishop Rich, I believe your words to be in error. Else Christ's glory could be stained by the actions of a man. Was it not such prideful, overweening defense of Our Lord that caused His angel Lucifer to fall?" Gregory's mild eyes penetrated Rich's hostile glare. "Archbishop, your words shake Hell itself. You are in error dangerous to your soul. I recommend you to fulfill your desire to defend the Church by reforming your own monks of Canterbury. Leave this matter to us. Please, go from our presence now. We will speak with you later."

The dumbfounded archbishop was directed to the door, as Pope Gregory turned to the Curia. "Let us be chastened by the lesson of our brother's overzealousness. And beg Our Lord's forgiveness for his words."

After some moments of silent prayer, Pope Gregory asked Simon gently, "Is there to be a child?"

His head bent, Simon nodded.

The Pope turned to the Curia, "We see how, through our archbishop's error, Satan works for the damnation of two souls: in the birth of a child in indissoluble sin, and in the excommunication of the man before us. Repentance is due, yes. But *not* the casting away of a man who has flown to us for our aid. No soul is lost to sin, if it repents and truly yearns for salvation."

The words were like a burst of light into Simon's darkness. By a miracle of kindness, he was being drawn back from the doors of Hell and embraced with mercy. Tears broke from his eyes in a torrent. Unable to speak in this so unexpected grace, he reached for the Pope's thin hand and covered the papal ring with kisses.

Gregory murmured over him, "Mercy, my son, is the way of Our Lord."

When at last Simon could wipe his face, he stood and bowed deeply.

The Pope spoke quietly. "Sire Montfort, a vow to serve Christ is a solemn thing. Yet we have granted relief in the past, as your letters from the emperor and King Henry remind us. Our sister is not lost to the Church. Neither shall we turn you or the child from Christ's shelter. As for the money you offer, the Lord provides our needs by many, and sometimes strange ways. We are rebuilding the Vatican's walls for our defense. This day at lauds I prayed funds could be found to pay the stonemasons. By such miracles as Christ in His bounty sheds on us, the sum you offer is the very sum we asked. Not more, nor less, but like the manna that Our Lord required Moses to have faith in day by day."

Gregory looked among the faces of the cardinals of the Curia.

Many were frowning.

"In the eyes of the world," he addressed them, "I would do better to reject what this man offers, and apply to moneylenders for the funds we need. But I believe that's not what I'm to do." He nodded to Simon, " We accept your offering, and grant the annulment that you ask, for thereby three souls will be healed, and the Church's needs met. It will be said by many that the Pope has sold a bride of God for gold. So be it. To be Pope is to be target of the small of faith," a sad smile creased his cheeks. "I ask only, Sire Montfort, that you pledge yourself to take the Cross, and defend our Church and Christendom."

Simon knelt again and kissed the offered ring, as Gregory held out his hand. "Most gladly, Your Holiness! My hope is that my life may be of service to Christ, and to you."

Chapter Thirteen

KENILWORTH
1238

AT THE WALLS OF MILAN, Simon took part in one pitched battle with the English forces under Henry d'Urberville. Then the contest settled into siege. He camped with the English by the city's gates until mid-June, when his promised six weeks of service to the emperor were done. Then he returned to Rome.

The Pope had shown him great mercy. As he ruminated during the long hours in the camp, Gregory's kindness he felt was a grace of which he was deeply unworthy. But he had been granted a second chance.

At the Vatican, he received the beautifully inscribed document with its heavy golden seal. With the precious annulment in hand, he embarked for England, very different from the man that he had been when he arrived in Rome. No longer the unwilling novice in the world of sin, he felt as if his soul was given back to him.

The first days of August were already spent when he reached Dover. Without stopping at London and Henry's Court, he went straight on to Kenilworth.

Kenilworth had been one of the finest holdings of the Crown. The square castle's sloping walls seemed planted in the earth, defying wars and time. But time will have its way.

From an island bounded on the north and east by a deep channel, on the south and west by a wide lake called the Mere, the fortress rose, a red mass of sandstone. Four square towers braced the mighty central tower's corners, rising a story higher than the roof, carrying their banner-poles a hundred feet above the placid surface of the Mere.

A bailey wall enclosed the island on three sides, sloping to the water's edge. On the fourth side the wall crossed the island, dividing it into an inner court and a broad outer yard. Within the court, a little chapel stood opposite a small foyer-building that sheltered the staircase to the tower's raised ground floor. Like many ancient fortresses, the tower was built upon a man-made heap of earth, now entirely contained within its square walls.

The outer yard provided ample space for stables, barns, paddocks and an orchard. A road crossed the yard from the inner court's gate to a causeway carried on a dam across the Mere. At the far end of the dam there was a sluice, covered by a swing-bridge. From the bridge, the road passed through woodland to the manor's fields, and to the village of Kenilworth.

The castle had not been inhabited for decades. When, in March, the Countess Eleanor arrived, the Mere was a slough of reeds. The bridge was rotting. Much of the dam's road surface had tumbled down into the marsh. The orchard was a thicket of briars. Of barn and stables there were only rotting beams. The chapel's walls, with no roof to protect them, were crumbling. The gate's arch was fallen, and the roof of a corner tower had collapsed.

Lady Mary held tightly to the countess's trembling hand as the two women, dismayed by what they had seen thus far, went up the steps of the foyer and entered the castle's hall.

Though stern on its exterior, the building once had been handsome within. The entire main floor of the central tower was the hall. Opposing sets of three soaring arches pierced through the thickness of fourteen feet of stone in the north and south walls. To admit abundant light while giving siege defense, the arches flared down to long, narrow arrow-slits in the walls' outer faces. Within, tall steps rose from the floor to the arrow-slits, forming a triangle of steep window seats between the arches' angled walls. But the white plaster was flaking, leaving the red stone exposed. Daylight from the arrow-slits, reflecting from the scrofulous arch walls, was livid and morose.

"Here's a good tile floor," Lady Mary observed, straining for a hopeful note.

Eleanor's servants, following her from Odiham, brought in bundles from the packhorses and wagon, as Mary explored and Countess Eleanor stood stupefied.

Opening the door to a small storage room in the corner tower to the right of the entrance, Mary jumped back as a rat scurried out. She opened a similar door to the entrance's left and saw nothing but blackness. There was no floor. The toes of her shoes were at the edge of a pit. The waiting woman mustered her self-control and announced bravely, "What a fine, cool place you'll have to keep your wines!"

Eleanor was standing in the middle of the hall, looking about like a shipwrecked castaway as her servants heaped her leather sacks of clothes and casks of household goods around her.

Mary cautiously opened another corner tower door across the hall. This small room was a latrine. A stone ledge served as seat, with an open shaft behind it. Light poured from above. Turning her head, she saw two higher levels, each stepped back so that matter dropping from above would fall clear of the seat below. "Look, a latrine! How airy and convenient!" she reported brightly.

At the fourth door Mary exclaimed, "Here are the stairs. Come, my lady. Let's see the upper chambers."

Like explorers in a cave, the women climbed the dark staircase. On the landing, a moldering partition of wood paneling faced them. The partition formed a passageway with a single door opposite the stairs. Eleanor opened it and went in, as Mary ventured further up the stairs.

The chamber the countess entered was dusty but ample, with a steady north light beaming through small windows cut in the deep stone. The floor was sturdy, and the ceiling was sound, with traces of old paint. But the dreariness was as palpable as fog. Eleanor placed her hand upon the growing mound of her belly and tears came to her eyes. She stood for some time, frozen with hopelessness until Mary reappeared.

"Come see," Mary urged, standing at the door and motioning the countess to come with her. "The stairs go up to the roof where there's more little rooms in the towers. Don't bother about 'em now. But look at these chambers!"

She led the countess to where the paneled passage opened at a right angle to a second passage burrowed through the thickness of the castle's southern wall. This passage gave entry to two more large rooms, the last with small windows that looked westward over the Mere. The view was lovely, but the floor was rotten, and the ceiling, hung with moisture-beaded webs, was on the verge of collapse.

"You'll use the first room for now. I'll have your bed and chests put there," Mary said decisively. "But won't this chamber be lovely when it's fixed!"

The countess looked at Mary, her eyes wide with helplessness. "Perhaps we should go back to Odiham."

"Nonsense. What's needed is a bit of scrubbing and a few repairs. It'll give us somewhat t' do before the baby's born."

"A great deal to do," Eleanor looked around her, confounded. But the prospect of something immense to occupy her, to keep her mind from drifting toward Rome and her unknown fate, dawned upon her as perhaps not such a bad thing after all.

"It's a fine place," Mary insisted cheerily. "And we can make it comfortable again."

Five months later, when Simon and his squire emerged from the green shade of Kenilworth's forest, the road before them was newly smoothed; the great castle and its yards were a hive of busy workmen.

Full of joy at homecoming and the good news he brought, Simon spurred his horse to gallop. New bridge-planks clicked under the horse's hooves. In the outer yard, he passed a barn that filled the air with the perfume of fresh-sawn wood. Young cherry trees were planted in the cleared and pruned orchard. A mason was resetting the cornerstone of the gate's arch. In the inner court, a slater fitted slates into the chapel's new roof. A rose garden with a turf seat was by the chapel door. Kitchen, laundry and brewing sheds stood in a neat row beside a wattle-fenced kitchen garden green with lettuces and herbs.

As Simon and his squire passed the gate and reined their horses to a halt, the kitchen boys, Garbage and Slingaway, who knew Simon from Odiham, came running, shouting welcome.

Simon gave his horse's reins to Slingaway and dashed up the foyer steps, entering his new home for the first time.

No one was in the hall. He turned around slowly, awed by the splendid room. The walls were newly plastered and whitewashed. The great arches, now bright white soaring arcs, filled the room with clear daylight from their long arrow-slits. Opposite the entrance was a wooden dais with a finely carved oak table and two chairs. Above them, drawn in red paint on the white wall, was the immense fork-tailed lion rampant of Montfort. Simon laughed with delight.

A corner door suddenly was flung open and Lady Mary trotted in from the stairs. "Well here you are at last!" she gasped, quite out of breath. "When you didn't come back sooner, we worried ourselves into a fit till we heard that you was in Milan."

"Where is she?" Simon asked.

"She don't come down the stairs these last few days. Too steep for her. Her balance ain't good. I told her, 'No, you stay up here. I'll go fetch him!'"

Simon was already through the door and climbing the stairs two at a time.

Eleanor was at the landing waiting for him. She threw her arms around his neck and kissed him, and he kissed her.

She drew him into the chamber, "Look at me! Any minute now, Lady Mary says. Oh, I'm so glad you're back!"

Simon kissed her again and again, and looked at her and kissed her again. "You're enormous!" he grinned.

"I mean to outdo that Berber camel driver's daughter," she laughed.

"Ambitious wench," Simon teased. "Look what I have for you," he brought from his robe the vellum document with the gold papal seal.

Eleanor began to shake. "Oh, God be thanked!" she whispered. For months the issue of the annulment had been so terrifying that she had not let it enter her mind. Now the full sense of her peril fell upon her. She began to quake and weep.

Simon helped her to her bed. "He's granted it! All's well." He looked at Lady Mary, unsure what to do.

Mary took her mistress's hand and rubbed it hard. "Come now! Don't be cryin' an' doin' the baby harm. Besides, it seems 'tis good news that he brings!"

Sternly admonished, Eleanor wiped her tears. Her smile emerged like a pale sun after a rainshower. "Tell me... We were so very frightened when we heard Archbishop Rich had gone to Rome. I begged Our Lord that the Pope wouldn't listen to him."

Simon unrolled the document and put it in her hand. "Your prayers were surely heard. I can't repeat the words Rich used, but they turned against him as if by a miracle." He kissed her long brown braids and her neck as she read.

"I've been so very much afraid," she whispered. "Oh, thank God!" She pressed the annulment to her breast.

Two days later Eleanor's labor began. Early in the hours of the morning she gave birth to a boy.

After all was done, Lady Mary summoned Simon to the room. He held the infant in his arms and softly called him Henry. Eleanor smiled, seeing the little red-faced bundle against Simon's red-lion-dappled robe. "Such a gentle lion," she murmured, and she fell asleep.

In the days that followed, Eleanor recovered, nestled in her newly painted chamber, amid new bed curtains that made the room quite cheery. The baby Henry nursed and slept.

For Simon, all that he had ever hoped for, and far more, was gained: marriage, family, a splendid home. Even his titles were under firm promise from his brother-in-law the king. A life of peace and happiness miraculously seemed won. Perhaps all was forgiven him in Heaven. He gazed with fatherly amaze at the sweet, pretty child that was his son. He looked upon his wife, so wise, so loving: she in whom alone his heart found rest. He roamed over

Kenilworth: the bastion, the yards, the Mere and manor lands: a property as lush and beautiful as any he had ever seen. The castle, strong and simple in its form, surely was the handsomest of castles that he knew. And the Mere was as a mirror, doubling the beauty of it all.

He was astounded by his good fortune. A nagging sense of his unworthiness lingered, but he tried to dispel it and embrace his happy fate. And quite often he could, returning to Eleanor from rambles about Kenilworth with his face shining like a boy's with pure and innocent delight. But at other times, lonely evenings as Eleanor was lying-in, he was troubled by an annoying sense of doubt.

It was not long before his doubts found cause.

King Henry, in his thoughtless generosity, had bestowed Kenilworth where, even were it sound, it could not be afforded. Simon had barely more than half an earl's income. Eleanor, whose dowry never was returned by Gilbert of Pembroke, had no income at all beyond field rents at Odiham and occasional gifts from Henry.

Yet the countess had spent freely – on credit – to restore and furnish Kenilworth.

Word of Simon's immense loan from the Hospitallers spread. With his return, a stream of creditors arrived, each hoping to collect his debt ahead of the rest. Collectors came for payments owed to cabinetmakers, ironmongers, drapers, and dealers in materials from timber and paint to stone and slate.

The workmen at Kenilworth came and asked for payment too, lest there be no money left for them. Their clear message was that no work would be finished unless they were paid. Simon was forced to place them first on the list for any funds he raised.

Bills came for silver serving trays and goblets not yet delivered. These Simon cancelled. But very quickly all the credit he could raise against his Leicester rents, due in September, was spent. Rents years' in advance became entailed.

Moneylenders and collection agents made camp in Kenilworth's outer yard. Even the Hospitallers sent two of their knight-clerks to see to their investment. The castle was besieged by creditors.

Then, as if those debts were not enough, there came a letter from the Bishop of Soisson. He demanded that Simon pay his church two thousand and eighty marks. This was the interest-fattened, two hundred mark debt Simon had still owed to Ranulf when the old earl died. At Ranulf's death, the bill had passed as settlement of a debt Ranulf owed to the Count of Brittany, Piers Mauclerc. Without informing Simon, Mauclerc had discounted the debt to a moneylender of Cahors for quick cash. The Cahorsine, also not informing Simon, held the bill five years while it grew compound interest at sixty percent per year. Then he sold the swollen debt to the Bishop of Soisson, making the church collection agent for both principal and interest.

Simon refused to pay any more than the original debt. He had not sought the loan, and Ranulf had given it interest-free. The bishop answered him with threat of excommunication if he refused to pay the interest as well. Simon would be excluded from the Church, cast from salvation, and his lands placed under interdict. All churches in his domain would be closed. No marriages, no funerals or baptisms could be performed.

Simon wrote back to the bishop, accusing him of extortion in the service of usury. He flatly refused to pay more than he felt he owed. Usury was a subject on which he was adamant.

The bishop replied with excommunication. In Soisson, the ritual was read, bells were rung, candles were inverted and their flames stamped out on the cathedral floor. Simon was damned to everlasting Hell.

The Jews Simon disbursed from Leicester might consider this a just revenge. But Simon thought it was absurd. He wrote to Grosseteste, asking him to lift the interdict and excommunication, and baptize his son.

Grosseteste now was the Bishop of Lincoln. He agreed to lift the interdict and to perform the baptism. But he wrote back to Simon angrily. "Did you suppose you could commit the sins you have, and there would be no retribution? Justice is done. If not for your debt, then for your crime of simony in Rome. Excommunication is what you have earned."

If Simon thought he had escaped his sins unscathed, here was his answer. Hellsmouth opened wide, and laughed. He was excommunicate after all, consigned to the damned despite the Pope's mercy.

In his heart, Simon felt the truth of Grosseteste's accusation. The brief happiness he had enjoyed was undeserved. He was far fallen from the man he meant to be; he was unworthy of the grace the Pope had shed on him. At twenty-five, he had failed in life's most crucial tests. His successes were a mockery. Sinking toward despair, he turned to his wife for comfort: the prize for whom he paid the price of his soul's peace.

But, to her mind, he perversely courted excommunication. "Just pay the debt," she urged.

"With what!" Simon exploded in frustration. "You've spent all we could ever hope to have. And more!"

"Don't shout at me!" The countess, sitting in her bed, covered her ears with her hands. "It's you who left your debts unpaid!"

Simon was livid. He felt an urge to strike her. He turned and left the chamber, running down the stairs to be alone in the hall until he regained self-control.

Later he returned to her. But she repeated he was wrong, and urged him once again to pay the debt. They shouted at each other, and this time when he left her it was with the awful dread that he did not know this woman who possessed so harsh a tongue.

Where was the gentle, wise Eleanor whom he had thought he wed? Only months before, his entire being was consumed with love for her. A dreadful thought occurred to him. Perhaps the troubadour was right: marriage was passion's swift cure. Even the prize of love seemed snatched away from him. Wanting to feel his love again, to reassure himself, to laugh at that foolish notion, he went back to her chamber.

But Eleanor was sullen, fearful of the rage in him she had not seen before. She was struck with doubts as troubling as his. They said little to each other. Uncomfortable, they kept their eyes averted. Their love, the thing most certain in the world, suddenly seemed very frail.

Simon left the chamber feeling empty, utterly abandoned and alone. Lady Mary comforted her mistress, but Simon had no one to comfort him. Sitting at the table in the hall, he brooded in a gathering cloud of despair, as he labored with his inventory lists and debts.

In September, the king and queen arrived at Kenilworth with a small, discreet retinue. Simon, obeying the king's intent not to announce the birth until a proper time had elapsed since the wedding, had sent word to Henry secretly of his success in Rome and Eleanor's safe delivery of a baby boy. He told the king they wished to name the child for him. Henry was delighted. He came as quickly as he could to serve as godfather at the christening.

The little royal entourage picked its way through the shabby siege in Kenilworth's outer yard. The grass was trampled to mud, and the mud was littered with travelers' sacks, cooking pots, urinals, and the droppings of the debt-collectors' freely wandering mules and horses. Men talked loudly of trade and interest rates. Some played dice or tended campfires. A carpenter had built a shed against the bailey wall. Within, two white- robed Hospitallers sat reading their breviaries.

King Henry and Queen Eleanor rode through the gate and found Simon and his steward, deMesnil, waiting for them in the court.

"What are all those people doing here?" Henry demanded, as Simon held his stirrup for him to dismount.

"They're trying to raise money by plowing Kenilworth into the mud," Simon smiled, straining to be affable. "You've come at a difficult time."

"We thought we'd come at a joyous one," the queen replied, as deMesnil helped her from her horse.

In the hall, Henry looked about the newly decorated room, pausing at the great red lion on the wall. "Is that the latest fashion?" he asked with a wave of his hand.

"Eleanor had it done when I was in Rome. It's quite handsome, don't you think?" Simon said bluffly.

"Not my taste," Henry made a sour face to tease. "Where's my sister?"

"She's upstairs with the baby. Wait till you see him! He grows bigger every day." Simon's whole joy now was in his son. The king and queen followed him up the dark staircase.

Henry kissed his sister on the cheek as she sat in her curtained bed, "You're looking perfectly fine," he commented as the queen kissed her too.

"I feel well. But Lady Mary says I must rest here a week longer."

The baby's nurse, a plump, ruddy-faced country girl, brought tiny Henry.

"So my nephew's to be named for me?" King Henry beamed, clearly very pleased.

"Let me hold him," the queen whispered, gazing on the child with a look that verged on greed. She had been married for three years without conceiving. Court gossip had concluded she was barren. Her pretty face glowed as the infant was put in her arms. "He's lovely! You're so fortunate."

"Oh, you'll soon have a fine son of your own," the countess said lightly.

But her words touched Queen Eleanor with unexpected force. She started to cry.

Seeing her remark's effect, the countess quickly said, "Sister, forgive me!"

"No matter. It's just foolishness," the queen shook her head. But her feelings, long pent, were past repressing. Tears ran down her cheeks, wetting the silk veil that framed her face.

Henry looked at her, embarrassed, and walked out of the room. Simon followed him. The nurse took the baby. Lady Mary put her arm around the queen, guiding her to a chair at the bedside.

"I'm so sorry..." Queen Eleanor apologized, wiping her tears with her fingertips. "Henry's very eager to have a son. Especially now..." At the countess's questioning look, she went on, still dabbing at her tears. "The mutterings... That Richard is so prudent, so wise. And

'What a pity Richard isn't on the throne!'" She pursed her lips. "If Henry had an heir, their mutterings would cease!" She tried to sound angry, but her shoulders shook and she broke into tears again.

Below, in the hall, Simon saw to the arrangements for his royal guests.

"I can stay just for a day," Henry said. "As far as the Court knows, only my sister is here and the baby is still due. I don't want to risk their learning otherwise."

Every moneylender and merchant in the Midlands knew Simon was back, but Henry held fixedly to his project of concealment.

"But perhaps it would be good for the queen to visit for a time," he suggested. "The Court upsets her... as you see."

Simon bowed slightly, "We would be honored to have her as our guest."

"The church bells weren't rung for us as we came through the village, and I saw the church was shut. What's happening here?"

"I've been excommunicated, and my lands put under interdict, because I haven't paid a debt the Bishop of Soisson is trying to collect. Debt bloated by Cahorsine usury," Simon said wearily. "As if my creditors in England weren't enough." He didn't want to discuss the issue. He feared, after the conflict with Archbishop Rich, the king's interference in a matter that involved the Church could only make the situation worse. "Bishop Grosseteste of Lincoln has agreed to lift the interdict, and will perform the baptism tomorrow."

"He'll lift your excommunication?" Henry asked.

"That... will be resolved some other time. " Simon said evasively, clearly wanting the topic dropped.

Henry, not lacking sensitivity, let the matter pass, but made a mental note to help however he could. "Well... I'll change out of my traveling clothes and have a bath."

"I'm afraid you'll have to go down to the baths in the village. Our furnishings don't include more than a washbasin as yet."

Henry, with deMesnil and two servants, went off to the bathhouse in the village, and Simon returned to his table heaped with bills.

A little later, Queen Eleanor came down to the hall. She had removed her veil. Her thick blonde hair fell in loose curls across her shoulders. She seemed calm now. "I hope you'll forgive my outburst," she said almost shyly.

"My lady," Simon rose from his table and bowed. "You need no forgiveness," he said politely.

Gesturing for him to sit again, she came and leaned against his chair, so close that he could feel her body's warmth. "Your son is beautiful," she murmured.

"Yes," he said, very ill at ease in her closeness. His attraction to her had not lessened; and too he feared that anything might set her off again.

Bending over him, she surveyed the heap of bills. "No one lives without troubles, do they?"

"I've noticed that, whenever I think someone has a perfect, happy life, I don't know much about them," Simon smiled. His eyes met hers for an instant, but he quickly looked away. "Has Lady Mary shown you and your ladies to your chamber?"

"Yes. It's quite pleasant. This is a lovely place." She straightened. Her woolen riding robe fit tightly over the curves of her bosom and hips. "I can see all across the lake from the chamber's windows. And there are hardly any flies." She walked to the nearest arch, climbed to its highest step and sat, peering out the arrow-slit.

Simon's gaze followed her. "You haven't made acquaintance with our mosquitoes yet. And the frogs in the Mere were so loud in August that Eleanor hired a boy to beat the water to quiet them." He had never been alone with the queen before. He realized he was staring, and he looked away. "But Kenilworth is beautiful."

"You should be very happy here," the queen turned toward him.

His answer stuck in his throat. In truth, he was far from being happy.

That evening Grosseteste arrived. He looked at Simon coldly and said not a word to him. Chagrined, Simon withdrew and kept himself apart. His excommunication formally made him unfit company for anyone in the good graces of the Church.

The baptism was performed the next morning in the chapel. Simon could only watch the ritual from outside the open door. King Henry and Queen Eleanor served as godparents. Lady Mary, squire Peter, Thomas deMesnil, the queen's Lady Alice and the servants of Kenilworth were witnesses.

A light breeze came through the doorway, lapping the long white satin cloth in which the child was wrapped. The baby cooed to the bishop's murmuring. All went well until Grosseteste, placing his hand upon the child in blessing, paused. He frowned as if he saw something deeply disturbing. Something distant, far beyond the reach of his hand to the child's head. The words came from his lips, "This child shall not outlive his father, but shall die on the same day, and by the same hurt."

The gathering of witnesses stirred, shocked by the words. The king and queen exchanged perplexed looks, doubting their ears. Simon went pale. Could the bishop's anger go so far as to cast such a curse upon his child? Rage rose in him, but sank to horror as Grosseteste seemed to wake as from a trance. The bishop continued with the blessing, apparently unaware of what he had said. The words were prophecy.

Queen Eleanor, cradling the infant in her arms, glanced to Simon with a frightened look. Standing by the door, he could do nothing but look away. Anxiety swept over him. Anxiety and guilt. Even the child, his one remaining source of happiness, now had the taint, the spoilage, of all things dear to him.

The bishop left directly after the ceremony. And no one spoke of the ominous words.

Chapter fourteen

QUEEN ELEANOR
1238

King Henry left Kenilworth the next morning. Queen Eleanor remained.

In the days that followed, angry words flared constantly between Simon and his wife as more bills arrived. He took loans and made every arrangement that he could to satisfy the besiegers in the outer yard. And their numbers thinned. But the work was like salt grinding in a wound.

One afternoon, his temper raw, he went up to the countess's chamber with a stack of slips of debt clutched in his hand. Eleanor sat comfortably amid the pillows of her bed. The queen sat on a chair beside her, keeping her company.

"What are these!" Simon held out the fistful of bills.

"What?" his wife looked up, startled. "What are they?"

He threw them in her lap.

Blinking at his anger, trying to ignore his rudeness, Eleanor smiled weakly to the queen. She took up three of the bills and read them. "These are for my bed's new draperies, summer and winter. This is for Lady Mary's chamber." Mary occupied the little tower room at the end of the passage.

Simon roughly took the slip from his wife's hand. "At a cost of thirty pounds?" he asked caustically.

Eleanor looked up, tears coming to her eyes. "The cloth is so fine. She wanted it. I couldn't say no."

"How did you suppose it would be paid for? And these!" He picked up several of the slips at random from the bed. "Sixty pounds for mason's stone. Forty pounds for unseasoned timber! What is our forest for, that we buy green wood elsewhere? Twenty pounds for thirty iron pots. Thirty! Do we feed an army here?" He glared at her, then read the next slip. "Two dozen rosebushes!"

The countess turned to the queen in meek appeal. "I so love roses. Don't you?" But the queen bit her lip and looked down. Raised in a family in bankruptcy, she understood Simon's dismay too well.

Finding no support, the countess turned on her husband. She summoned all her fragile strength and burst to shrieking. "Stop placing blame on me! You don't know what it was like here! Filthy! Everything in wreckage! You were gone. If you failed with the Pope, maybe you were never coming back!" She clumsily wiped her tears with the palms of her hands. "I couldn't bear to think of it. So I thought about our home, and kept myself busy."

Simon stared at her, confounded. With a gesture of exasperation, he glanced to the queen, who was looking at him sympathetically. "What would a king's daughter know of debt!" he bellowed, and he left the room in fury.

The queen arose and followed him. Going down the dark staircase after him, she called softly, "Please, don't be angry with her." He stopped at the bottom step and looked back up. She came down to where the light from the open doorway brought her past the deepest shadows of the stairwell, and she touched his hand.

"She's nothing but a spoilt child!" His voice reverberated in the stairway's stone shaft.

Queen Eleanor took his hand in her two hands and pressed it to calm him. Her silent, gentle gesture had effect. It bridged his isolation. His rage broke to despair. "I love her. But this is a nightmare she's wrought!"

"You must forgive her," the queen urged, still pressing his hand. "She was thinking only of your new life together."

"Our life? She's stifled it! And for what? Kitchen pots and bed curtains!"

The queen looked in his dark eyes and said softly, "Of course you're right."

Meeting her gaze, Simon felt steadier. The touch of her hands was soothing.

Pressing his hand more firmly, she murmured, "You must cherish a heart that loves more than it reasons."

He cast his eyes down, away from her gaze. He found his heart was racing, but due to rage or what he did not know. He returned the pressure of her hands, then drew his hand away. "Thank you... for your advice." His voice was husky, his tone warmer than he had intended. Embarrassed, he laughed shortly. "Everyone's abandoned me, though I sorely need counsel."

Queen Eleanor studied his manner and her lips bent to a smile. She and Simon stood on the stairs, silent for some moments. The very air between them seemed vibrant. At last she said, "I must go back to her. May I tell her you forgive her?"

He nodded.

She turned and, with a toss of her bright hair, ran quickly back up through the darkness of the stairs.

Simon went back to his worktable, amazed to find that he was feeling buoyant. Almost happy.

At supper that night the countess remained in her chamber as usual. But the queen joined Simon in the hall. DeMesnil had gone to Leicester. Lady Alice kept company with Lady Mary and the countess, so the queen and Simon dined alone.

"Tell me of your trip to Rome," Queen Eleanor insisted, in a playful mood after her second cup of wine.

"I told you and Henry..."

She grasped his wrist. "Of course you did. But what you *didn't* tell..." Her eyes shone with a naughty sparkle in the candlelight. "Truly, does the emperor have a harem?"

Simon blanched, and avoided her steady gaze. "If I knew of it, I'd be a poor guest to gossip of my host's household. "

The queen looked at him closely, and he looked away from her. She narrowed her eyes teasingly, "You do know, don't you! Are they very beautiful? Dark-skinned, dark-eyed sultanas?"

A hot blush rose to Simon's face. "I was in Milan most of the time..."

She dug her nails into his wrist. "Don't try to put me off."

"Ouch!" he pried her fingers from his wrist, and put her hand upon the table. But her hand remained folded in his as he said low, "There's none in Rome who can compare to England's queen."

His words were a gallantry, but the inadvertent warmth of his look was sobering to both of them.

She drew back, slipping her hand from underneath his as she gave a nervous laugh. "I beg pardon. I fear I ask questions that belong to your confessor."

Recovering himself, Simon shrugged peevishly. "I have no confessor. You forget, the Bishop of Soisson's marked me a sinner, outside the law and righteousness, and decent Christian company. I'm a man you ought to shun."

The queen's eyes flashed, "The Church of Soisson's put a wolf in bishop's clothes!"

He laughed at her blunt outburst. "I agree." He lifted his goblet and drank as in a toast. "It's good to hear someone else say what I think."

They went on talking for some time, long after the meal was cleared away. But the heated moment when he held her hand did not occur again. She jested, and he laughed freely at her wit, as she made mock of Henry's courtiers and the English lords. Both foreigners, aware they were resented, they came to feel a bond of understanding. Simon's pain lifted. She made the little circle of the table in the candlelight into an island free from cares. For the first time in many months he felt at ease. They sat together, laughing and talking long into the night.

When she parted from him to go up to her chamber, he took her hand and pressed it to his lips. "Thank you. You've cheered me."

Glancing away from him, she murmured, "You, too, have made me happier than I've been." Then she turned and went quickly up the stairs.

Simon went back to the table and drank another cup of wine. The burdens he was bearing had been lifted for a while. The queen's face lingered in his mind, filling him with a strange mix of sadness and excitation. And a soothing warmth. He closed his mind to thought so he could savor the sensation, and extend the freedom from his cares for a few moments more.

The next day was hot and sunny, a last breath of summer in September. Feeling restless, Simon took a respite from his work and went out for a ride.

As he ambled through Kenilworth's woods, he saw a white veil hanging upon the branch of a tree. Dismounting and leading his horse aside from the road, he plucked the veil from the branch and went into the woods to investigate. Beneath a large, old oak he found the queen sitting, her back resting against the tree trunk as she read a book. Astonished, he asked, "My lady, how did you come here?"

Looking up at him, she squinted against the dappled sunshine. "I walked. The people in the yard were perfectly polite."

"Where's Lady Alice?"

"She had a headache so I sent her back. It's refreshing and cool here.

"You shouldn't be alone."

"Then will you join me?" The queen made room for him to sit on the soft hillock of moss that made a comfortable seat at the tree's base.

He uncinched his saddle and put it on the ground, then used the cinch to hobble his horse, letting the animal graze on the moist grass that grew where sunlight reached the forest floor. Returning to the queen, he sat beside her.

Ill at ease in this odd privacy, he cast about for something to say and hit upon, "What are you reading?"

She handed him the little, leather-bound volume. He wrinkled his nose in mock disapproval of "*The Knight of the Cart*" and returned the tales of Lancelot to her. "I prefer *Ivain*."

"Are we to talk of books?" she asked archly.

"Not if you don't wish. What would you talk of?"

She was silent for some moments, as if struggling with indecision. Finally she said, "Last night I came to feel that I can trust you."

She paused as if a cord of reticence were fraying; then, with an uncertain smile, she went on. "I see you have your cares, as I have mine. And I too need a friend's counsel." Putting her hand on his, she looked at him almost pleadingly, "But I must ask your word that you won't speak to Henry, or to anyone else, of what I'm going to say."

Simon looked at her, uncomfortable about what might be coming next. But he nodded and said low, "You have my word."

"What do you think of Richard?"

The question took him by surprise. "Prince Richard? He's intelligent, earnest..."

"Yes. I didn't mean that." She brought the words out slowly, "Do you think he is *ambitious*?"

He realized what she meant. "I don't know," he said honestly.

She gazed up toward the beams of sunlight flickering through the leaves, and said softly, "I'm terrified of him."

"Henry can defend himself."

"Do you think so?" She looked at Simon straightly, her eyes wide with her fear. "I think the hurt alone of seeing his brother's hand raised up against him would destroy him."

The thought seemed ludicrous to Simon, but he took her hand to comfort her. "You underestimate him."

"Do I?"

"Henry can keep what's his as well as any man. Far better, for he is a king."

"I see," she bent her head. "No one knows him as I do. No one can help me." Tears choked her voice. She turned and pressed her face to Simon's shoulder. He placed his arms around her, trying to be comforting.

They sat for a long time. He didn't know what to do, and dared not move. He felt her tears soaking his robe. Sitting, holding her crying in his arms, he rocked her as one would a frightened child, and whispered gently, "Hush, don't cry. Don't cry."

He sat a long time holding her in his arms. Time drifted in the gentle comfort of the moment. She raised her head, brushing her damp hair from her face, and kissed him on the lips. Without thought, he returned her kiss with a kiss, long and sweet, that wrapped them both away from all the pain and threat that the world offered them. She drew him to lie with her on the mossy ground. And the passion he had felt since he first saw her flooded through him like a sweet, heated wave, drowning thought, cares, cautions and restraints.

In the blue of the evening, Simon, leading his horse by the reins, walked with the queen across the causeway back to the castle. Their bodies sang with love spent, and spent, and yet still ringing in their nerves.

Late that night, Queen Eleanor came to the small tower chamber where Simon slept during his wife's lying-in. He was awake and looked up when the door opened, but he did not move or speak. The queen let her cloak fall, and lay down beside him. In the moonlight on his pillow, her hair shone like a golden sea through which his fingers swam.

Every night after that she came to him.

Days went by. The countess, deemed strong enough by Lady Mary, left her chamber and went about her household duties normally. Simon was aloof, silent and brooding. The countess thought his mood was due to his anger at her spending, and she blamed herself.

The queen, for her part, was far more able than Simon to conceal her guilt. Or, seeing their passion as *courtesy's* ideal, forbidden love, she felt no guilt. She was bright and happy, spending afternoons with the countess, playing with the baby Henry on the rose garden's turf seat.

Her duplicity amazed Simon. But he was glad for it. His wife and the household suspected nothing. The queen's visit passed, for her, in sunny autumn days of seeming innocence. Slow, languorous, tantalizing days that drew after them long nights of passion sated.

Simon, looking through the hall's arrow-slit, watched his mistress and his wife happy in the sunlight with his infant son. Guilt worked in him. The dreadful truths weighed heavily. Adultery. Adultery with his lord's wife. Adultery with the queen. Treason. In his heart,

Simon despised Henry and always had. His passion for Henry's wife in some part sprang from that same pit of feelings. But those speechless depths could not hold him in deafness long against the shouts of reason.

One night when the queen came to his room, Simon was sitting on a chair beside the window, looking grimly out at the sky. She brushed back his dark hair and kissed him on the lips, then tried to draw him to the bed. But he would not move. "It's time you left," he said quietly.

"Is it?" she asked, holding his hand to her breast. "Do you love me?" her voice quavered. "You've never said..."

He said nothing and looked away from her.

Still pressing his hand, she recited the words of the ancient tale, "Sire Tristan lay with Isolde of the White Hands for her beauty and her high birth, and that she had the same name as Isolde the Fair. But he could not love her."

Simon brought her hand to his lips and kissed it, saying softly, "I do love Eleanor."

Tears came to the queen's eyes. She clutched his hand a moment more, then left the room.

Chapter Fifteen

GUILT
1238-1239

THE QUEEN LEFT KENILWORTH THE next morning.

Her absence sharply ended Simon's dream. Guilt struck him with full force. The power that passion could hold over him, its strength to blind him to all else, was glaringly made clear. He saw his damnation writ large in Hell.

How had he permitted himself such heedless, mindless, dangerous pleasures? Had his excommunication, his exclusion from his faith, so obliterated every sense of what was right and wrong? And if it had, what vile and corrupt man was he becoming? What further wrongdoing might be within his scope? This new man seemed to grin within him with sardonic hope. Self-loathing filled him with a cramping nausea of the soul, a revulsion that he yearned to vomit forth, an infection that his spirit retched to cleanse. Yet his cast-out state blocked all chance of confession and redemption.

Time, the passage of days and even minutes, brought him such unbearable, increasing pain of mind that his former melancholy pangs of shame and guilt seemed merely sentimental. He thought constantly of suicide.

In agony of spirit, he left Kenilworth to beg Grosseteste to see him. He walked the eighty miles to Lincoln barefoot, wearing the long, coarse hair shirt of a penitent.

"What does the buyer of indulgences want with me?" Grosseteste asked caustically, when his clerk told him that the lord Montfort had come.

But when he saw Simon in the hair shirt, his face stubbled with beard and streaked with dirt and tears, his feet bloody and bruised,

the bishop relented. Simon was the son of his heart. He had meant
to chastise him only for a while, for an act he believed cynical and
politic in Simon's reaching for his titles. But the sight of him wrung
Grosseteste's heart.

Simon fell to his knees, "I beg you, father, if Heaven can have
mercy on a sinner such I've become, lift my excommunication and
hear my confession, before I do mortal damage to myself with my
own hands."

Grosseteste was aghast. He raised Simon up and had him sit on
the bench, beside him. He ordered his clerk to fetch washcloths
and a basin of water.

After the monk had washed Simon's face and bleeding feet, and
left the room, Grosseteste said gravely, "Tell me of your audience
with the Pope."

Simon recounted what had happened at the Vatican.

Grosseteste listened thoughtfully. When Simon finished, the
bishop pressed his pale, creased brow with his fist, then shook his
head. "I have presumed. This was clearly Our Lord's doing, and
I'm much at fault."

"Father, I beg you, hear my confession," Simon pled.

Grosseteste lifted the excommunication.

Simon knelt by the bishop's feet. "Father, father, I have sinned..."
Like the overflow, then bursting of a dam, his confession came
pouring out into the bishop's ear.

Grosseteste was shocked and very shaken. In his own youth, he
had suffered but lightly from temptations of the flesh, enveloped
as he was in the classroom and the cloister. He sat for some
time, absorbing Simon's words. Two glistening streaks of tears
marked his cheeks, for he loved this man and had high hopes
for him.

"I'm not without blame in this," the bishop said at last. "When
you begged to join our brotherhood, I cast you back with no thought
of the dangers. For the sake of a vision that you would do great
things at Court, I left you undefended. I lost sight of your soul. For
this I stand blamable before Heaven. But Pope Gregory spoke truly.
No one is beyond mercy. You must tame yourself, and guard your

every thought and act. And pray, so long as you live, to be cleansed of these sins."

He prescribed a harsh penance. Simon was to scourge himself on holy days, and whenever he felt tempted in thought. As for deeds, such must never happen again. He was to say the prayers of all the Hours, including waking in the middle of the night to say the prayers at midnight and at lauds. He was to spend three hours of each day reading the Bible or the works of saints. And, to remind his body of its shame, he was to wear a hair shirt always, next to his skin.

Simon returned to Kenilworth no longer desolate, but with new hope, though of a stern shade. His tormented marriage had seemed to him Heaven's condemnation for his union with a nun. Now he saw his marriage as his shield from further sin. He was determined to cease bickering.

He told Eleanor his excommunication had been lifted. She took note of the hair shirt and his rising in the night to pray, and assumed it was the price Grosseteste required for the lifting of the ban.

Simon's pain of spirit did not find relief at once. But gradually, with Grosseteste's remedies, and faith that even he could be restored to Heaven's grace, he began to find ease for his battered soul. When thoughts of the queen rose in his mind, he applied the whip to his offending body.

With his wife, the sharp edge of his temper was scoured away by his guilt. He said no more about the debts. He was gentle, striving to make amends for the betrayal that she did not even suspect. Eleanor, who blamed herself for his dark moods, was overjoyed at his new kindness.

Once more Simon could find delight in the baby Henry, who cooed and generously wet in his arms. And he looked upon his wife with gratitude for her innocent love.

The fields of Kenilworth were past their harvest. Winter wheat was being sown. From the barn came the incessant hiss of threshing flails. The kitchen garden Eleanor had planted in the spring, yielded great bunches of herbs. They hung like an inverted thicket in the rafters of the kitchen shed. Beneath the drying herbs were crocks of quinces and medlars in honey. Wicker trays were spread on the shed's thatch roof, their loads of late peas, beans and sliced apples drying in the sun. The woods were turning to the burnished tints of autumn. Wild swans swam in the Mere, drifting like white clouds across the water's limpid sky. And the massive bastion of the castle rose in the reflection, a block of red stone topped by the red lion banner of Montfort.

Thoughts of the queen taunted Simon: imps that he cast out with the lash and prayer. But neither he nor his wife spoke of her until some weeks had passed since his return from Lincoln. As he sat in the hall with the countess one evening, watching her dandle little Henry on her knees, she brought up the subject of the queen's visit.

"Poor Eleanor. It's not a happy life for her. She wants so much to have a child." The countess looked from her son to Simon, "I oughtn't to repeat this, but she told me Henry's impotent."

Simon stared at his wife. Then mortifying shame sent a hot blush to his cheeks. Abruptly he got up and left the hall. He realized that he had been used.

October came, and Simon still had not gone to Court. He dreaded it. But his return from Rome, and the granting of the annulment, had not yet been formally announced. Letters came from Henry summoning him, then demanding that he come at once.

On the fourteenth of October, Simon arrived at Winchester where the king was holding Court.

The See of Winchester was vacant. Henry wanted the queen's uncle William chosen as bishop, but the monks of the chapter refused. To persuade them, Henry summoned his courtiers, especially his hated foreign friends, his Poitouvins, Savoyard and Provencals, everyone who had a large appetite. Winchester Castle's store of food was soon consumed, and Henry made his Court the monastery's guest.

It was an extreme measure. The longer the Court stayed at Winchester, the more of the monks' grain and ducks and chickens went to the royal feast. And the more of the monks' costly Bordeaux wines were drunk. To the monks' horror, the king declared that he would stay until the chapter relented. Until Christmas if need be. Henry knew well how to conquer clerics: not by the force of arms, but the force of stomachs – a strategy that put his victim in the wrong for grudging hospitality.

Simon reached Winchester, where wine was flowing freely, and found the king in a bibulous, congenial frame of mind. The papal annulment of the Countess Eleanor's vows was read aloud to the assembled Court, bringing all questions of her marriage's propriety to an end.

After the reading, Henry, rising from his chair a bit unsteadily, announced, "Lord Montfort, you bring news welcome to us all! After so long an absence from England, you must be eager to go home."

Simon doubted there were many left who didn't know he was long back, but he bowed to the excuse that Henry gave for his extended absence from the Court.

"We'll not require your attendance until February when, God willing, our sister will have been delivered safely of her child." Henry was as intent as ever on concealing the true cause of the marriage. He gave his goblet to Mansel and came down the dais steps, taking Simon by the hand. Then he turned to the Court, "We shall invest the lord Montfort with the titles, Earl of Leicester, Steward of England, at our Candlemas Court."

During the brief audience, the queen searched Simon's face. But he kept his gaze on Henry. Then, taking his leave, he crisply wished her well and bowed to her as any subject might. He had expected the sight of her would fill him with loathing. It did not. Instead, he found he pitied her, he understood her and, perhaps worst of all, he loved her still.

In November, happy news rejoiced the land. The queen, feared barren, was to have a child.

King Henry wrote to his sister at Kenilworth: "Lady Alice found a physician who prescribed prayers at the tomb of Saint Edward and a tisane of foul-tasting herbs. Success at last! I'm having the saint's tomb moved to our abbey church at Westminster, to have him near our bedchamber. The child, if it's a boy, will be named Edward."

The countess, almost giddy with delight, read the letter aloud to Simon.

His face turned ashen. He said nothing, but that same afternoon he gave away his robes with the embroidered lions, his scarlet riding-cloaks and robes lined with fur, all of his fine clothes. From that day onward he wore penitential robes of plain black wool.

At Kenilworth, the winter days and months passed quietly. Every night, Simon roused when the bell of the nearby abbey struck midnight. Through the dark hours, he sat in his chair by the table in the hall, a candle lighting his book as he read *Templum Dei*, on confession, and other works that Grosseteste sent him on the subject of contrition, or the lives of saints. He felt some comfort in the writings of Saint Francis and Saint Augustine, but though they had been sinners, none had sinned as he had.

In late November, old Bishop Stavensby of Coventry and Litchfield came to visit. He had heard the Montfort child was due. As he was traveling past Kenilworth, he came to offer to perform the baptism. The child he saw seemed far advanced for a newborn, but the countess had no wish to tell the chatty bishop that little Henry was three months old, and already baptized by Bishop Grosseteste. So Henry was baptized again.

At the little celebration that the countess gave that evening, Stavensby began to cough and sneeze. By morning his was very sick. There could be no thought of his continuing his journey right away.

The bishop stayed at Kenilworth. Doctors were summoned, but his feeble lungs grew worse. On Christmas Day he died.

It was a strange visitation, Stavensby coming to Kenilworth to die. The weeks of Advent Simon spent in prayer at the gentle old priest's bedside, his own spirit's battle sobered by the sight of an impeccable soul's last struggle with the body.

At the beginning of February, Eleanor and Simon attended Court for Simon's investiture. Henry was still at Winchester, much to the monks' dismay.

In a full and formal ceremony, Simon received his titles: Earl of Leicester and Steward of England.

Later, at a feast given in his honor, Simon was seated by the queen. Fingering his black woolen robe teasingly, she asked, "Earl Montfort, why such somber dress on your most festive day? Has the jewel of our Court so soon grown tarnished in dull marriage?"

Simon met her eyes and said quietly, "It is not marriage, my queen, but life that tarnishes."

Queen Eleanor drew back her hand. "You oughtn't to take life so to heart," she pouted charmingly. "*Courtesy* maintains that we are only mortals. You would still have us be angels."

"I still believe your *courtesy* in error, though I've learned its power far too well."

"Are you two arguing again?" Henry broke in affably. "I thought you'd made your peace."

"We had indeed, my lord. Or so I thought," the queen smiled to her husband. "But the Earl Montfort is quick to forget."

The next morning, Simon begged to be excused from Court. He and the countess returned at once to Kenilworth.

Eleanor was pregnant with their second child. In the warm days of spring she sat out-of-doors with the baby Henry and his nurse, watching the swans gliding on the Mere, their little cygnets puttering after them. Lambs played in the newly greening fields, cavorting about their sheared mamas, and all the white fluff that the sheep had shed the orchard seemed to have put on.

The destriers that Simon bred at Leicester were brought down to Kenilworth. As knights of the Leicester Honour came to pay their fealty to their new earl, they looked over the horses, bargaining with deMesnil for their prices.

Then, in May, a fissure cut across the peace of Simon's life.

Thomas, the Count of Flanders, the eldest of Queen Eleanor's several uncles of Savoy, came to England to visit his niece – and to collect on Simon's debt of two thousand and eighty marks. As even excommunication brought no payment, the Bishop of Soisson had offered the bill at discount: and found a buyer in Count Thomas's wife, none other than that Princess of Flanders, Johanna, who once had been Simon's betrothed.

Vindictiveness might have had some part in Johanna's motives, but Thomas realized that, with his niece's marriage to King Henry, he could bring royal force where spiritual had failed. He wrote first to Simon, demanding the two thousand and eighty marks. Simon again offered to pay the two hundred, and not a penny more. He informed Thomas he had not sought the loan from Ranulf, and had been given it interest-free.

As soon as he reached England's Court, which was still lodged at Winchester, Thomas insisted that King Henry force Simon to pay the debt in full.

Henry knew little of the history of the debt, but he knew quite well his brother-in-law's financial straits. He wanted to help, although he was, as always, deep in debt himself. Without a word to Simon, he bullied and harried Thomas till the Count agreed to just five hundred marks. Then he paid the five hundred at once, getting Thomas's receipt before the count could recover and protest.

Then Henry summoned Simon to Winchester.

Simon received the royal summons as a thing both dreaded and expected. His crimes of adultery and treason must be known. How long could Henry think the queen's pregnancy a miracle? He bade farewell to his wife and child, and somberly made arrangements with his steward deMesnil, like a man who believed he never would return.

At Winchester, as he was led to the king's private chamber, Simon steadied himself with sterner bravery than ever he had needed in battle. He deserved a sinner and a traitor's death, and he was prepared. He even felt relief that the secret of his guilt and shame was broke open at last.

To his great shock, he found King Henry in a merry mood.

"Five hundred marks!" Henry announced proudly, presenting the bill to Simon.

Simon stared at the slip of parchment, then at Henry. His nerves, strung to the fraying point, snapped in irrational fury. All that he had braced himself to face was vanished, leaving his old outrage at Soisson in its place. "How dare you negotiate my debt? I don't owe five hundred marks! I owe two hundred. It's cost me excommunication, but I will not relent. Those cursed Cahorsine leeches must be stopped!"

"Ah, the tyrant of the Leicester moneylenders is now waging private war against Cahors?" Henry laughed. "I should have known. But now what's done is done. You owe me five hundred marks."

"I'll give you two hundred. No more!" Simon could not stop himself. His fear, his guilt, pent up for months, sent his emotions past suppressing. "How could you meddle in my business, when you knew nothing of it!"

Henry lost patience at last. "You do not speak to me so! By Saint Edward's head, you'll pay me the five hundred marks! Or you can pay the full two thousand and eighty! And I'll wring it out of you myself!"

"I won't have you meddling in my business!" Simon hotly retorted.

"Then pay the two thousand and eighty! I'll send my sheriffs to collect it at the end of the month!"

At the end of May, as Henry threatened, sheriffs and bailiffs appeared at Kenilworth and Leicester. They confiscated horses worth five hundred marks. Henry had relented, taking only the value that he actually had paid. Simon was livid but he had no recourse.

Henry, for his part, was unfazed in his love for his friend. As soon as the matter was settled, Simon was forgiven.

In June, church bells rang and all England celebrated. After only seven months of pregnancy, the queen had given birth to a miraculously fine and hearty boy. A joyful letter went from Court to the Earl and Countess of Leicester, summoning them to the baptism at Westminster. Henry appointed Simon to be one of the child's three godfathers.

Chapter Sixteen

THE BIRTH OF AN HEIR
1239

"I'M LENDING YOU THE LONDON manse of the See of Winchester for the summer. You should be quite comfortable there, if golden wine-ewers and jeweled goblets make anybody comfortable." Henry chatted volubly to Eleanor and Simon as they strode through the corridors of Westminster Palace. "The former bishop, my tutor, did his best to feather, or I should say gild, his nest. Once William's made bishop, the table service and furnishings will be sent here. But until then you might as well enjoy the wealth of Winchester." The king was in high spirits.

They passed a chamber heaped with presents: a carved ivory saddle with padded and embroidered saddle cloths; enameled and jeweled caskets; intricately chased gold goblets, trays and candlesticks; a Bible with a jewel-encrusted cover. All were gifts from England's high clergy and lords. Though gift giving was customary at the birth of an heir, no value was set, as it was for the Great Aids: the knighting of the heir and the wedding of the king's eldest daughter. This sumptuous outpouring was a response to the miracle of Saint Edward – and was a measure of the widespread relief that Henry finally had an heir.

"Look at this. Perfectly splendid!" Henry waved gleefully at his new treasures. "Yet lord Gilbert," he turned to his sister, "that vile Pembroke relative of yours, actually had the effrontery to send a bolt of common cloth! As if just anything would do at the birth of my son. I was so annoyed I sent it back. I did the right thing, don't you think?"

"I'd have had him thrashed," Eleanor said earnestly. Gilbert of Pembroke was the one person in the world whom she hated. His refusal to return her dowry was the cause, in her mind, of every trouble that afflicted her.

"Well, I can't do that, much as I'd like to," Henry laughed, walking on. "It's turned embarrassing. The Earl of Gloucester's taken Pembroke's part and goes about saying, 'God gave us this child, but the king sells him to us.'"

Simon, in a somber mood, spoke for the first time. "My lord, the embarrassment is hardly yours. Shame belongs to anyone who's slow to rejoice that you have an heir. How has Richard taken it?" The queen's fears and Pembroke's behavior piqued his concern.

Henry beamed with relief at Simon's words. He had feared that Simon's dark looks meant the matter of the debt still rankled. "My brother may be my worst critic, but in his heart he's right and true."

The king linked his arm in Simon's arm familiarly as they walked from room to room. "Surely there are some who aren't pleased that I have an heir and Richard's further from the throne, but Richard seems delighted. It's almost annoying, having a brother who is so good! Sometimes I look in that righteous face of his, and wonder what Fate had in mind, making me the elder. Actually, I think he's glad he's not upon the throne." Henry's drooping eye twinkled, "This way, he gets all the credit and none of the blame. Nobody remembers Richard's errors. Everyone learns mine by heart and can recite them back to me. He'll serve as godfather with you tomorrow at the baptism."

They reached the chamber that had been converted to a royal nursery. Henry, beaming proudly, showed Simon and Eleanor his miraculous new son.

The sight of the child brought unexpected feelings in Simon. The infant was the prettiest that he had ever seen, and would be king of England. He let his gaze rest on the boy with a certain pride, its blond-fuzzed head and giggling face a refined version of his own little Henry. Love, and a protectiveness toward this small being, crept into his heart.

The next day, June 20, 1239, the baptism was performed in the small, modest chapel of Westminster Abbey. Before the altar stood the gorgeous, just-completed tomb of gilded stone and checkered tiles housing the relics of Saint Edward the Confessor. Garlands of roses draped the tomb, and pungent incense clouded it, as if the saint himself were celebrated as the child's father. The Bishops of London, Norwich and Carlisle assisted. The papal legate Otto gave the blessing as the godfathers, Simon, Prince Richard and the Earl Humphrey de Bohun stood close together, their six hands cradling England's new prince over the baptismal font.

Bohun noted Simon's hands were trembling. "Are you all right, Lord Montfort?" he asked. But Simon, sickened by the thought the saint within the tomb could see his guilty soul, didn't answer.

The legate, pouring water on the infant's head, recited, "I baptize thee Edward, in the Name of the Father, and of the Son, and of the Holy Ghost."

As they left the abbey chapel to return to Winchester House, the countess Eleanor gave a deep sigh. "We all can breathe more easily now that Henry has an heir. And such a lovely baby. So very like our Henry, I think." She smiled and pressed her husband's arm, "But then, I see your face in everything I love."

Simon brought her hand up to his lips and kissed it. But he did not smile.

At the king's insistence, the Earl and Countess of Leicester were to remain at Winchester House all through the summer. Like many mansions in London, the house stood by the Thames, its garden sloping to the water and a boat landing.

Mornings, before she went to Court, the countess Eleanor, now weighty with her second pregnancy, would sit in the garden with little Henry and his nurse, watching the busy traffic on the river. Barges passed slowly with the tide, laden with bales of hay, building-timbers, firewood, cattle for the butcheries on London Bridge, and barrels and cases of merchandise of every kind. Ships, each with its huge, single sail furled, glided with a sweep of oars like the pinions of wings. A multitude of small sailboats darted hither and thither, delivering passengers then coasting along the river's edge, waiting to be hailed by new customers. Baby Henry squealed with joy, reaching out his tiny hand as if the river's traffic were a toy for him.

At Westminster, the countess Eleanor sat by the queen's bedside as she lay-in. And in Court, Simon held a place of high honor, seated on the dais steps by King Henry's feet.

Gradually, as day followed day with the king and his Court in a high state of happiness, Simon's anxieties fell from him like a suffocating cloak cast off in summer sunshine. All the chief lords and ladies of England were at Westminster. The queen's uncle, Thomas of Savoy, came again from Flanders. But even his presence among the feasters could not dampen Simon's good cheer.

It was a time of festival, with hunting parties in the woods of Hyde, torch-lit regattas on the Thames, and feasting every night. Simon took part in all of it as the king's brother-in-law and most-loved friend.

On the morning of August 9th, the celebration of the Churching of the Queen was held. It was again in the small chapel of Westminster Abbey. The occasion marked the first entry of the queen into the church after her pregnancy, and it was preceded by her first confession since her pregnancy was known.

Queen Eleanor went to the confessional with what onlookers thought was more than ordinary gravity. She emerged pale, reaching for her Lady Alice's hand for support. Edmund Rich, the Archbishop of Canterbury, left the booth, his plump face both grim and oddly excited. Confession put upon the priest who heard it the strictest ban against revealing what he heard. But the archbishop sought out King Henry at once.

The gracious ritual at the church door, as the queen made her entry, was delayed for half an hour. Queen Eleanor seemed very much upset. Many thought she must have left her bed too soon, she seemed so ill. At last the doors were opened, and the queen, accompanied by her ladies and the courtiers, passed within.

As she knelt on the altar steps, her back to the nave and the noble onlookers, Archbishop Rich stood over her. The words of blessing came from his mouth with the flatness of rote. The queen trembled so perceptibly that her veil shook. Stranger still, King Henry scowled and strode back and forth across the altar's dais, glancing toward the door, disrupting the archbishop's incantation with his nervous pacing. Even the least astute of Henry's courtiers sensed that something had gone very wrong.

The Earl and Countess of Leicester arrived late. Coming in the rear door of the nave, they entered quietly, not to disturb the ritual in progress at the far end of the chapel.

As soon as he caught sight of them, Henry stopped his pacing and called out, "So! The Earl of Leicester does dare show his face? Here, among decent Christians?" His drooping eye and the corner of his mouth twisted in a bitter grimace. "To think I've loved you as a friend! And you dare face me?"

Archbishop Rich ceased speaking. The queen sank to the altar steps, covering her face with her clasped hands. The courtiers stared at Henry, then turned to look at Simon.

Countess Eleanor looked from her husband to her brother, utterly confused. Henry surely knew that Simon's excommunication had been lifted. Else he could not have served at the baptism.

Simon went pale. His throat closed; he could make no answer. Henry's words – so long expected – seared him. Numbly, he gripped Eleanor's arm, turned and left the chapel. He guided his wife back to the boat landing where the little boat they had hired for the day was waiting. He ordered the boatman to take them back to Winchester House. He had no idea of what to do.

Eleanor sat on the boat's thwart, wringing her hands. "What's come over Henry? Is he mad? What have we done?"

They reached Winchester House, but its gloomy opulence in the August heat was oppressive. The countess sat, wracking her mind for explanations. The nurse brought little Henry to her, but she gestured testily for the child to be taken away. Simon stood by the window, mute and staring at the river.

Soon there was pounding at the door. Royal bailiffs forced their way in past the porter and squire Peter who answered the knocking. The captain of the bailiffs read his orders, "Earl Montfort, by order of the Crown you are evicted from this place. You, your family and possessions are to be gone at once."

"Peter," Simon turned to his squire, "pack as best you can, and return with the countess to Kenilworth." He started toward the door.

"Where are you going!" Eleanor cried.

"I must see Henry!"

"In the name of Heaven don't go to him now! He's out of his mind! He could send you to the Tower! Wait till he comes to his senses," she pleaded.

"I must see him now! I may have no other chance."

"Then I'll go with you!"

"No! Go back to Kenilworth!"

She grasped his hand and said firmly, "I'm going with you."

"I don't want you to witness this!"

"My being there might bring him to his senses. I will not stay here!"

She told the nurse to bring the baby. Then, with little Henry in her arms, grasping the nurse by the wrist and bringing her along as well, she left the house with Simon. Behind them, as Peter, Lady Mary and the servants hurried to pack, the bailiffs tossed the Montfort's traveling chests and sacks into the street.

Simon entered the chapel with his family. Eleanor held little Henry, with the nurse following close behind. The milling, murmuring courtiers fell silent as they saw Simon come in. Leaving Eleanor, the baby and the nurse by the door, he walked forward toward the king.

Henry, seeing him, came down from the dais. The courtiers parted, making an open path between them.

Simon knelt at Henry's feet. He tried to speak, but no words came. Tears filled his eyes.

Henry, his lip curled in hatred, looked down at him. "My faithful friend! My liegeman! Always so ready to serve!" He began laughing bitterly. "It seems there is no limit to your serving!"

Simon, his head bent, whispered, "My lord, I beg forgiveness..."

"Forgiveness!" Henry shouted. "You seduce..." But abruptly he stopped speaking. The lords, the high clerics, all his Court was listening. Already he had said dangerously too much. He needed this heir.

Stifling his rage, banking its fire with all the strength he had, Henry said in a loud voice for all the Court to hear, "You seduced my sister! And when I found it out, against my will I gave her to you to avoid the scandal." Shaking from the strain, he looked about. The queen was crouched by the altar, her face turned away. Archbishop Rich met his searching eyes with an approving nod. Henry drew strength from Rich, and bellowed till the stone walls resounded with his voice. "And, lest her holy vows impede the marriage, you went to Rome! With presents and great promises, you bribed the Roman Court to do what was forbidden!"

The whole assembly broke into confusion. The king seemed to have lost his mind. All this was long well-known and long forgiven, with months of close friendship between the earl and king since then.

Archbishop Rich alone looked on calmly.

Prince Richard, pushing through the crowd, reached Henry. "For God's sake, Henry! What do you mean by this!"

Henry was quaking with emotion. Fending off his brother, he blurted out his accusations for the Court to hear. He beckoned to Archbishop Rich, "The archbishop knows the truth. He warned the Pope! But truth was overcome by Roman greed…"

Tears dripped from Henry's twisted face. He looked down at Simon doubled over at his feet, then looked among the crowd. Thomas of Savoy caught his glance. Gasping for breath, his gaze locked on Thomas, "… and when you failed to pay the money, you were excommunicated…" In confusion, shaking as if a fit were coming on, he looked wildly back to Rich, who opened his cloaked arms to receive him. Embraced in the archbishop's golden cope, Henry sank on Rich's chest, sobbing and raving, "… and to increase your wickedness, you named me as your surety. And I knew nothing! I knew nothing of it!" His last words blurred into convulsive weeping.

The Court burst to loud talk. No one could understand what was happening. Had Henry gone mad?

Simon, his hands covering his face, remained crumpled at the feet of the king and the archbishop. Prince Richard grasped his shoulder, pulling him up to stand, and whispering in his ear, "In the name of Heaven, leave here! For my sister's sake! Go! Before Henry can do more we'll regret."

Staring at Richard, Simon moved mechanically toward the door and went out. The countess, and the nurse holding the baby, hurried after him.

Simon ran to the landing where the little riverboat, hired for the day, was waiting. But as the boatman was about to push off from the dock, Simon realized he could not go back to Winchester House. And bailiffs soon would come for his arrest at Kenilworth. No place in England would be safe. He asked the boatman, "Can you cross the Channel?"

The boatman blanched. "I had 'er out t' Margate onc't, fishin' t' sea."

"Take me to France, and I'll reward you!"

The boatman was a game fellow, and such an offer from an earl came to poor men only in their dreams. "There's a good wind. We have the tide. I don't mind riskin' drownin', m'lord, if you don't."

Eleanor, slowed by her pregnant weight, and dragging the dazed nurse along, reached the landing.

The boatman looked from her to Simon as she gestured to be helped aboard. "What about the ladies and the babe?"

"We're going too!" Eleanor insisted.

Simon looked at his infant son in the nurse's arms, then at his wife, her belly large with their second child. "You'll be safe at Kenilworth. I'll send for you. You're in no danger here."

"You'd save yourself, and leave me to face Henry's madness? It's our marriage he rails against! I'm no safer here than you are!"

"Oh, dear God!" Simon cried, "Cannot my wife and child be spared?" He looked at her pleadingly, "Eleanor, it's not our marriage... God help me! It's not you that Henry accuses me of seducing."

"I don't want to hear this! I won't!" Eleanor covered her ears. Her eyes looked terrified. "This is all madness!"

"Believe me, Eleanor," Simon begged, "it's you I love. Do as I say!"

"I'm going with you! Whatever befalls you, I share." The countess thrust out her hand for the boatman to help her aboard.

The little boat set sail and passed on down the Thames, bearing away the Earl and Countess of Montfort, their baby and the nurse.

Summer's long evening slowly stretched toward night, spreading a golden-pink light on the sea, as the tiny river boat glided swiftly with the wind and tide out from the river's mouth into the open waters of the Channel. The English summer night, lingering in northern twilight, dimly lit the dark sea till clouds gathered in the west. Then the waves grew choppy. The nurse clung to the thwarts, frightened out of her wits, as watery hillocks rose like curious heads bobbing up to peep over the bows.

The Channel's dark volume began to dance and pitch as the wind rose. In the strengthening gusts, the boatman furled the straining sail for it was pressing the bows downward. The tiny vessel wallowed, swayed, then rode up on the water's back, only to dive into the next dark trough. Water rushed over its side as another gleaming mound of sea rolled toward it. With the surge, the boat rose again, then slid down from the crest, filling to the waling. With the next wave, the boat wallowed, sinking beneath its load of passengers.

Simon bailed. The boatman tied the steering oar and bailed. The baby Henry shrieked. Eleanor pressed him to her bosom to keep him warm in the salt spray. Water soaked her robe and swirled about her knees. With the bailing, the river boat rode a little higher, up and up to tip over a surging crest then skim down the wave's slope, only to fill with sea again. Simon and the boatman bailed. The screams of the baby shrilled above the hissing of the wind and spray and the roaring of the sea.

Night darkened the sea and air into a single blackness splashed with phosphorescent foam. Climbing a towering mass of water, the boat heeled and nearly capsized at the crest. Against the shining spume, Simon could see the dark shape of his wife huddled with their child. The prayer of Jonah came to his lips, "Thou hast cast me into the sea. The waters compassed me, yet Thou hast brought up my life from corruption." And he prayed that Heaven grant a miracle to keep the little boat afloat till morning, and to land.

The chill water cavorted like mountains at play, tossing, pulling at the boat as if urging it to join them, to dive and swim free of its human load. Softly, the boat would yield to the water's invitation. Then with a shudder it would be borne up again as by some unseen hand beneath. All night the little vessel tried to loose itself and sink into the dark below. All night it hovered on the surface, lashed with spray and dashed by sheets of foam. But as the yellow haze of dawn pushed darkness from the sky, the rough sea calmed.

The boatman, standing on the waling, set the sail. Searching the horizon in the early light, he could see only water.

Then, as morning grew to its full brightness, a thin line appeared in the east where the glaring blue sky met a dark seashore. By noon the battered little river boat, with its drenched, exhausted passengers, touched land on the Flemish coast.

End: Book I

Book II

THE EXILE

Chapter Seventeen

EXILE
1239

"Is this how my brother comes home? Glorious?" Amaury eyed Simon's salt-stained robe and unshaved chin. "To me it looks more like disgrace. What did you do? Murder somebody?"

"No," Simon replied, his head bent, his voice stifled with shame.

"Yours must be the briefest enjoyment of an earldom ever!"

"Amaury, don't mock me."

"But I will! I suppose you're going to say you haven't got a penny, and I must pay these folk who've fished you from the sea." Amaury waved toward the Thames boatman and the little cluster of Flemish fishermen who had brought Simon and his family down the coast and up the Seine to Montfort l'Amaury. The men loitered by the entrance, behind the countess and the nurse who held the whimpering baby.

Simon kept his gaze averted from his brother's lacerating look. "I'll repay you as I can."

"How do you mean to do that?"

"I can't go back to England. I thought perhaps I could join you." Amaury, as Marshall of France, was preparing to go on crusade to the Holy Land.

You don't expect me to pay your travel expenses to Palestine. You don't even have a horse!"

"I gave my promise to Pope Gregory that I would take the Cross. Believe me, brother, I need the absolution that crusade grants."

"I don't doubt that! But it's hardly my concern. You may stay here. Serve as my steward till I come back, and I'll consider that repayment for what you still owe for the horses that you bought from me. I doubt I'll ever see any other payment."

"Amaury! Please let me go with you!"

"You have no armor. Nothing! Go back to England and equip yourself, if you must go on crusade. I have neither the time nor means to do it for you!"

"I can't go back to England!"

"Very well. Then look after Montfort l'Amaury."

That evening, after bathing and dressing in fresh clothes found for them by Amaury's squire, Simon and Eleanor went to the hall for supper.

A contingent of crusaders was meeting at the castle, assembling under the marshal, before joining with the forces of the counts of Champagne and Barr and the duke of Burgundy.

The tall, narrow, gray stone hall was crammed with trestle tables and benches crowded with men. To Amaury's right, at the table on the dais, sat the guest of honor, a sleekly handsome, dark haired man in his forties: Count Thibaut of Champagne. A large force was assembling at his city of Troyes. Thibaut had come to finish arrangements with Amaury for the transport of supplies.

Eleanor, then Simon, sat to Amaury's left. Loaves had been cut, trencher slices served and the first course was in progress. Everyone ate heartily and talked of the crusade.

"I've levied a duty on spices at the fair, "Thibaut was saying. "The merchants must carry our grain and other supplies to Marseilles for shipment to us in the East. As that's provided, your packhorses can be used at once." So the conversation went, intent and businesslike. Neither Simon nor Eleanor had any part in it.

The high stone vault of the hall was muffled with bright-colored banners that drooped from the shadows down toward the yellow glow of candlelight below. There were banners with the blazons of Beaumesnil, Harcourt, Coucy, Nogent, Vernon, Nonancourt, and many more: Norman families Simon had known since childhood. All had sons going to the East with Amaury. The men were merry, easy in a lifetime of friendship, sparked with the excitement of setting out together for honor and adventure in a distant land. The ancient hall, gloomy and decrepit as a hag, was gay in her borrowed heraldry. Her rough-hewn walls sang with echoes of the men's raised, eager voices.

In the days he had spent traveling from Flanders, Simon had set his hopes on joining this crusade. He sat brooding, picking at his food, half-listening as Amaury and Thibaut made their plans. He had never liked Thibaut. Thibaut called "the poet" for the torrid love poems that, in his youth, he had written to Queen Blanche. Thibaut's much vaunted but chaste passion for the Queen of France always had sent Simon into fits of pique. But now the sight of him, and the gnawing thought of his own particular guilt, made him feel sick.

As the feasters grew raucous with their wine, goliards arrived, students from the University of Paris who earned their living singing bawdy songs. The gaily dressed, be-ribboned students dashed in with their tambourines, their lute and pipe and drum; and the knights welcomed them with a roar of greeting.

Simon took no notice.

The drum rattled to the fast beat of an *estampie*, then slowed to the plaintive heartbeat of a *chanson d'amor*. Then, with a racket from the tambourines, the goliards' sly, salacious verses skipped to a rollicking *gigue*.

Eleanor laughed freely. The knights bellowed with laughter.

Simon picked at the raspberries in front of him, unhearing. He was sunk in his own thoughts. But the words of one lewd song bore in on him. He found himself listening to its refrain.

> Were the world mine
> From the Mere to the Rhine,
> All would I resign
> To have the Queen of England in my arms.

Simon turned deep red and choked on the raspberry he was swallowing.

Amaury, rosy-cheeked with wine, reached past Eleanor and pounded him on the back. "My brother strangles at the mention of love," he laughed to Thibaut. "If it weren't for me, he never would have married!"

Simon stopped coughing and looked at his brother. "What do you mean?"

Amaury was very drunk. He grinned, "Who do you think sent you those notes? And that pretty barge, did it get there by itself?"

Simon looked questioningly at Eleanor.

She looked at him, as perplexed as he at Amaury's remark. "You sent me a note, sealed with your lion seal, bidding me to meet you."

"I sent you no note. I have no lion seal. Only Amaury's seal shows the lion of Montfort. Mine's a hunting portrait."

"You didn't ask me to meet you?"

"I thought you asked me!"

They stared at each other. Then Eleanor burst to laughter and tears at once. "Your brother arranged our meeting?"

"Cupid," Amaury raised his goblet in a salute to himself.

Simon, pale and scowling at his brother, put his arm protectively around his wife." "How dared you do such a thing!"

Thibaut broke in, "Thank him, Simon. Not every brother would have done as much."

Simon cast a withering look at Thibaut.

But Eleanor, wiping away her tears, nodded, "Yes. Indeed! Thank you Amaury!" She turned her gaze to her husband, "I'm so grateful to him. Aren't you?"

Her moist eyes searching his, Simon yielded and said softly, "Yes. I suppose I am."

"A drink to Amaury!" Thibaut announced. The cups all around the hall were filled, and the toast was drunk. Then the goliards went on with their songs.

Simon and Eleanor sat holding hands, their fingers intertwining as they talked and laughed about what each had thought that afternoon when they had met upon the barge. And the talk of the crusade went on around them.

Someone arrived late at the table on the dais. There was a flurry of movement, a shifting to make room as he joined them.

"Well, Piers, you've come after all!" Thibaut greeted him.

"I just arrived. You don't mind if I sit, dusty like this?" the newcomer asked. He was a tall, blond, genial-looking man in a fine but travel-stained riding robe.

"Sit down, and be welcome," Amaury said affably.

Simon looked up from his wife; the smile faded from his lips. The man who had just come was Piers Mauclerc, the count of Brittany. It was Mauclerc who had inherited the two hundred marks debt that Simon had owed Ranulf. It was Mauclerc who sold the debt to the Cahorsine moneylender. Simon suddenly stood up, nearly overturning the trestle table. In his hand he gripped his dining knife. "Mauclerc! I could kill you!"

"Simon! What are you doing here?" the startled Mauclerc's eyebrows raised in astonishment.

"Well you might wonder! Thanks to you I've suffered excommunication! You and your damned Cahorsine moneylender!"

"If it's about your debt to Ranulf, let me explain..."

"I don't want your explanations!" Simon brandished the knife.

Amaury grabbed Simon's arm, "You come to my door in disgrace! And now you threaten my guest, under my own roof?"

The stir at the table on the dais caught the attention of the entire room. Knights turned this way and that on the benches, craning to see what was happening.

"Simon, let him be!" Eleanor pleaded.

Thibaut stood, and forced his way between Mauclerc and Simon. "Piers has taken the Cross. You challenge a man whose life is pledged to God!" Through clenched teeth he hissed, "Did your excommunication so bind you to the service of the Devil?"

Thibaut's words tore through Simon. He let the knife drop. Covering his face with both his hands, he pushed his way from the table on the dais, pushed past the gaping men sitting on the benches and ran out of the hall.

In the castle yard, servants hurried with bowls and salvers from the kitchen sheds. Clusters of soldiers crowded the yard, sitting and squatting on the ground. They talked loudly and cheerily as they ate their suppers. Simon forced his way through them until he reached the gate. From there he ran past the stables of the outer yard, where grooms were packing gear. He ran on down the village's steep, cobbled road, past heaped sacks of provisions piled in mounds against the walls of houses. He ran on until he was alone, beyond the village, at the foot of the hill, out on the dark empty field of the tiltyard.

At the far end of the field the old dummy of the jousting quintain hung on its tall post, its wooden arms outstretched. Simon wandered across the grass and leaned against the quintain's post. Wiping his wet eyes, he muttered, "Lord have mercy on me."

The sky above was clear and black, sparkling with unmindful stars. Reaching up, he gave the quintain's paddle-arms a turn. The grinning dummy swung around, as he looked up at it. "You didn't teach me what I most needed to learn," his voice came softly from the knot of pain in his heart.

The quintain smiled its foolish grin.

"What am I lacking? ...Self governance you say?" Simon let out a bitter laugh and made a bow to the quintain. "There indeed is no excuse! But what do I do now? Stay here? Serve as steward until Amaury returns? And after that? What then?" The words fell like stones at his feet, and his spirit fell with them. He sank down to the grass and cried.

When the tears stopped, he remained a long time kneeling in the grass, weary, all spirit spent. At last he sat back and wiped his face. "Don't think of the future? But what of hope? Of honor? What of my family?" He shook his head, "There is no hope. No honor. Nothing for my family. I've thrown it all away."

He gazed up at the weathered quintain, its arms stretched out against the starry sky. "Everything but faith you say? Heaven, help me," he whispered. Kneeling on the grass, he made the sign of the Cross upon his chest. "My Lord, can you still hear me? I thought to live by faith. But I've failed and failed and failed again. And all I've gained has turned and cut me. I have no pride... no will left. I'm blind. Defiled. Empty. Have mercy on me, Father! Defiled as I am, I am still Yours." He held his arms spread wide. "Do with me what You will."

Chapter Eighteen

THE MESSENGER
1239-1240

AMAURY, HIS KNIGHTS, HIS TRAIN of foot soldiers, servants, pack horses and wagons left Montfort l'Amaury. Simon and Eleanor watched the broad column of the march, and the broader swath of dust it churned, diminish, then disappear beyond the low hills to the east. Then they went back to the castle to begin their life in exile.

Simon sent a letter to his steward, Thomas deMesnil, telling him where to send their clothes and whatever money could be raised. In a few weeks a little convoy came: Lady Mary on her mule, with two packhorses led by the squire Peter. They brought clothes, Simon's armor and a half-barrel of silver pennies: all that remained of the earl's rents.

Lady Mary also brought a letter from deMesnil. It told how the servants had returned to Kenilworth with what they could salvage from the king's bailiffs and street thieves. But they were evicted from there as well. Kenilworth was confiscated by the Crown. Under the steward's lead, the beset band of domestics had withdrawn to Leicester where they were now, so far undisturbed. DeMesnil added that, for as long as he could, he would collect the Leicester rents and send them on to France.

Simon wrote to Bishop Grosseteste, begging him to take his servants under his protection.

The remainder of the summer passed quietly in France with almost all the barony gone on crusade.

Paris was a day's ride east of Montfort l'Amaury. Simon's parting with Queen Blanche had been decisive. It was necessary that, as he was in France again, he present himself at Court at once. He and

Eleanor went to Paris. To his relief, Queen Blanche wasn't present when they were admitted to the great, double-gabled royal hall.

King Louis presided over a nearly empty Court. His almoner was with him, but Louis dismissed him and the few pages and attendants who were present, so that he could greet the earl and countess privately.

Louis, at twenty-six, was tall, large-boned and deep-chested. He wore his straw-blond hair cut chin-length with a fringe across his broad brow. His mouth, a version of the narrow jaw and V-shaped lips that marked his mother's House of Castile for a thousand years, gave him a mildly bemused look. But the steady kindness of his eyes deprived his lips of any hint of irony. This day, Louis wore a plain, close-fitting robe of dark blue wool, belted at the waist with a knotted cord. Though he often wore no emblem of his office, he had a thin gold circlet with four fleurs-de-lis over his hair. It was as close as Louis came, on ordinary days, to dressing regally.

Queen Blanche had raised her son in an unwavering light of faith. He had been taught to look on every act and thought as holy, a service to the Lord. Simon and Louis, as playmates, had been the best of friends, though Simon thought that Louis was too mild. But Louis, with a child's wisdom, perceived his friend's flaws: he saw the stern rigidity of Simon's faith would not fit life. Though as devout as Simon, Louis was more kind. He was to be Saint Louis.

The King of France greeted his friend's return in his usual, perceptive way. He was not at all surprised. He had supposed Simon's unbending will would meet conflict with King Henry. What amazed him was that it had taken nine years.

"Welcome, Earl of Leicester," Louis grinned warmly. "Too much time has past since I last saw you. And I'm glad to meet your wife, the lady for whose love you've shaken Rome." Noting the countess's advanced pregnancy, he added, "I see you've lost no time getting a family."

"This will be our second child," the countess said, proudly placing her hand upon the mound of her belly.

With a little backward counting, Louis realized why Rome had been shaken. Simon's robe of penitential black seemed added confirmation. Louis knew so brittle a nature as Simon's eventually must break. Considering the way in which the rupture struck, he was relieved. A man of Simon's capabilities could have broken far more dangerously. The King of France smiled genially, "Our blessings on your first and second child. May Leicester prosper to support them."

"I fear they can expect nothing from England. I shall not live there again," Simon said bleakly.

"Surely that's not so. Or won't be so for long. From what I've heard, you're not a liegeman whom King Henry can afford to lose."

Putting aside his bantering tone, Louis shifted to the familiar *thou*, used only for menials and the closest friends and family. "Simon, thou art welcome in France. Thou hast my love, unchanged. But so much love have we for you," he pointedly shifted to the distancing royal *we* and *you*, "that we would not have your king find cause for offense, as when you were accused of spying. Though, Heaven be our witness, you have not done it," he laughed. "So long as your liege is owed to King Henry, come to us here only in his service."

It was intended as a generous gesture. If Simon was discouraged, tempted to admit failure, willing to give up his claim to the earldom of Leicester for some place as a pensioned courtier in Paris, Louis would not let him.

"If I renounce King Henry, and offer you my liege?" Simon asked, stunned to see the one door he had hoped might open, shutting in his face.

"I have no earldom to offer you," Louis met his eyes earnestly.

"My father's lands of Toulouse and Foix..."

"We cannot reclaim them from Count Raymond. However much a rebel he once was, he's a loyal subject now."

Simon tried to protest, but Louis would not hear it, "Make your peace with Henry. He has more means to reward your services than I ever will."

A pained laugh came from Simon's lips. "Never again will King Henry wish to reward me for my services."

"I have faith that time will heal whatever is amiss," Louis said confidently. "Until then, risk your fortunes no further by visiting our Court." He dismissed Simon and Eleanor, but as they left he called out after them, "My love goes with thee, Simon. Give King Henry time."

Barred from the crusade, and now from Louis' Court, Simon withdrew to a small chamber in the tower of Montfort l'Amaury. The window of the tower, high above the hilltop, gave a broad view of the fields of Normandy. In the distance tiny specks, the autumn reapers, moved, gathering in the grain-harvest under a vast September sky.

But Simon did not look out of the window. He sat with his face buried in his hands, his mind trying the corners of the labyrinth that was his life. The turns all came to the same burning wall, and the wall seared him with shame.

The countess sought herbs that would cure melancholy, but they had no power over melancholy with such real and ample cause. And her tender care only shamed Simon the more. Day after day, squire Peter sat on the floor outside his master's closed door, talking loudly to the servants as they passed so that they couldn't hear his master weeping.

In late September, Eleanor gave birth to another boy. Simon was called to see his second son. He came, his eyes red, his face haggard, and stood by the bedchamber door. Eleanor held up the newborn child for him to see. She smiled encouragingly, "Shall we name him Simon?"

Simon shook his head, turned away and went back to his chamber.

The boy was christened Simon. As much as his brother Henry was a good and quiet child, the infant Simon was the opposite. He cried and pinched his nurse's breast and would not be consoled. It was as if the strained life into which he had arrived poisoned his very being.

Autumn turned to frigid winter. The expanse out Simon's window danced with snowflakes, then cleared to a sweep of white under a brilliantly blue sky. But now the window's wooden shutter was closed tight against the cold. Peter kept a brazier stoked to warm the little room. The piercing shrieks of the baby rang through the stone chambers. Simon, gaunt and listless, sat with his face hidden in his hands. Time passed for him in a continuum of pain. His thoughts, too agonizing, sank into a deep, mindless and endless sorrow: such might be the true quality of Hell. To burn would be to feel, an ecstasy compared to this rigid torment – numb, featureless and frozen as the snowbound world outside.

One afternoon a horn's notes sounded on the icy air. With the lords gone, a horn was as unlikely in that snowy landscape as a bluebird's call. Simon rose stiffly from his chair and opened the shutter. A frigid breeze blew in. Across the whiteness below, the figure of a lone knight was coming at a gallop from the Paris road.

"Peter!" Simon cried, roused from his lethargy.

In an instant the squire came from where he was sitting just outside the door. He peered out the window for his weak sighted master. "A knight with a red cross upon his cloak," he reported. "His horse's mantle is red with a saltire in gold."

Simon knew the heraldries of Norman France as surely as he knew his alphabet and Latin. "Harcourt," he muttered, puzzled. "Back from Palestine? "

The sight of Harcourt lit a spark. For Simon in his depression, movement had been like wading through a wall of snow. But Harcourt's return ignited a glow, and the glow hollowed through his frozen soul until it lit a flame of curiosity he was surprised he still possessed. His movements quickened. "Peter, bring my washbasin. I must dress."

By the time Simon had washed, dressed and come down to the hall, everyone at Montfort l'Amaury knew Harcourt was arriving. Eleanor ordered the cook to prepare a small feast for their visitor. The table and three chairs were arranged on the dais. Lady Mary saw to it that the courtyard by the castle door was swept.

Then Harcourt's horse's hooves were heard clattering upon the paving stones.

A moment later, before a brazier heaped with burning logs, squire Peter helped John Harcourt shed his snow-caked cloak emblazoned with the red cross of crusade. Harcourt bowed to Countess Eleanor, then warmly pressed Simon's hand. They had been good friends when they were boys. He fetched a parchment from the blousing of his robe. "I bring a letter from Amaury." But he gave the parchment to Eleanor, not Simon.

As the countess unfolded the letter and began to read it, Simon burst out in annoyance, "My brother holds me in such contempt that he doesn't write to me, but only to my wife?"

"Simon, the crusade is lost!" Eleanor looked up from her reading, her eyes were wide with shock. "Amaury is in a Saracen prison. He asks me to beg Henry for an army to rescue them."

Simon took the letter from his wife, scanned it, then turned to Harcourt. "How can this be?"

"We had fools for leaders," Harcourt said curtly.

"Thibaut?"

"For all you may not like him, Simon, Thibaut is no fool. The Duke of Burgundy was chief in our undoing."

Peter brought a stoup of wine, and Mary brought three goblets. Harcourt, Eleanor and Simon sat at the table. After the wine was poured, Peter and Mary lingered. Amaury's servants gathered in the shadows of the hall to hear what had become of their master.

Harcourt took a sip of wine and began his tale.

"We reached Acre at the end of September and held meeting with the lords of Outremere, as they call our Christian kingdom there. It was decided we should strike Egypt first. Then, with the south and west in our control, we would march north upon Damascus. The Outremerines, the Orders of the Templars, the Hospitallers and Teutonic Knights – everyone was in agreement. Even the time was propitious. The Saracens were fighting a civil war. The Sultan Ayub's forces were divided, attacked by Ayub's uncle, Ismail, who had usurped Damascus. Ayub could spare few men to counter us."

Harcourt took a long drink from his goblet. Lady Mary refilled it, and he went on. "Food was scarce along our march. There'd been a drought. A drought in that land is parched indeed! Supply gave us concern. When we were three days march from Acre, Piers

Mauclerc learned of a caravan passing just to the east of us. With his friends he went out secretly. No one knew till he was gone, or I suppose we would have stopped him."

Simon frowned, "Mauclerc..."

"The caravan turned out to be immense and heavily guarded. But by a miracle of Our Lord, Mauclerc caught them so much by surprise that, after only a brief fight, the guards all fled! Piers' hardest task was driving back so many fine horses and treasure-laden camels to our camp. Was ever a knight so blessed!"

Simon's scowl could have melted stone.

"These were the sultan's soldiers and supplies?" the countess asked.

"No, no. A caravan of merchants, unarmed once their guard took flight."

The countess glanced to her husband, confused that crusaders attacked and plundered disarmed men. Simon was displeased with the tale on many counts.

Harcourt, oblivious of their looks, went on, "Everyone envied Mauclerc. Our courage was fired by his luck. We all prayed for a chance at such glory. But it surely was the Devil who heard our prayers."

Harcourt drank more wine and held out his goblet for Mary to refill it again. Clearly his nerves needed fueling for the telling of his story.

"A few days later one of our Arab scouts came to the Count of Bar and told him that the enemy was sighted coming out of Egypt. Ayub's army, he swore, was just a thousand men. The count told the Duke of Burgundy, your brother Amaury and your cousin, the Outremerine lord Philip de Montfort. Beyond those few, they kept their news secret, believing that their own hundred knights and thousand foot soldiers could destroy Ayub. They would gain a brilliant victory and outshine Mauclerc's glory.

"They left our camp late at night, but a soldier on watch told Thibaut of their movements. Thibaut rushed from his tent to stop them. He argued with the duke that the scout's report might be a trap."

Harcourt drank very deeply. "Philip de Montfort scoffed at him, claiming that he knew the sultan's forces, and that the scout spoke truly. The duke, the Count of Bar and Amaury trusted him. Philip is native to the land and should have known. But Thibaut was the wiser.

"When the duke and his friends left with their men, Thibaut roused the rest of us to march at once to Ascalon. It's a ruined place, but its broken walls offered the nearest shelter. By morning we reached Ascalon and built a barricade as best we could. Thibaut had told the duke he would go there, and no further, till our forces reunited."

Harcourt's voice lowered, his face was flushed with wine. "We had barely set up camp at Ascalon when the Outremerine lords came dashing in. The story they told was piteous! And worse still was the account that Amaury sent by messenger to Thibaut.

"Much of the night, the duke and his followers rode along the sands of Gaza's beach. Just before dawn the guide told them to halt. He said the sultan's army was near. They should rest for the remainder of the night in the soft dunes. They would have battle in the morning. He did not say that the sultan had five times the thousand men he claimed, and that they lay in wait just on the dunes' far side. The duke had his men make camp and sleep within the very lion's jaws.

"The sultan's archers surrounded our men as they slept, leaving only the sea at their backs. The Outremerine lord Odo waked and saw what was happening. He roused the duke, crying for retreat at once.

"But from that place there was no swift retreat. The duke's horn sounded, and was answered by a flight of Ayub's arrows. Drowsy foot soldiers, waked from their sound sleep, stumbled in the soft sand and fell down, struck dead by Saracen shafts. A few knights reached their horses and mounted. But in the dunes the heavy destriers pawed sand deep to their bellies. They wallowed, easy targets for the Saracen's bows. Their riders fell, bristling with arrows. The cries of dying men, the neighing of wounded horses, was answered by the hiss of an unceasing rain of arrows.

"The Outremerines whipped their light Arab ponies from the dunes and dashed away to save their lives. But your brother Amaury the Marshall, the duke and the Count of Bar stood ground with their men.

"They were forced into the sea. Waves, red with blood, broke round their legs. Volley after volley of Saracen shafts drove through them. They brandished their swords, but the enemy was far out of reach. The Count of Bar sank to his knees, his body pierced by more than twenty shafts before he fell and reddened sea-foam covered him. Your brother was pierced in the thigh and shoulder.

"When the archers' work was done, the Arab cavalry came swiftly and cut down all who could yet lift a sword. Every Christian who survived was taken to the Sultan's prison at Damietta."

There was silence when Harcourt ceased his tale. Then a soft murmuring came from the shadows where Amaury's servants stood. Mary sent the servants to the kitchen to bring supper.

Softly, Simon asked Harcourt, "What does Thibaut mean to do?"

"He doesn't dare attack Ayub, with his reduced forces. Another defeat would mean the end of rescuing the prisoners. I've applied to King Louis. But most of France's lords who could bear arms were with us." Harcourt turned to Eleanor, "Our hope now lies in England."

Chapter Nineteen

THE CROSS
1240

IN THE VILLAGE CHURCH OF Montfort l'Amaury, Simon pledged himself to the crusade. Eleanor sewed the red cross of crusade on his black robes.

Simon was transformed. His weeping and his lethargy were ended. Vitality flowed back as if the sun shone, melting winter's paralyzing chill. He had no doubt what he must do. Nor did he lack spirit to do it.

Weighing the risks of returning to England to arm, he wrote to the knights of the Honour of Leicester, asking them to join him on crusade. He hardly knew them. It was not a war declared by England's king, and his own claim to any leadership at all, exiled as he was, was very doubtful. He had small hope they would respond. To his amazement, nearly all the Leicestermen returned pledges to join him. As King Henry's foreign friend, Simon had been hated. But Englishmen now saw him as a martyr, the victim of their mad king's whim.

Eleanor went to England, directly to King Henry's Court with Amaury's plea.

Westminster Hall was dismal. Simon had suffered, but Henry suffered too. His face had a dull, ashen pallor. The droop of his left eyelid was draped with dark creases. His mouth hung slack as if in a constant sneer.

Queen Eleanor, beside him, was beautiful as ever but seemed worn with cares.

There were few courtiers. Prince Richard talked with the clerk Mansel. Several bishops, Walter Cantaloup among them, had brought a petition.

The Countess Montfort knelt on the dais steps as Mansel read Amaury's letter aloud.

When the clerk finished, King Henry was quiet for some moments then gave his reply in careful, measured tones. "We see no need to aid these French knights. Outremere is a kingdom of our ally the Emperor Frederic. This crusade went without his consent, and in disregard of his wishes. We'll not invade his lands as well."

"Henry, there is deeper matter here than politics!" Richard burst out. He seemed more tense, more florid than when Eleanor had seen him last. "It is our duty as Christians to aid our brothers who fought to free Jerusalem. That the emperor lost the Holy City, and now fails to give aid to those who would recover it, is a shame to him!"

"Richard, stay out of this!" Henry snapped.

"I won't say what you ought to do with England's armies, brother. But neither shall I be stopped from doing what is right!" Richard retorted. "Before the Court, and with God as my witness, I pledge myself to the Cross. I will go to Palestine."

Eleanor grasped Richard's hand and kissed it. "Bless you, brother!"

Henry glared, furious. But the oath was out and there was nothing he could do if Richard persisted. "You're a new man, Richard? Bent upon heroics?" he asked acidly. "We cannot let you go alone. England can ill afford another Richard-with-a-lion's-heart wandering in foreign lands and being seized for ransom. We give you leave to raise an army, but," he added meanly, "you shall do it at your own expense entirely."

Eleanor looked from one brother to the other. She bowed her head to Henry, "May I beg one more favor? That you grant my husband peace, that he may come to England to arm for Palestine?"

Henry scowled. But before he could answer, Bishop Walter Cantaloup spoke up loudly. "Surely, good king, you would not hamper a knight pledged to the cross?"

Henry glared at the bishop, but waved his hand in grudging permission.

The queen watched the proceedings silently. After the countess left, Henry leaned toward her and muttered, "I suppose you're pleased he's coming back."

"My lord," the queen whispered, "when will you cease to believe the lies spread by those who would have Richard on the throne?"

At Montfort l'Amaury again, Eleanor told her husband of King Henry's promise of peace to him for the crusade. But Simon knew that any offer of peace from Henry would be very fragile. Cautiously, he wrote to Richard, offering to place himself and his knights of Leicester under the protection of the prince's crusade. The prince accepted. Simon then wrote to Peter de Montfort, his cousin in Gloucestershire, asking him to meet him with an armed escort.

In March Simon landed secretly on England's coast. Peter de Montfort, with a well-armed band of Leicestermen, greeted him on the rocky shore with his own destrier, sent on by deMesnil from Leicester. Surrounded by his bodyguard, Simon rode to Windsor where King Henry was holding Court.

The mood of the Court was as oppressive as when Eleanor had visited. Courtiers spoke in hushed tones, fearful of being noticed. Henry lashed out at everyone viciously and unexpectedly. Even the bailiffs moved as if the floor might gape and swallow them.

Simon entered the hall with his cousin Peter and his guard, all dressed in chain mail, with swords at their sides and the red cross of crusade sewn on their surcoats.

"You come into my presence armed?" King Henry asked, his tone laden with sarcasm.

Simon knelt before the royal dais. "We come armed for Christ, to tell my lord King Henry that the earl and knights of Leicester have pledged themselves to Prince Richard's crusade." He bent his head, "We come to beg your blessing."

"Is our blessing of worth to you, Montfort?" Henry asked caustically.

"Though I may be your most unworthy subject," Simon bowed his head lower, "yet you are my king."

Henry looked at him coldly.

But the queen stood up and in a clear voice said, "The blessing of the Crown be upon you, Earl Montfort. Go in peace, and may your life be spared in the Holy Land."

The Court was tense. The queen looked defiantly at Henry.

Simon saw that staying any longer would be perilous. He arose, bowed and with his guard left quickly.

As Simon reached the stable-yard, there was the sound of running feet behind him. A page caught up and placed something into his hand. Out of breath, the boy recited, "My lady the queen asks that you take this to the Holy Land, to have it blessed at the Holy Sepulcher. She prays you bring it back to her for the salvation of her soul."

Simon looked at the object in his hand. It was a small gold cross. He said softly, "Tell your lady that I will. And I pray for her redemption, as I pray for my own."

While his liege knights were arming, Simon went to Leicester to raise what funds he could for his expenses on crusade. Whether the holding was still his or not, he sold the remaining forest lands of Leicester's chase to the Knights Hospitallers, getting a bill of credit for a thousand marks, to be paid to him at the Hospital at Acre, in Palestine.

As Earl of Leicester, he was commander of the knights of the Honour of Leicester, but he had as yet no knowledge of what combat skills his liegemen might possess. To see how bold and deft, or how ill-suited for warfare, they might be, he announced that he would hold a tournament at his fief of Ashby de la Zouche, where a broad field made a ready jousting ground.

Word of the tourney spread all over England. Not only the Leicestermen, but knights from as far as Northumberland and Devonshire came to display their prowess before the Earl Montfort, the hero of the wars in Wales. The earl's abuse and exile by King Henry only stoked their ardor. Tents and pennants in bold colors bloomed on Ashby's fallow field and, when that space was filled, lined the road's wayside as well.

Henry's increasingly erratic rule had angered all of England, But no one had suffered more publicly and seemingly unjustly than the Earl Montfort. A spirit of revolt was rising, and Simon had become its signal martyr, his name a watchword for outrage at King Henry. Men flocked to Ashby to defy the king.

Simon was amazed so many came. As he sat with deMesnil on the raised platform of the viewing stand, watching the tourney, his steward explained to him, "They see King Henry as unjust, and you, my lord, his most outrageous victim."

Simon peered thoughtfully at the contenders battling on the field. Finally he sighed, "So be it. I care not what they think, so long as they will fight Ayub." With a holy purpose as his focus, all else now seemed irrelevant. That Heaven had seen fit to grant his prayer to serve, and now gave him an army, seemed an act of God that set all rationality aside.

There were jousts and hand-to-hand combat with swords, both mounted and on foot. Many were the men who left the field with cuts and bruises. The less skilled were winnowed away. In the main, the Leicestermen did well. The best of the strangers joined their ranks. What the forming company of knights held in common was contempt for King Henry, and a glowing notion of the Earl Montfort. These men would become the core of Simon's loyal followers: in the East and for decades to come.

That night, after the tourney there were bonfires, drinking and a feast. Around the blazing fires there was much discussion of the king's ill treatment of the earl. John Botevelyn, a knight of the Leicester Honour, told how even the flag of Leicester had been confiscated by the Crown. Consternation burst into loud shouts against King Henry.

"Down with Henry! We must have a flag!" the knight of the Leicester fief of Ivanhoe bellowed.

Thinking quickly in the storm that he had roused, Botevelyn offered, "I know where we can find a flag. One hangs in Hinkley church."

Ivanhoe and several sturdy, drunken volunteers came forth to go and seize it.

Botevelyn led his little band at a wild gallop cross-country to Hinkley, where they broke down the church door. Indeed a flag hung in the nave, an ancient flag of Hinkley, moldering and full of gaping holes. They took it anyway. Proudly, Botevelyn presented the prize to the Earl Montfort.

The rag was piteous. Simon frowned.

"My lord," Botevelyn urged, "we must have a flag. All the better that it has no virtue in itself. Our victories will make it glorious."

Simon laughed warmly at Botevelyn's spirit, and appointed him the bearer of the ragged cloth.

In May Richard's army departed. The prince would take ship from Provence to Palestine. Queen Eleanor had smoothed matters with King Henry by having Richard's army act as guard for the safe conduct of presents to her mother at Aix, a task that Henry could not well refuse.

The Leicester knights, not ready yet, would travel separately to Palestine by way of the port of Brindisi, in Italy. At Prince Richard's request, the Emperor Frederic had given the crusade his blessing and his best harbor for embarkation to the East.

Simon attended Richard's leave-taking with the other onlookers. King Henry showed his disapproval by bidding his brother farewell privately and not appearing on the quay. There was an elite gathering nonetheless, a crowd composed of England's highest lords, both leaving with the prince and bidding him farewell.

The Archbishop of Canterbury, Edmund Rich, was there. He urged in public what he clearly had pled often to the prince alone. "You're abandoning us, Richard. The Cross has need of you, but England has need also. With you gone, our land is like a vineyard with no wall. Every passing stranger will be free to pick the fruits of English toil."

The prince rested his arm fondly on Rich's shoulder, but said loudly for everyone to hear, "Even if I had not taken the Cross, I would leave now. It's supposed that I can stop the wrongs that

England suffers. *But you know I cannot.*" His words had a sad ring, and a freight of meaning.

Observing the faces near him, Simon saw the lords' expressions tense, bitter with anger and unstrung with disappointment. He saw what lay beneath the prince's words: Richard was refusing to support the overthrow of Henry. With Richard gone, the rebel lords would have no one to champion. It was the clearest proof of Richard's loyalty. England was at the verge of civil war.

The prince's ships set sail. The lords and clerics standing on the quay watched as though their hearts were drawn to tender threads across the water as their one hope against their king left them, and the white flock of his sails grew small across the dark waves of the Channel.

Two months later, Simon and his Leicestermen departed from England. The countess and the Montfort children would leave Montfort l'Amaury and join them in Paris, then stay at the emperor's castle at Brindisi, as Simon and his army went on to Palestine.

Chapter Twenty

OUTREMERE
1240

ACRE WAS DRY AND DUSTY beneath its blaze of sun. Little by little, the starkness of the East impressed the traveler: the whitened houses of the Greek Islands, the pale earth of Cyprus. Yet the absolute sky, dust and sea of the Holy Land came as a shock. On seeing Palestine for the first time, the Emperor Frederic had remarked, "If this is God's Promised Land, He hasn't seen my Sicily."

To arrive at Outremere was to wish that one were home again, to see a brook, a meadow, a voluptuous green tree.

Simon debarked at Acre on October 13th, just three days after Richard had arrived. Outremere was in confusion. The Outremerine lords, descendants of crusaders settled for a hundred years in Palestine, had joined Thibaut and the Templars in making treaty with Ismail, the usurper in Damascus. But the Hospitallers had played off the Arab civil war, making a separate treaty with Ayub, and gaining the release of the prisoners. Thibaut changed his allegiance to support the Hospitallers' pact; and most of the prisoners, Amaury among them, were set free.

The Templars and the Outremerines considered Thibaut's shift as treachery. Rather than face their fury, Thibaut left at once for France. Most of the rescued men left with him. Amaury was gone, and the immediate goal of the crusade was met, before Richard and Simon landed.

But the Holy City was still held by Ayub. And the Christian factions of Palestine were split and arguing among themselves. All Outremere, except the emperor's own Order of Teutonic Knights and his appointed governor Filangieri, was in rebellion against the empire. The Outremerine lords held that Frederic wrongly claimed the kingship for himself, from the regency he held for his son Conrad, the child of his deceased wife Yolanda, Queen of Jerusalem.

Though the Templars, Hospitallers and Outremerines all saw Frederic as a common enemy, the result of Thibaut's treaty was that the Hospitallers were split off from their league.

When Prince Richard wrote to Frederic asking his permission for the crusade, the emperor had agreed, making one stipulation. The prince was to bring Outremere back to submission to the empire. With the Holy City to be won, and peace to be made among the Christian factions, Richard's crusade did not lack for work.

As his knights, their servants, horses and provisions came ashore, Simon went to the Palace of Acre to announce his arrival. The buff stone hall was teeming with sun-browned men, shouting, glaring fiercely and gesturing like angry barterers in a bazaar. Templars in their long white robes, Teutonic Knights in black emblazoned with a white cross, Hospitallers in white robes crossed in red, magnates of the Acre Commune and lords of Outremere in Arab headdress, all furiously bellowed at each other. The din was deafening.

Richard stood on the dais with a few familiar English faces gathered around him as, against the noise, he tried to shape a plan for his crusade. The tight furrow of his brow eased when he saw Simon coming toward him through the crowd.

Richard had heartily disliked Simon when he was Henry's foreign friend. But now the sight of him in Acre was most welcome to the prince. The Montfort family had branches everywhere. It was Simon's cousin Philip de Montfort who was leader of the rebel lords of Outremere. Richard saw Simon as the very mediator he needed.

"Your brother is on his way home with Thibaut," the prince told Simon, shouting to be heard. "A few prisoners are still held by Ayub. We're marching south toward Jaffa tomorrow, to try for their release and the return of Jerusalem. Don't suppose you've come too late. You're just in time."

"In time to join this snake pit?" Simon asked, looking around the hall. "I thought Acre was Christian. This seems to be the tribe of Ishmael, every man's hand raised against every other man."

Richard laughed dryly. "Actually there are factions: five of them. Six if we're included. They're just all mixed together at the moment."

So that he needn't shout, he showed Simon out onto a terrace that overlooked the harbor. In the relative quiet of the terrace he outlined recent events, cursing Thibaut roundly for the mess that he had left behind.

"What we must do is force Ayub to ratify our treaty with Ismail in Damascus. That will reconcile the Hospitallers, the Templars and the Outremerine lords. But the rift between the emperor and Outremere will take more care. I'm looking to you to deal with that. Your cousin is the arch-fomenter of the troubles. I want you to work from within his league for peace."

Simon winced at the duplicitous commission. "I've never met Philip, I've no idea what sort of man he is. Is he in Acre?"

Richard went back to the hall's doorway and pointed. "He's right there. The large blond man dressed in purple."

Simon laughed, "It's a wise man who recognizes his own kin. He must take after his mother's side of the family."

"I count on you in this," Richard pressed. "And remember, we march south in the morning."

Simon made his way through the tumultuous throng to reach Philip. Though the Outremerine was his father's brother's son, he felt an aversion to him, the innate distaste he felt for any man who plotted against his king. And he was ill impressed with Philip's bad counsel and his flight from the debacle in Gaza. But Richard had come far to rescue Amaury. Simon felt it only fair to try to do as the prince asked, even if it meant consorting with rebel cousins.

"Greetings, Philip," Simon bowed. "I'm you cousin, Simon de Montfort."

Philip's broad face beamed in a bearish grin. "Simon! We've just seen Amaury off, and now you're here!" His gravelly voice was warm and garrulous over the noise around him. His Outremerine accent had a disarming ease. "Come to rescue your brother I suppose. Came with Richard? Where've you been?"

"I only just arrived. My men are still debarking."

"When you get them billeted, come out to supper. We're at Toron, ten miles north on the inland road. You'll see Montfort Castle half way there. We sold it to the Teuton Knights a few years back, and live in town now. The Teutons call it 'Starkenberg'," he wrinkled his blunt nose. "It's still Montfort to me."

That evening, when his knights' tents were pitched among the olive groves on the outskirts of Acre and all was arranged for the morning march, Simon with Botevelyn and Peter de Montfort, rode out to Toron to keep Philip's invitation.

Philip de Montfort was one of the richest lords of Outremere. He owned sugar cane plantations and two factories, in Acre and in Tyre, where sugar was refined into white, cone-shaped loaves for export to France. His Toron house was grand and airy, columned in the Persian style with porticoes and cloisters. It was not unlike the emperor's Roman villa, but here the Orient was genuine. And, unlike in Rome, it was chaste, though lavish in its luxury. Its decoration was as far from Rome's licentiousness as pure, abstract forms could be from lurid heathen art. Burly, blond Philip, a perfect Norman in his stature and with his flaxen hair, seemed odd in this exotic place, but he was born to it.

Seated on an ornate chair inlaid with ivory, Philip received his guests in his Moorish hall. The room's walls and floor were coruscated with designs of stars and triangles on tiles glazed in blue and white. At the center of the room a square pool sent a fountain of thin-streaming water up to cool the hot, dry air. The coffered ceiling was deep-cut and gilded in an intricate network of spangles interlocking in a marvelous geometry. From the boss at the center of each coffer hung a lamp, its oil scented with civet. Six lamps shed six regions of light. Beyond the lamps' glow, silvery moonlight poured through shutters of sandalwood pierced with flowery tracery. The moon cast a lacy palimpsest of light and shade upon the tiles' blue patterning. Hot breezes through the shutters bore a spicy odor, adding pungence to the oil lamps' sweet perfume.

When Simon arrived, in addition to Philip there were three men present, sitting upon the floor on satin cushions. They were John, Lord of Arsuf; Balian of Ibelin, the Lord of Beirut; and Peter de Vielle Bride, the Master of the Templars in Palestine. It was the core of the rebellion against Frederic. But to the eyes of Simon and his Englishmen, the meeting looked more strange than sinister. After the fashion of Outremere, the sturdy men all wore caftans of dainty, flowered silk.

Simon introduced his cousin Peter de Montfort and his flag-bearer Botevelyn.

Philip, delighted to find yet another kinsman in Peter, explained that Balian and John were his cousins, sons of the John known as "the old Lord of Beirut." John and Helvis, Philip's mother, were the offspring of the great crusader, Balian of Ibelin. In Outremere, introductions often brought on genealogies, for ancestry was politics.

Philip summoned his steward, an elegant, turbaned Ethiopian as black as ebony. He came in bearing caftans for the newly arrived guests, as a courtesy of the house.

In the chamber where they changed their clothes, Peter held up the delicate silk garment embroidered with carnations and butterflies, before pulling it over his head. "I should bring one of these to my wife. If this is what the men here wear, what do women wear?"

"Nothing at all I'm told," Botevelyn, who had been to the East before, replied.

"What do you mean, 'you're told?'" Peter asked.

"You never see 'em. Not the better sort at any rate."

"And the others?"

The expert on the East rolled his eyes, "They don't wear anything either."

When they were dressed in their flowery garments, the three were led back to the hall. Philip had left his chair for a cushion on the floor with his guests.

Supper was served in Moorish fashion, on a pile of carpets rather than a table. Each course was offered in huge bowls of pale green Chinese celadon, a precaution of the host, for it was believed in Outremere that poison would crack celadon. Everyone helped himself from the communal dishes, using his own jeweled dagger to spear his food, or simply using his fingers. Napkins and finger-bowls of rose water were given to each guest.

The feast was pungent, heavily spiced, and every course was mutton. Each looked different but, to Simon, they all tasted the same. Happily, between each course the specialty of Palestine was served: sherbet. The sherbets were made of snow brought by swift camels from Mount Hermon and flavored with orange or lemon juice. No lord of Outremere would dine without his sherbets, or would drink his lemonade without it being packed with ice.

Not long after the feast began, Philip turned to Simon, apologetic in his blunt way. "This about your brother being captured. I'm really sorry it happened, but there was nothing we could do. The damned Arabs were everywhere!" His easy dialect and earnest manner were disarming. "We got out and saved our skins. You must hold that against us. But if Ayub had taken us, it wouldn't have been a stay in prison. It would've been the end of Outremere. We've got our families to look out for. Crusaders come and go – now don't take this amiss – but we live here!"

Simon nodded. He found his cousin's politics distasteful, but he did not think Philip was a coward.

Philip grinned, cuffing Simon's shoulder in a friendly, bearish way. "You leave Acre with Richard tomorrow?"

"Yes."

"Good! You'll let us know what he's doing with his friends the Hospitallers."

The words took Simon aback. Philip's outspoken manner was as odd to him as were his flowery robes. The Outremerine's quick assumption that he would be his ally truly astonished him. His oath of liege bound him closer to Richard than did his blood tie with Philip. But, as Prince Richard already had learned, in Outremere the bond of family came first. Philip assumed his cousin would be on his side.

"The prince is going to try to force Ayub to recognize the treaty that you've made with Ismail," Simon explained, though he was sure they knew already what Richard intended.

"That's what he says. I'll believe it when I see it!" Balian's tone was surly.

"Richard's a man of honor," Simon objected.

"So was Thibaut. So was Filangieri. So is everybody," retorted the grim Balian.

"Was Filangieri at the Council today?" Simon carefully diverted the talk from Prince Richard.

"Filangieri's cooped in Tyre. He dares not stick his nose out of his gates, for fear of us," John of Arsuf replied. "It's his fault we lost Jerusalem! He's the emperor's toady, but he didn't rebuild the city's walls. Ayub just rode right in."

Simon was shocked. "Does the emperor know this?"

"Nobody across the sea can rule a country that's constantly at war," Philip said bitterly. "The Holy Land is our responsibility!" He tapped his broad chest. "Simon, I tell you, what we have to do is put Queen Alice of Jerusalem back on the throne. Then we can defend this country the way we see fit! Palestine's our homeland. We know better how to keep it than somebody who sits off in Italy or Germany, fancying that he's a Roman emperor!"

Simon was ever more amazed at Philip's clumsy candidness. "Queen Alice is the great-grandmother of Prince Conrad. She's quite old, is she not?"

"She's one of us. And a fine lady!" Balian said defensively.

"What do you plan to do about Filangieri?" Simon asked.

"Let the dog cringe at Tyre," Peter the Templar spoke in crisp, courtly French untainted by the Outremerine accent. "So long as he doesn't interfere with us, we won't invite Frederic's attack by bloodying our hands with his pathetic governor."

"What worries us is Richard," John put in. "What kind of treaty will he make with Ayub? It wouldn't be the first time crusaders traded our lands for some undefendable arrangement for Jerusalem, then went home claiming that they'd 'won the Holy City,' leaving us to fight it out."

"Why don't you go with Richard and take part in the negotiations?" Simon asked.

"You saw today what happens when we get together with the Hospitallers," Philip replied. "Richard thinks of us as enemies already, because of his alliance with the emperor. But you're close to him. You could present our side, without the Hospitallers meddling."

Simon found himself thrust squarely in the role that Richard had commissioned him to seek. But he was ashamed to return Philip's blunt honesty with duplicity. "You've been so forthright with me, I must be equally with you. I'll do all I can with Richard to secure the safety of your borders. Yet, though I see the justness of your grievances, loose-ruled as you are by the emperor from Italy, I will not work for the overthrow of his rights. As for placing Queen Alice on the throne, I will resist you in it if it comes to that."

Philip smiled, disappointed. "You're a good man, cousin. We appreciate your speaking your mind. And we'll be glad of your help with Richard. Just give us time. You'll see that we're right."

The remainder of the evening was spent with maps and talk of strategies against Ayub, the ideal borders for defense, and which castles were most needed. The Outremerines, for all their easy-seeming ways, were masters of military strategy. In their hundred years in a hostile land, they had learned every means by which a few armed men could dominate.

Simon listened to them closely, fascinated. He recognized their skills and meant to learn all that he could from them. In comparison, what he had learned from Louis' military tutors dwindled to archaic simplicity.

When the conference was done, Peter de Vielle Bride offered to ride back to Acre with Simon. Aloof towards most men outside of his Order, he respected Simon, thought he could be useful and, in his own peculiar way, he was attracted to him. "Have you ever ridden a dromedary?" the Templar asked.

"Is it like a camel?" Simon recalled the sorry creature the emperor had given to King Henry and the shaggy beasts of burden he had seen that day on the streets of Acre.

"It is a finely bred riding-camel. Riding a good dromedary is like sitting on a hilltop, and sailing through the air at the same time. Fastest animal I know. I have mine here, and I've just bought a superb one from Philip. You may ride her back to Acre if you wish."

"I accept the offer," Simon grinned gamely.

Their horses and the two dromedaries were brought to the villa's courtyard. Simon gave his horse to Botevelyn to lead back to camp and went to inspect his exotic mount. In the moonlight, the sleekly groomed animal had the pallid color of an oyster. She looked down her nose disdainfully at him.

"Ugly thing," Simon observed. "And I don't care much for its expression. How do I mount it?"

"She'll bow to you. Place your foot on her neck and climb up." The Templar uttered a syllable in Arabic and the animal obediently dropped to her knees. Simon clambered up. With a lurch, the dromedary stood again. Then Simon and the Templar, on their tall mounts, were gliding through the villa's gate.

"No point in trying to put your legs around her. You sit cross-legged on top like this. The skill is all in the balance," the Templar prompted.

They shuffled through the streets of Toron easily. But as they passed the city gate, the Templar gave another brief command, and both the dromedaries broke into a ragged trot. Simon was bounced mercilessly. He was amazed to find that, each time he came down, the beast was still beneath him. Disgusted with the thumping she was getting, the dromedary hurled her legs out to a wide, swift run, taking Simon off across the desert in the dark.

The next morning, Peter de Montfort found Simon soundly over-sleeping in his tent. "How was your ride?" he grinned as he poked his cousin awake.

Simon opened his eyes reluctantly. "Never accept the offer of a dromedary," he grumbled. He had been thrown, and had to walk the animal to Acre, returning her to the highly amused Templar just before dawn.

Simon's Leicester knights assembled with Richard's troops outside the walls of Acre and the crusade began its march. Simon rode with Richard, reporting on his meeting with the lords.

"So you're already the appointed spokesman for the interests of Outremere?" Richard smiled cynically. "You certainly have a skill for gaining others' confidence."

Simon was stung. "It's not my skill, but their despair of an equal hearing that made them quick to accept me. And if we are to do anything of lasting value here, we'd do well to embrace their plan for Palestine's defense. They've lived their entire lives here in the midst of war. They know the problems of terrain and military tactics better than anyone else could."

"Your point is made," Richard said placatingly, as Simon seemed quite heated. "The Jordan River, you say, must be the border for Jerusalem to be secure?"

Simon brought out the map Philip had given him and handed it to Richard, who spread it out over his horse's neck to study as they rode.

"In the north, the border should extend to the Sea of Galilee and include the city of Tiberias," Simon reached across and ran his finger in a line along the map. "Ismail holds Mount Tabor, here, but not securely. Ayub is moving against him from Syria. From the Sea of Galilee, the border should taper to the coast, with Beaufort and Sidon as its outer-works as stipulated in the treaty with Damascus. The southern border should extend from Gaza to the Dead Sea."

"What are these forts drawn in red?" Richard asked.

"Those are held by Ayub or Ismail. The blue are Outremere or the knightly orders."

"Your cousin's a dreamer if he thinks we can negotiate the Saracens back to the Jordan for this whole length of the river. Do we need that middle part? Samaria and Nablus?"

"They're less crucial. But we'll do best to demand it all, if only to have something to relinquish in the bargaining."

"Very well. We'll ask for it all. Initially." Richard folded the map and gave it back to Simon. "I've sent word to Ayub to have his ambassador at Jaffa. If he isn't there, we'll march upon Damietta. But I hope we can negotiate," he added wistfully. He had never gone to war before. Arguing was his skill, not battle.

For a time, the conversation lapsed as they rode through the empty, beige landscape beside the sea. But Simon was troubled. At last he said, "I want to thank you for what you did at Westminster. I believe you saved my life."

The prince did not respond for several moments. Then, "I don't know why Henry's angry at you. And I don't especially want to know. When you return to England, I hope we can be better friends."

"My prince," Simon said earnestly, "I beg you to count me as your friend, though I'll never return to England. Your mounting this crusade to save my brother has put me very deeply in your debt."

"You may be sure I didn't come this far to save your brother," Richard said with a sad mile. "I came for myself. This past year very nearly brought me to my ruin. Henry has been more maddening than ever. And, last winter, my wife and son both died of pleurisy."

"I'm so very sorry... I didn't know." Simon was much moved. Richard's clandestine marriage for love had paralleled his own.

"It's sometimes more than I can bear," the prince went on, "watching the sovereign power that our grandfather built, day by day erode in Henry's hands." He seemed glad to have someone to whom he could talk, someone who was not going back to England. "It's not that I see Henry's errors more clearly than others do. But only I am safe to speak against him. Even so, I'm powerless."

"You're very loyal," Simon said with deep respect for a man who, troubled past enduring, could usurp the Crown but didn't.

"Loyal?" Richard looked at him. "You think that I do right? I don't know. Sometimes I think I'm just a coward." He turned his horse abruptly, spurred it to a gallop and went riding back to view the line of march.

The Master of the Hospitallers, seeing the prince leaving, came up and joined Simon. That morning Simon had collected the thousand marks for his letter of credit from the sale of his Leicester woods. The Hospitaller wanted to discuss further finances. After the niceties of greeting, he came to the point. "This campaign could cost that thousand very quickly, Lord Montfort," his face was long and solemn. "I want to let you know that, if you need it, we're willing to extend you credit for another thousand marks at our best terms. I can give you twenty percent per annum now. Our lowest rate. We're committed to this effort, and want to do all that we can to help."

Simon smiled curtly at the Hospitaller's unswerving eye to business, even on the march, and wondered what the interest rate would go to on the battlefield. "How very generous of you. I'll remember your offer, " he said coolly. The Hospitaller's opposing order and its master, Vielle Bride with his infernal dromedary, rose higher in his liking.

The next day the crusade reached Jaffa.

At the time of Thibaut's signing of the treaty, forty days had been allotted for the exchange of prisoners and the putting of the terms of peace into effect. The time was only now nearing its end. With some prisoners still held, Richard feared Ayub might not mean to fulfill the pact.

But hardly had the prince reached Jaffa and made camp when, punctually upon the fortieth day, the ambassador arrived with the remaining prisoners. The Christians, pale, tattered and with bandaged wounds, were a stark contrast to the gorgeously dressed Saracen escort. The ambassador was swathed in crimson damask and cloth of gold, with a scimitar in a jeweled sheath, and a damascened helmet that streamed crimson ostrich plumes.

The sultan's magnificent spokesman was admitted to Richard's tent. The prince girded for tough bargaining. Forming his ruddy, sun-scalded face into its sternest look, he insisted upon full compliance with the treaty made with Ismail. Then, bracing himself, he demanded all the lands of Palestine that the Outremerine lords had specified. Jerusalem must be released at once, with all territories held by Islam from the western coast to the Jordan, from Sidon and Beaufort to the Sea of Galilee, and from Gaza to the Dead Sea. He put on the fiercest expression he could muster, but was ready to negotiate far back from those requirements.

To everyone's astonishment, after the prince relented in regard of Nablus, the sultan's ambassador agreed to everything he asked.

"Give me the map!" Richard, trying manfully to hide his shock, called to Simon, who was standing nearby. Point for point, the prince detailed his demands, using the Outremerine's map for reference. The ambassador confirmed each point, growing agitated, but not contradicting.

When all that Thibaut and the Outremerines wished was granted, Richard managed to put on a tone more menacing, and a face more glowering than any member of his staff had ever seen before. He rumbled at the ambassador, "Sultan Ayub does well to grant me what I ask!"

The ambassador left with every appearances of deep relief, dipping a courtly bow. Richard, his rosy face relaxing, stared before him in dumbfounded amazement.

Simon said low, "Can the Saracen civil war be so fierce that Ayub will grant us anything, rather than fight us as well?"

Soon the truth was known. It was more strange than anyone imagined. The Sultan Ayub's astrologer had predicted that King Richard of the Lion's Heart one day would return; and when he did, he would lay-waste all of Islam if he was not appeased. Richard was mistaken for his uncle.

The prince called for a feast to honor the astrologer who single-handedly had won his crusade for him.

Chapter Twenty-One

JERUSALEM
1240-1241

PRINCE RICHARD SENT SIMON BACK to Acre with report of the victory. Then he marched his troops to Ascalon to rebuild the city's walls as a strong point for his southern border. Palestine was won. Now it must be secured and governed.

At Acre, Simon's news touched off frantic celebration. "To the Lion-Hearted!" was the cheer, "May he live forever in the memory of the Saracens!"

But when Simon told the lords about Richard's move to Ascalon, the mood changed quickly and completely.

"Ascalon belongs to the Templars!" the Grand Master Vielle Bride protested. "If Richard means to give it to his Hospitaller friends, he had best think again!"

"I don't believe he has any intention of giving it to the Hospitallers," Simon offered, amazed at the Templar's assumption.

"And when he leaves?" Balian spat. "The Hospitallers have wanted Ascalon for years. Go back and tell Richard to stay out!"

"You yourselves said Outremere must hold that southern strong point!" Simon countered.

"*We* must hold it," Philip de Montfort bellowed, wagging his thumb at himself, Balian and Vielle Bride.

That night the Hospitallers' headquarters in Acre was sacked and there were riots in the streets. Simon rode fast to Ascalon.

"I never intended to hand Ascalon to the Hospitallers," the prince insisted. "What madmen are they in Acre? For that matter, what difference should there be if the Temple or the Hospital holds

Ascalon when, but for the work I'm doing, it would be nothing but a heap of stones?"

"Clearly our reasoning is not theirs," Simon said dryly. "But you had best appoint a commander for Ascalon who's neutral to both Orders."

In the next weeks, Richard's men set the great blocks of the dismantled castle into place, and the prince searched Outremere for an acceptable commander. He hit upon Walter Penninpie, the titular Mayor of Jerusalem, appointed by Filangieri but generally well liked. Penninpie was not allied with any of the Orders, and was only grudgingly a servant of the emperor.

"That leaves Jerusalem without a mayor," Richard said wearily. He studied Simon for several moments. "You truly don't intend to return to England? Would you consider staying here? I think you might do well."

Simon felt as though the earth itself shifted beneath his feet, as the meaning of Richard's words reached his attention. "My prince, you would consider me for Mayor of Jerusalem?"

"Why not? The Orders and the lords of Outremere hold nothing against you. And you served the emperor honorably in Milan, so you're not unknown to him. I think I couldn't find a better man. You will consider it?"

"Good prince, there is no work on earth that I would treasure more than serving the Holy City." The prospect was staggering, as if the Gates of Heaven were opening to him. Truly, he felt no fate could compare in sweetness to the honor of serving the royal city of the Lord, the age-old goal of pilgrims, the place most precious to Christianity.

A messenger was sent at once to Penninpie, who already had replaced the Moorish commander at Jerusalem. Then Simon, with his commission from the prince in hand, rode to Jerusalem with Peter de Montfort and the Leicestermen. The tattered flag of Hinkley flew proudly in the lead. From the shore at Ascalon, they traveled the ancient road up into the dry, brush-covered slopes of the mountains.

"Simon, do you see how the shepherd walks before his sheep here? They follow him, instead of his driving them along with dogs," Peter de Montfort observed. "A rather gentler notion of 'the Lord is my shepherd,' isn't it?"

Simon said nothing. He was lost in the sensation of being in Jesus's own countryside, traveling in the way of pilgrims before and after him. His whole heart sang at the sight of the parched hills, the dry, contorted trees, the shepherds with their following flocks. As his horse paced the road that King David as a boy had walked, Roman legions had marched, and Christ and his apostles no doubt knew well, tears came into his eyes, tears of amazement at the fate that had brought him here. A backward glance at his life was as dizzying as looking down a dark pit out of which, miraculously, he had flown free. Less than a year ago, he had been weeping in his tower room with no future, and shame filling his past.

The Holy City rose in the distance like an immense crown set by the Hand of God upon the mountains. The dome of the Temple Mount, the Church of the Holy Sepulchre, church spires and minarets melded in Simon's hazy view to the ornaments of a diadem. He dismounted, removed his shoes and walked the remainder of the way barefoot, his gaze fixed on the city as tears flowed from his eyes.

Peter de Montfort took his horse in lead. The Leicester knights were silent, moved by the sight of their commander walking on before them like a pilgrim penitent.

Jerusalem's walls, towers, even the fortress itself lay in ruins. Simon observed the city's wrecked defenses as he walked toward King David's Gate. The emperor's flag flew from a hastily rebuilt rampart.

Walter Penninpie stood in the courtyard to receive the English. "Welcome to Jerusalem, Lord Earl," the amiable, departing mayor took both of Simon's hands. Noting his dusty, bruised feet, he added, "Jerusalem will do well to have a man of faith to govern her. Politics has not treated her well." He ordered one of his own men to take the faded, tattered flag of Hinkley and raise it beside the flag of the emperor.

The ancient, holy city of Jerusalem was a dead city. Its streets were empty, its lanes were an eerie, silent labyrinth. Shreds of awnings fluttered over tradesmen's vacant market-stalls. Pigeons strutted, pecking crumbs from the floors of ransacked and abandoned shops. The windowless walls in the quarter of rich villas formed desolate, winding canyons. Above the houses' walls, tangles of leafless branches stretched against the sky. The skeletons of roses, myrtle and orange trees showed where lush roof gardens had been. Within the villas, soft dust carpeted the floors, unmarked by human footprints.

The Moslems of Jerusalem had fled when the city fell to the Christians, and the Christians had fled when Ayub marched in. With Ayub holding the city in the midst of civil war, no one dared return.

Only in the holy places, tended by those souls so sturdy in their faith that war's horrors were but a thin shell of life's illusion over the Eternal Truth, did a daily routine persist. The Temple of the Rock's broad esplanade was swept. Mass was said in the Holy Sepulcher. Bells rang from the church-belfries. And from their slender towers muezzins called the times of prayer over the empty city.

The day after Simon and his knights arrived, Penninpie and his guard left for Ascalon.

Simon, feeling the need to purify himself to face the honor and the trust placed in his hands, went, dressed only in his long, penitent's hair shirt, to the Church of the Holy Sepulchre.

There, surrounded by monks from every part of Christendom, the old Archbishop of Tyre, the highest prelate in Outremere, was saying Mass. He had come to give thanks for the return of the Holy City into Christian hands.

Simon quietly knelt in prayer.

When the Mass was done, one of the monks who had seen Simon's arrival with his troops, murmured to the archbishop and indicated the kneeling penitent. The archbishop placed his hands on Simon's head in blessing. "Lord Mayor, may you serve our Lord so that He rejoices in your work. May all blessings be upon you in your care of this city where He preached and was crucified."

"Father, I've sinned grievously. I am unworthy."

"King David sinned grievously," the archbishop smiled. "He lusted for a married woman, and he sent her husband into battle to die. I doubt you've done as wickedly. Our Lord chooses his favorites, not by their purity, but by the mystery of His own wishes, which are beyond our fathoming. He has called you here. Trust that He knows why."

Simon kissed the old archbishop's hands in thanks for his words and felt strengthened by them.

As mayor, Simon held his Municipal Court in the ancient citadel. But he did not presume to live there, that was for the emperor alone to grant. As soon as work and time permitted, he took a solitary walk through the streets that Jesus must have walked to His crucifixion. He kissed his fingertips and touched them to the old stone walls that might have witnessed Jesus's passing with the cross. Beyond the gate called "Golden," he sat in the Garden of Gethsemane, then climbed the Mount of Olives.

And there he found the home of his heart. It was a rambling, spacious house with thick, whitewashed walls. It had wide windows with crude timber lintels, and shutters smoothed and whitened by centuries of wind-blown sand. The only color within the house was the windows' broad vistas of the sky above, the green of Gethsemane below and the heat-shimmered Holy City on its neighboring mount.

Simon sent to Brindisi for Eleanor and his family to come at once. Here they would live.

He walked through the city every day, studying what needed to be done. His cousin Peter followed him, making copious notes, as squire Peter lugged a heavy leather bag of wax writing-tablets.

With his notes in hand, Simon pondered and prayed, and consulted the Archbishop of Tyre, who soon became his confidant.

"Pilgrims have begun to come again," the archbishop told him. "Above all, they need food and shelter."

Simon assigned his Leicestermen the task of repairing and cleaning the empty villas to serve as hostels for the pilgrims. When his knights complained about their lowly labor, he reminded them that the legions of Rome were not above such menial work in building an empire, and theirs was a finer task in Heaven's eyes. Their grumbles ceased.

Word spread quickly that the Holy City was in Christian hands again, and the flow of pilgrims increased to a flood. Everything was needed, from food and clothing to cooking pots, saddles and blankets.

Simon proclaimed that shop stalls in Jerusalem were to be had for a year free of rent to any merchant who would make repairs and bring his wares for sale. Within days, new awnings unfurled over the lanes, stone-hammers echoed and the swishing of brooms was everywhere. Among the first to come were dealers in pottery and copper. Passing by to Damascus, they turned their caravan aside to take advantage of the chance to secure city shop space of their own. They filled their allotted stalls with shiny copper cooking pots, earthen jugs and bowls.

Rug merchants came, their camels grunting under loads of rolled carpets. Peasants came as soon as they could pick their crops. Through the city gates they led donkeys heavy-laden with baskets heaped with fruits and vegetables, harvested from gardens in the valleys. Soon the shop-fronts displayed oranges and lemons, dark red pomegranates, great bunches of figs, dates and herbs, and swags of onions woven into ropes by their long leaves. Leather sacks of camel's milk sat propped like weary travelers leaning against one-another. Blankets set upon the ground cushioned huge cream-colored ostrich eggs. There were fish, poultry and butchered sheep. Screes of grain, dried fava beans and nuts spilled from the newly stocked and overflowing shops into the market lanes.

Simon re-established the ancient market days. On Tuesdays, shepherds arrived with their flocks. Geese, chickens, peacocks and pheasants squawked and shrieked from swaying clusters of crates precariously tied onto the backs of camels. Bedouins brought their sleek, tassel-bedecked ponies for sale at the horse fair by the city wall.

Within weeks of Simon's edicts, the streets were filled with men from all over the East: Arabs in billowing burnooses; Armenians and Greeks in white tunics of cotton; Syrians and Persians in rich caftans and pantaloons; Outremerines in their French street-clothes of long robes or short surcoats and hose, but with their heads wrapped in turbans for protection from the sun.

Not only the churches, but the mosques and synagogues were filled with worshippers. Donations brought the sacred sites of all three faiths into repair. The Dome of the Rock was gilded anew. Every minaret proclaimed the times of prayer as shopkeepers set out their mats and knelt to face toward Mecca. The Wailing Wall resounded not only with cries, but with earnest discourses as friars tried to persuade Jews that the Savior had come, and Jews insisted that he hadn't. Simon, who had driven Jews from Leicester, listened now to the Archbishop of Tyre, and learned that in the Lord's own city all this was as it should be.

Weeks became months, and Jerusalem swelled with life. Larger caravans brought ever-richer merchandise into the city. Celadon, pearls, spices and bolts of silk came from the Orient; dried cherries, almonds, honeyed apricots from Egypt, with cotton cloth of gauze so fine it was transparent. Thick woolen carpets woven in intricate designs, and tough brown mats of camel's hair came from the wandering Arab tribes. From Medina came high camel saddles, tasseled halters and fringed reins. Heavy silk brocades embroidered with gold thread came from Damascus, along with scimitars with blades so sharp that they could cut a flower-petal drifting in the air.

Moneychangers came, ready to convert the coin of any land in Europe or the East. And pilgrims came in ever-greater numbers, praying at the holy sites, giving alms, then buying at the shops.

As Mayor of Jerusalem, Simon made trade easy, and housing for the pilgrims free and plenteous – which increased trade, and brought streaming donations to the churches. He put a tax on certain sales, and set aside the proceeds to rebuild Jerusalem's defenses. Every day he walked the streets and battlements, talking with the workmen, the shopkeepers, the pilgrims, learning what more needed to be done. His cousin and his squire followed, taking notes.

People warmed to their new mayor as he moved among them. They brought their disputes to his court, sure of a fair settlement. And, feeling he was fair, they abided by his judgments. There was little crime. Those who could work found ready employment, those who could not found generous alms. Jerusalem, called the City of God, and the City of Truth, at last had peace and prosperity.

At Eastertide the city overflowed with the faithful. They came in greater numbers than ever before in living memory. Christians who long had planned to make the pilgrimage now hurried by land and sea to Palestine.

Simon watched the dormant, war-exhausted city come to bud, then bloom and bear abundant harvest in his care. His friend the Archbishop of Tyre, with shining eyes spoke of the New Jerusalem, as if the New Millennium had come.

For Simon, there could be no greater happiness, no surer sign of his return to grace. He did not credit himself with the achievement that he saw around him. But the joy he felt in being the Lord's agent was past words.

Soon after Easter, the Countess Eleanor reached Acre. She had been pregnant once again when Simon left her at Brindisi. She came with Lady Mary, three nurses and three sons.

Simon met her at the wharf and kissed both of her hands, his eyes full of love at having her here with him. Then he swept up the new infant from its nurse's arms. "Who's this?" he asked his wife. "You *will* outdo that camel-driver's daughter!" When they had parted, she hadn't known she was pregnant again, though they had spent sweet nights together on the way from Paris to Brindisi.

"He's named Guy, for you uncle whom, I hear, was a great lord in the Holy Land," Eleanor explained, not sure he would approve her choice.

"Guy!" Simon laughed. "You have broad shoulders for your size. I dare say you will be a great knight."

The baby stared at his father, blew saliva bubbles and kicked in sheer delight.

Little Henry threw himself against his father's legs and hugged him. Simon knelt and kissed the boy's cheek. "I'm two-and-a-half!" Henry announced proudly.

The nurse took tiny Guy from Simon's arms as he stood up again and looked to his middle son, Simon. A year-and-a-half old, the boy clung to his nurse's neck: his face was red from crying but he was asleep now. His long-suffering nurse clearly hoped he wouldn't be awakened.

Simon nodded to her, and turned back to Eleanor. "I've taken a house. It's plain, but it is on the Mount of Olives where Jesus sat and taught. Can you imagine!"

"Not so long ago I couldn't have imagined that we would be *here*. And that you would be the Mayor of Jerusalem!" Eleanor laughed in bliss, and took her husband's hand as they walked from the quay.

The countess settled comfortably into the villa on the Mount of Olives. Simon had bought only the most essential furnishings: a table, a few chairs, a simple rope bed: no more than he had needed for the few hours he spent at home each night. After her troubles at Kenilworth, Eleanor was determined to resist the impulse to redecorate beyond the basics necessary for her servants and the children. The house remained stark and white but for its glorious vista of the Holy City.

Within a few days of her coming, Eleanor received a visit from three Outremerine ladies, the wives of Balian of Ibelin, John of Arsuf and no less a personage than the Princess Maria of Armenia, Philip de Montfort's recent bride. They arrived at her door like three sultanas in curtained camel-palanquins.

Botevelyn had been wrong, the ladies dressed. They wore robes cut in the French fashion but of Eastern cloth far richer than any ever seen in England or in France: sumptuous damask in a deep ruby hue, sewn with dangling pearls; silk shimmering in iridescent green and blue; cloth-of-gold embroidered with silk flowers so vivid and so finely-wrought that they seemed real. And over this grandeur of fabrics, the ladies wore quantities of golden chains tasseled with strings of pearls and strung with jewels like beads. Their veils were swagged with ropes of yet more jewels, and gaudy jeweled baubles hung from their ears.

Such glitter prodded Lady Mary to mutter, "T'is a wonder that, with so much weight upon their heads and necks, they can still stand." But what shocked Mary most was that they kohled their eyes and rouged their cheeks and lips. "Heathen dancin' girls!" she grunted. "Astonishin', hearin' 'em speak French."

Eleanor was fascinated. Nothing she had ever seen in the Courts at Westminster or Paris remotely could approach what these women displayed merely for a social call. Touching the Princess of Armenia's golden robe, she begged, "Tell me where you find such stuffs as this." That very afternoon she found herself with Princess Maria, clinging to the handrail of a camel palanquin, and peering from that dizzying height down into the new silk-stalls of Jerusalem.

Simon was prospering. Sales taxes from the markets, after the emperor's share and the fund for the city defenses, went to the mayor's purse. Give as he might to the churches as donations, and to the poor in alms, he still had an income far beyond any he had enjoyed before.

Though he had no wish to let the luxuries of the East invade his home, when Eleanor fearfully showed her new-bought bolts of emerald samite, flowered golden baudekin and griffin-patterned white damask, he felt such sorrow for the deprivations she had suffered due to him, and such unwillingness to broach again the issue of her spending, that he smiled, "Have what you will. We can pay for it now."

Eleanor's relief turned into giddy merriment at all the beautiful clothes she would have. And Simon was happy in her happiness. Though she never decked herself with ropes of jewelry, soon the Countess de Montfort blazed like a sun in her new robes, set off against the stark white of the house.

Simon loved to see her so well pleased. But, for himself, he went on wearing penitential black.

In May Richard prepared to leave for England. Most of his army, including Peter de Montfort and the Leicester knights, were going with him. A convocation was called at Acre for all the lords and prelates of Outremere, the Masters of the Orders, and the magnates of the trade communes, to hear how the prince, the emperor's surrogate, would leave the governance of their land.

The crowd was orderly and quiet, intent to hear what Richard would say. Their civility was a credit to the prince's months of management. Penninpie and Simon stood on the dais, at either side of the prince.

Tanned, his red hair glinting gold, his eyes ice-pale from the harsh sun, Richard looked over the now-familiar faces in the hall. "When I came here, Palestine was in disorder, the infidel supreme. I leave you now at peace, with all restored into your hands. I pray that you keep peace among yourselves. If you do not, if quarrel separates and weakens you, the Christian world is cut off from her root."

A soft murmur of agreement passed through the assembly. The prince went on.

"I've searched for men who would serve you well, and help you keep the peace; in whose hands I could leave your governance."

Richard paused, looking among the upturned faces. "As Jerusalem is the capital and throne of Palestine, and as the lord Montfort has shown himself so able in that city's care, I leave him as your acting governor."

The hall broke to excited shouts, daunting at first till it was clear the din was cheering. The Archbishop of Tyre, in the fore, raised his hand in blessing.

Simon stared, uncertain what to think. Richard had said nothing to him of his intent. He was stunned. Richard turned to him, his broad smile beaming.

Simon could only stammer, "My lord, ... I didn't expect this."

The prince raised his hands to quiet the deafening roar of approval. He motioned to his clerk, who handed him a parchment. "I see," Richard grinned, when the room had quieted, "that my choice of the lord Montfort is in accord with your wishes. I offer this petition to the emperor, to be signed by each of you, requesting that Simon de Montfort be confirmed as your Viceroy!"

The prelates, the magnates, the Outremerine lords and the Masters of the Orders erupted in a cheer that made the stone walls reverberate like rolling thunder.

Richard turned to Simon after the assembly calmed. "I don't doubt that the emperor will grant it. You've proven your abilities. May you be Viceroy of Palestine."

Simon could say nothing. He looked to his cousin Philip, who stood near the foot of the dais. The Outremerine smiled broadly and nodded, and his smile was echoed on all the faces near enough for Simon to see.

"Thank you," Simon whispered, so overcome that words were hard to utter. "I came here only to free my brother. But Our Lord's ways are unknowable. I will serve you, with His help. My life could know no greater happiness." Tears streaked his cheeks as Richard embraced him.

With the title of viceroy, Simon's power was as complete as a king's. He could summon armies to make war, or negotiate a peace. He could set policy for trade, for taxes, for all business of the state. It was the perfect solution to the emperor's distant, ineffectual rule. And the factions were content, for Simon gave to each fair hearing, though he was bound to none.

As he had immersed himself in the care of the Holy City, Simon delved into the broader task of governing Palestine. He consulted with the trade magnates and made new laws to aid commerce. The taxes, which increased with increased trade, he set to restoring the defense-works of Palestine's borders.

With the Masters of the Orders and the lords of Outremere he studied past campaigns, learning the points of vulnerability, which had been tried decade after decade in a land always at war. His late-night readings turned to chronicles of Palestine's battles. The archbishop lent him the works of his predecessor William of Tyre. Balian lent him a study of King Richard's campaigns, and a tattered notebook of the writings of his grandfather Balian's squire Ernoul, on the Christian debacle at the Horns of Hattin.

Simon visited the three knightly orders' chief citadels: Kraak de Chevalier, Starkenberg and Carmel, and studied their innovative defense-works: battlements, ringed wall within wall, impregnable, defendable with only a few men. Here, in unceasing war, every flaw of strategy and structure had been probed.

Simon shaped not only his military strategies, but his politics for the Holy Land's defense. His readings gave him insights into the complex history of alliances and hostilities that formed the several factions of Christian Palestine. Carefully, he contrived to have the Orders and the Outremerine lords so interwoven in his plans as to be inter-dependent. So long as they supported one another, so long would the Holy Land remain in Christian hands.

To the Jews and Moslems he offered his court's judicial services, if they wished to use them. Otherwise, he left to themselves all those whom he regarded as infidels. The Jews, he believed, must be preserved and defended in the hope they might some day convert by their own choice. As for the Moslems, their freedom to worship and to conduct their trades was crucial to the peace.

On days when the work of his court wasn't too pressing, Simon devoted his time to his friendships with the leaders of each faction.

He played tennis with his cousin Philip. Their rackets were bent hoops strung with gut, their ball a goatskin sewed tight over wadded leather. Simon was not good at the game. His quickness of response could only partly compensate for his weak eyesight. But when Philip won as usual, he swore that Simon let him, hugged his cousin bearishly and loved him all the more for it.

Simon took part in tournaments with the Teutonic Knights. His skill at jousting, where the target was far larger and less swift than Philip's tennis ball, won him their admiration. With the Teutons' Master, he talked of the emperor. "A genius in numbers and in sciences," the solemn German murmured, "a pure scholar. A blessing to our Order and to the world." Simon nodded in sober agreement. He was sure the German had not met the emperor in person, or ever seen the artwork on his Roman villa's walls.

With the Master of the Hospital he spent hours discussing finance, to the gratification of the Hospitaller if not to Simon's amusement. Compound interest ceased to be a mystery to him. He came to understand the workings of a bank, what was the needed return on investment, and what truly was usury.

Far more enjoyably, Simon went hunting with the Master of the Templars, Peter de Vielle Bride. In the desert, on light Arab ponies, they pursued gazelles with lithe, swift hunting dogs. The Templar's heart was in his eyes as he watched Simon dashing across the sands on the tassel-streaming Arab mare he leant him. It was not by chance the Templar was called Vielle Bride, the Old Bride, but he was too wise to let his warming passion come to words or deeds.

As Viceroy, Simon was accepted by the leaders of each faction. They were drawn together through him. But with each, he walked a careful line: to serve their interests within reason and without partisanship. Trusting him, they came to trust each other. To the clergy, Simon listened always and attentively, and made the Archbishop of Tyre his confessor. It was he who guided Simon, both in spirit and in politics.

Simon kept his focus on the holding of the Holy Land for Christendom as his one goal. The trade, the military strategies, the politics were only means. A New Jerusalem indeed seemed shaping in his hands.

Since much of his time was spent in Acre, Simon took another house and brought his family there, although the house upon the Mount of Olives remained his retreat, and his vantage point to watch over the Holy City's progress.

Evenings, in either home, he spent with Eleanor. On hot summer nights they sat in their roof gardens, cooled by sea winds at Acre, or the balmy, orange-blossom scented breeze that wafted from Jerusalem. The countess invited friars to discourse to them, or trouvers to sing the old, familiar songs of France.

One night, listening to a trouver's plaintive song of the lush beauty of the woodlands of Auvergne, Simon took his wife's hand. "Do you miss England?"

She looked at their little sons playing around their feet, and smiled, "No. Not at all. I've never known so much contentment as we have here. And you?"

"I find it hard to believe we've found such goodness, such happiness. Pray God our whole lives may be spent here."

Months went by. With each ship's arrival at Acre, Simon looked for a letter from the emperor to confirm his viceroyship. But there was no response.

Filangieri had returned to Frederic's Court. The one person beyond the reach of Simon's campaign for unity had been Filangieri. To befriend him would have meant losing all the rest. Simon guessed whatever influence the fallen governor had at Frederic's Court would not be used in his favor. Yet he felt certain that Richard's commendation, and the petition signed by every man of influence in Outremere, must outweigh any counter-argument Filangieri could deploy. He waited patiently.

At last in October, when Simon had been in Palestine a year, a ship came from Genoa with an ambassador from the emperor. Before the convened Court at Acre, he delivered to the lord Montfort a leather packet of documents bearing the Holy Roman Emperor's seals. Among the documents was an order making Walter Penninpie the Governor of Palestine. Simon was rejected, his viceroyship denied.

When the letter was read aloud, the roar of outrage from the lords and magnates in the hall was terrible. The Templars and the Hospitallers shouted and waved their fists in protest. The Outremerines brandished swords and uttered curses at the emperor. The magnates threatened to cease sending their taxes to Frederic. Even the old archbishop muttered imprecations. Only the Teutons, the emperor's own knightly order, kept silent.

Simon waved for the meeting to quiet. When the din subsided and he could be heard, he said, "We all hold Sire Walter Penninpie in high regard..."

A deluge of shouting interrupted him.

When there was sufficient quiet for him to be heard again, Simon went on, "I too am deeply disappointed. I shall go to the emperor myself and beg his reconsideration. Until then, Walter Penninpie is our emperor's choice. You must obey him, as we all must obey those who rule over us."

Simon was even more dismayed than the Outremerines. He had served the emperor well and thought he was highly regarded by him. There was such recent cordiality between them that Frederic had lent him the villa in Brindisi, where his family lived for months. What could have happened? A flicker of a thought crossed his mind: he had told Scott his place and time of birth to cast his chart. But whatever the chart might claim, surely such foolishness could have no bearing upon this. More possibly, King Henry's hatred countered Richard's commendation. He must find an advocate strong enough to counter Henry. He would apply to King Louis.

When he told her the news, the Countess Eleanor was in a state of fury. "Has the emperor no gratitude! You and Richard have done more than anyone else in our lifetime to secure the Holy Land! Just the huge tax monies that you've sent should make Frederic embrace you as his viceroy!"

"So reason would have it," Simon said bitterly. "But if neither Richard's commendation, nor the petition – nor the tax monies as you point out – can sway the emperor in my favor, I must find stronger allies. We'll go first to France and enlist Louis' aid. You might go on to England to try to soften Henry."

"I don't want to leave here!" Eleanor protested.

"We will be back. And with our future secure."

Simon was confident, though the decision to leave was a hard one.

He savored his last visit to the Holy City's winding, stone walled streets with their brilliant-colored awnings saturated with the sun. Even the heat and sweat of Palestine had come to feel sweet to him. Standing on the city wall, he turned his face up to the beating sunshine and felt its heat draw at his skin, its light glow scarlet through his shut eyelids. The heat seemed to draw all stress away until he felt as languid as a lizard. How could these people be so given to war amid such generous warmth? For a few moments, the past and future fell from him like worn and suffocating cloaks in the eternal present of the moment. He was lured so far out of himself as to enjoy a mindless, simple sensuality of penetrating warmth. This place surely must be near to Paradise: man in his primal nature, at one with God's earth.

A few days after the Acre meeting, Simon received an invitation from his cousin Philip. "A farewell feast I suppose," he remarked to Eleanor, and he told the waiting messenger he would attend. The foremost of the lords of Outremere, Vielle Bride and his chief lieutenants of the Temple, the Archbishop of Tyre, and all the leading prelates and magnates of the trade communes would be the guests. They were to meet at Philip's hunting-lodge on the shore of Lake Merom.

At sunset on the appointed day, the guests assembled at the waterside. A flotilla of small boats was waiting to ferry them out to a tented banquet barge. The sun's brilliant disk, fast sinking in the west, tinted the lake to flaming gold, then red. Far out in the rippling glare of the lake's surface, the floating pavilion was a dark, hunching silhouette with pennants fluttering from its peaks. Night came quickly as the boats took on their passengers. The sky faded to mauve and stars appeared. Lamps were lit within the pavilion, winking through the silken walls and blending with the stars, as the night deepened and the barge vanished in the darkness of the lake and sky. A flare was set to mark the barge's bow, to guide the boats bearing the last of the guests.

Simon, the Archbishop of Tyre and Peter de Vielle Bride were first to reach the barge. Philip met them on the deck. His steward, magnificently dressed in a crimson caftan and a white turban with ostrich plumes, greeted the guests with silver wine goblets, serving them wine from a silver ewer shaped like a lion with rubies for eyes.

"To our family!" Philip toasted, his arm around Simon's shoulder. "To Montfort!" He proudly led his guests into the pavilion.

The banquet tent was sumptuous, excessive even for the East. And everywhere that Simon gazed, he saw the Montfort colors and the Montfort heraldry. The tent's walls were red silk with rampant lions worked in silver thread. Over this rich fabric, swags of white silk-gauze, embroidered with red lions, hung in artful draperies. The tent-poles were sheathed in silver wrapped with scarlet ribbons. Upon the floor, carpets woven in a pattern of red fork-tailed lions rampant were heaped to serve as tables in the Moorish style. Cushions of crimson samite, tasseled with silver beads, provided seating for the guests. Overhead, silver oil lamps, hung on crimson cords, were scented with regal frankincense. And at the center of the banquet room a rampant lion, sculpted out of ice mixed with attar of rose and dappled with red rose petals, cooled and perfumed the air.

"It's all just for tonight," Philip beamed with a wave of his hand. "I've been planning this for a long time."

"Indeed?" Simon smiled, a bit abashed. Clearly the feast was not to honor his departure. "What are we celebrating?"

"Our family," Philip said expansively. "Tonight is the Montforts' greatest night!"

Other guests were entering the tent now. Philip closely watched their expressions, delighted by their awe. When all were seated on their cushions, the host ordered his steward to begin the feast.

At the stern, two pages liveried in scarlet folded back the tent's flaps to form an entryway. Through the opening, scarlet-clothed musicians marched playing a loud fanfare on screaming battle schawms. The brass band trod a circuit around the room and then marched out. Behind them, black-skinned slaves, dressed as knights in cloth-of-silver shirts and leggings to suggest chain mail, held up flaming wooden swords with chunks of lamb impaled down to the hilts. The steward rushed to pluck the fiery morsels off the charring blades. He heaped the lamb into vast celadon bowls which the slaves carried to the guests.

Helping themselves with their dining-knives, the guests pricked the sizzling gobbets and waved them about in the air until the hot meat cooled.

Philip turned to Simon. "This course is for the Montfort valor."

"How clever," Simon nodded. He took a long gulp of wine to arm himself against his cousin's gross ideas of elegance. To Simon, brought up at the austere Court of France, the lavish vulgarity of the feast's display was very far from pleasing.

When the guests had eaten their chunks of lamb, the tent-flaps were opened and a second march of slaves came bearing trays of little silver dishes. Each dish held a lemon sherbet molded as a lion's head with pomegranate seeds for eyes.

Simon smiled. The sherbets' artfulness amused even him. And the wine was mellowing his mood.

"You like the sherbet?" Philip, at his elbow, grinned. "Wait till you see the next course! A dish fit for a king!" He winked gleefully to the archbishop, who sat nearby.

More wine was served. Slaves, now costumed in exotic, flowing robes in hues of blue and green, brought in a gilded table. The screeching brass band marched through once more, followed by slaves liveried in blue and green and bearing above their heads huge nests made of spun gold. On each nest sat a peacock, its luminous, green-eyed golden tail flowing over its bearer like a cloak. The nests were set upon the table, the gorgeous tails draping to the floor. The steward carefully lifted the sapphire-feathered skin from each bird's back and served the peacock pies beneath. A sigh of wonder filled the room.

Philip was enchanted.

"Is this for the Montfort pride?" Simon asked archly.

Philip fixed him with a sterner look than Simon had seen before in his cousin's eyes. "No. For false modesty."

Simon drank heavily to stifle his displeasure, and not offend his host again.

The sweet, rich wines of Hebron were poured, round after round, and the pageant of the meal went on: orange sherbets in the form of castles; sturgeons from the Sea of Galilee, minced in a salad with their roe and served in a golden boat much like the ship that had brought Simon to Palestine, as Philip happily pointed out. On shield-shaped golden salvers, doves were served, stewed in wine with candied fruits and violets. Roasted gazelles were brought in by six slaves in white caftans with splendid gold and crimson sashes and toy scimitars.

"They represent the Sultan Ayub, laying the riches of Palestine at your feet," Philip murmured in Simon's ear.

Last, there was a gilded marzipan formed as the City of Jerusalem. When the steward lifted up the Dome of the Rock there was a frantic flapping of white wings as doves flew out. The birds fluttered about the room as servants lurched everywhere to catch them. At last the avian effect was caged and the room quieted.

The feast was done. The guests were filled with awe and utterly sated.

Philip got to his feet, more than a little wobbly from his wine. "Now!" he called loudly to draw the room's attention. "Now it is time for our toast! I toast to my cousin, Simon de Montfort! Who's brought us safety and prosperity. To the king for whom we've prayed!"

Simon smiled and nodded as goblets were lifted to him. He was feeling very genial from all the wine he had drunk.

"This is the hour for which we've waited!" Philip bellowed. "For which we all have prayed!" He beckoned to the steward, who came bearing a crimson cushion on which sat a golden crown. From the circle of the crown's base, three jeweled bands curved up to hold an orb surmounted by a cross. It was the true Crown of Jerusalem.

Simon looked at it with interest, at first supposing it another marvelous work of marzipan. But it weighed down the steward's hands more heavily than sugar could.

Philip was standing over Simon. "We, the lords and the Commune of Outremere – empowered since the founding of our kingdom to elect our sovereign – have voted." He took the crown into his hands and lowered it toward Simon's head.

Sober in the instant, Simon bolted from his seat, nearly knocking the crown from Philip's grip. "No!" he shouted, moving beyond Philip's reach. "I have no rightful claim to be your king!"

"The kingship rests in our vote, And we've chosen you!" John of Arsuf insisted.

"When I first came to Palestine," Simon retorted, "I told you I would oppose any attack upon the emperor's rights! Do you think you can tempt me to usurp his Crown?"

"It's Frederic who's the usurper!" Balian of Ibelin shouted.

The old Archbishop of Tyre rose from his seat and laid his hand on Simon's arm. "Viceroy Montfort, you hold Outremere in unity. A unity that no one else has achieved. We need your rule. The Holy Land depends on it."

"Father, you flatter me," Simon said as gently as he could. "It is not my ability, but the Will of God that keeps the Holy Land at one and safe."

"Your religion is too nice for reality!" Philip broke in. "Can it be you don't know the worth of what you do?"

"I know that I will not be made the tool of treachery!" Simon threw back.

"You speak from creditable loyalty," the archbishop pressed. "But does not loyalty to God come first? The emperor left Our Lord's land undefended. You were sent to us. You alone can meet our need."

Simon looked into the eyes of his confessor and friend. "Father, if I accept this Crown, I bring you war with Frederic. And I bring shame upon Prince Richard who has protected and trusted in me."

He looked about the room. Even to his nearsighted eyes it was clear that the black-robed Teutonic Knights were absent, as were the red-crossed Hospitallers. "There are neither Hospitallers nor Teutons here. I'd bring you civil war with them as well! Philip," he turned to his cousin, who still stood holding the crown, "give me a boat to take me from this place at once!"

"You're not leaving!" Philip bellowed.

Simon raised his eyebrows. "You offer me a Crown, cousin, then tell me that I may not leave? What strange respect you pay me! Or, Philip, is it not really as your puppet you would have me reign? No more sovereign than old Queen Alice!"

Philip stared, speechless. Slowly he turned to his steward. "Get him a boat," he grunted. "Let him turn his back upon his family and the Lord's land."

"May God forgive you," the archbishop murmured as Simon passed by him. "I truly believe that you were meant to stay with us."

Simon paused. "Father, I will return when the emperor has granted my viceroyship. But I will not steal a Crown!"

Chapter Twenty-Two

THE RETURN
1242

IN JANUARY OF 1242, TEN weeks after the feast upon Lake Merom, Simon and his family reached France. The sky was iron gray. Soft, dark folds of clouds rolled and a wind from the north blew sleeting rain as they climbed the steep, cobbled road through the village of Montfort l'Amaury. Even the shuttered cottages that lined the road seemed to have withdrawn into their winter sleep. It was a somber change from the never-ending blaze of summer sun in Palestine.

At the castle, Amaury did not meet them. A young man came with the servants who hurried out the door to take their horses in the wind-swept yard.

"Welcome, Uncle Simon," the youth greeted rather shyly. "Your squire reached us only a short time ago to tell us you were coming.

"John?" Simon asked hesitantly. He had not seen his brother's son since the boy, at age five, had been sent to serve as page in a German margrave's Court.

"You don't remember me, "John blushed, "but I remember you quite well. And you," he turned to Eleanor, "are the good countess who pled with King Henry for the forces that went to my father's rescue."

As the baggage wagon was unloaded in the yard, John led Simon and Eleanor into the castle. Lady Mary, Eleanor's servants, and the three nurses with the three small boys followed.

"Your father isn't here?" Simon asked, disappointed at not finding Amaury in the hall.

"My father's dead," the youth said quietly. "He contracted a fever in the sultan's prison and died in Italy on his way home."

"Oh," was all Simon could say. He was shocked. The mere existence of his brother filled some place of comfort in his spirit that he hadn't been aware of till this moment. Despite what seemed to be an ever-growing world of cousins, his brother was his one kinsman who was true family for him. He had not loved Amaury. He certainly had never missed him. But his absence now seemed as palpable as the loss of a limb.

And there was another pang: a younger brother's unquenchable frustration. He had looked forward to his brother's welcome, to talking with Amaury of Palestine, to having his brother's praise at last. Returning pilgrims would have told him of his achievements there. But if Amaury died in Italy, he might never even have known that he had gone to rescue him.

The young Count of Montfort made every effort for the comfort of his guests, but Simon would stay only a day. The castle no longer felt like home, it had passed on to a virtual stranger. Leaving Eleanor and the children to John's hospitality, he rode to Paris at once to enlist the aid of France in his petition to the emperor.

Pilgrims returning from the Holy Land had indeed spread word of Simon's good works. The greeting Simon found at Court was a hero's welcome. Queen Blanche arose from her seat, came down the dais steps and walked through the hall with both her hands outstretched to him. King Louis followed and embraced him.

"What brings the triumphant Viceroy of Palestine to us?" Blanche asked, her face aglow with a proud, motherly smile.

"I've come to beg your help, good queen," Simon bowed low. "But I must speak of the matter only privately." Her eager greeting of him with the honor he did not possess wracked him with embarrassment.

Blanche ordered a chair brought and had Simon sit beside her on the dais during the Court's session. All afternoon, the Ministers of France, men Simon had known only as lofty personages when as a page he served the Court, came to congratulate him. Too conscious that, despite all he had done for peace in Palestine, he had failed to secure the viceroyship, Simon found their praises far more painful than pleasing.

The ordeal reached its peak when the Archbishop of Rouen, Odo Rigaud, the Minister of State, drew a jeweled ring from his own finger and pressed it into Simon's hand, saying, "Take this as a small token of our gratitude for making the Holy Land and Our Lord's city safe."

Simon gently pushed the archbishop's hand away. "Your Excellency, I regret that I cannot accept your gift," he murmured, "but pray for the Holy Land. And pray for me."

Later, meeting with Queen Blanche, Louis and the archbishop Rigaud in the queen's chamber, Simon told them of his rejection by the emperor, and of his intent to petition Frederic with their aid.

He stood with his back to the blazing hearth, dark and tall in the firelight. Louis, somber beside him, leaned against the mantel, the profile of his broad, milk-white face skimmed by the firelight. Rigaud hovered at the edge of the hearth's glow, beside Queen Blanche who sat in a high-backed chair, her solemn face lit by the full light of the fire. The three listened gravely.

Simon described his management of the Holy City and of Palestine, and the strong favor that the Orders and the Outremerines showed him – though he omitted their attempt to crown him King of Jerusalem. "By God's grace, I was given means to hold the disparate factions in unity. Having a leader accepted by all, and in attendance day by day, is the only means for Palestine's defense," he urged. "I've come to beg you to join with Prince Richard, to use your power and influence to sway the emperor to grant the viceroyship of Palestine to me."

Blanche's long face was pensive. Louis and Rigaud kept a tense silence. The queen spoke quietly, "This is a poor time for you to ask us to join in any way with Prince Richard. And our influence with the emperor is at low ebb. Our support, I believe, would even damage you in that quarter, although our Christian goals should be the same." She looked into Simon's shadowed face. "We are at war with England."

Simon looked from Blanche to Archbishop Rigaud and Louis. "Has Henry invaded Normandy again?"

Louis glanced down, abashed. "No. The fault is mine. I opened the aggression."

The archbishop explained, "King Louis bestowed the province of Poitou upon his brother Alphonse."

"I hardly see fault there," Simon said caustically. "Henry ignores the fealty he owes to you as Poitou's overlord. The fault, if any, has been your twenty years of patience."

"Would that it were so simple as that." Louis gave a pallid smile.

"King Henry had given Poitou to his brother Richard," Rigaud continued. "The province was bestowed on Alphonse just as Richard was in Palestine rescuing our knights."

"I see," Simon raised his eyebrows. "That was not well done."

"To say the least," Louis laughed curtly, turning his back to the fire and clasping and unclasping his hands behind his back; it was a nervous gesture that his subjects saw rarely, but dreaded. "I'd gladly return Poitou to Richard, but the problem has become compounded. At Christmas, Count Hugh of La Marche – whom you may know is Richard and Henry's stepfather – tried to murder Alphonse. I've ordered the count's arrest and trial. His wife, the Queen Mother Isabel of England, has demanded that her sons protect him. Henry is arming to regain Poitou – and in his parents' defense."

"So it is war with England?" Simon saw his hopes for his petition to the emperor sinking in the flood of these new events.

"And more," Queen Blanche added. "Count Raymond of Toulouse and Count Thibaut of Champagne, who has lately inherited the kingdom of Navarre upon our southern border, have joined in an alliance with La Marche, Castile and England. We face war with our neighboring kingdoms a well as civil war."

"We've issued a full call to arms for the spring," Louis smiled sadly.

"I regret that you had best forget our help with Frederic," Blanche met Simon's gaze.

"Without it, I'm alone at the emperor's Court, against Filangieri who is a favorite of the emperor and who has already proved himself more than a match for Richard. The Outremerine lords and Templars, whom Frederic hates, probably have compromised me further by their favor." Simon's heart was clutched into a knot of frustration. "Clearly, despite the evidences of my success, petitioning the emperor without strong aid is futile."

Simon was utterly stymied. His brilliant prospects suddenly were gone. All he had done in the East meant nothing in this world of chaotic politics. Further, the consequence of Amaury's death was that, if ever he had nurtured hope of regaining a share in Montfort l'Amaury, that hope was gone now, too. Everything had passed to John. With his holdings in England confiscated, Simon had absolutely nothing left.

Slowly, he asked in a low voice, "May I remain here, with you at Court, until such time as matters change? It seems I've nowhere else to go. Perhaps I may be of some use in your Poitou campaign?"

The words gave spark to the glimmer of a thought, a hope that long had lived in Simon's heart. "Louis, permit me to lead the force against Toulouse! Give me a chance to avenge my father's death and win back Toulouse from Count Raymond. Perhaps that's why Fate's brought me back. To do my father justice!"

"I have no wish to conquer anyone," Louis said mildly. "My only goal is to bring Count Hugh of La Marche to trial. I don't mean to deprive Count Raymond of lands that are his by ancient right."

"He strikes at you," Simon burst out, "and yet you let him keep his sword to strike again?"

"His people love him. He governs Toulouse well."

"He's treacherous!"

"I know he is! But I do not want war!" Louis shouted, roused to anger at last.

Simon's frustration soared past control. "Want it or not, you have it! Or will you let Count Raymond make a mockery of France! Let him cancel the victory my father gave his life to win for you! Are you afraid to fight?"

A sharp blow struck Simon across the mouth.

Louis stood in front of him, straight, shaking with anger. Forcibly he quieted himself, saying with measured restraint, "Forgive me that I struck you, Simon. But, though I may not be your king, I will have your respect!"

Simon wiped blood from his lip. His face burned with anger and humiliation. He looked from Louis to the archbishop and the queen, then turned away from their shocked faces. He pressed his fist to his bleeding mouth, and watched the fire in the hearth for several moments. Louis was his last remaining friend. He wished the flames could consume the rash words he'd spoken.

When he turned around again, he said hardly above a whisper, "I beg your forgiveness. To repay your years of kindness to me with such words... I beg pardon! ...Louis, can you understand that I'm desperate for my life! I've lost everything in England, and now the East is gone from my reach too. My wife and three sons have no home. Grant me permission to regain my father's lands, if I can."

The depth of Simon's despair softened his three listeners. Louis had never thought to see his friend so stricken. Quietly, the King of France said, "Stay, then. Help me plan our campaign in the south. I cannot promise you Toulouse, but I will find some recompense for you."

Simon began attendance at King Louis's Court, and rented a house in Paris for his family. He had some funds brought from Palestine, and could use as money the credit of his service to the king. With these assets, he and Eleanor could live modestly for a while, but not indefinitely.

In the spring, the lords of France assembled in arms. A city of tents stretched across the open fields from the Saint Honore Gate to the Bois de Boulogne. The army was immense. It was Louis' intent to muster such a force that Henry, impossibly outnumbered, would agree to terms.

Simon would lead a contingent of the march. Daily he met with the king and the chief lords of France, planning the campaign. The great double-gabled hall was filled with tables covered with maps of Poitou, scrolls containing lists of names of men-at-arms, lists of supplies and reports of the enemy's preparations. A small army of clerks labored over the documents, and came and went with their arms laden with more documents.

Though the lords who had returned from Palestine held Prince Richard in high regard, the prospect of gaining lands in Poitou was a strong lure. But more, their outrage at Count Hugh's attempt upon Alphonse's life was intense. Hugh was not loved in France. And his Lady Isabel, Countess of Angouleme and Queen Mother of England, was thought a madwoman, a trait it was believed she had passed on to her son King Henry.

As Henry's victim, Simon found here, as in England, a strong sympathy for him that left him much chagrined. He alone knew that his exile was well earned.

Simon was surrounded by a glow of popularity at Louis's Court. He was the native son returned, the hero of the Holy Land and seemed, along with Alphonse, a target of the insane English Royal House.

Though Louis was not given to jealousy, the regard verging on worship that Simon was receiving made him uneasy.

In June, just as the army was ready to move south, a messenger arrived from King Henry. But the letter that he carried was not for the King of France. It was for the Lord Montfort.

To avoid any question of his loyalty, Simon gave the letter, with its large, dangling royal seal of red wax, to the Archbishop Rigaud to unfold and read aloud for everyone to hear. It was a summons to military duty.

Simon burst out laughing. "King Henry confiscates my lands, I live in exile, yet he asks my services?" He took the letter from the archbishop's hand and flung it at the messenger. "King Henry will see me at the head of troops quite soon enough!"

"I must have a written answer," the messenger begged as he picked up the letter and the pieces of the royal seal that lay shattered on the floor.

Simon turned to a clerk. "Write my answer. I send my regrets." His tone was sarcastic. He returned to studying a map that lay unscrolled on the table.

But Louis seemed troubled. He took the letter from the messenger and read it again for himself. Frowning, he turned to Simon, "It seems that Henry offers you reconciliation. You ought not to reject him."

Simon looked up from the map to Louis, eyebrows raised in doubt that he had heard rightly. "What would you have, my lord?"

The lords and the archbishop also looked at Louis in amazement.

"Of course I'm not eager to lose you to King Henry," Louis explained clumsily. "If we weren't so well prepared, it would be folly to relinquish you to him now. But this could be your chance to recover your lands and titles. I won't stand in your way."

A murmur at the king's self-sacrifice and generosity spread among the courtiers.

"There is no chance that the King of England means to restore my titles," Simon said flatly.

Louis held the letter out to him. "From what I read here, it seems that's not the case. He, at least, is ready to forgive." There was an edge, a challenge in Louis' tone. He added earnestly, "Simon, whatever I can offer you in France cannot compare to your earldom in England. And too, for my own reasons, I would have you on good terms with Henry. If there had been a mediator at his Court, this war would not have happened."

Archbishop Rigaud, grasping at Louis' reasoning, nodded in agreement. "Lord Montfort, it might be wise for you to go to King Henry, for all our sakes."

"You would order me to go?" Simon asked Louis, incredulous.

"No, but we strongly ask it." Louis used the royal "we" deliberately.

"I know your plan of war!"

Louis smiled. "Knowing the full count of our forces should move the English to negotiate."

"If I do serve England, I must do so honestly. If it comes to fighting," Simon gave Louis a piercing look, "I must fight you with all the strength – and all the knowledge that I have."

Louis met his gaze. "I know your sense of honor far too well, my friend, to expect any less." The king broke to a playful grin familiar to his childhood sparring-partner. "Go to Henry! And I'll beat you if you fight me in Poitou!"

Louis left no choice. Simon departed the next day. Only his squire Peter accompanied him, leading a fine destrier that Louis gave him, and a packhorse laden with his armor. His own warhorse, like most of his possessions, had remained in Acre.

Simon and his squire rode south to the appointed meeting place at Pons, in Poitou.

"Sire, this venture makes me very much afraid," the squire admitted when they had hardly passed beyond the walls of Paris. "King Henry may be luring you into a trap."

"That's probable," Simon said tersely.

"Yet you still go?"

"I must."

"Sire, I beg you, don't go into the king's tent. Only meet with him where you can be seen by everyone."

"You would defend me from murderers?" Simon smiled.

"I would," Peter answered. "But Prince Richard and the other lords would give you better help than I if they saw you in danger."

"I'll take your words to heart."

Simon no longer had the protection of the Cross. He would be meeting Henry in his own dukedom, where the king could do with him as he wished. Murder seemed improbable, but arrest and execution for an act of treason loomed as highly likely. Henry need not cite any cause other than his service to King Louis. Yet Louis, apparently oblivious of this risk, gave him no alternative. Simon was coming to feel strongly that Fate toyed with him, smiling, raising him upon her wheel, only to whirl him down to destruction as the heights of success came into sight.

It was exceptionally hot for June as Simon and Peter rode through Orleans and Tourenne. The fields of sprouting wheat wilted with drought. At Poitiers, already there were signs of war: newly repaired city walls, burnt crops, rocks strewn in the roads, a quiet of expectation and of dread.

In eight days of unhurried travel Simon reached the English camp. He sent his squire to announce his arrival, and to say that the earl would meet the king only in full view of the camp.

Henry emerged from the door-flap of his tent, smiling. He was thin but heartier than when Simon had seen him last, at his brief visit to England's Court before arming for Palestine. Henry wore a brilliant suit of mail and, over it, a crimson surcoat embroidered in gold thread with the three strutting lions of Plantagenet. Prince Richard, the royal clerk John Mansel, the queen's uncle Peter of Savoy – who gloried in the title Earl of Richmond, William Longspee the Earl of Salisbury, and Roger Bigod the Earl of Norfolk gathered around to witness.

Henry held his hand to his brow, shielding his eyes against the harsh sunlight. He smiled up at Simon, who rudely remained mounted. "We thought you mightn't come. We're glad you did. Richard tells us there is not your equal in the world for strategies of war."

"What strategies the prince has had from me he knows weren't mine, but the work of the lords of Outremere." Simon brushed the compliment aside. He dismounted and approached the king. "You summoned me. I've come. What do you want of me?"

"We've summoned all the earls to service."

"Does that include me? You've seized my lands and rents. I live in exile. Will you make good my losses?"

Henry's lip curled cynically. "Can you make good mine?" His idle-seeming comment was lost on everyone except Simon, who understood it perfectly. Any child that Henry fathered was blocked from the Crown by the bastard in the royal nursery.

But the king moved on lightly from the remark. He had other concerns, more pressing at the moment. He shifted his stance then said, "We'll offer you a mercenary's pay, for the present. If you serve well, we will consider your full restoration." He tipped his bearded chin up in a haughty-seeming way, but actually so that his drooping eye could better study Simon.

Simon met his gaze. A chill sweat broke on his forehead. It appeared that degradation, rather than arrest and trial for treason, was what Henry had in mind, at least at present. "What wage do you offer me?"

"We thought that you would name your price."

Simon drew breath. Could Henry really want him back? Richard's advocacy would weigh far more here than it did at Frederic's Court. The prince might be his rescuer again. Henry seemed no more intent upon revenge than to offer a demeaning game of bargaining. He would play it if, before these witnesses, the earldom of Leicester could be in the balance. "Six hundred pounds," he said, "for no more than three months service. And firm guarantee that all my rents and titles will be restored at the end of that term."

Henry didn't flinch. "You'll have your six hundred. Send your squire to collect it when you will."

"My king, I require your full pardon for the past. And your further promise that no actions will be taken against me."

Henry met him with a clear, straight look and said coolly, "You have it."

The bargain was witnessed by the prince, the royal clerk and three earls. Simon was astonished. Fate seemed to have spun her wheel again.

Richard stepped forward to bring the tense moment to a quick end. "I don't doubt you've heard stories of the cause of this campaign." He took Simon by the arm, leading him toward his tent. The meeting with the king and earls disbursed.

"I know of Louis's gift of Poitou to his brother, and of the attempt upon Alphonse's life." Relieved by Richard's intervention in the tense meeting, and feeling that the prince had been his savior and advocate yet again, he followed Richard gladly.

"You should know our side." Richard's tone was pointedly friendly. Reaching his red and gold striped tent, the prince raised the tent-flap and they went in. He offered Simon one of his folding campstools and they sat as they had many times in that same tent in Palestine. A servant brought them wine. Richard began his version of the story.

"You've heard the gossip. I would have you know the truth, however bad it is." The prince spoke openly, candidly. "Louis has his claims to Poitou, as I have mine. Nonetheless, we could have come to some agreement. But, foolishly, my mother's husband, Count Hugh of La Marche, acknowledged Alphonse's claim."

Simon listened, drinking his wine. His nerves, strung tight from the encounter with King Henry, were gradually relaxing. He began to realize that the prince was very drunk, in the controlled stupor of a man who must lead, but is tried past bearing.

Richard held his cup for his servant to fill to the brim. He took a long drink of the wine, and spun out his sordid account. He seemed to take some comfort in confessing to a man he held in high regard.

"Mother flew into a rage when she heard that Hugh had pledged to Alphonse. Mother's rages are formidable. She tried to strangle Hugh. It took three men to pull her off. To placate her, Hugh promised to go to Alphonse's Christmas Court and withdraw his liege. But mother, it seems, didn't think that was sufficient. She gave Hugh's servants a deadly poison for Alphonse. The plot was found out and Alphonse's bailiffs tried to arrest Hugh at the feast. The old count threw a candlestick down on the table, setting the cloth on fire, and escaped in the confusion." Richard forced a laugh, "Fairly adventurous for an old man!"

"Or for anyone," Simon smiled, though he was not charmed by the story. He felt a surge of pity for Richard, a great prince burdened with such a mad family.

Richard sensed his sympathy. "Mother and her husband are like two bad children, grown old at their wicked games. To our misfortune, larger matters hang upon their games than on child's play." He gazed upward, "It is one of the Great Commandments, 'Honor thy father and thy mother...'" Then, leaning forward, he looked closely in Simon's eyes, breathing his wine-breath in his face. "Do you understand? I confess that rightness is all on Louis's side. But we cannot forsake our parents."

Simon's dark lashes shaded his eyes. He looked down at the ground, avoiding Richard's stare. "I've sold my sword to your side. But know this, Richard, I'm many times indebted to you for what you've done for me. I will do all I can for you."

Richard looked relieved. He stood and stretched. And Simon stood. Their conference was over.

"Count Hugh assures us he has an ample army," the prince yawned. "The castles of Poitou are strong. Especially Frontenaye, where Hugh's eldest son commands."

"What force from England have you brought?"

Richard dodged the question. "Hugh urged us that he needed only money. But I argued that it was an ill part for the Crown to serve only as banker. We should come ourselves."

Simon smiled, "If you mean to keep your army's numbers secret from me, I well understand, but I can be of little use to you beyond the strength of my own arm."

Richard met Simon's eyes with a pained look. "Simon, I trust you. I'm not holding back. What you see here in Pons is our whole English force."

"I saw only a few hundred tents as I rode in."

"It was hard enough for Henry to raise money from the barons, much less men for this venture. We have three hundred knights and seven earls. Eight, with yourself included."

Simon looked at him in disbelief. "Louis is leading thirty thousand men! This camp is not a guard sufficient for the safety of the king's person, much less conduct of war!"

"Our chief force is to be the army of La Marche, with reinforcements from Toulouse, Castile and Navarre. We're to meet them at Tonnaye and Tailleberg, two days march from here. Still," Richard admitted, "we know we are outnumbered. We've sent a plea to the Archbishop of York to raise more men. It is for them that we remain waiting here. So long as Henry was in England, the barons wouldn't bestir themselves for him."

"The king has placed himself in jeopardy – this is how you recruit?"

Richard squirmed. "The Poitouvins have blocked the roads and burnt the fields to slow Louis' advance."

"I saw it. And wondered what the Poitouvins expect to eat this winter."

"English money and French plunder," Richard shrugged. "But the tactic is our best ploy. Henry has sent an embassy to Louis, reminding him that the breach of the truce between England and France was his, not ours. I pray that the annoyance caused his march, and our appeal to his honor, will weigh with him to return Poitou to me and leave mother and Count Hugh alone."

Studying the prince, Simon saw an able man crushed by frustration, trying to keep some dignity in the face of shame upon shame. Yet he was firmly loyal to his family. He pressed the prince's sturdy hand, "I'll help you Richard. In every way I can."

Chapter Twenty-Three

TAILLEBERG
1242

LOUIS' VAST ARMY LEFT PARIS and marched slowly toward Poitou. Very slowly.

The little English camp at Pons waited for reinforcements, and the answer to King Henry's embassy to Louis.

Summer heat shimmered over the parched slopes. In the camp the earth grew hard and dusty under foot. The bright colors of the tents faded in the sun's blaze. Count Richard of Pons claimed he was hard-pressed to find provisions. Food had to be brought from ever-greater distances. The prices the count asked for the loaves of bread, salt meat and eggs that his people brought climbed daily. He was making a good profit from the war.

Henry and his army waited. No word came from England. But every day there came reports of the steady advance of the French.

The English sweated in the Poitou heat and waited.

Simon dined with the earls, Prince Richard and the king each day. It soon was apparent that Richard was his only partisan in Henry's circle. The other lords were annoyed, even dismayed, to find the detested Frenchman back among them. Tempers were short in any case, and Simon's presence made him an apt target for their barbs. As for the king, he seemed to take a certain pleasure in their discomfiting his former "foreign friend."

For Simon, his two-year respite from their hostility made their jibes all the harder to bear, but he tutored himself to ignore them; he drew inward and said little. Unlike in the past, when he had let his temper have free rein, he had a wife and three sons to consider. Three months of such self-discipline was a small enough price to pay to gain the return of his English lands and titles. These lessons in humility and self-restraint even seemed fitting: a divinely just and lenient punishment, considering the cause of his exile.

As for Henry, he was bearing the ordeal of waiting for his reinforcements well. More than well, he seemed ebullient. His challenge to the King of France had sent the frail, patched kite of his assurance beating high into the wind. Even with Simon he was almost genial at times. One sweltering afternoon he went so far as to suggest they share a game of chess.

Taking a rook that Simon, a good courtier, politely left ill guarded, Henry remarked as if off-hand, "The queen came with us. She's staying in Bordeaux." He raised his head to watch Simon's expression, "She is with child."

Simon smiled, unruffled. "More children make for a secure succession. May you have many sons, my lord."

Henry seemed satisfied, took Simon's queen and won the game.

At last word came to Pons that the new recruits in England had reached Dover and were ready to embark. The boredom of the camp lifted. Swords and pikes were sharpened as the men readied to move out.

But more days passed with nothing. Then an English knight and an archer straggled to the camp. In mid-Channel their ships had met the French. As they maneuvered for battle, a storm had blown up from the west, dashing the English vessels onto the French coast. The newly recruited army that had been so long awaited was shipwrecked and captured, or drowned. There would be no more reinforcements from England.

The mood in the Pons camp turned grim, waiting now for Louis's reply to the embassy.

Louis no longer kept them waiting. His courier arrived with his offer. The earls gathered in the king's tent to hear the message read. King Henry had his clerk Mansel unravel the wax-sealed tab and read aloud.

"To Henry, by the Grace of God, King of England, Lord of Ireland, and to all his people, Louis, by the Grace of God, King of France, bids greeting. As we are reminded by you, and as we agree, peace between two neighbor kingdoms such as ours, fellow Christians and lately united in war in the Holy Land, ought not to be sundered for light cause. To the end of fashioning a proper, lasting peace, we therefore propose a truce of three years, and offer, as the sign of our good will, full restitution of the Province of Poitou to the Lord Richard of England. And, further, we offer restitution of the Dukedoms of Normandy and Anjou, taken by our forefathers from John Plantagenet.

"However, we will not abridge our right of justice over our own vassals, the Count and Lady of La Marche who, as no subjects of England, ought not to concern our neighbor kingdom, or obstruct our peace."

As Louis' terms were read, the earls in the king's tent looked by degrees relieved, then jubilant at its generosity. There was so much excited talk that the last words passed almost unheard. Simon was astounded at the extent of the offer, even aggravated that Louis took so supine a stance after such immense preparations for war.

Nearly overcome with relief and joy, King Henry began to dictate his reply.

But he had hardly begun his answer when a second courier arrived. He came from Frontenaye and bore a letter from the Queen Mother Isabel. It was delivered into the king's own hand. Henry's fingers trembled as he fumbled to unseal it. He finally gave the letter to Mansel to open and read. The clerk read the letter loudly and clearly, as he had the one before. The king, the prince and eight earls heard:

"To her cherished son Henry, by the Grace of God King of England, Lord of Ireland, Duke of Normandy, Anjou and Aquitaine: Isabel, by that same Grace Queen of England, Countess of Angouleme and La Marche, sends her Maternal Benedictions and Prayers. By all the Angels of Heaven, by the Weeping Mother of Jesus, do you leave your Mother to the mercy of the French? Do not turn your back upon your Mother's cries..."

Mansel stopped reading and looked to Henry. But Henry nodded pettishly for him to continue. The clerk read on reluctantly.

"...lest all the Devils in Hades drag you down to the Eternal Agony that you would thereby earn."

Mansel's voice trailed off. He looked again at the king. But Henry snapped, "Well? We'll hear the rest of it!"

In a low voice Mansel read, "Be you Cursed Forever if you have not the Natural Love in you to stand between your Mother and her Executioners. Our Enemies close in upon us! How can you bear to hold your forces in delay?"

When Mansel ceased reading, everyone was silent. An icy air had settled in the tent. The earls looked to their king.

Henry sat in his chair, ashen.

The Queen Mother's courier finally broke the silence. "Good King Henry, what answer will you give?" he begged.

Barely above a whisper, Henry said, "We go to relieve Frontenaye." A nervous flicker darted across his brow. He said louder, his voice tight, ""We march to Tonnaye and Tailleberg to gather the forces of Toulouse, Castile, Navarre and La Marche. Then we march on Frontenaye."

Everyone present knew this was madness. But no one said a word. Not even Richard. And with him silent, no one else dared speak.

The next morning the camp at Pons was a vacant field of trodden earth. A day's march brought Henry to Tonnaye, on the River Charente. There, reinforcements sent by Thibaut, now King of Navarre, and by King Alphonse of Castile and Count Raymond of Toulouse, waited to join him. England's strength grew from the mere three hundred who had sat in the dust of Pons, to a modest army of almost a thousand men. But they were still far short of Louis' thirty thousand.

At Tonnaye, the sight of the forces waiting there raised the English spirits. With these knights and foot soldiers, and Count Hugh's vast army waiting at Tailleberg, there might be hope.

As the Tonnaye tents were being lowered and the combined armies formed to march on to Tailleberg, three riders on spent, lathered horses galloped into the camp. They were King Henry's half-brothers of La Marche: Hugh LeBrun, Guy de Lusignan and William de Valence. Hugh, the eldest, was eighteen. William, the sweet-faced youngest, was just twelve. Frontenaye, Poitou's chief stronghold, had been in their keeping. They were guided through the confusing maze of the camp to King Henry.

The boys were breathless, wide-eyed with fear. They threw themselves on their knees upon the ground before Henry. "Frontenaye is taken by King Louis!" Hugh cried. "We fought well, brother," he pleaded, clearly terrified, "but the French brought a great trebuchet and breached our wall!"

"Don't punish us," the youngest bawled. "We did our best!"

King Henry had never seen his half-brothers before. He stared at them, shocked that they were so young, and were so much afraid of him. "Children," he said softly, "my children..." He reached down, drawing William to stand up. The others stood, wiping their tearful faces. William sobbed uncontrollably.

"So young, and yet so brave for me," Henry said gently. He held William to his breast, pressing the boy's wet face against the gold-embroidered lions of Plantagenet.

"Mother's safe," Guy, the dark-haired middle boy, assured Henry. "But Louis marches to meet you at Tailleberg."

King Henry nodded. He put out an arm to gather the two older boys to him as well. "So, we have lost Frontenaye, and Louis comes," he sighed with paternal kindness. "We will march together to meet him."

Tailleberg was a handsome city, walled, tile-roofed and turreted, perched on a hill on the north bank of the River Charente. Between the hill and the swiftly flowing river was a long, narrow field. In front of the town, spanning the river was a fine, ancient Roman bridge of stone. Across the river, to the south, lay broad meadows.

Late the same night of the day they left Tonnaye, King Henry's army marched through the meadows and approached the bridge. On the flat land below Tailleberg's walls, and along the north bank of the river as far as eyes could see, there were lights: the watch fires of an immense army. The English observed the seemingly endless camp with satisfaction.

"You see," Henry beamed to Richard, "It would have been a coward's part to accept Louis' terms. He dared not face the army of La Marche."

Gazing at the numberless points of light in the darkness, Richard nodded. "It would seem that you're right."

There was a break in the army's steady forward movement, a commotion in the vanguard. The march came to a halt.

"What? What? Why are we stopping?" Henry demanded.

By the light of the army's flares, two riders could be seen coming down the line of march at speed. The Marshall Roger Bigod, leader of the vanguard, galloped with Count Hugh himself.

"Welcome, father!" Henry greeted cheerily when the count reached him.

The count's horse shivered and stumbled as it was reined-in. Its eyes were bleeding, blood foamed from its nostrils and mouth. Hugh slid from the saddle just as his horse's knees buckled and it fell. The old count pointed, panting for breath, "Across the river... France's army! Louis holds Tailleberg!"

"By the head of God!" Richard bellowed, "We nearly camped with them!"

Henry stared. In a low voice he asked, "What do we do?"

"Stay where we are, and rest as best we can," Richard answered. "We will have battle in the morning."

In a few hours, the blue haze of dawn revealed acre upon acre of tents across the river. In the first light, King Henry, Prince Richard, Roger Bigod and Count Hugh stood by the river, surveying the enemy. It was a daunting sight. The more daunting to the four who knew that behind them slept but one man to each thirty of the French. The army of La Marche had not arrived.

"What of your promises now, father!" Henry demanded of Count Hugh. "When we were in England, you wrote that you would have such an army as could fight King Louis with no fear! Where are they?"

"What army?" the old count looked surprised. "I never made such a promise."

Henry, Richard and Roger Bigod stared at him.

"You did, sir!" Richard fumbled in the blousing of his surcoat and brought out a packet of letters tied with cord.

Count Hugh opened one letter, then another, and shook his head as he read. "I never wrote this. Not any of this!"

"Father, what... what is this I hear from you?" Henry stammered. "Haven't you sent to me, begging me to come and meet your army here? Where is your army?"

"None of this is my doing!" Hugh insisted. "This is your mother's work. By God's Throat, she's contrived all this without my knowing!"

Not waiting for another word, Prince Richard unbelted his sword and handed it to Bigod. He spoke to his guard stationed at the bridgehead, then walked across the bridge.

The French camp was waking. A shout went up, and then another and another as the red-haired prince of England was seen walking toward Tailleberg, alone and unarmed. Several French knights, men he had rescued in Palestine, ran to meet him as he stepped from the bridge. They formed an escort around him to bring him to King Louis.

The King of France was sitting at breakfast in the tower of Tailleberg's castle. Admitted to Louis's presence, Richard said at once, "Good king, I come to ask for truce."

From his window Louis had a good view of the river, its farther bank and the little army encamped there. He touched his mouth with his napkin and motioned for the meal to be taken away, then turned to Richard. "I offered you generous terms. You flouted them. Why should I grant you truce?"

"For no reason but that it is I who ask it." Richard met the King of France's gaze. He could offer nothing more. But the weight of France's debt to him for his rescue of their knights spoke loudly.

Louis had no wish to conquer England even though the English king lay helpless in his grasp. What he wanted was a permanent, negotiated peace. He knew that resigning the Queen Mother to justice was a hard demand, however generous his other terms had been. "We honor you, Richard," he said after some moments of thought. "You saved our people in the Holy Land. And, as this is Sunday, we should do a good. We grant you truce. But for today and tonight only."

"Our Lord's blessing upon you, good king," Richard bowed and turned to leave.

"Lord Richard!" Louis called after him, "We've granted you truce for this day and night for you to have time to deliberate. Night brings counsel with it."

"On that account I asked it," Richard answered. He bowed again and left.

It was mid-morning when the prince entered King Henry's tent. "What does Louis say?" Henry asked. His tone was hollow, his face was gray and the muscles of his brow were clenched tight.

Richard whispered in his ear, "Louis offers us truce. But for tonight only. He expects us to accept his terms tomorrow. Which is what we must do, if we stay here. And his terms will not be so generous this time."

'What should we do?"

"As soon as darkness comes, we must retreat."

The order was given to the army's captains to be ready to withdraw after dark.

In the bright afternoon sunshine, Richard and the earls Roger Bigod, Peter of Savoy, William Longspee and Simon stood on the riverbank. Across the river, the long streamers of red-orange silk: the Oriflamme of Saint Denis, the battle flag of France, was set at the bridgehead. Simon watched its flame-like ribbons curling and uncurling in the breeze, and he remarked grimly, "I pray Louis won't miss us until morning. But he needs no scouts for this distance. Only his own eyes and ears."

"Wishing you were in the other camp, Sire Montfort?" William Longspee asked sardonically. He was King Henry's cousin, a son of one of Henry II's bastards by his mistress Hela. He had always detested Simon.

"No, Earl William," Simon smiled, ignoring the pointed insult as he had been schooling himself to do. "I was thinking how the terrain of our retreat might be used to our advantage. South of the meadows, the roads are narrow and the vineyards on each side are too woody for the maneuvering of troops. Louis must keep to the road, following us in an extended line. His vanguard will be vulnerable for he can't deploy a flank. We may yet give him trouble."

The Count of La Marche had joined them and was listening attentively.

Longspee's look was cynical and bitter. "It seems strange to me that a man who has grown up with another, enjoying his largesse, would plot against his friend."

"Isn't loyalty bound to liege, regardless of affection?" Simon countered. "As for fighting Louis, we grew up fighting each other. It would give me the greatest pleasure to defeat him now, outnumbered as we are."

Longspee frowned. "As for your loyalty, Sire Montfort, we know you're serving as a mercenary, and mercenary loyalty is to whomever pays the most. For the rest of your nice words, we'll see how much your heart is in them when the fighting comes." He turned and stalked back to his tent.

"Carping old bastard," Bigod muttered after him with more truth than he intended.

Longspee's words were the kind of insult Simon had borne all his years in England. Watching the earl's retreating back, he remarked thoughtfully, "His point of view is natural enough. It's I whose lot in life is strained."

"Tell us more of how we can turn our retreat to advantage," Count Hugh pressed.

"We can't risk it," Richard said decisively, utterly cold to his stepfather. "We must withdraw to Bordeaux as quickly as we can."

"It's a long way from here to Gascony, and we're not provisioned for a steady march," Roger Bigod warned.

"We should reach Sainte by tomorrow. Then we'll see what our next stage will be." The prince's stern tone admitted no further discussion.

That night the English camp was abandoned. To avoid the risk of capture, King Henry, Prince Richard and Peter of Savoy, with the wagon of the royal treasury and an escort of knights, rode at once toward Sainte. Simon, Bigod, Longspee and the other earls: of Hereford, Warwick, Surrey, and Oxford, and the captains of the forces from Castile, Toulouse and Navarre, stayed with the army.

The sky was black. The stars in the clear air were a swathe of sparkles in the heavens. Forms in the dark landscape merged into shadows. In the camp no lights but the campfires were allowed. The tents were left standing, and only the most needed gear was packed. Talking was in whispers for the wind blew from the south, carrying every sound across the river. In the darkness beyond the glow of firelight, by touch alone the soldiers harnessed horses, strapped bundles onto packhorses and loaded cases of arms into wagons. The sightless, silent work was slow and fumbling. When the last of the rear guard moved out it was nearly dawn.

Louis was wakened in the small hours of the night and told of movement in the English camp. He went down to the riverbank and watched. Above the rushing of the river's flow, the jingle of harnesses was unmistakable though all that could be seen was the campfires' orange glow upon the flanks of tents.

King Louis gave the order for his army to pursue the English after dawn.

Chapter Twenty-four

SAINTE
1242

AFTER A NIGHT OF FORCED marches, the soldiers of Henry's army began to straggle wearily into Sainte. More came throughout the day, exhausted. In the darkness they had wandered out of the way on the unfamiliar roads. Some had marched double and triple the distance to find Sainte. They fell down in the narrow, winding alleys, sleeping wherever they fell. A wagon freighted with arms had gone off the road and overturned. Its cargo was abandoned in the panic of retreat.

"What now?" Roger Bigod asked as he, Simon and Richard walked through Sainte with flares that night, inspecting the condition of the army. Bigod held his flare high. The light, reflecting from the stone walls of the houses, showed sleeping bodies crouched in doorways and littering the lanes. In their hurry to abandon Tailleberg, numbers of soldiers had lost parts of their armor. Many had lost their swords.

Richard's eyebrows pinched in worry. But he said calmly as they walked the streets, "A few days here to re-arm and rest, then we'll march to Blaye."

"If Louis doesn't reach us here before that!" Bigod gave a harsh laugh.

"He should have closed upon us already," Simon observed gravely.

"Louis will wait for the trebuchet and siege cat to be brought from Frontenaye." Richard replied, with the authority of one who knows.

Simon looked at him, astonished. "Good prince, why do you say this?"

Richard smiled broadly, "My good deeds in Palestine serve me well. My informants are the best. We will reach Gascony, and the French army will not overtake us."

They were walking by the city wall, a low structure not more than ten feet at its highest range.

"I pray we move on soon. My lord, look at this," Simon ran his hand along the mortar between the wall's rough blocks. It was as soft as sand and fell away at his touch. "A siege here would be brief. A trebuchet will breach this easily. Then there'll be fighting in the streets with a force thirty times our number, and the walls will be our deathtrap. It would be better to camp in the open fields than to stay here."

Looking down the dark street at the wretched, sleeping bodies that were his army, Richard shook his head. "It will be days before we can re-arm and move these men."

The next morning, as Simon was crossing the square by the town's north gate on his way to join the king and earls at breakfast, he heard shouting in the distance. Just audible, then drifting clearer were the sounds of battle.

John de Plessis, the Earl of Warwick, was running toward an alley of stables. He shouted to Simon, "The Count of La Marche engages Louis' army on the road! The fighting has begun!"

Simon ran to the alley and the shed where his horses were stabled. A groom started to bring his palfrey, but he cried, "My destrier!"

The groom loosed the big warhorse, kept saddled with Simon's helmet and shield hooked to the saddlebow, and he cinched the girth tight. The horse pranced nervously, pricking its ears in excitement. Simon mounted, turned the horse around in the narrow alley, and spurred to a gallop.

Other knights were pouring across the square toward the town's north gate. Their shouts and the clatter of their horses' hooves drowned the distant sounds of combat. At the city gate Simon's mount, a gift from Louis, was near the lead of the sortie.

A mile north of Sainte, the level land narrowed to a breadth no wider than the road as the road made a long curve around the base of a hill. Here, on one side, was a steep slope dense with briars, and on the other a sharp drop into the swift Charente. The road was just wide enough for vineyard carts to pass, or fourteen horsemen to ride abreast.

Simon's destrier outran the other horses, and kept the lead as the charge crowded in the narrow curve around the hill. The sound of fighting was clear and loud, but the battle was still out of sight. Then suddenly around the curve there was the Oriflamme, the dust, the shouts, the din of clashing metal, and a churning knot of men and horses.

Simon and the English knights came full-gallop upon the French. Foot soldiers scattered from the running horses and scrambled through the brush on the hillside. The French knights' horses in the vanguard shied. Rearing, they toppled backward with their riders, splashing into the Charente. Weighed down by their armor, they quickly sank and drowned. A few of the French spurred their mounts up the hill, tangling their mantels in the thorny bushes.

Simon closed in the fight. His sword struck shield. But the velocity of the English charge pushed him on. His second blow was deeper among the French. His third cut his way deeper still. Soon he was surrounded, beyond his own men and the fighting was in earnest. He slashed to one side and the other, keeping his horse turning, wheeling to give no target while his sword flashed like a windmill's arms in a gale. There was no thrust and parry. All around him steel blades swung, yet no one could come near him as he whirled and flayed and worked his horse backward toward the English.

Then, leading the English forward, he cut his way among the French again. He took no notice how he struck. His sword rang hard on parry of steel blade or shield, or bit through mail. Familiar blazons of Chevreux, of Meaux, of Dreux came fast one after another. But he saw only the parries, strong or weak with clang on blade or grate through mail. Beyond the brilliant steel, surcoat-colors shifted: blue, red, yellow, white, red and red and red. Simon made no count of wounds he dealt. He met blade, parried and struck. His sword was red, his glove and chain mail sleeve were soaked with blood. Moments, or hours, passed, rung on the cacophony of steel on steel. Eventually the press around him eased, and then fell back beyond his reach.

A siege cat, a wooden wall on wheels, was drawn across the road. Near it, on the hill, a single knight upon a fine horse draped in blue with golden fleurs-de-lis stood watching. It was Louis. The slope was full of French crossbowmen. But Louis stayed their shot.

Simon saw he was alone in the road. His horse was treading on the bodies of the fallen. He turned about and pressed his spurs to his horse's flanks, and it sprang ahead toward Sainte. From behind the wooden barricade, men ran out to the wounded and the dead.

As Simon reached the English and La Marche's men they gave a joyful shout, and all galloped back to Sainte.

Dinner that afternoon in Sainte was festive, each knight telling how and whom he had struck, and how many prisoners he had taken. Simon sat silent, his nerves still ringing at high pitch. He had nothing to say. Apart from a blow he'd given the knight of Chevreux, he had no notion whom he'd struck or how. He had returned, his surcoat red as a butcher's apron, the chain mail of his right sleeve stiff with blood. He sat, clothed in his black robe, at the king's dinner as his squire worked to brush his armor clean. The merriment of the feast came to him only distantly. The chamber, the knights seated at table, all lay beyond the vision of flashing blades and bloody hands and helms still playing through his nerves.

"My lord Montfort, I owe you an apology." William Longspee was standing before him. "Never in my life have I seen such battling as you did today!"

The Earl of Salisbury's words took everyone's attention. Men who had hated Simon, who had called him foreign leech and traitor and Queen Blanche's spy, now gushed forth stories of his bravery. Humphrey de Bohun, the Earl of Hereford, told how blood had spattered around Simon like a hailstorm of crimson. Peter of Savoy declared the lord Montfort had come upon the French like a lion on a coop of hens. Roger Bigod claimed he saw Simon strike the knight of Pontoise with a blow that split his helm and head in half.

Simon listened with detached interest, only gradually realizing that it was he whom they were praising – that he had won this day a hero's fame. Never before, not even when he fought the Welsh, had these men had a good word for him. He wished the ringing of his nerves would stop so he could enjoy his triumph. He smiled, nodded, even laughed with embarrassment as the rain of praises showered over him.

That he had severed souls from their bodies, that families had lost fathers and sons, was not Simon's or any of the lords' concern. With the donning of chain mail came a tacit pact: an agreement to be killed or kill. Death was not a tragedy. Only how one's life was lived, and what might come after death, were worthy of a knight's grief.

An envoy from the French arrived. King Louis had withdrawn his army to a meadow three miles north of Sainte. The envoy gave King Henry the list of prisoners held by France, and Louis' offer of exchange.

Henry gave the list to Richard. "How many prisoners do we have?" the prince asked the clerk Mansel.

"As the lord Montfort gave no quarter," Mansel said wryly, "we haven't so many more than the French have of ours. The most noble are John de Barres and the Seneschal of Boulogne. We hold twenty of the French in all."

Richard turned to Henry, "It seems a fair exchange."

The King, subdued in spirit, nodded. He alone showed no joy at the victory.

"Tell King Louis we agree," Richard commanded the envoy. "We will release our prisoners to him at sunset, if those he holds are brought then to the city's northern gate."

The envoy bowed. But instead of leaving, he went to Simon and bowed again. "I bear a message also for the Earl of Leicester from the King of France. And a gift. He sends a hogshead of his best wine, with his congratulations."

Simon burst out laughing and the tangle of his nerve reknit. "Give him my thanks. I'll enjoy the wine at Christmastide. But if he means it as a Trojan horse, take him this empty cup from me. It holds the better beverage for war." It was a private joke, rising from a long-standing dispute between Simon and Louis: Simon held that fine wine never should be spoilt with water; Louis, that unwatered wine was bad for health and slowed the eyes and hand. The gift was Louis' way of saying Simon's eyes and hand were all too swift. The envoy left with the empty cup as answer.

"My father," King Henry turned to the old Count of La Marche after the envoy was gone. He spoke in a controlled and careful manner. Richard watched him worriedly. "My father, when you saw the French, why did you attack, instead of warning us?"

"I saw the chance to strike them by surprise," Count Hugh said simply, proud of his bold move. "It seemed best, rather than to lose the chance."

"Your purpose was to reconnoiter only!" Henry's voice rose stridently. "We were not warned! But for our brave knights, we could have been taken!"

Old Hugh stared at the king, his creased cheeks growing livid. "They were stopped by my men first! I thought to save you from another hasty flight, and have your thanks. But I see you still hold your deluded hopes against me!"

"Whose fault is it that we're here at all?" Henry shrieked back.

"I tell you, it's not mine!" Hugh retorted.

"Father, you lie!" Richard bellowed.

The old count stood up from his seat, his face purple with rage. "I lie? You're both as mad as your mother!" He threw his napkin down and strode out of the hall.

His three sons watched him go, but stayed beside King Henry.

Hardly was Hugh gone when Count Raymond of Toulouse arrived. He brought a small company of reinforcements. Henry studied the brief list of names, his expression a mask of dullness that barely concealed his pain.

Taking the king's unhappy look to spring from the brevity of his list, Raymond spoke up quickly. "With money, I could raise far more men. My Touloussaines have overcome the French before.

Even when far outnumbered," he added with a pompous swelling of his chest and a glance toward Simon.

"With cowardly devices," Simon muttered to Bigod who sat beside him. Simon's father had been killed by a stone hurled from a mangonel mounted on the walls of Toulouse. He well knew his father's old enemy, and detested him.

Raymond heard the remark. Slowly, insolently the count looked Simon up and down. "Montfort's with you again, good King?" He turned back to Henry, his tone full of venom. "What use can more soldiers be to you, my lord, when you persist in harboring French traitors?"

"Lord Raymond, if anyone is to be called a traitor, look to yourself!" Simon retorted between clenched teeth. "You're a traitor to your liege lord King Louis, and a traitor to your ally as well! You were to bring us fighting men. Instead you come and ask us for more money!"

"Montfort, enough!" Henry shouted, his voice quavering. He was fast losing his last threads of self-control. Coughing to steady himself, he went on, "After today's battle, no one doubts your loyalty to us. But we are grateful for the aid the Count of Toulouse offers. The more so..." his throat was gripping shut with stress, "...more so when those most close to us have failed. We mean to aid Count Raymond every way we can," he forced his last words out as if he were choking.

Raymond saw his chance and took it. "I need three thousand marks."

"It will be given you," Henry waved his hand, hardly hearing the huge sum.

"Henry!" Richard protested. But the king turned such an aching look upon his brother that Richard bridled, only saying, "At least, I'd ask the count where and when, in what quantity, how armed and how supplied, this force would be that we are buying for three thousand marks."

"Richard," Henry pleaded, his voice cracking and his body twisting, "we mustn't challenge our faithful friends with such hard questioning."

A smile turned the corners of the Count of Toulouse's lips.

To all the English it was clear the count was making the most of the king's weak moment to fleece him. There was a long, painful silence.

King Henry's fool, Henry of Avranche, who lately had become a fixture of the Court in camp, broke the silence with a shaking of his belled scepter. "Our king is very like to Christ," he winked sagaciously.

"How are we like Christ?" Henry turned to the fool, so relieved and flattered that his throat began to ease. "Is it that, like Him, we put our trust in faith?"

"Oh no, my lord," the fool wagged his head solemnly. "But that Christ, at the age of thirty, was as wise as on the day that he was born."

This theology of divine omniscience, brought to bear on Henry, roused titters among the lords.

Stunned, Henry's mouth fell open. Rising from his chair, he struck the fool across the face with the back of his hand. "Hang him! I want him hanged!" he shrieked and his voice broke again.

Bloody-nosed, Avranche scrambled from the room.

Henry moved as if to go after him. But Richard caught him by the arm, and he sank back in his chair. At the restraint, all spirit seemed to leave the king. He doubled over, clutching himself as if he were in pain, and began rocking to and fro.

Richard said softly, "I'd like to know the particulars of the force Toulouse promises, brother, so we can know how best to use them."

Henry turned his face away. With his head bent so low that his chin pressed against his chest, he gave a stiff nod.

Richard, Toulouse and Bigod went aside and talked.

It was decided that, until Toulouse's reinforcements could be brought, the army would remain in Sainte, regrouping and rearming. Simon and Bigod would stay with the army. Hugh LeBrun was made the seneschal for the king's household in Sainte. The king, the other earls and the prince would keep in motion at a distance, to avoid the risk of capture. The wagon of the royal treasury was sent on south under guard.

Before dusk and the appointed time for exchange of the prisoners, before Louis could attack again, the king and his company left Sainte.

The royal party rode a circuit of Pons, Herbizi and Archiac.

On the morning of the third day, they neared Sainte again to see how the army was faring. The Earl of Warwick rode ahead, returning to the king and prince with word that France's force was still encamped three miles to the north. They hadn't moved. Sainte had not been troubled. So complete was the quiet that Hugh LeBrun invited the royal company to breakfast. King Henry and his entourage rode into the town.

Sainte's squares, its cobbled streets and lanes, its rag-stone walls and red-tiled roofs were washed in summer sunshine; all was peaceful. Soldiers sat on doorsteps, sharpening their weapons. They waved and shouted welcome as the king rode by.

Hugh LeBrun was standing before the bishop's manse, which had been requisitioned for the English headquarters. "Welcome back, brother," he greeted. "As you can see, all's well."

Henry looked tired. He dismounted and put his arm around his half-brother Hugh. Leaning on the youth, he went into the house. A long table was set up in the hall. The king, the prince and the eight earls were seated.

Roger Bigod reported on the progress of re-arming. "All our men are accounted for, though we're still short of arms. If Toulouse's men arrive soon, we should be able to march south in good order."

"Louis has made no move at all?" Richard asked.

Young Hugh spoke up with an odd smile. "There's sickness in his camp. It's said the King of France himself is sick."

"Warfare upsets his tummy," little William de Valence, the youngest of the brothers of La Marche, clutched his stomach in mock torment.

Before the child had a chance to enlarge upon his rude remark, there was a loud commotion at the house's door. A knight, in the surcoat of Coucy, forced his way past the guard, shouting, "I know

Prince Richard's here! I must speak to him!" and the knight broke into the hall. Seeing King Henry at the table, a thin gold coronet over his hood of mail marking him regally, the knight came and knelt before him. "Good King Henry, you are betrayed! The Count of La Marche has surrendered to King Louis!"

"By the head of Solomon! Whatever did we come here for!" Roger Bigod bellowed.

The French knight turned to Richard, "Louis has pardoned the Count of La Marche, taken his lands in holding and sent him against Count Raymond of Toulouse for his betrayal of France. Now Louis marches on you here in Sainte."

Hardly had the knight finished speaking when Guy, the middle brother of La Marche, came running in shouting, "Flee! Everyone! They've turned against us! The aldermen of Sainte are opening the city gates to Louis!"

In an instant Simon was on his feet and moving toward the door.

"Where are you going?" Henry demanded, sitting as still as stone. His face was drawn, expressionless.

"To have the bells rung for retreat!" Simon exclaimed. "Before our soldiers are trapped here by Sainte's walls!"

"We've given no command to retreat," Henry said rigidly.

In the desperateness of the moment the words broke from Simon's lips: "Are there not locks and iron doors enough for you at Windsor, if you must be locked up!"

The whole company stared, shocked at his words.

Then the French knight begged again, "King Henry, you must flee!"

The spell was broken. The whole room suddenly was in headlong movement. Benches toppled, the table was overturned and the breakfast scattered on the floor as everyone got up at once and ran.

Richard hurried Henry out, the king still glaring at Simon. In the jostling at the door as everyone tried to squeeze through at once, the golden coronet was knocked from Henry's head and trampled under foot.

A quarter of an hour later, Louis, with his Marshall and Ensign, entered the house. The abandoned breakfast was strewn everywhere amid the wreckage of the broken table and benches. The King of France bent down and picked from the doorsill the crushed coronet of gold.

"The Crown of England lies shattered at your feet, my lord," the young Ensign smirked.

Louis cut him short. "It is no matter for your smiles."

Chapter Twenty-five

BLAYE
1242

HENRY, HIS EARLS AND ENGLISH knights fled south, past the border that divided the province of Poitou from the province of Gascony. They reached the town of Blaye that night. The English foot soldiers and squires, abandoned by the fast riders, tried to follow, then surrendered to the French. The companies from Castile, Toulouse and Navarre surrendered to King Louis with no attempt to flee. The victorious army of France marched south in slow pursuit of Henry.

Where the Garonne and Dordogne rivers join and widen to the estuary of the Gironde, the quiet waters meld with the sea, flowing around several wooded isles. Guarding the estuary's northern shore, where the land rises to a cliff, was the castle of Blaye, a cluster of crude towers of buff stone and Roman tile. Blaye was an ancient sentry-point guarding Gascony from the north and west.

Below the castle, the land was level along the estuary's bank. A quay stretched its retaining wall in front of a wide street of warehouses filled with tuns and hogsheads of the region's wines. But no fine mansions adorned the town, despite Blaye's busy trade. The merchant magnates of the wine exporting industry lived across the estuary and upstream in the city of Bordeaux. Blaye castle stood alone in rough, decaying grandeur.

Rudel, Blaye's lord, a sick, dying old man, had long since ceased to take an interest in his fortress's care, had ceased to take an interest in anything except the hawks he watched from his bedchamber window as they glided in the air-currents high over the Gironde. When Henry and his disheveled entourage reached Blaye, Rudel had himself brought to the hall to greet his king. "My lands, my castle, use them as your own," he said with an antique, parchment-dry courtliness as fragile as his graceful, thin white hands. Then he had himself carried back to his chamber, and his door locked securely to establish his neutrality should battle come.

King Henry, Prince Richard and the eight earls shared cramped quarters. The knights who succeeded in reaching Blaye made do with sheds constructed out of scraps of wood and thatch. Their tents, their gear, their clothes had been lost on the road from Tailleberg, or were still at Sainte. There were no comforts. Necessities were scarce. But, with nothing left to lose, further retreat could be swift.

The squires, too, were left in Sainte and taken by the French, so everyone had to fend for himself. None save the knights and lords, the clerk Mansel and the redoubtable fool Avranche, had been able to follow the king's desperate retreat.

The English looked forward to negotiations with the French, when their squires could be ransomed. In the meantime, local folk offered their services to cook and do washing for a fee. Laundering was problematic since none of the English had a change of clothes. But most found their culinary lot improved, with stews of fish and local sausages in place of their squires' pots of barley mush and boiled dried meat.

Still, the amenities were few. The cliff 's edge served as a latrine, giving a foul scent to the landward breezes when the tide was low. There were no baths and water was scarce, apart from the muddy estuary itself. Even among those who could swim, few cared to strip naked before the warehouses and take a plunge to wash away their sweat. Soon everybody stank.

Richard sent the Poitouvin knight Giles Argentine to scout the French movements. The next day Argentine reported, "King Louis camps at Cartelegue. His men are suffering from fever. Even the King of France himself is known to be sick."

Henry's half-brother, Guy de Lusignan, standing beside the king's chair, nudged his brother Hugh LeBrun. William, the youngest, covered his face with his hands.

Henry, though listening dull-eyed to Argentine, notice the boys' movements. He pulled William's hands down from his face, uncovering a broad smile. "Why do you smile, William?"

"When the French came to Frontenaye, we were cleaning the latrines. We dumped the filth pots down the wells!" the boy squealed with delight.

Henry began to shake. He laughed. Tears started to his eyes. "You stopped King Louis! You poisoned the wells!" he roared. "The French drank foul water! My army couldn't stop them, but you did!" His whole frame shook with spasms of laughter. He hugged the three boys.

The lords cast their gazes away from Henry, mortified by his glee at such a vile victory. Richard looked down at the floor, his face red with shame for his brother. Simon looked at the La Marche boys with the beginnings of loathing.

Henry settled into Blaye, unwilling to go further. A Court of sorts was convened in the castle's hall. Richard's spies began arriving with more news of the French camp. Most of Louis' huge army was sick. The King of France was confined to a cot and could not be moved further. There was no risk of the army of France advancing.

But Louis did not have to march to gather victories. The lords of Poitou, learning of his leniency toward old Count Hugh – and of King Henry's debacle – hurried to his camp to pledge their liege to France. Louis was conquering Poitou even from his bed.

King Henry, his hand pressed hard against his cheek, listened to Richard's spies' reports: all recitation of betrayals. Day by day he seemed to shrink -- like a leaf hunching, twisting, blanching in a flame, the distorted shape still holding form, but ready at a touch to turn to dust.

Then a courier came from Parthenay with very different news. "Good king," the monk bowed obsequiously, "my master, the Bishop of Parthenay, wishes to cleave to you. But he is fearful of a French attack. He begs, if you could spare five hundred pounds of gold to fortify his walls, he'll be your faithful subject always."

Henry roused. His dull eyes seemed to clear. "Here's someone loyal to me?" His spirits rose. He looked to Richard, "Give the bishop what he asks." His treasury wagon, having left Sainte for Blaye at once after the first encounter with Louis, had arrived safely. He ordered his Poitouvin knights, Giles Argentine and Drogo de Barentin, to accompany the monk to Parthenay with the five hundred pounds of gold.

Five days later Barentin and Argentine returned on foot, their horses and their helmets lost, their surcoats torn, their faces cut and bruised. They knelt before the king, heads bowed, reluctant to speak.

"How came you to be hurt?" Prince Richard demanded.

All pride and haughtiness gone from him, Barentin looked to King Henry. "Don't count the Bishop of Parthenay a friend, my lord. Knowing of your generosity to Toulouse, he only meant to rob you of your gold, and make fools of us."

"What are you saying?" Henry's hands began to shake.

Argentine steeled himself, and said in a voice so low that only those nearest to the king could hear, "We went into the cathedral at Parthenay, unarmed as custom holds is proper in a church. The bishop took the gold we brought. Then he ordered us seized, mocked, and beaten by a dozen of his stout monks. He already had pledged himself to France."

Henry pressed his fist hard against his cheek and began rocking to and fro. He moaned with a strange, forlorn sound, clutching himself as he rocked.

The English lords watched him in shocked silence.

Simon, serving as steward at the door, came in to announce that Hertolt, the Royal Castellan of Mirebeau, had come. Seeing Henry, he stopped speaking in mid-sentence.

"The king's not well," Richard said carefully. "Keep Hertolt outside the door."

Henry crooked his arm tightly over his head. The pitch of his moaning rose and fell in a tuneless, nasal humming as he rocked himself.

His courtiers stared, frozen by the sight. Roger Bigod went to him. Tenderly, the gruff earl put his arms around his king. "Don't carry on so, my lord," he spoke as gently as a mother to her child. "It's the Bishop of Parthenay who'll burn in Hell for this. Not you."

Henry grasped Bigod's hand and pressed it to his lips. Tears ran from his eyes, but the moaning and rocking ceased.

Bigod cradled Henry in his arms, softly murmuring, "Be still, my lord. Be still." Though he might brashly insult his king in Court, he loved Henry and could not bear to see him so wounded.

Henry quieted. His fit seemed to pass. He sat upright in his chair and wiped his eyes. Seeming more in control of himself than he had been for days, as though he had drawn new strength from sturdy Bigod's embrace, he turned to Richard, "The Castellan of Mirebeau has come?"

"If you don't wish to see him..."

Henry beckoned, "Send him in."

Hertolt's castle lay directly in the line of march from Louis' camp at Cartelegue to Blaye. The royal castellan knelt before Henry. "My king, your Majesty knows how fortune runs against us. Can you send me no soldiers? I have no hope without your aid!"

Hollow-eyed and fragile, Henry studied him," Do you want money?" he asked heavily.

"My lord, I must have fighting men! It's far too late for me to find mercenaries anywhere."

A faint, sad smile turned Henry's lips. He had found an honest liegeman. "You see, Hertolt, what knights we have." He gestured at the lords in the room, a gesture that included the shabby camp out in the yard, "Barely enough to guard ourselves. Even our Lord Christ was betrayed by his friend. Can we expect any better?"

Henry seemed to have finished speaking, but as Hertolt began to rise, he said slowly in a voice of deep, chill sadness, "I loved the Count of La Marche. I loved him as my father. But it's you, not he, who is loyal to me. Whatever you hold for England's Crown henceforth is your own, by our gift." He slumped back in his chair, as depleted as an emptied sack. Then suddenly he sat bolt-upright shouting, "Save yourself, Hertolt! Do all you can to save yourself! I can do nothing for you." He fell back in his chair again, rocking to and fro, his arm bent tightly around his head.

After Hertolt left, Henry shut himself up in a small chamber behind the hall. He would admit only two people through the door: Simon, and the fool Avranche. "It is proper," Henry muttered, "that the Steward serve me with his washbasin, to see that I don't stink. And the Fool must bear me company, as he's my only equal here."

In the small, whitewashed and sparsely furnished, hot and gradually fetid room, the king sat on his cot hour after hour, staring at the floor. His drooping eye sagged until the lower lid showed pale and liquid as an oyster. The painted image of a soul transfixed in the agonies of Hell could no better depict such utter despair.

Once, Henry looked up at Simon with an anxious look and asked about his royal coronet, lost in the flight from Sainte.

"Another and a better one is being made in England," Simon answered in a reassuring tone. His feelings for Henry were far from love, but seeing his liege lord, his king so battered and so fallen, even touched him with compassion. For the first time, he could fathom the crushing burdens of a man not bold or brilliant, yet born to responsibilities he never sought. He was moved to pity.

Henry went on eyeing Simon, and chuckled, "You speak to me as if I were a child. I'm not so bad as that. Only very sad."

The fool Avranche diligently tried to cheer the king. But he had small success until one afternoon when Henry found two courtiers who suited his black spirits perfectly.

The Countess Garsende of Bearne and her son Gaston arrived. Though she was told that the king saw no one, the countess insisted she was the king's aunt, and would not be refused.

"Do I have an aunt of Bearne? " Henry asked Simon vaguely.

Simon didn't know, but Peter of Savoy sent word to the king's chamber that Garsende was in fact an aunt of Queen Eleanor. Henry allowed her to be shown in.

The Countess of Bearne's stupendous form filled the narrow doorway. Her body and each feature of her face were puffed, except her eyes which sank into their fleshy lids like two black snails withdrawn into their shells. Her son was as immense as she, and swaggered as he walked, jiggling his fat as if its movement should intimidate the less- portly.

Avranche hissed in Henry's ear, "They're physicians, truly. Most accomplished leeches!"

The shadow of a smile turned Henry's lips.

Avranche made a low bow with elaborate flourishes, "O, mistress of the tender skills, speak. Our king bids!"

Garsende fluttered and colored pink as a rosebud at the fool's flattery, missing his puns on "leech" and "tender" in their monetary meanings. But Henry let out an uncontrollable guffaw. Simon had to cover his mouth with his hand and look away to keep from laughing.

"My lord, most gracious king," the countess tried to bend her shape. But bowing was impossible. Her face grew redder with the strain until she ceased the effort. "We, your loyal kin of Bearne, have flown to your protective wing..."

Avranche raised his arm, wing-like, as if taking measure, then shook his head dolefully. Another laugh bubbled from Henry's sunken chest.

Perception began to waken in Garsende that the fool was not her friend. She scowled at him, pursing her lips and narrowing her tiny eyes. Her face took on a flush until it seemed no face at all, but a lumpy scarlet pillow.

Henry's mouth fell open at the sight. A pant of laughter broke from his pale lips. Then more. His laughter grew, bringing more grotesque displeasure to the countess's livid flesh, and more hilarity from Henry. She was the perfect image of Greed, the Deadly Sin that was so much the cause of his misery.

When he could calm himself, the king managed to say, "Lady, pay the fool no mind." He asked her coaxingly, coyly, "Tell me, what is it you would have of me? Perhaps the fame of my generosity has reached even to Bearne?"

"Most gracious lord, indeed!" simpered the countess, still only dimly aware of the jest in which she nonetheless was playing her part flawlessly.

"How much do you want?" Henry murmured seductively.

"Dear king! Your kindness quite outruns your fame, " she gushed, flustered.

Henry eyed her as if making calculations and then said, "I'll grant you thirty pounds a day. That ought to be enough to keep you in your present state."

The countess took her "state" to mean her noble dignity, not her massive form. Making an effort to bow again, she failed, and dipped a solemn nod instead. Gaston, beside her, could barely contain his joy.

Henry smiled majestically upon the pair. "We wish to see you every day, to keep always before our eyes a reminder of mankind's true nature."

The Bearnes were costly fools to keep. Their rate of maintenance per day was more than a whole company of mercenary knights would be. But sight of them seemed like a poultice, drawing Henry's pain away. Seeing them, he could place all fault in mankind and see himself as virtuous, abused for his largesse. The Bearnes enabled him to forgive himself. In gratitude, he coddled Gaston and Garsende like a pair of grotesque lapdogs fed sweetmeats.

As the days went by, more and more reports reached Blaye of the spread of fever among the French. Too sick to march, King Louis' immense army lay festering in the growing filth of its encampment. Five thousand foot soldiers and eighty knights were dead of dysentery. Louis himself was thought to be near death.

King Henry permitted Richard to send Simon as his envoy to King Louis, to seek terms of truce.

The reek of the French camp was overwhelming. The local peasantry, who would have tended to the soldiers' cooking, washing and provisioning, stayed away due to the stench and fear of the disease. Only a few nuns from a nearby convent braved the foul atmosphere to care for the bedridden. A nun conducted Simon to the King of France's blue and gold striped tent.

Louis, lying on a camp cot, raised his hand weakly as Simon entered. His eyes were red with fever. His fine blond hair lay in thin, sticky strands across his forehead. He looked at Simon and smiled, then shut his eyes and murmured, " You were right. See what comes of putting water in good wine."

Simon sat on a stool beside the cot. Louis' appearance shocked him. He was certain he was seeing him alive for the last time. He pressed his friend's hand, then kissed it as tears came into his eyes. The once-strong hand remained in his. He clutched it as if, by holding Louis' hand, he could pour his own vitality into his friend and raise him from death's grip.

Louis answered with a smile. He spoke slowly, keeping his dry, burning eyes shut. "It was a marvel, watching you fight on the road to Sainte. I should never have let you go to Henry. When have so few men stopped thirty-thousand?" He gave a little laugh at the memory, and opened his eyes to look at Simon. "What do you call that, that spinning your horse, and striking every-which way?"

"I call it, trying my best not to be killed," Simon grinned.

"It was very messy. Barbaric," Louis' lips stretched to a smile that seemed more a grimace. Then, "You've come from Henry to ask a truce?"

"Yes."

"Tell him we grant it. Where's my clerk? Have him write it down. I want a truce for five years. If I die, that will give my mother time... and my little son."

Simon pressed his lips to Louis' hand again. "I pray God spares you," he whispered.

Louis studied his friend for a long moment. Then he sighed and shut his fevered eyes again. "Simon, serve Henry patiently. I love you well. But he needs you." He motioned for the clerk, whom the nun was bringing in, and dictated to him the terms of a five-year truce. When the task was done, all of Louis' strength was spent, and he dozed off in the stupor of his sickness.

Simon returned to Blaye bearing the offer of truce, but heavy-burdened with the sight of Louis. Seeing what the boys of La Marche had wrought by fouling the wells of Frontenaye, he was filled with disgust and rage. But Louis' words stayed with him. He must try to be patient with Henry.

The truce for five years was accepted. In the next weeks, the army of France slowly dispersed. Louis was carried back to Paris on a litter. The war in Poitou had come to an end.

Chapter Twenty-Six

BORDEAUX
1242

THOUGH THE WAR WAS DONE, Henry stayed shut up in his chamber at Blaye, until one morning when a courier arrived from Bordeaux. Peter of Savoy, who received all communications to the king, consulted with Prince Richard then, after the messenger was carefully tutored, Savoy urged Henry to hear him.

"I bring you happy news, good king," the courier bowed low. "Your queen is delivered of a daughter."

Henry drifted up from his reverie. A smile glimmered in his eyes, "A daughter? And all's well?"

The courier glanced to Savoy, then added cautiously, "The queen is better. She urges that, as soon as your own health permits and your tasks here are done, you hurry to her with all speed."

Henry brightened. "We will leave Blaye tomorrow. We've sat here in our sorrow long enough. In Bordeaux, with our queen, we will regain our strength."

The next morning, the English abandoned their camp of huts in Rudel's yards, and marched on to Bordeaux.

The great city was a very welcome sight. After London, Bordeaux was the richest city in all Henry's domains. Battlements and turrets of creamy golden stone and steep roofs of gray slate stood in sharp outline against the searingly blue southern sky. Pennants fluttered, trumpets blared from the towered barbican of the Begueyre Gate. Street criers shouted the coming of the king. People crowded the ways and leaned from windows to see the royal entourage pass by. They cheered and waved their welcome.

Henry, haggard and aged far past his thirty-four years, seemed heartened by the greeting. He nodded to the smiling faces along the street and in the windows above. "Here are the worthy subjects of a king," he sighed to Peter of Savoy, who rode beside him. "Let Louis have Parthenay. And all of Poitou!"

After escorting the king to the Hotel de Ville, the knights and lords were free to find their own lodging.

Relieved of his long, close company with Henry, Simon took a room at an inn. His squire Peter, left behind in the precipitous flight from Sainte, had been allowed by Louis to return to Paris and the Montfort household there. Simon, fending for himself, left the inn to find a bathhouse, to wash away the dust of Poitou and the sweat of the king's hot, confined chamber at Blaye.

Bathhouses were luxurious: spas for married couples with sensual tastes, and trysting places for courtesans. The bath at Bordeaux was in an undercroft with a low, groined ceiling. Arches with massive pillars stood in files, forming aisles. There were no windows. Thick white candles in tall iron candle-stands lit the steamy air, checkering the room with warm light and secluding shadows. At one end of the room the maw of an immense hearth blazed. Hung from chains over the fire were cauldrons of hot water bubbling with essences of lavender, rose, lemon and civet. Along the aisles, draped booths of heavy crimson curtains stood, enclosing waist-deep wooden tubs. At the side of each tub, the bathhouse provided racks for towels and clothing, and a table with bowls of scented lumps of soap from Spain, fresh fruit, goblets and a carafe of wine.

The bathhouse was completely taken over by the English come from Blaye. Its languid atmosphere was sundered by the rollicking mood of the men, who cavorted like boys at last released from school. They threw back the booths' draperies, giving free view of their white arms and torsos, their sun burnt faces, and their hair and beards peaked with soapy foam.

Drunk on the bathhouse's good Bordeaux wines, the husky, red-haired knight Richard de Gray made loud jest of his friend John Eyvile's slender anatomy.

Drogo de Barentin, Giles Argentine and Nicholas de Meulles, the king's most trusted Poitouvins, pelted each other with fruit lobbed through the perfumed mist. The low arches rang with a deafeningly merry din.

In the midst of the carousal, a young troubadour, dressed in the parti-colored motley of his trade, sat leaning against a pillar and playing upon a pipe. His long, blue satin sleeves spread round him like bright butterfly wings on the wet stone floor. He bent and swayed with his music, but he might have been a dumbshow for all he could be heard.

Simon found an empty booth nearby, undressed and climbed into the tub as an attendant filled the tub with hot water.

Now and then a few notes of the pipe floated above the noise. The melody was sad. From the booth next to Simon, Peter of Savoy chided the troubadour, "Not so pathetic, boy! Play us a cheerful tune. We're in a celebrating spirit."

The youth stopped, and began again. But again his rhythm slowed. At last he stopped entirely. Turning to his audience of one, he pled, "My lord, I cannot. My heart's too heavy."

"Your lady loves somebody else?" Savoy teased him.

"I am a Touloussaine. You haven't heard, sire? King Louis has renewed the so-called holy war against the Albigensians and Count Raymond."

His words, though barely audible, caught Simon's ear. He knew that Louis had sent old Hugh of La Marche against the army being raised by Raymond of Toulouse. But, closeted with Henry, he didn't know that Louis had renewed the war against the Albigensians: his father's crusade. The news struck him like a thunderbolt. He washed quickly, straining to hear more.

Nearby, Count Hugh's son Guy de Lusignan knew all about it. For him, his father's part in a crusade exonerated his abandoning King Henry and attacking Henry's ally. "Weep, troubadour!" Guy sneered. "Your heretics are dying!"

"Guy Lusignan," the youth in motley met Guy's eyes and spat upon the floor, "so much as *that* do I fear you witch-spawn of Melusine!"

Melusine was sacred. Ancestress of Lusignan and of La Marche, she was said to be a nixie, transforming herself into a flying serpent and soaring out her castle window to her coven on Saturday nights.

At the pointed insult, Guy sprang from his tub and in an instant had his hands around the troubadour's throat, battering the lad's head against the pillar. Simon and Savoy leapt from their tubs, and pulled the cursing, flailing Guy away.

Simon, taking up his towel and his clothing as he went, dragged the troubadour out of the bath hall. In the anteroom he threw the youth down roughly, dried himself and began to dress. "Do you mean to be killed?" he demanded.

"The Lusignan are all witch-bastards," the troubadour muttered, rubbing his bloody head and getting to his feet uncertainly. "The whole House of Lusignan's a nest of vipers. I've lost my pipe." He staggered back toward the hall.

Simon caught him and pinned him against the wall. "Are you mad? He'll kill you!"

The youth gave a sly smile. "If he kills me, I shall go to Heaven, and my murderer to Hell."

"You'll go to Hell!" Simon retorted. "Or does your faith teach that you may tempt others to damnation, and thereby save yourself!"

The troubadour made no answer.

Simon finished dressing, paid his bill, and took the youth out with him to the street. "Troubadour, you've made such enemies today that you had best leave Bordeaux."

"I've lost my pipe," the youth grumbled.

Simon took several silver pennies from the purse on his belt and gave them to him. "Find another. And may Christ save you from yourself."

The troubadour's lips bent in a smile at the sight of the money in his hand. "May Christ save you too, sire," he grinned and sauntered away, whistling his melancholy tune.

Simon went at once to the Hotel de Ville. A heavily armed bailiff challenged him at the door. He identified himself, insisting that his business was urgent, and he was admitted to the hall.

Henry, alert, tense and pale, sat at supper with Prince Richard. The spirit of the meal seemed far from the easy jubilation of the royal entry to Bordeaux.

But Simon was too preoccupied with his own thoughts to notice. He bowed to the king. "My lord, the war for which you summoned me is done. Though the three-month term of our agreement is not yet fulfilled, I ask your leave to go to Toulouse. My father's war against the heretics is renewed. God willing, I hope to avenge his death."

Henry stared at Simon. Then his mouth fell open and he uttered a loud, piercing shriek. Simon was so startled by the sound that he thought somehow the king had been struck a blow. But Henry began crying, "Don't go, Montfort. Don't leave me now."

Clearly the king was mad again. Simon glanced to Richard.

Richard's face was stern and solemn. He said in a low voice, "Rebels against England's rule have tried to kill Queen Eleanor. She was found in the double agony of both childbirth and poisoning."

Simon was stunned. In a strained voice he asked, "Is she still alive?"

"Yes. We pray and hope she will recover, but she's very ill. Archbishop Malemorte of Bordeaux has been praying for her without cease for the last two days."

"Stay, Simon!" Henry pleaded. "Stay and avenge her!"

"My king," Simon said tensely, "were my father's ghost to rise and summon me, I would first see this crime avenged." He had striven long and hard to cool his memory of Queen Eleanor, but the thought of anyone presuming to touch her life roused him to fury.

Seeing Simon's enraged expression, Henry, satisfied, slumped silently back in his chair.

In the days that followed, Queen Eleanor remained confined, recovering very slowly. Her household was cross-questioned in the search to find her poisoners. The tainted supper was traced to two servants who had fled. They were both native to the village of Veyrine.

While the inquiry into the crime against the queen pressed forward, the royal Court at Bordeaux filled with petitioners. Every sort of Henry's subjects came: from poor pilgrims to the lords of Gascony, and higher.

Among the first to arrive was the Queen Mother Isabel. She met with Henry in his private chamber, her four sons of La Marche gathering around her like chicks clustering by their hen. In addition to Guy, Hugh and William, who were still in attendance upon King Henry, she had brought her youngest son, Aimery de Lusignan.

"They have no home!" she cried to Henry. "That wretch their father, sitting at Toulouse, has given everything to Louis. He's abandoned us! His own sons have nothing!"

Henry began to tremble. "Mother, I'll see to it that my brothers never suffer want."

"Resign my province of Poitou to them!" she regally commanded. "Poitou was my dowry! I brought the province to England. It's only right that my children should have it now!"

Poitou had passed to England two generations earlier, when Eleanor of Aquitaine brought both Poitou and Gascony, the paired duchies of Aquitaine, to her husband Henry II. Isabel brought only Angouleme, but no one cared to trim her claims down to the truth.

Richard, as holder of Poitou's title before its seizure by King Louis, was stung. His florid face flushed redder. "Mother, if we do regain Poitou, the province has an overlord! Unless you'd have Henry disown his full brother!"

Isabel squinted her small eyes first at Richard, then at Henry. "To think I've given birth to two such selfish wretches!"

Simon, an inadvertent witness to the family quarrel, seeing Henry stricken and Richard choking with rage, offered in a mollifying tone, "Good lady, the king is even now hard-pressed to carry out the business of the state within his assets. If Poitou is regained, its taxes will be needed."

The queen mother turned toward him, astonished. She gave Simon a moment's careful scrutiny, then coldly said, "I see. The truth is, Sire Montfort, you set yourself against me! You mean to divide me from my sons. The renowned warrior!" she spat. "Perhaps you'd even like to cast the blame on me for your failure at Tailleberg?"

Simon recoiled. But Richard's apoplectic look gave him strength to restrain himself. He said stiffly, "Madam, you favor your sons unequally. You know the needs of some, but not of others. The king has need of Poitou, if it's recovered. For that matter, my wife, in this defeat, has lost lands that are her birthright as well. Were Henry to transfer all rights in Poitou to his brothers of La Marche, my wife's, as well as many others' rights, would be impaired." Henry collected Eleanor's Poitou rents but rarely sent them on to her.

Grateful to Simon for this cool and rational argument, Henry looked to his mother with a helpless shrug. "What's mine I would give freely, but I cannot give away what is Richard's and Eleanor's. I'll find some recompense in England for my young brothers."

Isabel was not appeased. She turned again to Simon. Pursing her lips into a creased rosette, she hissed. "So. You have succeeded! No doubt you think your sons, as the king's nephews, should have a larger share of royal favor. The coming of Henry's brothers is inconvenient for you, isn't it!"

"I don't oppose any of your children, madam," Simon strove to be keep his self-control. "But I must serve the interests of your eldest son, who is my king, and your daughter, who is my wife."

"Don't talk to me so haughtily about your king and wife! I know your kind!" Isabel smiled viciously. "I know just how you came to call my daughter 'wife.'"

"Madam, I love your daughter!" Simon protested.

Standing beside his mother, young William chirped, "The earl who won his title on the battlefield of bed linens!" and he broke into giggles.

Simon slapped the boy across his face.

Instantly, Isabel struck Simon, shrieking, "How dare you touch my son!" She raised her hand to strike again, but he caught her wrist. "Let go of me!" she screamed. Like a hawk's talons, her free hand flew at Simon's eyes. He caught that hand as well, but not before her nails gouged his cheek. "Let go my hands!" Isabel writhed in his grip. "Will you lay hold upon the queen!"

"The Countess of La Marche, yes! Even my wife's mother, if she would scratch my eyes out!" Simon held her tightly as she struggled to be free of him.

Little Aimery ran from the room, crying for help. His three brothers hurled themselves on Simon. Richard tried to pull the boys away, as Henry shouted for them all to stop. Answering Aimery's cries, three armed bailiffs ran into the room with their swords drawn. Richard and Simon disentangled themselves from the boys and Isabel.

"Arrest him!" the Queen Mother pointed at Simon, whose cheek was bleeding.

"On what charge, mother!" Richard demanded.

"Treason!" William de Valence shouted, thinking of the worst thing he could say.

Simon glanced at the boy and gave a short laugh.

"There's no need for you here," King Henry told the bailiffs quietly, gesturing for them to leave. They sheathed their swords and went away, and Henry turned to Simon, "You'd best go as well. I'll summon you later."

Simon left, following the bailiffs out. The four Lusignan brothers watched him go and Guy called after him, "Montfort, we won't forget this! Ever!"

Later that day, a royal bailiff summoned Simon from his inn. The clerk Mansel met him in the Hotel de Ville and led him through corridors and rooms until, at the opening of a door, Simon found himself in Queen Eleanor's private chamber.

The queen lay in a high, canopied bed. Several of her waiting-women hovered nearby. Henry sat on a window seat with a large wax writing-tablet propped on his lap. He was drawing, but he glanced up and nodded with a smile as Simon was shown in. Then he turned back to his tablet and continued drawing.

Seeing Simon, Queen Eleanor held out her frail hand.

This was the first time Simon had seen the queen since his audience at Windsor, before going to Palestine. She had a death-like pallor. Her skin seemed transparent and as pale as pearl. Her silvery blue eyes were enormous in her gaunt face.

"I hope my lady is feeling better," Simon said gently. The memory of her lying in his arms seemed as distant and unreal as a sweet, haunting dream. Seeing her so ill made him achingly sad. The sight of Louis dying, and now this, made him want to weep – and strangle poisoners.

Queen Eleanor smiled, her pale lips forming their sweet bow. "A little. Thank you," she whispered. "What accident has left its mark upon your cheek?"

"No accident. It was a lady's anger," Simon grinned.

"Your wife's?"

"She's not here."

"Ah, this is more interesting," the queen said teasingly.

"Mother did it," Henry looked up from his drawing, obviously listening.

"Oh." The queen lowered her voice, "You've met the Gorgon, and you're not yet turned to stone?" Her eyes took on their familiar playful twinkle.

"No," Simon found himself smiling broadly. Her wit, her appeal as a fellow outsider, still drew him to her. He had never succeeded in completely banning her from his thoughts. He still wore penitential black for good reason.

"Did you bring back my cross?" she whispered, too low for Henry or her waiting- women to hear.

Simon reached inside his black woolen robe, and brought out the small gold cross from where it hung on a fine chain around his neck. Drawing the chain over his head, he said in a low voice, "I had it blessed at the Holy Sepulcher, as you asked." He placed the cross into her upturned hand.

With a look of happy surprise, she grasped his hand before he could draw it away. "Keep it!" she whispered. "Go on wearing it for me."

"No." Simon flushed, realizing that the cross could be seen as a love token, though his mind had not permitted him that thought until now.

She let go of his hand and closed her fingers over the cross in her palm. "Then I'll wear it for *you*," she smiled languidly. Her gesture, her tone of voice, were as potent as if she yielded her body to him.

Simon blushed; he couldn't speak. Had he repented so earnestly, only still to be so moved by her? Was he such a fool that he had failed to see, within his heart, the reason why he wore that cross? He stood as confused as a boy caught in a shameful act. He was furious at himself. But, looking at her pale blue eyes gazing at him, he could not be angry with her. He glanced away, toward Henry. The king still sat on the window seat, concentrating on his drawing. But he saw that Lady Alice was watching him closely.

Queen Eleanor, seeing Simon's blush, murmured in a low, taunting tone, "Your heart is revealed, sir." She touched the cross to her lips, then pressed it to her breast.

Simon turned his eyes away from her. "I've repented. I thought, by the blessing of the cross, to be free."

"But you are not. Do you think of our nights...?" she whispered. "Ah, yes you do," a quiet, triumphant laugh tinkled from her teasing smile. "You cannot even look at me now."

Henry had left the window seat and was coming toward them with his drawing tablet. "You're whispering?" he asked, more slyly than suspiciously.

"I'm begging the Lord Montfort to avenge me," the queen answered. "Is that not why you had him brought to me? That I might stiffen his resolve?"

Henry looked from her to Simon, but instead of prickling at the charged tension between them, he said instead, "We place our trust in you."

Simon, caught in a net of confusion, could only nod. Was she being seductive simply out of her own nature, or was she enticing him at Henry's bidding? Did it matter? Whatever the case, his mastery of himself was far from what he had supposed.

Henry rattled on, "We're going to march against the rebels at Veyrine. Our knights will leave as soon as my new battle flag is ready."

The battle standard of Plantagenet had been lost, like so much else, at Sainte. "This is to be my new flag," Henry proudly showed his drawing. "It's a dragon, such as King Arthur had. You've seen how Louis' Oriflamme flickers in the wind like flame? The streamers of my dragon's tongue will lap the wind like a serpent." He spoke with childlike glee. "You'll be with us, as you were at Sainte?"

Simon understood his words to mean that he was to lead the assault. "As you wish, my lord." He was glad to be dealing with the straightforward issue of a military action. The purpose of his visit concluded, he left the chamber without allowing himself so much as another glance in the direction of the queen.

In a few days, the flag was finished and the force of English knights, led by the Lord Montfort, left for Veyrine. King Henry stayed in Bordeaux.

In a week, Simon and the knights returned with the rebels' heads on pikes, for all rebels in Gascony to see.

A celebration was held in honor of his swift victory. Simon, now the hero of Veyrine as well as Sainte, was seated beside the king and addressed with his full titles, Earl of Leicester, Steward of England. His rents and honors were officially restored.

Simon felt profound relief. The crushing weight of an unknown future at last fell from him. All that he had lost in England was regained. Louis had been right. When the Court left Bordeaux, he would return with his family to Kenilworth. They would have a home. With careful management, his sons would have an inheritance. Fate's wheel had turned again, and set him lightly on a pleasant, high plateau.

Nonetheless, he felt a nagging twinge of disappointment in the midst of the Court's merriment. Though he would not admit it to himself, he had hoped for a smile from the queen as payment for the gory vengeances he had taken at Veyrine. The mere sight of her would have been sweet, even if it was contrived by Henry.

But Queen Eleanor was not yet well enough to leave her chamber, and Simon was not summoned there again.

Much was made of the conquest of the rebels. Trouveres were paid by Henry to compose songs of the battle, and the knights whom Simon led received presents of gold coins from the king's own hand.

But it was clear the rebels who had poisoned the queen were only a symptom of far greater ills in Gascony. The entire dukedom, and especially the south: the Pyrenees and the Adour and Labour valleys, were in rebellion against England's rule. The lords of the Pyrenees beset the roads across their territories. They raided caravans and held travelers for ransom. Of even greater dismay to King Henry, the royal taxes he had counted on to pay the costs of his war in Poitou could not be collected.

Simon at first had supposed that, once the Veyrine rebels were punished, he could leave for the siege at Toulouse and the chance to avenge his father. But, with the restoration of his titles, his mercenary contract of three months was cancelled. He was bound again by liege to England's king.

And the Gascon troubles made it impossible for Henry to let him go. Simon was drawn into the business of the Court as the king's military councilor.

Unlike the time before his exile, when he was Henry's hated foreign friend, the English lords now held Simon in high regard. The battles of Sainte and Veyrine had won him their respect. In Court he wielded true power and influence. He was a hero now – England's foremost man of war.

Chapter Twenty-Seven

TREACHERY
1242-1243

AT THE COURT IN BORDEAUX, Prince Richard sought to find out all he could of Gascony's rebellion. He had received from his brother the title Duke of Aquitaine, which comprised both Poitou and Gascony. Beginning his investigations, he summoned the principal lords of the south, the Viscounts of Tartas, Soule and Gramont, who owed their fealty directly to him.

The first to come was Viscount Arnaud de Gramont, a dapper man of middle age, with graying hair and manners of exquisite civility. "My good king, my duke," he bowed to Henry, then to Richard with a flourish of his plumed hat. "The disorders of Gascony are the work of but one man – though I hesitate to name him."

"Tell us what you have to say, Viscount," Richard said coolly.

Gramont looked to Henry. "I hesitate from fear. He's very powerful."

"More powerful than England?" Richard prompted.

"And," Gramont bent his head, "you may doubt me. You hold him as a friend."

"We've found friends treacherous before," Henry sighed. "Speak out, good viscount. You have our protection."

"He is Thibaut of Champagne. Now King of Navarre."

"I do doubt you, Viscount!" Richard challenged. "Thibaut sent us troops at Tonnaye. Hardly the act of a fomenter of rebellion!"

"When he saw your... misfortunes in Poitou," Gramont chose his words daintily, "Thibaut summoned the lords of the Pyrenees to a meeting and persuaded them to break their liege to you, swearing to him instead. To bring the whole of Gascony into confusion, he has encouraged the lords to charge monstrous tolls on the roads that pass through their lands." Having presented this astonishing piece of information, Gramont shrugged his shoulders as if to say, "There it is. Believe me or not, as you will."

Simon, sitting on the dais step, took note. His old dislike of Thibaut fed his inclination to believe any ill of him. But he was the only one to consider Gramont's claims seriously.

Richard responded as if the stunning accusation never had been spoken. "You were summoned here, Gramont, because there are complaints against *you*. We're told you wrongfully hold men confined. That you seize property..."

"Lies. All lies," Gramont shook his head. "Lies spread by Thibaut."

Richard unrolled a long scroll. Referring to its entries, "You're accused of making raids by night. Here is a list of names of men who are held by you for ransom!"

"My bailiffs and I did make raids. Yes. To free poor prisoners, seized because they couldn't pay the new, abhorrent tolls. And we've restored the goods that were wrung from traveling merchants as payment of these tolls. It's I who am England's true friend," Gramont persisted with unruffled aplomb.

"You can bring us records, and witnesses who can vouch for what you say?" Richard held Gramont with a stern gaze. "We want a full accounting of the missing men, lists of your confiscations, and proofs that you have returned the goods to their rightful owners."

"My clerk is laboring on it at this very moment. Perhaps by November..." the viscount bent in an obsequious bow.

Richard lost his last reserve of patience. "Viscount Gramont, we have every reason to believe that you yourself are the worst offender!"

Gramont dropped to his knees at Henry's feet, "My king, I came here believing I would receive grace and kindness for my loyal services to you. But Prince Richard gives ear only to my lying enemies!"

Henry glanced to his brother, who was glowering at the prostrate viscount. The prince was unrolling another lengthy scroll of accusations from the families of travelers who had disappeared from Gramont's roads. The evidence against the viscount was heavy, despite his earnest pleas. Henry waved his hand for Richard to stop.

"Viscount," the king said gently, "it's best for men to set their lives in order, not by force, but by their own free will. We mean to show you every mercy. Give us a full accounting on the first day of December. Free anyone you hold wrongly imprisoned. Make restitution of properties, and we will hold no further inquiries."

Richard spun on his heel away from Henry, and looked up at the ceiling in exasperation.

Gramont rose to his feet. "Most gracious king," he murmured as he bowed. He shot a narrow, hateful glance at Richard as he left the hall.

The same procedure followed with the Viscounts of Tartas and Soule. They swore, as Gramont had, that Thibaut was the cause of the disorders. They too were given until the first day of December to render their accounts.

The prince's inquiries delved deeper. More Gascon lords were summoned to Bordeaux. With dogged earnestness Richard probed, calling for witnesses, demanding accounts. On some days, Thibaut and the Gascon lords all seemed equally guilty. On other days, the evidence seemed lies and calumnies, and the lords the most innocent of men. The only certainty was that the taxes could not be collected. Gascony was a mystery, a conundrum, a frustration.

The queen was never at the Court. The earls Peter of Savoy and Roger Bigod joined Simon on the dais steps to hear the testimonies, and add their share of baffled opinion. Life in Bordeaux settled into a routine as, month after month, Richard's hearings trudged onward.

Seeing he would be in Bordeaux for some time, Simon rented a villa not far from the city. It was a rustic, rambling, tile-roofed and buff-stuccoed house with a stable, a garden of herbs, a lawn kept tidy by a few sheep, and an extensive vineyard. He sent for his family.

In a few weeks Eleanor arrived from Paris with their three sons, Henry, Simon and Guy, and Lady Mary with servants and a wagon laden with the Montfort's possessions that had come with them from Palestine.

Magnificent in her splendid silks from the East, the Countess Eleanor made her first appearance at her brother's Court since she had pled for her husband's safe-conduct to arm for the crusade. Her transformation in two years left her brothers dazzled.

Henry arose from his chair and came down the dais steps to take her hand. "Is this the russet nun I knew?"

"The cygnet has become the swan," Savoy offered gracefully.

Simon was much pleased by his wife's reception. He had forgotten that Eleanor once had seemed plain, her large features discordant in the soft rounds of her young face. As the angles of her profile took on strength, she was becoming comely, even stately. Hers was a beauty that, from small beginnings, would surpass the prettiness of others' youth, and reach bold handsomeness, when their faces had long since sagged in middle age.

But of this growing beauty, Eleanor herself was ignorant. She dressed lavishly to overcome the plainness she still saw in her polished copper hand-mirror. The effect was extreme, gorgeous. She stood in Court in a brilliant green damask robe shimmering with seed pearls.

Her brothers stared in awe.

The weeks of the southern autumn and mild winter passed. The queen at last returned to her normal routine of life. Simon attended Court one day and found his customary place upon the dais step was right beneath her gaze. Her illness had imparted a pallor, a delicacy that added an ethereal refinement to her loveliness. The beauty that was hers before, was now so much enhanced that none could look on her without feeling compelled, not only to love, but to protect her.

For Simon, her nearness was excruciatingly distracting. He steeled himself to avoid her glance; but the effort that suppression of desire took, left him in a state of constant, uncivil annoyance.

As the king's military strategist, until it was decided what to do in the disordered land, his services were not particularly needed. He begged liberty to spend his time away from Court, at his villa in the country with his family. King Henry was not sorry to let him go.

Simon began to teach his little son Henry to ride. The boy was four, a quiet, alert child who spoke in solemn whispers. His brother Simon was unruly, sullen and given to sudden tantrums. But Guy, sturdy and toddling at two, was determined to do everything his eldest brother did. He screamed until his father lifted him onto his palfrey's high saddle. Once on horseback, the infant quieted and balanced himself carefully, fingering the reins, and grinning broadly with a smile that showed his tiny teeth.

Simon stayed away from Court, finding peace and refuge from temptation in his rural villa with his family.

But one day the Countess Eleanor asked brightly, "Ought we not to do something to celebrate the queen's recovery? I think an afternoon in our fresh air would be a pleasant change for her."

"What have you in mind?" Simon replied, in a tone intended to discourage.

"We have our return to England soon to celebrate as well," she went on not the least bit daunted. "We must invite the whole Court here."

"I think not..."

"Oh, but we must! No one should think that we still hold a grudge."

The invitations were issued.

The day of the Court's visit to the villa of the Earl and Countess of Montfort was warm and sunny. The earth basked in the generous Gascon springtime. Countess Eleanor arranged to have the feast served in large, rented tents.

The king, the queen and Prince Richard arrived in the midst of a grand parade of English lords and knights and Gascon courtiers.

The royal table was sheltered by a tassel-bedecked tent, its sides tied up with silken ropes for a full view of the lawn and vineyards.

The villa's first strawberries, roast fowl and lamb, and the renowned sausages and cheeses of the region, were served with wines from the villa's own cellars.

Simon, seated beside the queen as etiquette required, spoke little. He seemed in a dark mood, his face slightly flushed. Queen Eleanor did not take it amiss. She made no effort to force conversation. His heightened color, and his silence, told her all she wished to know of his susceptibility. Beneath the cloth, she gently placed her hand upon his thigh.

Her touch ignited an ordeal of shame, and of desire. Despite his penitence, Simon could not bring himself to end at once the sweet sensation of her touch. But fury at his own weakness prevailed. He pushed her hand away and glanced at her with a stern frown, risking that his look might be seen by Henry, seated just beyond her.

With an expression of mock pouting that Henry could not see, she drew back her hand.

As the courses of the feast were completed and the guests began to stroll about; little Henry came running to the royal table. "May I ride my pony for the king and queen to see?"

Simon would have said no, but the queen turned from the table and held both her hands out to the child. "My godson! You don't remember that I held you once. Yes. Do let us see you ride!"

Simon nodded his consent, and the boy went running toward the stable. In a few moments he was back, atop his pony. His feet still far above the stirrups, he gripped the pony's mane with his small fists. Turning his mount this way and that, he nudged it to a trot.

The queen watched, delighted and enthralled by the earnest little rider. As if thoughtless in an excess of happiness, she clutched Simon's hand as it rested on the table in full view of everyone. Henry noticed. The Countess Eleanor noticed but thought nothing of it.

Simon pulled his hand out from beneath the queen's fingers. He was amazed at her boldness. He wondered if her near approach to death had brought her to mad disregard of caution. He glanced toward King Henry, thinking that this baiting, like the summons to the queen's chamber, might be at his instigation. But Henry was frowning.

Gaston de Bearne, the queen's rotund Gascon cousin, came to the royal table. Genially, he leaned his bulky shape between the queen and Simon. Noticing the sparkle in her eyes as she watched the little rider, he asked, "Prince Edward is the same age?"

"No," Queen Eleanor said wistfully, "he's almost a year younger." Edward had been left in the care of the Archbishop of York, who was acting as Regent of England in the king's absence.

"Your eyes speak clearly of your yearning. How much you must miss him, my dear coz," Gaston gurgled.

Queen Eleanor glanced down, a rosy flush spreading over her face. "You think you can read my thoughts, Gaston?"

The Count of Bearne dropped his voice to a murmur and whispered into the queen's ear. "I cannot understand, coz, why Henry strips himself of everything for Richard, when he has a son and heir of his own."

A frown darted across the queen's brow. "What do you mean?"

Gaston pressed himself more tightly in between her and Simon, whispering even lower, "Henry heaps so many titles on his brother, one would think he had no son of his own. No proper heir. What does he leave for Edward?"

The queen's frown deepened to two distinct furrows.

Gaston took note. He'd found the point of vulnerability for which he was probing. "I beg pardon," he cringed. "Have I upset you?"

"Not at all," she insisted. "What you say is true. But Edward is so young..."

"Wasn't Henry a king at nine?" Gaston said slyly. "Duke of Gascony would be a pretty title for the little prince."

Queen Eleanor turned toward Gaston, astonished. "Would the lords of Gascony countenance such a thing? He's still a very young child."

"I assure you," Gaston smiled unctuously, "we of Gascony would gladly give our fealty to Edward. We would endear ourselves by long service to our future king." He knew the Gascon lords would accept Edward. They would be rid of Richard. With an infant in England as their overlord, they could be sure of benign neglect and easy governance for years to come.

Having planted the idea in the queen's mind, the Count of Bearne withdrew, nodding to Simon.

Warmed to desire despite himself, and furious at Gaston, the last person to whom he would feel grateful for sparing him from sin, Simon glanced toward the queen.

But she was distant now, preoccupied. Watching little Henry maneuvering his pony on the lawn, she mused, "The archbishop writes that Edward takes a great interest in horses and weapons. He says the prince will surely grow to be another lion-hearted king."

Henry, watching Simon and the queen, his old jealousy rising, remarked cynically. "Edward won't learn much of weapons from the archbishop. When we return to England, we should send him to you, lord Montfort. Yes!" He gave a dark laugh, "You must bring him up, as if he were a son of your own."

The queen and Simon both looked sharply at Henry.

The king smiled and ate a strawberry. "What better way to ready the prince to retake lands we've lost to France, than to have him trained by one who was schooled with the enemy?"

The Countess Eleanor, at the farther side of Henry, took up the offer eagerly. "We're deeply honored that you would entrust the prince to us. How sweet it will be for our boys and Edward to grow up together!"

"Henry, please," the queen pleaded. "I would have Edward with me." She reached for her husband's hand, but he drew back from her.

"Good! We will arrange it." Though Henry's lips smiled, his eyes remained coldly fixed on Simon. "When you are settled again at Kenilworth, Edward will be sent to you.

Simon and the queen exchanged tense glances.

Only the Countess Eleanor was happy.

End: Book II

ḣistorical context

THE FOLLOWING NOTES ARE FOR the reader who wants to know what is accepted history. The dialogue, with a few exceptions that I've noted, is not to be found in historical sources. The only named characters in The Courtier and The Exile who are not historical are Lady Alice and Lady Mary.

It was February of the year 1229: The records of King Henry's Court have Simon arriving in February 1230, whereas Simon himself reckoned the year as 1229. The discrepancy arises because the Court of England dated the year from January 1ˢᵗ, whereas common record keeping after the manner of the Church dated the year as beginning at Easter. Hence, by some reckoning the year was still 1229 in February, though the following April was in 1230. This difference in calendrical customs gives rise to frequent confusions.

Though he would have been very young for such a mission, I believe Simon was only sixteen at this time: that he was born in September of 1213 at Carcassone. Political circumstances would have made it highly desirable for Queen Blanche to have a trusted agent in King Henry's Court. And after his brother Amaury's failure, no one else had Simon's potential opportunity.

Some historians believe Simon to have been twenty-one in 1229, based on the Cernay *Cartulair* which, for 1209, records that the Countess Montfort had been blessed by God with *"filios multos et pulcros."* In addition to Amaury, there was a brother who died young and a middle brother, Guy, who was wedded to the Countess of Bigorre, in the Pyrenees, during their father's wars in the south. He had died before this story begins. In any case, what the *Cartulair* records seems not so much a statement of fact, as a conventional phrase supporting the general divine favor enjoyed by the father,

Simon de Montfort III. The son who concerns us here is of course Simon de Montfort IV.

I use for physical description of Simon his hunting seal. The ivory on the cover may also be of Simon, as a penitent. Contemporary writing describes him as handsome, dark haired, quite tall and very nearsighted.

He was Norman and noble: Simon's mother, Alis de Montmorency, was descended illegitimately from William the Conqueror, through Henry I by his mistress Rosamonde, who was poisoned by Eleanor of Aquitaine. *L'epouse de Simon de Montfort...*, M. Zerner, Brussels, 1992.

This earnest faith, and his family's service to the Crown: Amaury, then in his twenties, had taken up their father's war. Deeply in debt from the hiring of mercenary troops, and hopelessly losing the war, he ceded all the family's hard-won territories: Toulouse, Foix and Narbonne, to the Crown of France. It was normal practice for a royal Court to take as semi-hostage a young member of the family of a lord or prince with whom the king had made a treaty.

Margaret Wade Labarge in *Simon de Montfort*, London, 1962, p.22, hints at the probability that this is what happened, though actual documentation so far is lacking. The transfer of the Montfort child to the Court, especially after his mother's death in 1221, would have been normal, and it would account for Simon's excellent education, his lifelong closeness to Louis, and the preferment he enjoyed at the Court in Paris. His brother Amaury sent his own son to be brought up in the court of a German margrave.

"Let's have a joust for it." Civil disorder in England at this time was dire. It had been growing worse since the largely absentee reign of King Richard the Lion Hearted, and had dissolved into civil war during his brother King John's reign.

While the political unrest had been quieted by severe measures brought about by the young King Henry's guardians, the relative peace was gained at the expense of placing foreigners, the king's subjects from the English duchy of Poitou in France, in key positions in the government, and particularly in the local peacekeeping offices of the county sheriffs.

As the sheriffs were allowed to keep most of the fines they charged, the Poitouvins grew rich, especially to the loss of members of the rural knightly class who might have expected to hold the office of sheriff themselves. Further, the barons often were cheated by such trickery as being summoned to serve on judicial benches in several far-flung places on the same day. When they failed to appear, the summoning sheriff could fine them for their absence. Practices such as these were driving some lordly families into bankruptcy. The reign of King Henry III is the period of the "wicked" sheriffs such as the Sheriff of Nottingham, the archenemy in the tales of Robin Hood.

Palsy marred the young King's face: "one of (the king's) eyes was half-closed and almost hid the pupil." *The Chronicle of William de Rishanger*, The Camden Society, 1840, p.75.

The Treasurer, Peter de Riveaux: Peter de Riveaux was the nephew, or illegitimate son, of the Poitouvin Bishop of Winchester, Peter des Roches, who had been Henry's guardian. Riveaux was Clerk of the Wardrobe and Treasurer of the Chamber. These two offices together controlled the royal finances. When he became Treasurer of the Exchequer as well, he was in complete control of the government's finances and did not have to account to anyone, resulting in fiscal disaster for Henry. For a fuller appreciation of Peter de Riveau and the financial functioning of the Court of Henry III, see T. F. Tout, *Chapters in the Administrative History of Medieval England: the Wardrobe, the Chamber and the Small Seals.* Vol. 1, 1920-28.

our cousin Ranulf, Earl of Chester: Ranulf was a nephew of Simon III. See Bemont, Charles, *Simon de Montfort*, The Clarendon Press, Oxford, 1930, p.3, *footnote 3. your brother's been here about this already*: Amaury appeared before King Henry repeatedly for his own claims; then repeatedly renounced his claims in Simon's favor, the last being as late as April 11, 1239 (*Layettes* no. 2739.) See also below.

---

answer finally came from King Henry: *Royal Letters,* vol. I, p. 362. Some historians have taken Henry's letter to Simon, dated April 7 as the King of England prepared for war in France, to mean he had made promise of the earldom to Simon at the time of Simon's visit to Westminster, the preceding February. But Simon's actions, approaching Ranulf as he did, and not responding to Henry, would indicate he did not believe Henry's April offer, or anything preceding it, to be in good faith.

summons came for Amaury: Henry III disembarked on the coast of Brittany on April 30, 1230, with intention to regain Normandy. H.R. Luard, Rolls Series, vol. III, p. 190; Berger, *Histoire de Blanche de Castile*, p. 200

the heretics in southern France: The Albigensians were a sect similar to, and perhaps derived from, the Manichaean heresy, which held that all matter was evil. Their leaders, called Perfects or Cathars – who were often of noble houses – led lives of poverty and simplicity, and argued the virtues of their faith with consummate skill. Their itinerant preaching gained them thousands of converts at a time when the Catholic Church was struggling with corruption. The lords of the southern duchies of France particularly sheltered them. See the note below: *"she would commence a Court of Love."*

The Dominican monastic order was founded to provide men of comparably pure lifestyle and well-educated preaching to counter them. But when a papal legate to the Albigensians was murdered, Pope Innocent III declared a crusade against the heresy, offering much the same advantages of financial credit and absolution from sins that a crusade to the Holy Land would provide, at far less inconvenience.

The result was a thoroughly disorganized torrent of northern knights and barons descending upon the south. The Albigensians fled before the invasion, six thousand of them taking shelter in the large church in Bezier, under the supposed rules of safe sanctuary. The invading northerners, not observing sanctuary, heaped wood against the church, set it aflame and killed everyone inside.

In the aftermath of the burning, no one wanted to take responsibility for these out-of-hand "crusaders." Simon de Montfort III was already well respected for his role in the Third Crusade: he refused to take part with his fellow crusaders in the sacking of Constantinople and instead went on alone with his own knights to Palestine. When he offered to take over leadership of the Albigensian crusade, the Pope confirmed him. A brilliant military leader, with the aid of mercenary troops hired in the north he conquered large regions of southern Gascony and Province. See J. Sumption, *The Albigensian Crusade,* London, 1978.

the song of Simon de Montfort: The *Chronica Johannis de Oxenedes* of John of Oxford, ed. H. Ellis, Rolls Series, 1859, p.144, provides the Song of Simon de Montfort the Crusader. The *Annals of Dunstable,* Vol III, p.33, records that English lords, rebelling against King John in 1210, *elected* Simon de Montfort III their king on the basis of his fine reputation. These Annals often reported hearsay that was not supported by other sources. Nonetheless, the notion of "Simon de Montfort" as king entered the folklore of England and came to be looked upon as prophecy.

Henry now had claim to Simon's loyalty: August 13, 1231 (1230). *Royal Letters,* Vol. I, p. 401. *Close Rolls 1227—1231,* p. 543: Simon receives "full seisen," but not titles: "The king accepts the homage of Simon de Montfort for all the land of S. de M. his father and sometime count of Leicester, to hold from the king the *honour* of Leicester." King Henry does not refer to Simon as Earl of Leicester, but merely as *"nostro Simoni de Monteforti." Royal Letters,* Vol.I, p.497. Due to calendrical issues, 1231 here is counted as 1230.

Amaury repeatedly renounced his claims in England, first by document when Simon arrived at King Henry's Court in late 1229-early 1230, and last at the Easter Court at Westminster in 1239, after Simon had officially received his titles at the King's Candlemas Court in Winchester the preceding February 2. Repeated official acts, and repeated mention of official acts, often obscure the clear timeline of events.

As evidence in his trial before King Louis in 1260, Simon wrote a brief autobiography beginning with his first arrival in England. Here is his own account in Bemont's translation: "First, our lord the king says that he has done me great goodness in that he took me for his man, because I was not the eldest. So that all may know just what this goodness was, my brother Amaury released to me all the rights that he had in my father's inheritance in England, if I could secure it, in the same manner that I released to him the inheritance which I had in France. I went to England and prayed my lord the king that he restore to me my father's inheritance. He answered that he could not do it because he had given it to the earl of Chester and his heirs by charter. I returned therefore without having found grace. The following year my lord the king crossed to Brittany, and with him the earl of Chester who held my inheritance. I went to the earl at his castle of Saint Jacques de Beauveron. There I prayed him that I might find the grace to receive my inheritance. He graciously agreed. The following August he took me to England with him and asked the king to receive my homage for the inheritance of my father, saying that I had a greater right to it than he. All the gift which the king had given to him he renounced in this manner. And the king received my homage." Bemont, Charles, *Simon de Montfort*, Paris, 1884, Slatkine-Megariotis Reprints, Geneve, 1976, p.333.

broad fields furrowed in long waves like the sea: The three-field system was a form of agriculture sustained for well over a thousand years. The fields were of very large size, giving a cleared and open aspect to Britain's landscape. Julius Caesar reported, almost a half-century before Christ, that Britain was chiefly open land under intense cultivation.

On each manor, one field would be planted with wheat, the second with legumes, and the third would lie fallow, with animals grazing and depositing manure. The three fields' uses were rotated annually. The "spring" field was planted with oats, peas beans and barley, replenishing the nitrogen the wheat had drawn from the soil the previous year. After the year of legumes, the field would lie fallow for a year then, the year after that, it became the "winter" field, planted with wheat to begin the cycle again.

By the thirteenth century, the fields, from centuries of plowing, were carved into broad, deep ridges often so large that a man could barely stride across one at a time. The huge fields were not fenced, but the corners of their perimeters were marked with posts or palings, hence the expression for wrongdoing: to "go beyond the pale."

Villein, or *housebondsman,* (husbandman) was the term designating commoners who, by inheritance, had a house in the *village* and shared in the use of a manor's fields. Since some of the ridges within each field would have better soil than others, the villeins drew lots (a handful of marked straws) each year to determine which set of ridges each would work for that year. The ridges in each set would not be side by side, but distributed throughout the field, again to equalize the distribution of the best land, but also to accommodate the large turning-radius of the plows used.

Each plow was drawn by six oxen: three villeins might share a plow and each have two oxen to contribute to the team. Some of the ridges in the fields belonged to the lord of the manor. The villeins paid the lord in service by plowing and harvesting his part of the land. By custom, the lord returned the favor, supplying his villeins with beer (a *beer bid-reap*) or, on manors where the custom was less generous, water (a *water bid-reap.*)

The villeins might also owe their lord chickens, eggs and other staples on specified occasions such as Christmas, as well as fees for grinding their wheat at a water or wind-powered mill the lord provided. See Homans, *English Villagers of the Thirteenth Century,* Russell & Russell, New York, 1960.

no thriving town: Leicester was an exceptionally unfortunate town. Most recently, in 1173, by order of King Henry II, Leicester had been besieged, razed and depopulated as punishment for its earl, Robert Blanchmain's, supporting the queen, Eleanor of Aquitaine, and her son Richard the Lion Hearted. On Richard's ascension to the throne, the Earl of Leicester was forgiven, and rebuilt his hall. But the town recovered very slowly and sporadically, being still sparsely populated within its walls as late as 1722.

Leicester had been a major Roman town at the crossing of two of the most important of the Roman legions' roads in Britain. Fine mosaic floors of wealthy Roman villas have been excavated in and near the city. Massive stone arches, perhaps a part of the Roman baths, still stand. After the conquest of Britain by the Angles and Saxons, and the division of Britain into the *heptarchy*, the "seven kingdoms, in 753, Leicester became the capital city of the kingdom of Mercia. The name "Leicester" derives from "Legre-caestre," Lyger, or Legre, was the old name of the River Soar. If King Lear is not to be looked upon merely as mythical, then Leicester was the site of his castle.

In 874, Leicester fell to the Danes. Its Roman walls protecting its perimeter were destroyed and the city became incorporated in the Danish "five boroughs," which included Nottingham, Lincoln, Derby and Stamford. In 920, Ethelfloeda, the daughter of King Alfred, succeeded in raising an army and driving the Danes from Leicester, Derby and Nottingham. She caused the Roman walls to be rebuilt with an assortment of stone and tile cemented together with an especially sturdy mortar that adhered in clumps, making any subsequent reuse of the stones all but impossible.

After Ethelfloeda's death, at Castle Tamworth in 922, Leicester passed back and forth between the Anglo-Saxons and the Danes, resulting in further demolition, no longer repairable thanks to Ethelfloeda's mortar.

In 1068, the Saxon, Earl Edwin of Coventry and Leicester (grandson of the storied Lady Godiva of Coventry and Leicester), surrendered and did homage to William the Conqueror. Leicester passed to Hugh de Grantmesnil, as Norman governor. After William's death, Hugh supported Robert of Normandy, rather than William's heir, William Rufus, or his brother Henry. When Henry succeeded as Henry I, Hugh retired to a monastery in France, and the king created Robert de Beaumont the first Norman Earl of Leicester. See *History and Antiquities of the antient Towne and once Citte of Leicester,* MS, Thomas Staveley, 1679; *History and Antiquities of the Town of Leicester,* John Throsby, 1791; *History and Antiquities of the Town and County of Leicester,* John Nichols, 1795. *History of Leicester from the time of the Romans to the end of the seventeenth century,* James Thompson, 1849. *Roman Leicester,* James Francis Hollings, The Literary and Philosophical Society, 1851.

Interestingly, despite the battering the town suffered, a merchants' guild was in existence in Leicester from as early as Oct. 9, 1196. See Stenton, F.M. "Documents Illustrative of the Social and Economic History of the Danelaw," British Academy, 1920, no. 347; cf. no. 392.)

you may choose whatever priest you will: Saint Mary de Castro (i.e. *of the castle*) Church still stands in Leicester. Unlike the other churches in the town, it was an appendage of the castle and hall: the lord of Leicester's own church.

above the doorway of an inn: I've placed this fictitious inn at the center of town, near the existing Church of Saint Nicholas, and named it for its location. Saint Nicholas, Bishop of Smyrna and the original of Santa Claus, became the symbol of generosity by secretly giving to two poor spinster sisters a bag of gold as they slept one night, thus providing them with dowries, and enabling them to marry.

Before there was widespread literacy and numbered street addresses, the images on inn- and shop-signs, and the statues prominent upon churches, provided neighborhoods with their identity. It was the custom for a lord staying at an inn to have his flag hung from a second story window, but Simon would have no flag as yet. Later, his flag of the red lion rampant on a white background would become the common inn sign of his partisans, and so comes down to us as a veritable cliché of medieval heraldry.

his name was Robert Grosseteste: See Francis Seymour Stevenson, *Robert Grosseteste, Bishop of Lincoln,* London, 1899.; A.G. Little, *Studies in English Franciscan History,* Manchester, 1917; J. McEvoy, *The Philosophy of Robert Grosseteste,* Oxford, 1982; *Robert Grosseteste, Scholar and Bishop,* ed. D. A. Callus, Oxford, 1955; R.W. Southern, *Robert Grosseteste: the Growth of an English Mind in Medieval Europe,* Oxford, 1986.

rents and fees due Leicester's lord: For a thorough discussion of the complex succession of the earldom of Leicester, see Bemont, *Simon de Montfort,* The Clarendon Press, Oxford, 1930, footnote 3, on pages pp. 9-10; also: *Dictionary of National Biography, s.v.* Beaumont; Bateson, *Records,* i.xi.

raise and train destriers: The term for warhorse was *destrier.* Customarily, when a wealthy knight traveled, riding his comfortable and docile palfrey, his squire led his warhorse on his right-hand side (dexter in Latin, hence destrier) as a gesture of honor paid the high spirited, elaborately trained and costly animal. The Percheron and Andalusian breeds are thought to be modern descendents of the Norman destrier. The Andalusian-type Lipizzans of Austria continue a gorgeous and theatrical version of the training a destrier would require, though a destrier would never leap into the air as Lipizzans do.

Destriers had to be highly aggressive to willingly run toward a fierce opponent, rather than behave submissively as a common horse might. Big and powerful to carry the weight of armor and withstand heavy blows, they could pivot in very short radius, move sideways into or away from an opponent, and perform such maneuvers as the elegant *caracole* of high steps turning from side to side, a move which can still be seen in parades. There was also the *petarade*: a swift outward kick of the hind legs, combined with a blast of flatulence that might usefully startle other horses during combat. See *petarde, Le Nouveau Petit Robert, 1996*; See also *Petit Larousse,* 1961. P.777 for the modern approximation: *"n.f. Suite de pets que fait un cheval en ruant.."*For *destrier, Petit Larousse, p 315:" n.m.(du lat.* dextera, *main droite) Autref., cheval de bataille (tenu de la main droite par l'ecuyer.)"*

Johanna had long lived at France's Court: For Johanna's history and involvement with Simon, see Kervyn de Lettenhove, *Histoire de Flandre,* reprint, July 17, 2009.; Elie Berger, *Blanche de Castile,* p. 210 and pp. 330-3.

Thou hadst best flee France: It was well known when Simon was at Henry's Court that he had seriously displeased Queen Blanche and dared not return to France. But the cause was placed on his seeking to wed Johanna, and later, Mahaut of Boulogne. See Guillaume de Nangis, *Recueil des Historiens des Gaules et de la France*, Vol. XX, p. 548. It is my belief the cause was his refusal to serve Queen Blanche from within the English Court. Queen Blanche was notorious for her surreptitious practices. After 1240, both Henry and Louis would use Simon openly and legitimately as a means to communicate with, and influence, each other.

Thomas deMesnil to serve as steward: regarding de Mesnil (or Menill) see Madicott, J.R. Cambridge University Press, 1994, *Simon de Montfort*, p.64. Thomas des Mesnil served Simon as his chief steward, his name appearing as witness on documents regarding the earldom and its holdings until 1247.

under the crumbling arches: the vicinity of the old Roman arches continued to be referred to as "the Jewry" until the twentieth century. See Fielding Johnson, *Glimpses of Old Leicester*, London and Leicester, 1891, pp. 9, 18, 68. I visited these arches, which are rather wide. The space they could afford is comparable to other cramped living- and work-space for medieval shopkeepers that I've seen preserved in the Shambles of York, in La Reole in Gascony, and elsewhere.

soon Simon was at the head of a mob: Lacking lordly titles, Simon didn't have the means to evict anyone as yet by command. And he had no knights or servants to assist in the eviction with physical force.

It's not doubted, however, that he did evict the Jews. But there was more than economics or racism behind this eviction. It cannot be coincidental that, in 1231, Grosseteste had just founded a house in London for the conversion to Christianity of homeless Jews (*domus conversorum Judeorum.*) Its location was the site of the present Public Record Office. Also in 1231, Grosseteste wrote *De cessatione legalium,* a treatise regarding the possible conversion of the Jews. See Bemont, *Montfort,* 1930, footnote, p.27; also, *Annales Monastici,* ed. H.R. Luard, Vol. IV, *Chronicon Thomae Wykes,* p.148; and Vol. IV of *Annales Prioratus de Wigorna,* (Worcester) p.448.

While it was supposed Jews would not convert to Christianity until the "Last Days," the twelfth-century writings of Joachim del Flor would have urged conversion soon. Joachim proposed three eras of history: the Age of the Father: the time of tribes epitomized by Moses; the Age of the Son: the rise of kings epitomized by Christ as spiritual king; and the Age of the Holy Ghost in which all mankind would participate in a collegiate, elective form of government as in monasteries. By using a count of twelve, rather than ten, as the basis for calculating centuries, Joachim placed the thirteenth century at the turning of the millennium: from the Age of the Son and kingship, to the Age of the Holy Ghost and the development of democracy.

The Franciscans were major supporters of Joachim's philosophy. In Paris, the Jacobin (Joachim > Jacob; pro-Joachim>Jacobin) monastic refectory was the chief center for the promulgation of Joachim's works. Five centuries later, the same location was later used as a center for the French revolution, giving its name to the revolutionary party: the Jacobins.

J.R. Maddicott, in *Simon de Montfort,* p.17, offers a photograph of a document by which Simon de Montfort expels the Jews from Leicester. Maddicott dates it to 1231-32. A document of this sort is elsewhere described as belonging to the year 1253, and written at the behest of Leicester's burgesses. The seal in the Maddicott photograph shows a shield with the rampant fork-tailed lion of Montfort, suggesting it post-dates the death of Amaury, the head of the Montfort family. See *Calendar of Patent Rolls, 1247-58,* p. 249; Bemont, *Montfort,* 1930, p. 27: *Roberti Grosseteste Episcopi Lincolniensis, 1235-53*; and H.R. Luard, Rolls Series, 1861, p.33.

it was the Countess Margaret's manse: Grosseteste advises the Countess of Winchester, Margaret de Quincy, not to receive the Jews, "whom the lord of Leicester had driven from the town, to prevent their crushing its Christian inhabitants under the weight of usury." *Rotuli Roberti Grosseteste, Episcopi Lincolniensis, 1235-53.* Ed. F.N. Davis, Canterbury and York Society, 1907-9.

he lent them money to buy sheep: From the early thirteenth century, Leicester began to figure significantly in the wool industry, and this commerce lasted until the development of synthetic fibers after World War II. There is little early record of the origins of this shift from the customary manorial three field system, apart from the villeins complaint to the Crown regarding the fencing of the fields, and a document sealed by Simon in 1239 regularizing some of his field arrangements with his "men of Leicester."

On May 3, 1239, Simon confirms the cession of the pasture at Cowhay in return for an annual rent of three shillings per head of cattle, and a colt of a hundred shillings' value once and for all. Further, by undated grants appended as supplement to this, he remits to his "men of Leicester" all the moneys paid annually for the earl's harvest, as well as for the admission of their beasts into the "defensa" (the fenced fields) of Leicester, and for carts carrying the grain of the townsmen to other mills than the earl's: in return the burgesses of Leicester are to pay him fifteen marks of silver (presumably annually.) Bateson, Mary, *Records of the Borough of Leicester*, 1899-1905, Vol. 1, p. 38.

Simon took on a squire: Mention of Peter the Barber is scarce. The *Calendar of Patent Rolls 1247-58*, on November 20, 1250, awards him rents at La Reole, in Gascony, forfeited by Etienne and Forton Piis, and directs Peter to pay a tax to the Crown consisting of two cheeses and ten pears.

villeins lodged official complaint: See Matthew Paris, *Chronica Majora*,Vol. III, pp. 318-19.

An alderman built a fulling mill: Woven woolen cloth required "fulling," beating to soften the cloth and raise the nap. Mills for this purpose were effectively "automated." Sets of hammers were powered by the turning of a mill wheel set in a river's flow. Cervantes has Don Quixote flee from a fulling mill in terror, believing that the mechanism, operating without a person in sight, must be animated by devils.

the old earl had died: Ranulf died on October 28, 1232. Harcourt, L. W. Vernon, *His Grace the Steward,* 1907.

Simon presented himself at Court: No such dialogue on the occasion of Hurle's historically factual romantic commission has come down to us. The few verbal exchanges at Henry's Court that have been preserved show a ribald wit which handily uses puns, biblical and classical allusions, and references to fables. These surviving dialogues have been attacked by scholars as the inventions of the chroniclers, yet they may be fairly accurate recollections of eyewitnesses.

Matthew Paris's *Chronica Majora* is the fullest, and one of the most respected of chronicles of the period. His monastery at Saint Albans, one day's ride on the principal road northward from London, has an underground passage to the ancient inn across the street. The passage is believed to have been used, perhaps daily, by Brother Matthew to gain the freshest news from travelers.

Since monastic chronicles were closed from contemporary inspection, the chroniclers were able to write of current events quite freely. And since they were charged with the responsibility of writing a history of the world from the Creation to the present moment, they took their office very seriously. Events from the Creation to the beginning of the keeping of the chronicle are dealt with rather briefly, but the day-to-day entries can be extensive, even to weather reports.

That Brother Matthew sometimes gleaned news directly from Simon is evidenced by the binding into his original manuscript (in The British Library) of a private letter sent to Simon by his nephew, John de Montfort, in Germany. The letter is the contemporary source of the term "golden horde" for the Asiatic invaders.

Initially, the *Chronica Majora* displays hostility toward Simon, but shifts strongly to his favor by the 1250's, even recording events that took place privately between Simon and King Henry which the chronicler could only have learned directly from Simon.

Simon began regular attendance at the royal Court: Simon's attendance at Court is increasingly marked by his witnessing official documents – the first in October of 1234 – until his mark of witness becomes the second-most prevalent, after the king's brother Richard.

His first witnessing is in regard of a change in the legal status of bastards, an issue Grosseteste addressed from the religious side by instituting a practice of having bastard children attend the wedding of their parents. The children were to be covered by a sheet until the end of the ceremony, at which they were uncovered, blessed and recognized as legitimate. Simon appears to have been serving as Grosseteste's spokesman at Court by bringing the plight of England's population of illegitimate offspring to the king's attention.

The furnishing of the rooms: There is no record of exactly how Simon achieved the royal favor he enjoyed. But Henry had artistic inclinations, evidenced by how he spent his funds, and Simon's familiarity with the Court of France would have been of keen interest to him. From this period in Henry's reign onward, the king's expenses show a consistent and costly interest in interior decorating. That he drew, is evidenced by a battle banner he designed when he was at war in Gascony.

the King's cursed foreign friend: on Simon's unpopularity and isolation: *Annales Monastici*, ed. H.R. Luard, Rolls Series, Vol. I, Tewkesbury,1864-9, p. 106; *Chronicle of Melrose*, "*alienigenarum inimicus et expulsor*"; Kingsford, *The Song of Lewes*, p.79, quotes Melrose to echo the description of Jesus, "despised and rejected of men." *Chronica de Mailros*, ed. J. Stevenson, Edinburgh, 1839.

his grandaunt Loretta: Powicke, F.M., "Loretta, Countess of Leicester." See also *Historical Essays in Honour of James Tate*, pp. 247-72 for the history of the "Recluse of Hackington," with contemporary sources. Loretta would live to be nearly a hundred, and be an advisor to Simon decades later.

Did I tell you that I'm learning to speak English?: *Chronicon de Lanercost*, ed. J. Stevenson, Edinburgh, 1839, p. 77, records that Simon did not speak English when he arrived in England. There is no indication that King Henry did either, though Prince Richard did. He was elected King of the Germans, "because he spoke their language." English and German, as spoken in 1250, were still mutually intelligible.

grandmother Eleanor held a Court of Love: The Courts of Love, founded initially by Eleanor of Aquitaine and her daughter Marie de France, adjudicated issues of love. Their precepts were drawn from Albigensian thinking as elaborated by the popular poets called troubadours. (More on the Courts of Love in the chapters The Court of Love and Countess Eleanor, and in notes below.)

if you mean Mahaut: Mahaut married Alphonse of Portugal, Johanna's former husband, in 1239. It's suggested by some historians that Simon sought to marry Mahaut to gain control of her fortune, evidencing his tendency to avariciousness. But Simon, in England and without a title, was at this time in no position to be a viable match for Mahaut: such a courtship initiated by him is highly unlikely. Rumors that he was courting Mahaut would, however, have served those who were seeking to prove he was an agent for Queen Blanche. Documents of the period often embalm current gossip, leaving the fruits of research to the biases of historians. See: Bemont, *Montfort*, Oxford, 1930, p.53; Berger, *Blanche de Castile*, p. 212.

our pageant wagon of the Miracle of Cana: The chief area of study of medieval theater has been of the play cycles, beginning with the brief Easter re-enactment of the three Maries' finding the angel at Jesus' tomb: the *Quem quaeritis*, which began to be performed in the tenth century. The religious play cycles, performed in and on the doorstep of churches, left remnants of text available to scholars. *Materials for the History of Thomas Becket*, J.C. Robertson, ed., Vol. III, London, 1877, p. 9, from the section *De ludis*, in the description of London includes a play on the life of Saint Thomas (Becket) circa 1170-82.

Tableaux, which had no texts to leave, are more problematic. Matthew Paris reveals that Saint Paul's Cathedral had a set-piece of imitation marble columns for its *Play of Adam*, which was set up at the gate through which King Henry's bridal cortege entered London. Later illustrations show Adam and Eve of this *Play of Adam* naked or nearly so.

There are numerous illustrations of tableaux, with elaborate scenery mounted on pageant carts, and sponsored by the craft guilds; but these date from the 1300's and later. Brother Matthew points up the problem: the clergy, through whom we have most of our records from the 1200's, disapproved of these portrayals of holy matters by the common people and avoided mentioning them. Still, the chronicler of St. Albans lets us know the guilds turned out for Henry's wedding progress with all their "usual display."

Fourteenth century illustrations of pageant wagons show some very elaborate affairs; might they have had simpler beginnings? That guild and parish pageant wagons existed as early as 1236, and took part in the entertainments of Henry's Wedding Progress, may be stretching Brother Matthew's laconic remark about "usual display," or is it?

already a Queen. She was sixteen: Margaret Howell, in *Eleanor of Provence*, Blackwell Publishers,1998, maintains that Eleanor was only twelve when she was wedded to Henry. Marriages did take place at that early an age, when the marriage brought a much-needed bond to a political alliance, and postponement of the ceremony might lose the advantage of the moment.

Frederic, the Holy Roman Emperor, married Yolanda, the Queen of Jerusalem, when she was only twelve. Such marriages normally were not consummated until the bride was of safe childbearing age. The emperor flouted that custom, causing Yolanda to die in childbirth before she was thirteen. For this he was looked upon by his subjects in the Holy Land as her murderer.

King Henry's own daughter was wedded to Alexander, King of Scotland, when both children were only nine. The royal couple wrote to Henry, complaining that their overseers were not permitting them their conjugal rights. Simon was dispatched to Scotland to tell them that, if they persisted, Henry would bring his daughter back to England and keep her there until she reached maturity.

King Henry gained no advantage in marrying Eleanor that would have justified his wedding a child. Furthermore, by 1238 there was great concern at the queen's failure to conceive, which would be nonsensical if she were only fourteen.

As for Eleanor's appearance, she and her sisters were all considered dazzling beauties. There is a stone portrait-head of her sister Sanchia in Aix en Provence that could be mistaken for an image of the young Britney Spears.

On the subject of medieval portraits in stone: the entry to the roof of the castle of La Reole, in Gascony, has a bas-relief carved over the doorway. It is a perfect head of the jug-eared, ("What, me worry?") character Alfred E. Neuman, who was the fictional mascot of the satirical *Mad* magazine, which originated in the mid-1950's. The castle, with its bas-relief, was built by Richard the Lion-Hearted.

bearing the King's washbasin: Matthew Paris, in the *Chronica Majora*, Vol. III, pp. 336-9, gives a disapproving description of the opulence of the coronation celebration. Apparently Roger Bigod tried to seize the honor of presenting the king his washbasin, but Simon retained the privilege. See also: *Red Book of the Exchequer*, p. 757.

she would commence a Court of Love: Courts of Love were forums for the doctrines of the Albigensians. The heretics believed each human soul was an angel, split in two. One half was flung to earth with the damnation of the Archangel Lucifer, yet the other half remained in Heaven. Such was God's grace that the half on earth forever yearned for reunion with its half in Heaven. This yearning was called love. Love was a divine gift, the means of mankind's redemption, drawing each soul to salvation. But it was a salvation unfulfilled so long as the earthly body lived.

The Albigensian adepts led lives of chastity, believing sexuality so much a sin that they would eat only vegetables and fish, as these two forms of life, they thought, bred asexually. The rite of passage from an adept to a Cathar, a "pure," required forty days of fasting, broken by a feast of fish and vegetables, then forty days more without food. To die of fasting was a grace, the sign of completion of the soul's earthly exile.

Troubadours, from the same regions of southern France where the Albigensians prospered, clothed the ideals of this morbid faith with the imagery of sexual desire. And the Courts of Love elaborated that desire into a Code of Love, which was termed *courtesy*. Passionate, unconsummated love between a man and woman was held by the Courts of Love to be the highest earthly good, drawing the soul toward its death on earth, and rebirth in Heaven. See *Love in the Western World*, Denis de Rougemont, Princeton University Press, 1983.

Good fathers of the Church: this entire exchange between Riveaux, the king and the lords is verbatim (in translation) from Paris's *Chronica*. The boldness and lack of decorum that England's Parliamentary meetings still may show has long historical precedent.

the Countess Eleanor of Pembroke, King Henry's youngest sister: Countess Eleanor was married to William of Pembroke on April 23, 1224. William died in 1231. At that time of his death, Eleanor and her governess Cecily de Sanford, a very devout woman, both took vows of chastity, administered by the Archbishop of Canterbury. They each wore a ring indicating they were wedded to Christ, but neither joined an order or entered a regular novitiate. Cecily retired to a convent. Eleanor received the royal castle of Odiham for her retreat. Matthew Paris, *Chronica Majora*, Vol. V, p. 235.

Henry III had three sisters, the eldest was only six when their father, King John, died. In addition to Isabel, wedded to the Holy Roman Emperor, and Eleanor, there was Joan, first betrothed to Hugh X, Count of La Marche. Their mother, Queen Isabel, had once been betrothed to Hugh. When she conducted her daughter to the wedding, she married Hugh herself and sent her daughter home. Joan was then married to the King of Scotland, but soon died.

Henry's sisters were considered one of his strongest assets for forming political alliances. Such marriages could range, for the bride, from acceptable to unpleasant, or even deadly as in the case of the Emperor Frederic's several wives. Eleanor had good reason to take holy vows to escape the hazards of being used as a political pawn. See *Royal Letters*. Vol. I, pp. 114-5.

Simon found his brother Amaury was there: Amaury was indeed at England's Court on embassy at this time. How Simon and Eleanor may have come together is not a matter of record.

a tournament in Cornwall: For the reader interested in discerning fact from fiction, this is a fairly accurate description of the private, country tournaments of the period, but there is no historical record of Simon's taking part in such an event. If he had, there would of course be no record since such tourneys were outlawed. He did first meet his cousin Peter of Gloucester at about this time.

the manor of Odiham: Eleanor had at least two properties of her own, at Kemsing and Wexcomb, apart from Odiham which she received from her brother in 1236 to provide her with a suitable home. Wexcomb had no hall when she received it after her husband's death in 1231, and the houses at Kemsing were burnt down. Neither Kemsing nor Wexcomb seemed to produce much in the way of income. Lands in Poitou were hers by inheritance, but I've found no indication that she received those rents at this time. She was essentially dependent upon her brother's irregularly fulfilled financial commitments to her, and his occasional gifts. *Close Rolls 1231-4,* p. 210 and *1234-7,* p. 131

At the time of William of Pembroke's death, his estate was worth 3,350 pounds a year. But Henry agreed, on behalf of his sister, to only 400 pounds a year from William's heir Richard, and 350 pounds a year from his second son, Gilbert. Henry stood guarantor for these payment to Eleanor.

Richard defaulted almost at once, but soon died in Ireland, purportedly due to actions Henry took at the instigation of Peter de Riveaux, his chief clerk of finance. For royal machinations against Richard of Pembroke in Ireland, see G. H. Orpen, *Ireland under the Normans,* Vol. III, pp. 67-70. The Pembrokes were relentless enemies of King Henry for good reason.

Richard's brother Gilbert proved even worse to deal with. Until the time of her death, Eleanor pursued lawsuits to try to gain her funds, including claims that her brother the king had accepted far too little on her behalf initially. See Labarge, *Montfort,* pp. 41-2 for a thorough discussion of the Pembroke estates' value, and Eleanor's claims.

Simon and Eleanor were secretly wed: Not so secretly that the exact date and place, and officiating clergy and witnesses escaped Brother Matthew's recording: *Chronica Majora,* Vol. III, pp. 470-1; also see: *Chronicon de Lanercost,* ed. J. Stevenson, ed. Maitland Club, Edinburgh, 1839, p.39.

objections to the marriage: The opposition to Simon's marriage is well recorded, as it was considered a major outrage. The fight between Simon and Prince Richard was actual, and resulted in Simon's having to publicly apologize and give Richard a present to make peace. The often colorful *Chronicon de Lanercost* claims Archbishop Rich was forced to flee London and, from a hill beyond the city, looked back to curse the Countess Eleanor, thus bringing on all her later misfortunes. *Lanercost,* pp. 39-40. See also N. Denholm-Young, *Richard of Cornwall,* Oxford, 1947, pp. 497-98; Stacey, R. C., *Politics, Policy and Finance under King Henry III, 1216-45,* Oxford, 1987, pp. 118-24; *Calendar of Patent Rolls 1232-47,* p. 209; *Annales Monastici,* Vol. I, Tewkesbury, p. 106, ed. H. E. Luard, Rolls Series, 1864-9

go to Rome!: Henry wrote to the papacy and the emperor in support of Simon's petition. Paris, Vol. III, pp. 479-80; *Calendar of*

Patent Rolls, 1232-47, p. 214, (H.M.S.O. 1906-). He also lent Simon 1,565 pounds for his expenses.

Hospitallers gladly granted him a loan: Matthew Paris places the loan at 1,000 pounds.

August was the true term of the countess's pregnancy: There is no doubt that Simon and Eleanor were wedded secretly on January 6. Simon was effectually absent-without-leave from the battlefield in Wales. The abruptness and secrecy of the ceremony also strongly suggest it was necessitous. If Eleanor knew she was pregnant, then, given time for travel, the child had to have been conceived in November, which coordinates with Simon's return to London to make report on the Welsh war and Amaury's visit on embassy. In which case, her pregnancy must have come to term in August, not November, the official time of the announcement of the birth.

letters from King Henry: regarding King Henry's letters in support of Simon in Rome, see *Calendar of Patent Rolls 1232-47,* p. 214. The emperor's support is mentioned by Matthew Paris, *Chronica Majora,* Vol. III, p. 480. Matthew is keen to point up the scandal of this simony.

Frederic II, the Holy Roman Emperor: the personality of the emperor and his history are from contemporary records, as are his experiments, his test of Michael Scott and Simon's visit to him to deliver letters from King Henry.

Frederic's interior decor is speculation based on the preserved chambers at Pompey which are the principal source of our knowledge of ancient Roman murals. However, this may be tantamount to describing a wealthy New York City interior based on what can be seen at Boca Raton.

That Simon was maneuvered by the emperor into serving with the English forces at Milan under d'Urberville, is history. This is, incidentally, the crusading ancestor mentioned in *Tess of the d'Urbervilles.* I've used the novel's spelling of the name, though the whimsy of 13th century spelling compassed such variants as Troubleville and Tupperville. Simon's son Henry, in writing his father's will from dictation, spells his own name "Henry" in five different ways on a single page. Regularized spelling is a convention that did not interest the medieval mind.

Where Simon stayed while in Rome is not a matter of record. It was contemporary gossip that the emperor kept a harem. So, actually, did the Sultan Djim, when he was a prisoner of the Borgias in the Vatican in the 1490s.

a clerk was reading Simon's petition: The arguments presented are not in the historical record. Archbishop Rich, though the architect of exquisite Salisbury Cathedral, had a reputation for brutality.

grant the annulment that you ask: the granting of the annulment of the countess's vows, on May 10, is recorded in *Entries in the Papal Registers Relating to Great Britain and Ireland: Papal Letters,* ed. W. H. Bliss, 1894, Vol. I, p. 172. See also Labarge, *Montfort,* p.50.

The Pope had written (April 18-23) to Richard of Cornwall, William Longspee and other English earls, urging them to come to the Vatican's aid against Frederic. When he was raising all the help he could against Frederic, it's not surprising the Pope granted Simon's petition, and attached Simon to the Church's cause against the emperor. See Labarge, *Montfort,* p. 56, footnote 4, and *Reg. Gregoire IX,* nos. 4095-96.

Simon would have been ignorant of the Pope's recruitment effort, since the private papal letters would have reached England after he left for Rome. Clearly he and Henry had no idea how serious Frederic's breach with the Pope was, or Simon would not have sought the emperor's help at Henry's behest.

the castle had not been inhabited for decades: See Bemont, *Montfort,* 1930, p. 59, and Simon's complaint against King Henry, reprinted in Bemont, *Montfort,* 1884, p. 333, document XXXIV. Few repairs had been made, and assets of the property had been skimmed off since 1207.

The tower of Kenilworth was "slighted" by Cromwell: it was packed with explosives and blown up. Today, only three walls remain standing. Additional buildings, including a grand banqueting hall, were built by Dudley, the Earl of Leicester during the reign of Queen Elizabeth I.

From lists of King Henry's expenses, I've reconstructed what was present in Simon's time. The tremendous debts that Simon faced upon his return from Rome suggest that Eleanor had a great deal of work to do to make the derelict property habitable. Notches in the existing stone walls indicate that there were supports for paneling, and there are of course holes in the walls for floor-joists and roof-beams. The corner towers still stand, and are as I describe.

Garbage and Slingaway: this defies invention. These were the recorded names of the kitchen boys in the Montfort household, preserved for us in Countess Eleanor's expense roll which was found inside the wall of the convent at Montargis when the building was damaged during the French Revolution. After Simon's death, Eleanor retreated to Montargis, where she died in 1275. See Labarge, *A Baronial Household of the Thirteenth Century*, pp 68-69..

a letter from the Bishop of Soisson: Bemont, *Montfort*, p. 60; *Letters Patent*, June 7, 1237; and transcribed in *Archives de la Chambre de comptes de Lille*, p. 270, no. 671. Jacques de Basoches, the Bishop of Soisson, had been trying to collect this debt from Simon for more than a year.

Exasperated, Basoches excommunicated Simon. He did not need papal permission. It is probable that after-the-fact, after he heard of Simon's trip to the Vatican and pledge to crusade, he sought papal support for the excommunication. If Simon had been fully under the protection of the Cross, he could not have been excommunicated for a debt. Basoches was sent a Papal Bull, dated September 10, 1238, supporting the excommunication. The bishop confirmed the excommunication in a letter to the Vatican bearing the late date of May 1, 1239. The occasion for this letter may have been to support the Count of Savoy's efforts to obtain payment of the debt, which by then Basoches had sold to him. Or it may have been a move to counter Simon's serving as godfather to the heir to England's throne.

a moneylender of Cahors: the increase of the Ranulf debt from 200 marks to 2,080 marks is well documented. The 2,080 debt (*duo milia et octigentas marcas*) sometimes appears as 2,800 marks, after a misprint in Bemont, *Montfort*, 1884, p. 263, where the letter from the Bishop of Soisson to the Vatican regarding the debt is reprinted.

An interest rate of 60% per annum was not uncommon at Cahors. The prominent moneylenders of that French city would have provided the most convenient means for Mauclerc to cash in the debt. Compared to their Christian competitors, the Jews gave some of the best loan rates available at that time. See also Labarge, p. 54-5; Bemont, *Simon de Montfort*, 1930, p. 60; *Royal Lettters*, Vol. II, p.16; *Calendar of Patent Rolls, 1232-47*, p. 185.

the King and Queen arrived at Kenilworth: for the royal visit in September, 1238, see Labarge, *Montfort*, p.51: "although the king himself spent some days with her (the Countess Eleanor) in September."

I don't know Labarge's source for this statement, though I believe it true. There appears to be a deliberate concealment of the king's location in early September. The *Royal Letters* and *Calendar of Patent Rolls*, which day by day record the location of the king throughout Henry's reign, both have large lacunae: from August 30 to September 12. The entries in the *Calendar of Charter Rolls* are mutilated beyond legibility from August 2 to November 8. These documents consist of "membranes," sheets of sheep skins sewn end to end to create one long roll for keeping the records of the Court. The *Liberate Roll*, from July 27 to September 6, is very deteriorated; the locations of the Court are particularly unreadable.

This wouldn't be startling if these records of the Court were badly deteriorated elsewhere and were otherwise filled with lacunae.

But such is not the case. Day by day, these contemporary records provide a very thorough picture of Henry's Court's location, activities and expenses.

The seemingly coordinated absence of information for the period from August 30 to September 6 suggests intent. I offer it as yet another piece in the circumstantial evidence of the queen's visit to Kenilworth in September 1238, and the resulting birth of Edward nine months later. Both King Henry and Edward I would have had good reason to want evidence of the queen's stay at Kenilworth destroyed.

she had been married for three years: the queen's apparent barrenness was recorded by Matthew Paris and others. Assorted nostrums had been tried with no effect. The political ramifications of Henry's failure to have an heir were serious in light of the efforts by Pembroke and other disaffected barons to put his brother Richard on the throne.

King Henry and Queen Eleanor served as godparents: See Bemont, *Simon de Montfort*, 1930, p. 37 footnote: "The sons (of Simon) were Henry, godson of Henry III..."

Robert Grosseteste's prophetic utterance at the time of young Henry's baptism was the subject of common gossip, though mentioned most often after the father and son's death. Believing the date of Henry de Montfort's birth to be in November, Brother Matthew records Stavensby's baptism of the child, and only later writes of Grosseteste's baptism of Henry and of the prophecy. The baptism by Grosseteste would support the birth of Henry before November: *Chronica Majora*, Vol. III, p. 518.

he walked the eighty miles to Lincoln: Simon must have made peace with Grosseteste at about this time. Exactly how it happened is not a matter of historical record.

The See of Winchester was vacant: Paris, *Chronica Majora*; H. R. Luards, 1872-83, Vol. III, p.498. King Henry's assault upon the

See of Winchester, as described by Brother Matthew, is the first example of the wry but effective tactics the king employed against his recalcitrant subjects. The chronicler also records Simon's arrival at Court on the 14th of October, 1238.

Lady Alice found a physician: There is an item in the record of royal expenses of a payment to a physician for prescribing prayers to Saint Edward and herbs to ensure the queen's fertility.

Simon's investiture: Simon's investiture was on Candlemas, February 2, 1239, and from that date onward he is officially titled Earl of Leicester. Paris, *Chronica Majora*, Vol. III, p. 524; *Layettes*, Vol. II, No. 2789. It is notable that Candlemas is one of the four ancient, pre-Christian holidays, as is the day of Simon's death, on Lammas, August 2.

Thomas, the Count of Flanders: See Labarge, *Montfort,* p. 54 for concise accounts of the peregrinations of Simon's debt to Ranulf's estate, and of the marriage of Simon's former betrothed, Johanna, to Queen Eleanor's uncle, Thomas of Savoy.

send my sheriffs to collect it: Simon's own account of his experiences with Henry is vivid regarding Henry's forcible extraction of payment for the debt. See Bemont, *Montfort*, 1884, document XXXIV, pp. 332-35. Written in 1260, the document was prepared by Simon as part of his plea before the King of France, when King Henry brought suit in France against him for treason. Entirely accurate or not, this work is Simon speaking for himself.

most loved friend: during this period, Simon appears more often than anyone else as witness to royal charters, indicating his almost constant presence with the king and the particular favor he was enjoying.

On the morning of August 9th: The *Chronica Majora* records the baptism, Vol. III, 539-40.

the celebration of the Churching of the Queen: Brother Matthew describes the event of the Churching of the Queen, and what was said by King Henry and Simon, with the explicitness of an eyewitness.

Simon, in his later trial evidence for King Louis, gives his own version regarding Henry's payment of his debt to Thomas of Flanders. He uses the debt, as Henry did at the Churching of the Queen, to obfuscate Henry's reasons for rage at him.

That the debt could not be the reason for the king's rage, is evidenced by Henry's subsequently lending Simon the Bishop of Winchester's manse for the summer and, up to the day before the Churching, having Simon witness more charters than any one else that summer – clearly Simon was by the king's side in a highly favored way.

The significant event occurring between Henry's evident friendliness toward Simon, and his outburst of rage at the Churching, is the queen's confession immediately preceding the Churching ceremony.

For King Henry's rampage, and Simon's flight from the Churching, see Paris, *Chronica Majora,*Vol III, pp.566-7; *Calendar of Liberate Rolls*, H.M.S.O. 1916-, pp. 311-12, 410; *Historia Anglorum,* ed. F. Madden Rolls Series, 1869-9, Vol. II, p.424.

In Bemont, *Montfort*, 1930, p.62, a translation of Henry's words, as recorded by Brother Matthew, is given as follows: "You seduced my sister before the wedding; to avoid scandal I gave my consent, in my own despite. You went to Rome to secure that the vow she had taken should not prevent the marriage, and you corrupted the Curia in order to obtain that which was forbidden. The Archbishop of Canterbury, here present, told the Pope the truth, but truth was conquered by the avarice of Rome and the presents which you lavished on them. Ay, you have failed to pay the money which you promised to return, and that is why you have deserved excommunication. To crown your folly, you cited me as security by an act of perjury and without telling me aught of it." Bemont publishes Simon's written recounting of the event as follows: "*la nuit maimes... il comanda que je fuisse pris a mene a la Tour de Londres e que le cumuns de Londres fust semons por mai prendre a mon ostel ou j'staie herbergez, mais li Rais d'Alemaigne* (Richard by 1260 had been elected King of the Germans) *qui la fu ne vout pas ce souffrir a cele nuit." Montfort*, 1884, p. 334. This, however, could refer to a later occasion when Simon was in mortal jeopardy due to the wrath of King Henry.

Amaury, as Marshall of France: Bemont, *Montfort*, 1930, p. 63- 4, foonote 1, discusses Amaury's campaign in Palestine in detail.

Were the World mine: this is an actual, popular song dating from this period, and is included in the *Carmina Burana*.

"I have no lion seal,": Simon's large seal shows a tall, angular figure with tousled hair, wearing a short riding robe, seated on a galloping horse and blowing on a horn. It's border bears the inscription: Sigillum Simonis de Mont... The best known document bearing this seal is dated to 1255. But since the seal does not bear his title, this seal's matrix may have been used by him from a much earlier date.

the Crusade is lost: Steven Runciman, in his A *History of the Crusades*, Cambridge, 1955, Vol. III, gives a thorough description of the politics of Outremere. Pages 213-17 describe this French venture in Palestine. Runciman uses the Germanic form of Amaury's name: Amalric.

England can ill afford another Richard-with-a-lion's-heart: King Richard I traveled, nearly alone, by the land route to and from Palestine. Tradition has it that Richard, on his way to the East, stole a hunting hawk from Leopold, the Duke of Austria. Steven Runciman offers more substantial reason for Leopold's rage at Richard: *A History of the Crusades*, Vol. III, p. 74. Richard had thrown down Leopold's banner at Acre, and Leopold suspected him of the murder of Conrad of Montferrat. In any case, Leopold seized

Richard as he passed through Austria, homeward bound, and kept him in prison until England paid an immense ransom for him. There was almost no one in England who didn't suffer from the exorbitant taxes that had to be raised to pay Richard's ransom.

he sold the remaining forest: The Curlevache incident: When, in 1239, Simon wished to sell his "noble forest of Leicester" to the abbey of Saint Mary-in-the-Meadow, he found that during the time he had rented it to the Leicester burgess, Simon Curlevache, the trees were cut down. Simon demanded from Curlevache 500 marks in reparations. Matthew Paris records this as "extortion." *Chronica Majora*, Vol. IV. p. 7.

Grosseteste, in a letter, urged Simon to be more lenient; he was giving cause for public opinion against him: "We have learned that you are thinking of punishing S., your burgess, with a severity disproportionate to his offense. Let not your severity be turned against him, or your justice be unappeased, but let pity mercifully exalt your judgment so as to give an example of kindness instead of cruelty." *Rotuli Roberti Grosseteste*, Davis, F. N., Canterbury and York Society, 1907-9, p. 141.

There is a story that when Curlevache refused to pay, Simon assaulted him, giving the burgess further cause for a case at law.

a tournament at his fief of Ashby de la Zouche: Sir Walter Scott makes a tournament at Ashby de la Zouche the opening setting for *Ivanhoe*. Ashby was a fief of Simon's, as was the manor of Ivanhoe; clearly Scott knew somewhat about Simon. The scene Scott depicts maddeningly confounds three centuries: the time of King John in the 1100's, this tournament in April of 1240, and costumes of the 1300's. Scott's aim was not to be accurate to history, but to fabricate tales that pointed up moral and ethical issues.

"You are abandoning us, Richard": The Archbishop's speech and Richard's reply are quoted from Matthew Paris.

Simon debarked at Acre: See Labarge, *Montfort*, pp. 55-59. Runciman, Vol. III, deals with Richard's crusade in pages 217-222.

Simon de Montfort be confirmed as your Viceroy: Bemont, *Montfort*, 1930, pp. 64-5, says "all we have [of evidence of Simon's time in Palestine] is a curious letter addressed to the Emperor Frederic by the 'barons, knights and citizens of the kingdom of Jerusalem', asking him to give them the earl as governor, until the young Conrad reached his majority. They will swear to obey him, 'as it had been the emperor's person'; they will suppress the bell, the councils and the captains of the commune, 'saving those who were there before the emperor was master of the country.'" The letter is dated June 7, 1241.

My father is dead: *Chronica Majora*, Vol. IV, p.180, records that Amaury contracted a disease in the Sultan's prison, and died on his return home, at Trapani, on June 1, 1241.

We are at war with England: Labarge, *Montfort*, pp. 59-63, gives an account of King Henry's war in Poitou. See also Bemont, 1930, p.65. The causes of the war historically were as I describe, bizarre though they seem. Actual events can be far more odd than one would write in fiction.

We will offer you a mercenary's pay: Bemont, 1930, pp. 65-6, footnote 3.

King of France bids greeting: See *Chronica Majora*, Vol. I, pp. 414 -28, for Matthew Paris's record of the war. The actual letters from Louis and the Queen Mother have not survived.

"What of your promises now..." The *Chronica Majora* reports this dialogue between King Henry, Prince Richard and the old Count of La Marche, Vol. I, pp. 420-21. I've followed Brother Matthew verbatim, and also the exchange between Richard and King Louis:

p. 421. The entire war in Gascony is given in the *Chronica Majora*, pp. 420-33. It is this record I've followed.

"Our King is very like to Christ": This is verbatim from Brother Matthew. Another episode involving Henry of Avranche survives. It appears that Avranche sat on a bench outside an inn and began to eat a supper he had brought with him. The innkeeper came out, demanding that he leave the inn's bench – it was reserved for paying customers only. The issue went for legal judgment. In court, the innkeeper's accusation was that the fool had the enjoyment of the inn's ambiance, in particular the aromas of its cookery, without paying. The judge upheld the fool's defense: that he could pay for the *scent* of the food with the *sound* of the jingle of coins in his purse.

"Are there not locks and iron doors enough for you at Windsor...": Years later in his testimony against Simon before King Louis' Court, King Henry recounts that at Saintes: *le conte dist ke les messons barres de fer a Windesore seroent bones a son eos a garder-le seurement dedenz."* Bemont, *Montfort*, 1884, p.341.

"your Majesty sees how fortune runs against us,": The *Chronica Majora*, p.431, gives Hertolt's speech, which I paraphrase for brevity, and King Henry's reply, which is given here verbatim.

the Countess of Bearne and her son Gaston arrived: see *Chronica Majora*. p. 431: "How the countess of Bearne came to the King of England at Blaye" for the outline of this episode.

"Most accomplished leeches": physicians were referred to as "leeches" because their often-used remedy of bleeding was done with the use of live leeches. The dialogue here is not from historical sources, but the daily sum Henry bestowed upon these would-be relatives is recorded by Brother Matthew as ruinous. "Tender," used to mean money, derives from *tendre* in Old French, meaning "to offer" – money particularly in the legal sense.

Bibliography

Primary Sources:

Montfort Archive, Bibliotheque Nationale, Paris. There is preserved, in this boxed archive of original documents, a brief autobiography by Simon written in 1260 in preparation for his trial before King Louis for treason against King Henry. (In the event, the trial was actually heard by Queen Margaret of France.)

Publications:
Calendar of Charter Rolls, Vol. I, 1226-1307, Public Record Office. Kraus Reprint, Neldeln/Liechtenstein, 1972.

Calendar of the Liberate Rolls, 1226-1240, Volume I, Public Record Office, 1916.

Calendar of Patent Rolls, 1232-1272, Henry III. Public Record Office. Kraus Reprint, Nendeln/Liechtenstein, 1971.

Eccleston, Thomas of, *The Coming of the Friars Minor to England, XIIIth Century Chronicles,* translated by Placid Herman, O.F.M., Franciscan Herald Press,Chicago, 1961.

Excerpta e Rotulis Finium in Turri Londdinensi Asservatis Henry III, 1216-72, ed. by C. Roberts, Public Record Office. 1835-36.

Exchequer: The History and Antiquities of the Exchequer, Madox, Greenwood, 1769-1969, Volumes I and II.

Grosseteste, Roberti, Episcopi quondam Lincolniensis Epistolae, ed. by H.R. Luard. Rolls Series, 1861.

Dicta Lincolniensis, ed. and trans.: Gordon Jackson, Grosseteste Press, Lincoln, 1972.

R. *Grosseteste Carmina Anglo-Normannica: Robert Grosseteste's Casteau d'Amour and La Vie de Sainte Marie Egyptienne,* Burt Franklin Research and Resource Works Series No. 154, New York, 1967.

Laffan, R.G.D. *Select Documents of European History, 800-1492,* Volume I, Henry Holt and Company, New York.

Matthew Paris's English History, from the year 1235 to 1273, translated by the Rev. J. A. Giles, Henry Bohn, London, 1852. See Kessinger Publishing's Rare Reprints. www.kessinger.net

Matthaei Paris, Monachi Albanensis, Historia Major, Juxta Exemplar Londinense 1640, *verbatim recusa,* ed. Willielmo Wats, STD. Imprensis A. Mearne, T. Dring, B. Tooke, T. Sawbridge & G. Wells, MDCLXXXIV (1684)

Matthaei Parisiense, Chronica Majora, Kraus reprint, 1964.

The Chronicle of William de Rishanger, of the Barons' War: The Miracles of Simon de Montfort. ed. J.O. Halliwell, Camden Society, 1840.

Royal Letters, Henry III, ed. W.W. Shirley, Rolls Series, 1862.

Strassburg, Gottfried von, *Tristan; with surviving fragments of Tristran, of Thomas,* trans. A. T. Hatto, Penguin Books, New York, 1967.

de Troyes, Chretien. *Arthurian Romances,* trans. W.W. Comfort, Everyman's Library, Dutton, New York, 1975

Secondary Works:

Baker, Timothy. *Medieval London,* Praeger Publishers, New York, 1970.

Bemont, Charles, *Simon de Montfort, Earl of Leicester,* translated by E. F. Jacob, Oxford, Clarendon Press, 1930

Simon de Montfort, Comte de Leicester, Sa Vie (120?-1265), Slatkine-Megariotis Reprints, Geneve, 1976. *Reimpression de l'edition de Paris 1884.*

Chrimes, S.B. *An Introduction to the Administrative History of Medieval England*, Basil Blackwell, Oxford, 1959.

Cosman, Madeleine Pelner. *Fabulous Feasts: Medieval Cookery and Ceremony*, George Braziller, New York, 1976.

Furnival. *The Babees' Book: Medieval Manners for the Young*, ed. Edith Rickert, Cooper Square Publishers, Inc., New York, 1966.

Green, John Richard. *History of the English People*, Lovell, Coryell & Company, New York, Volume II, 1878-80.

Homans, George Caspar. *English Villagers of the Thirteenth Century*, Russell & Russell, New York, 1960.

Howell, Margaret. *Eleanor of Provence, Queenship in Thirteenth Century England*, Blackwell Publishers Inc., Malden, Mass., 2001.

Johnson, Mrs. T. Fielding. *Glimpses of Ancient Leicester in Six Periods*, Simpkin, Marshall. Hamilton, Kent & Co., London, and John and Thomas Spencer, Leicester, 1891.

King, Edmund. *England, 1175-1425*, Charles Scribner's Sons, New York, 1979.

Labarge, Margaret Wade. *Simon de Montfort*, Eyre & Spottiswoode, London, 1962.
A Baronial Household of the Thirteenth Century, Eyre & Spottiswoode, London, 1965.
Saint Louis, Louis IX, Most Christian King of France, Little, Brown and Company, Boston, 1968.

BIBLIOGRAPHY

Gascony, England's First Colony, 1204-1453, Hamish Hamilton, Ltd., London, 1980.

Maddicott, J.R. *Simon de Montfort*, Cambridge University Press, 1994.

Nagler, A.M. *The Medieval Religious Stage*, Yale University Press, New Haven, 1976.

Nicoll , Allardyce, *Masks, Mimes and Miracles: Studies in the Popular Theatre*, George A. Harrap & Company, Ltd., London, 1931.

Painter, Sidney. *William Marshall, Knight-Errant, Baron, and Regent of England*, The Johns Hopkins Press, Baltimore, 1933.

Power, Eileen. *The Wool Trade in English Medieval History*, Oxford University Press, London, 1965.

Powicke, Maurice. *Medieval England: 1066-1485*, Oxford University Press, London, 1931.

Pye, N., ed. *Leicester and its Region*, Leicester University Press, Leicester, 1972.

Renn, Derek. *Norman Castles in Britain*, John Baker: Humanities Press, New York, 1968.

Runciman, Steven. *A History of the Crusades, The Kingdom of Acre*, Volume III, The University Press, Cambridge, 1955.

Salisbury-Jones, G.T., *Street Life in Medieval England*, The Harvester Press: Rowan and Littlefield, Sussex, England, 1975.

Slaughter, Gertrude. *The Amazing Frederic: Stupor Mundi et Immutator Mirabilis*, The Macmillan Company, New York, 1937.

BIBLIOGRAPHY

Waddell, Helen. *The Wandering Scholars*, Henry Holt and Company, New York, 1927.

About the Author

Since embarking on the research and writing of Montfort, in 1977, Katherine Ashe has written plays and screenplays on historical subjects from Columbus to the coal mining labor leader John Mitchell. She lives in rural Pennsylvania with her husband, journalist and theater critic Peter Wynne, and two dogs.